PRAISE FOR THE NOVELS OF JACK DUBRUL:

"A MASTER STORYTELLER."
—CLIVE CUSSLER

"STRONG, FRESH WRITING."
—*KIRKUS REVIEWS*

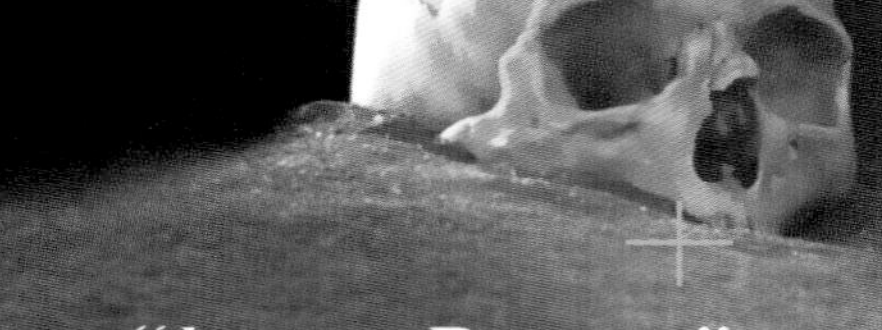

"ACTION-PACKED."
—*PUBLISHERS WEEKLY*

THE MEDUSA STONE

Jack Du Brul

AN ONYX BOOK

ONYX
Published by New American Library, a division of
Penguin Putnam Inc., 375 Hudson Street,
New York, New York 10014, U.S.A.
Penguin Books Ltd, 27 Wrights Lane,
London W8 5TZ, England
Penguin Books Australia Ltd, Ringwood,
Victoria, Australia
Penguin Books Canada Ltd, 10 Alcorn Avenue,
Toronto, Ontario, Canada M4V 3B2
Penguin Books (N.Z.) Ltd, 182–190 Wairau Road,
Auckland 10, New Zealand

Penguin Books Ltd, Registered Offices:
Harmondsworth, Middlesex, England

First Published by Onyx, an imprint of New American Library, a division of
Penguin Putnam Inc. Previously published in Great Britain as *Sun on Snow*.

First Printing, April 2000
10 9 8 7 6 5 4 3 2 1

Printed in the United States of America

PUBLISHER'S NOTE
This is a work of fiction. Names, characters, places, and incidents either are
the product of the author's imagination or are used fictitiously, and any
resemblance to actual persons, living or dead, business establishments, events
or locales is entirely coincidental.

For Lou,
my editor, my traveling partner,
my best friend, my mother

Acknowledgments

Once again, I am staggered by the help I needed to get this novel into readable form. First is Debbie Saunders, without whose love, support, and infinite patience I would not be able to work my craft. Second, of course, is my agent, Bob Diforio, the man who made this all possible. This time, I have a new staff behind me, Doug Grad and the rest of his team at NAL. Thanks a bunch, I won't let you down. I also need to thank Richard Marek, the sharpest and best editing pen in the business. I am in awe of his skill and insight. There are many others: Chris Flanagan, Kim Haimann, Sandy Preston, Sister Miriam Ward, and the list could go on and on. I really need to thank everyone who made my trip to Eritrea possible and acknowledge the people who make it such a wondrous place. I will never forget my time there.

I also want to thank the most important people in the publishing industry: the readers. Without you, I'm just a guy tapping at a computer. You have all my gratitude.

Author's note
For reasons of personal security, I did not go as far north into Eritrea as Mercer does in this novel so please forgive my discrepancies with the actual geography. Also, for the sake of the story, I've altered some rules of geology. Again forgive me.

THE MEDITERRANEAN AND AFRICA

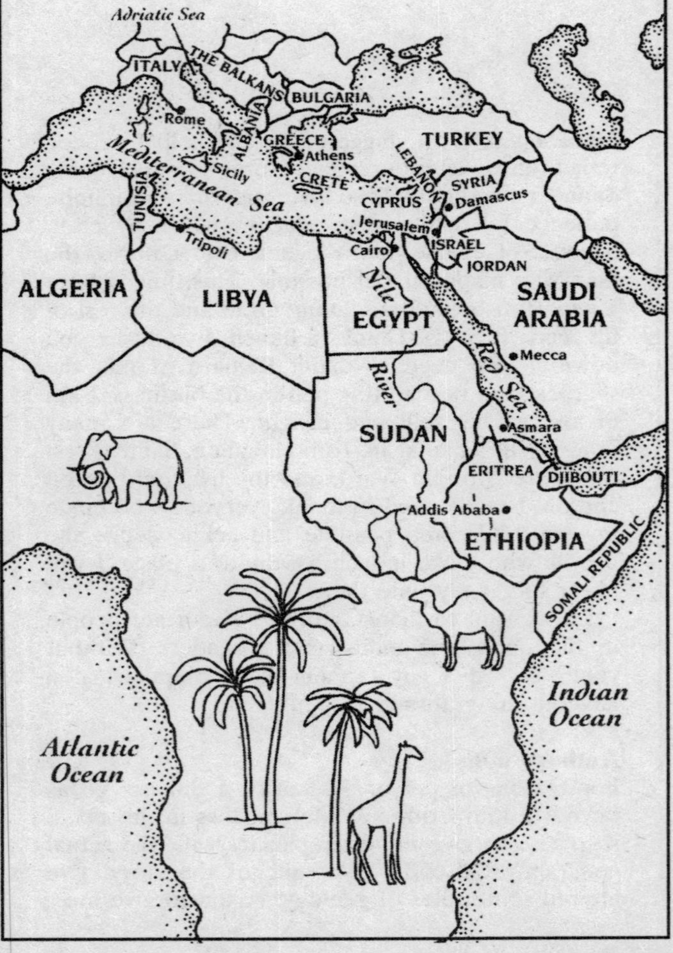

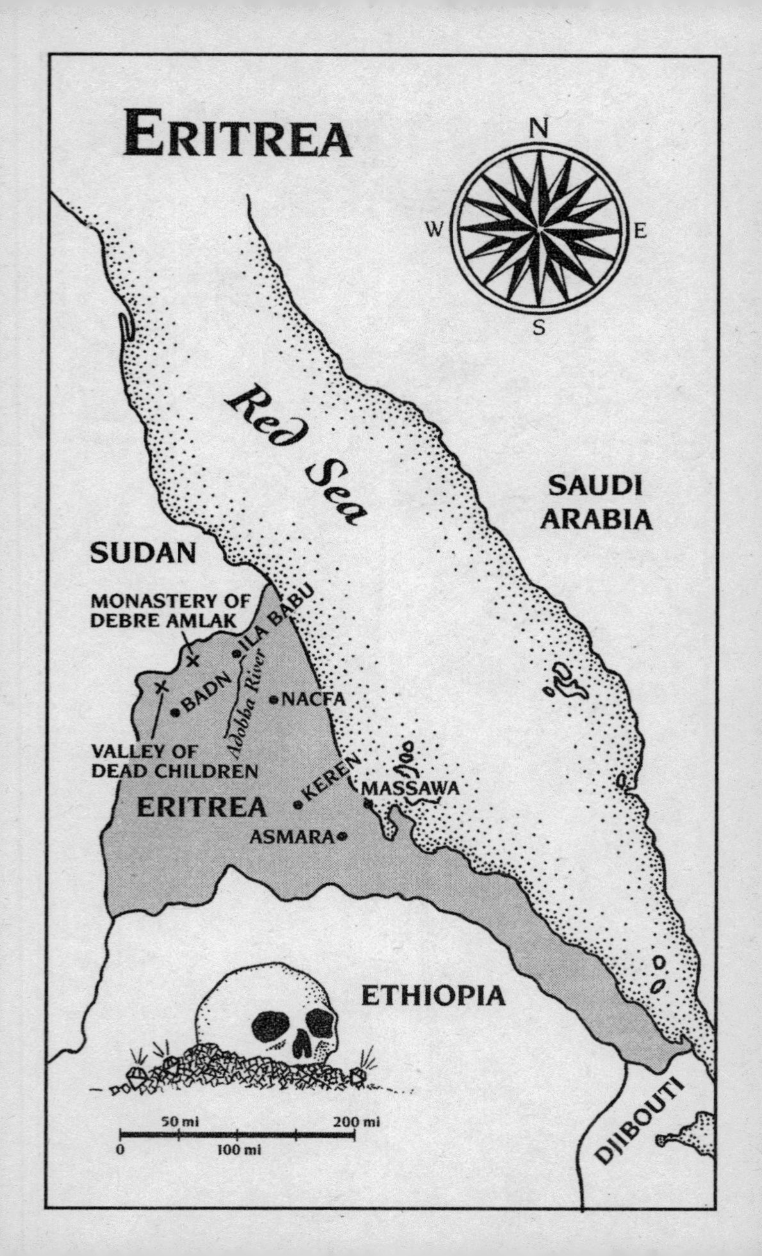
ERITREA
N
W
E
S
Red Sea
SAUDI ARABIA
SUDAN
MONASTERY OF DEBRE AMLAK
ILA BABU
BADN
Adobba River
NACFA
VALLEY OF DEAD CHILDREN
KEREN
MASSAWA
ERITREA
ASMARA
ETHIOPIA
DJIBOUTI
50 mi
200 mi
0
100 mi

Cape Kennedy, Florida
October 1989

Seated on his back for the last three hours and strapped to four and a half million pounds of explosives, Air Force Captain Len Cullins listened impatiently to the monotonous drone of the launch director. He assumed the lack of emotion was meant to reassure the flight crew, but he found the voice irritating beyond reason. With his first launch only two minutes away, Cullins still had time to fantasize about reaching through the radio link and strangling the director in his air-conditioned control center several miles away. The thought made him smile behind the dome of his helmet's face shield.

"*Atlantis,* this is Control. H-two tank pressurization okay. You are go for launch. Over."

"Roger, ground. We are go for launch. Out," Cullins intoned by rote.

The seconds dripped by, ground control and Cullins speaking in a prescripted speech devoid of any of the drama for what was about to take place. Outside the orbiter's heat-resistant windows, the deep black of the night shrouded eastern Florida. The stars beckoned and Cullins knew in a few minutes he would reach them. "Light this candle, for Christ's sake," he muttered.

"*Atlantis,* you are on your onboard computers. Over."

"Roger."

When Ground finally reached the critical final seconds of the countdown, Cullins could no longer hear the throb of the auxiliary power units or the fans and motors that hummed in the cabin. To him, all was silent in those last moments.

"Five . . . four . . . we have main engine start . . ."

Within a third of a second, the orbiter's main engines were pouring out a million pounds of thrust, white-hot exhaust searing the metal launch platform of pad 39A. However, all of this power did nothing except sway the *Atlantis* slightly forward on its mounts, what astronauts called "twang." From the pilot's seat, Cullins could not yet see the light from the controlled detonation of the liquid oxygen and hydrogen fuel, but the noise generated by the combustion shook *Atlantis* violently. For a brief instant he wondered just what the hell he had gotten himself into.

"Three . . . two . . . one . . ."

Just as the spacecraft righted itself from its expected wobble, the solid rocket boosters ignited, each of them putting out more than double the power of the orbiter's internal motors. It was as if Len Cullins and the other three men of the shuttle's crew had been collectively slammed against a wall. At the moment of ignition, thousands of gallons of water were dumped under the multiple exhaust nozzles in an effort to reduce the deadly vibrations caused by the roar of her throaty power plants. The water turned to billowing clouds of steam that reflected the fiery yellow exhaust.

"And we have liftoff." *No shit!*

In five seconds, the shuttle cleared the tower, and it was as if dawn had come to the Florida coast long before sunrise. The shuttle rose up and out of the mangrove swamps on a flaming trail of plasma that slashed the night like a knife stroke, chemical energy becoming kinetic so quickly that forty seconds after lift-off, the sound barrier was broken and then broken again only a few moments later. In two minutes, as the solid rocket boosters belched the last of their fuel, the orbiter was traveling four and a half times the speed of sound and was already twenty-eight miles above the earth.

While the onboard computers manipulated fuel flow into the *Atlantis'* internal engines to keep G-forces below three times normal, Len Cullins felt as if his body was being smeared into the contoured seat. Training had prepared him for this, but he still couldn't believe the feeling. So simple a matter as lifting a gloved hand from the armrest took nearly all of his strength.

"*Atlantis,* we have SRB separation."

"Roger. What a sight!" Cullins exclaimed.

The twin boosters attached to the bulbous external tank blew away from the orbiter like Catherine wheels, the last of their fuel spinning them in blazing arcs of fire and hot gas. And still the orbiter climbed, accelerating the entire time, past Mach ten like a mile marker on an empty interstate.

At an altitude of sixty-two miles, the crew was treated to the sun rising over the diminishing horizon. Even as they gasped like primitives at the reassuring sight, the *Atlantis* powered out of the atmosphere, to the realm where the Earth was little more than a painted backdrop, stripped of its warmth and beauty by the frigid vacuum of space.

"*Atlantis,* Ground. You are negative return. Do you copy?" Negative return meant that the orbiter was too high and too far downrange to land at their emergency fields in North Africa or Europe. Either *Atlantis* made it into space or died trying.

"Roger, Ground," Cullins replied to Houston Control, which had taken over the flight from Cape Kennedy as soon as the craft had cleared the launch tower. Ground Control for America's space program was located in Texas because of Lyndon Johnson's machinations during the program's infancy, a legacy that had since cost the agency millions in redundancies.

Eight minutes after the first rumble of the orbiter's main engines, they sucked the last of the fuel from the external tank, and suddenly a profound silence rushed in on the crew. It was at that exact moment, when the thrust of the engines died, and his arms lifted off his chair to float like swaying kelp in a tidal pool, that Cullins realized he had slipped Earth's bounds. He'd also done something every person in the world envied. He'd obtained a childhood dream.

"*Atlantis,* Ground. Go for ET separation."

"Roger. External tank separation . . . now."

Explosive bolts shoved the huge tank from the orbiter, and it began its long tumble back into the atmosphere, where it would harmlessly burn up.

"Gravity may be a law," Dale Markham, the payload specialist seated behind Cullins, joked. "But Newtonian mechanics is one hell of a 'get out of jail free' card."

Two hours after reaching orbit, with the payload bay doors open to vent excess heat, the crew got down to their primary mission task. They were already feeling the debilitating effects of zero gravity, and by tomorrow the crew would be about worthless. Therefore, NASA had scheduled a payload launch as soon as the shuttle had reached a stable orbit 250 miles above the planet.

Len Cullins and the other three men were still running on the adrenaline from the launch, yet nausea was becoming more than a nuisance and would soon impair them all. Videos and practice aboard NASA's converted Boeing 707 *Vomit Comet* could not prepare them for what it truly felt like to be in perpetual free fall. Sitting grim-faced in the pilot's chair, Cullins promised himself that he would not be the first to throw up the steak and egg breakfast prepared for them in Florida.

"*Atlantis,* Ground, prepare for transfer to Vandenberg for payload deployment." Vandenberg Airforce Base in California was in charge of the satellite in the shuttle's cargo bay, and its safe deployment was the principal mission for the shuttle's launch despite NASA's official press release about a communications satellite.

"Roger," Cullins said, and swallowed quickly, his stomach roiling just a few inches below his throat, his salivary glands on overdrive. "Vandenberg, go ahead, this is *Atlantis*."

"*Atlantis,* this is Vandenberg. We show green across the board for payload deployment."

"Roger, Vandenberg, we are go for payload deployment. Deployment is eighteen minutes." Cullins knew the window for launching the satellite from the cargo bay was very narrow due to the bird's particular mission. He switched to the internal radio net. "Dale, you've got eighteen minutes. How you doing back there?"

"Breakfast wasn't nearly as good coming up as it was going down, but I'm about ready," Markham replied.

Markham and the other payload specialist, Nick Fielding, were standing at the aft crew station, and until the satellite was safely away from the orbiter, total control of the shuttle had been turned over to them. Fielding would work the orbiter rotational controller that affected *Atlantis'* pitch, yaw, and roll, while Markham's specialty was the Canadian-built manipulator arm. Theirs was an exacting task due to the delicacy of the orbiter and payload and the effects of microgravity. Both men had heard the rumor that the Defense Department satellite, code-named Medusa, had cost two and a quarter billion dollars, and now its safety was their responsibility.

"Screw up this one, Dale, and we'll never see a tax refund check again," Fielding quipped as he used the joystick controller to lift the manipulator arm out of its storage rack.

"*Atlantis,* this is Vandenberg. Ground track has you nearing position, payload release in eleven minutes."

"Roger that ground, eleven minutes," Markham replied. He felt as though he was about to be sick again.

"You okay, Dale?"

"Never better." Markham belched wetly. "What's our attitude?"

"We're on the marks, nose down at 90 degrees," Fielding said.

"I still don't like this. The original mission planned for a full day of systems checks and practice with the manipulator arm before deploying the payload."

"We would have had it if the launch had gone off as planned yesterday. Blame Mother Nature for a windstorm, not the Air Force for bending their rules," Markham replied. "Besides, I don't mind saying I'll be relieved when this thing is out of the cargo bay. Have you heard what it can do?"

"Stow it, gentlemen, and get on with the task at hand." A

gruff voice came from behind them. Colonel Mike "Duke" Wayne was the shuttle commander and had the ultimate responsibility for this flight. Unlike the rest of the crew, the bristle-haired colonel had been in space before, on an early mission aboard *Challenger* also run by the Air Force in coordination with the National Security Agency.

Watching a video monitor and occasionally peering through the window, Markham twisted the manipulator arm until it had grasped the Medusa satellite's grapple, all the while aware of Wayne's steady gaze. Looking out over the cargo bay, the shuttle's vertical stabilizer was just a thin white line against the blackness of deep space.

"Four minutes, Lieutenant Markham," Wayne said.

"Roger," Markham replied without taking his eyes off the video feed from the manipulator's elbow camera, showing the satellite's orientation within the sixty-foot cargo bay. Until the Medusa was deployed and its solar panels and transceiver dish extended, it resembled a large, dark ice cream cone. Even with the cargo bay floodlights at full power, the satellite's skin appeared to be a darker shade of black than the space beyond, its radar-absorbing material seeming to consume light like a man-made black hole. The tip of the one visible sensor looked like the barrel of a large-caliber cannon, but was composed of intricately woven wires of what appeared to be gold.

Working the joystick like a surgeon, Markham lifted the Medusa out of its cradle. On land, the manipulator arm had less strength than an average man, but in the void, it could easily handle the eleven-ton satellite. Like the appendage of some monstrous insect, the fifty-foot arm eased the satellite upward so it hung suspended over the floor of the cargo bay.

Markham sucked in a breath in an effort to calm his churning stomach. A slight twitch on the controller could slam the Medusa against the side of the shuttle or launch it on an unstable orbit, and he was about to be sick. He safed the arm by locking it into position, reached for a motion sickness bag, and vomited.

"I've got the Medusa launch," Nick Fielding said, quickly taking over.

Markham smiled a weak thanks, his deep Florida tan faded to a sickly shade of green. As soon as he floated away from the aft crew station, Colonel Wayne stepped onto the variable-height work platform situated before the manipulator arm controls. "Vandenberg Control, this is *Atlantis*. We are prepared for payload separation on your mark. Attitude match confirmed." Wayne's brusque competence was like a steadying hand to Fielding, who didn't particularly want the responsibility of the launch.

"*Atlantis,* this is General Kolwicki. "Is that you, Duke?"

"Affirmative, sir. *Atlantis* standing by for countdown. We're all ready for our vacation."

Normally, NASA's tight budget called for orbiter crews to carry out scientific experiments after completing their primary mission objectives in order to maximize time in space and justify the staggering cost of launching a shuttle into orbit. However, the launching of the Medusa was deemed so critical that for the four days the shuttle was to remain in orbit, the crewmen were nothing more than sightseers, free to use their time as they saw fit. NASA had insisted that the crew remain in orbit for the extra days in order to perpetuate the deception about this military flight.

"*Atlantis,* this is Vandenberg Control. One minute from my mark for payload release . . . Mark."

Markham, Fielding, and Cullins might have heard rumors about the Medusa but only Wayne knew its true capabilities. Medusa wasn't just the single satellite in the cargo bay; it was an entire system, five platforms in total, four of them already in orbit and bearing down on the *Atlantis*. The final component, the satellite they were about to launch, was the crux of the system and had cost almost half of the $2.25 billion budget.

Designed to be the eyes of President Reagan's Strategic Defense Initiative, the Medusa was unlike any spy satellite ever built. Military planners knew that Soviet doctrine called for several silos and hardened bunkers for each of their nuclear-tipped intercontinental ballistic missiles. They could use these sites at random, secretly moving the missiles on trucks in an attempt to foil American targeting. Thus, a Russian launch could come from any number of places, many of them unknown or untargeted. It was a horrifying version of a card shuffle. Even with an unlimited budget, the Pentagon could not build enough laser defenses to cover all possible Soviet and Eastern European targets. In order for Star Wars to be successful, the U.S. needed to pinpoint the actual silos and bunkers where the rockets were housed at the time of launch. This way, if a launch ever occurred, the space-based lasers would already be locked on at the moment of liftoff and not waste precious seconds trying to acquire their target. To accomplish this, the Pentagon needed a new type of spy satellite that could look down from space and see through the rock and concrete and steel shelters and reveal Russia's most closely guarded secrets.

Medusa worked like a ground-penetrating sonar but employed charged subatomic particles rather than sound waves. The four receiver satellites that were currently orbiting in a diamond formation were poised to receive bounce-back information from the principle positron gun mounted on the about-to-be-released Medusa. Much of the science behind Medusa was beyond Wayne's understanding. He did know the Medusa mounted a plutonium reactor to create and fire the positrons and utilized the theorem of electromagnetic repulsion to receive the rebounded particles for collection by the other satellites. In computer modeling, Medusa could accurately detect a hardened missile silo, tell if it was currently storing an ICBM, pinpoint its command bunker and support tunnels, and even discover the underground piping conduits for power cables and dedicated communications lines. Medusa could see through the oceans as if they were glass and find nuclear submarines no matter how deeply or silently they were running. It was so precise that a detailed map of a mine field could be produced after just a few sweeps, beamed to a command post in real time, and give the exact position of every buried enemy explosive.

"*Atlantis,* this is Vandenberg. Targets now four miles distant, closing at eight miles per minute. They are two thousand feet above your orbit."

"Roger, Ground. Fifteen seconds." Colonel Wayne's eyes locked on the digital counter, his finger poised on the release trigger.

Because of the shuttle's attitude, the four receiver satellites were approaching *Atlantis'* belly, sliding by at a slightly quicker relative speed. The crew would not be able to see them until they had passed, appearing above the shuttle's tail on their silent journey.

"*Atlantis,* stand by for payload separation in . . . three . . . two . . . one. Mark."

Wayne jerked the trigger on the control stick at the same time Nick Fielding activated the maneuvering thrusters to ease the shuttle lower in orbit to avoid colliding with the satellite.

Even as Wayne was stowing the manipulator arm, the computers on board the Medusa woke to the commands of Ground Control. Like an umbrella, the satellite began to open, solar-collection panels extending that would charge the craft's internal systems and help in its attitude and orbital changes. The energy output of the plutonium reactor only powered the positron wave gun. Moving the satellite around the planet was accomplished with a solar/chemical rocket that would need fuel replenishment every one to three years.

Watching through a video screen, Wayne and Fielding stared in awe as the Medusa grew in size, panels built to exacting tolerances telescoping and unfolding like Japanese origami. In moments, the ice cream cone shape had transformed into a cruel phantom that was stooped over the earth like vengeful gargoyle. Medusa looked like Death, if Armageddon's messenger had been fashioned by man.

"Here come the Four Horsemen," Fielding muttered.

The four receiver satellites appeared over the shuttle's tail, faint glimmers against the star field. Just as they came into view, the Medusa received a command from Vandenberg, and a thin wisp of expended fuel pulsed from one of its jets. It accelerated away to join the others.

Len Cullins had come to the aft flight deck and looked over Fielding's shoulder. "Makes you wonder what we could accomplish if we spent our time creating rather than destroying, huh?"

Wayne looked at him sharply. "You even think that way again, I'll have you court-martialed."

"What the hell was that?" Alarm piqued Nick Fielding's voice. He was staring out the window, angling his body so he could track the hurtling satellites.

"What?" Wayne asked, turning away from Cullins.

"I saw a flash right behind the receiver birds, like the sun reflecting off something metallic."

"You sure?"

"Yes, sir. It was only for a second, and they're getting too far away to see clearly, but I definitely saw something."

Wayne opened a channel to Vandenberg. "Ground Control this is *Atlantis*. We have a visual of debris behind Medusa. Can you confirm? It appeared to be in dangerous proximity."

"Roger that, *Atlantis*." The ground controller could not mask the anxiety in his voice. "We just got a flash warning from U.S. Space Command at Colorado Springs. They're bumping up the power to their radar station at Cavalier Air Station in North Dakota, but preliminary telemetry puts it on a collision course. Stand by."

"What was it, Nick?" Cullins asked.

"I don't know. It didn't look big, but there's no way to really tell."

"*Atlantis* standing by," Wayne said to Vandenberg Control.

Several seconds ticked by. Only the sound of the shuttle's machinery and the low moans from Dale Markham punctuated the silence.

"Vandenberg Control to *Atlantis*. Duke, this is General Kolwicki. We want you to change attitude and increase the speed of your orbit to give us a visual assessment of what's happening. Whatever's behind the Medusa is so small we can't get an accurate fix."

"Yes, General. Changing attitude now." Wayne nodded to Fielding, who had moved back to his station at the reaction control system. Using small bursts of gas, the shuttle swung 90 degrees until it was in a head-down position facing the fleeing Medusa.

"*Atlantis,* ground track shows you gaining on Medusa at fifty feet per minute. Please increase orbital speed. Distance to Medusa, one thousand yards."

"Roger, Ground."

While Wayne and Fielding remained at the aft crew station, Len Cullins ducked back to the cockpit to look through the main view windows as they hunted down the unidentified object dogging their five birds. He slid into his molded seat and stared into the emptiness, trying to catch a glimpse of whatever Fielding had seen. He could hear Wayne speaking with General Kolwicki, the head of America's space command, through the communications net.

"Range, five hundred yards. Whatever's chasing our birds will overtake in fifteen seconds."

Cullins began counting backward in his mind. At eight seconds he could see the five satellites glimmering just above earth's hazy blue horizon. They looked like golden fireflies at this distance, their details lost in the planet's reflective glow. At four seconds, he could see them more clearly; the central bodies of the receiver platforms with their spiderweb collection dishes spread wide. At two seconds, he saw a dull silver flash behind one of the receiver satellites, so brief that had he not anticipated it, he would have thought it a chimera.

Ground control called out "Now," and a magnetic torque wrench lost during a Gemini space walk twenty-five years earlier, one of a hundred thousand pieces of space junk, passed through the collection dish of one of the satellites, latched on to a steel casing panel, and unbalanced the entire unit. The violence of the impact was lost in the void because there was no sound, but it hit with the force of a bullet and the receiver satellite began to tumble. As a horrified Cullins watched, it flipped three times before slamming into the main satellite.

"Oh shit, we're going to lose it." Cullins heard the unperterbable General Kolwicki shout.

"That's affirmative, General," Cullins said as he watched Medusa start falling toward earth.

Two hundred and sixty miles below the *Atlantis,* General Reginald Kolwicki watched America's most expensive military accident unfold. In just three and a half minutes, Medusa went from crowning achievement to unrecoverable debacle. Telemetry from the positron gun platform confirmed that the satellite was in a degrading orbit and that it would not respond to ground commands to fire its maneuvering rockets. It was falling, and there was nothing the forty assembled men and women in the control room could do to prevent it.

"Try the autonomous flight program," Kolwicki said to a computer technician who'd been typing furiously, trying to regain control of Medusa.

"No response, sir. The central processor is off-line."

"Are you getting anything from the damned thing?"

"Positron gun is on stand-by, and all encryption routines are nominal."

"Great. Medusa is about to burn up in the atmosphere, but it wants to still take pictures and keep the data a secret." Kolwicki growled at the irony. "How much longer?"

"Medusa will enter the atmosphere in twenty-five seconds. Total loss in thirty seconds at the most."

"Shit." A career military man who saw his career burning up in outer space, Kolwicki had no options. "What's the bird's position?"

"Over North Africa, tracking southeast. It'll burn up above the Indian Ocean."

"Might as well turn on the positron gun as she goes down. Maybe we'll gain something from this snafu." Kolwicki felt like a ship's captain knowing his command was going under and still ordering full steam ahead.

"Sir?"

"Just do it," he snapped.

Fingers flying in a blur, the tech snapped off several commands. The plutonium reactor keyed up, beaming supercharged positrons back to earth in a swath that cut across northern Africa from Chad, across Sudan and Ethiopia and finally to Djibouti and Somalia. In all, it took "pictures" of two thousand square miles, but its data was incomplete. Several passes over the same area would be necessary to gather enough information to allow analysis of the subsurface topography. It was only after the satellite began entering the atmosphere and the friction-induced heat climbed dangerously that Medusa shut down in an automatic safety mode to prevent a radioactive accident.

In Greek mythology, Medusa was a witch whose stare could turn men into stone. As Medusa fell from space and was enveloped in a white hot fireball of its own immolation, the satellite studied the barren African wasteland. Buried under tons of rock and stone, it saw something that man had hidden more than two thousand years ago in the hope that it would never be allowed to escape. Like its ancient namesake, Medusa's glance would bring death.

Northern Eritrea
January of this year

Jakob Steiner was beyond caring that he was about to die.

Death would be a welcome release from the torture of the past hour. His body was so racked with pain and the effects of dehydration that his will to live had evaporated as quickly as the sweat that had once poured freely from his skin. He had stopped sweating soon after his tormentors took up the chase, pushing him hard across the arid landscape. His khaki bush shirt and pants had once been wet with perspiration but now showed only white circles of dried salt under his arms and at his groin. At first he'd thought he was outpacing the *Shifta* bandits as they dogged him across the rocky desert, but quickly he realized that his initial burst of speed could not compete with the machine-like endurance of the terrorists. They'd managed to catch him easily and now lagged only a few paces behind. He could hear their boots on the loose soil, smell their unwashed bodies over his own stench.

They were toying with him. They could have killed him earlier with a shot from the AK-47s all four carried. Yet like a pack of hunting dogs, they chased him, hounding him with occasional shouts, pushing him beyond his own level of endurance so he ran on pure instinct, fight or flight. An hour had passed, an hour of unrelenting fear, and Steiner was reaching the point where he could not continue, when fight became a better option than flight.

Steiner hadn't had a drink of water since just before returning to his camp following another unsuccessful foray into one of the hundreds of box canyons in this part of the country. Zarai, his native guide, had remained in the Spartan camp as ordered whenever the scientist went exploring. Steiner gave no reason to the Eritrean, and custom demanded that Zarai not ask.

This morning marked the eighth day the two men had spent in the desolate region, a barren section of Eritrea's lowlands consisting of jagged ridges and mountains too steep and dry to be inhabited. Because there was nothing in these formidable canyons and plateaus to attract the agrarian Eritreans, the duo were almost certain to be the first explorers in the region since the Italian occupation prior to the Second World War.

Steiner had come into the camp shortly before eleven. A shrieking wind had picked up, throwing grit in his eyes and clogging his nose and mouth so he'd walked the last few miles with a bandanna tied around his face and his expedition hat pulled low. He could hear the nylon of his and Zarai's two tents snapping like the sails of a racing yacht.

For the first time since Jakob had begun his explorations, Zarai was not waiting for him in his usual position, hunkered over the low smokeless fire he used to brew endless cups of tea. In fact, the fire had been kicked out. The circle of stones ringing the pit was scattered across the space between the two tents, and Zarai's treasured teakettle lay haphazardly on the smooth sand. Steiner was too tired to sense any danger until he was pulling off his boots on the camp stool in front of his tent.

It was the smell that drew his attention first. The fine hairs on the back of his hands rose. He could feel the premonition of danger like a thousand centipedes marching up his arms to his chest. Jakob stood, his filthy, sweat-smeared socks whispering on the sand as he spun in place, sensing that he was being watched.

Without warning, Zarai came flying through Jakob's tent, propelled by some unseen force. Steiner staggered back, tripping over his own feet so that he fell heavily, his eyes unable to tear away from the sight of his guide dying just a pace away.

Zarai's face was covered with blood that had leaked from the sockets where his eyes had been. Fat black flies buzzed quickly back to their sanguinous meal, blanketing his head only seconds after his body came to rest. Zarai moaned weakly, brushing his curled hand along the sand in an effort to reach his mutilated face.

Jakob screamed, a high-pitched keen not unlike a young girl's, his stomach turning to oil. He crabbed across the ground in an effort to distance himself from his companion's pitiable figure.

Zarai clawed weakly at the ground again and went still, his last gasp no more than a whisper in the wind.

Then four greyhound-thin men came into the camp. They were dressed in stained and dusty uniforms, the camouflage pattern all but washed out, the cuffs, collars, and countless pockets showing frayed edges. While the clothing they wore was tattered, all four were in the prime of their lives, which for this part of Africa meant early twenties. Their matching Soviet assault rifles looked well cared for and greased.

The young men stood arrogantly, flat dark eyes regarding the cowering Steiner with contempt. Unlike Zarai, who had lighter skin and Arab features, a reminder of Eritrea's long association with the Middle East, these men were so black their skin had almost a blue tinge. Their features were classical negroid: high foreheads, thickened lips, and wide, handsome noses. While Steiner's field of expertise was archaeology, he recognized that these men were from Sudan, born in the ancient lands of Kush. Steiner knew enough of modern politics to know his life could not be measured in minutes.

A civil war had been raging in Sudan for decades, fought between the northern majority of Muslims against the Christians from the south. Sudan's small but appreciable animist population was caught in the middle. Relief agencies had been granted only sporadic entrance into the country to minister aid, so estimates of those killed were unreliable, but they ranged into the millions. In the past few years, driven by disease and malnutrition, many of those fighting in the south had turned to more mercenary activities—raiding aid shipments, plundering the camps of the quarter-million Eritrean refugees living in the country, and staging cross-border sorties for food or medicine and, more commonly now, to kidnap victims to be held for ransom.

Jakob Steiner lay on the ground, his socks stained the same dun color as his khaki clothes. His eyes were wide and fearful as he looked at the four men towering over him, four men who doubtlessly had perpetrated some of the despicable things Zarai had spoken of during their nights in the camp.

"What do you want from me?" he asked in German, his voice made raw by thirst and fear.

He got no reaction from the four terrorists, but noticed that one was carrying a large machete that hung from a hook on his belt. Zarai's blood was a red-black stain on the weapon's blade. He repeated the question in English. Again, the men looked at him blankly, ignoring the flies that had descended on the camp like a plague. Two jagged-wing vultures circled high above, gliding on the thermal updrafts produced by the sun hammering the desert.

"I have nothing," Jakob stammered. Even if the men didn't understand the words, they could certainly hear the pleading tone in his voice. "Just a little food, enough for another day or two, and just a small amount of money. I have more money in the capital, Asmara. I could send it to you, but you must let me go."

Silence, save the wind blowing across the camp.

"I am a scientist. I study ancient bones. I have no powerful friends. I am worth nothing to you as a hostage. Please let me go." Jakob was crying now, tears running into the dust caked on his face. "Please, take anything you want, but let me go. Do not hurt me!"

The four Sudanese did not react as his voice rose to a shrill whine. Then the terrorist with the machete, who was a little older than the others, kicked Steiner's boots across the few feet of open ground separating them from the Austrian scientist.

"You are a spy from America here to enslave our people," the cadre leader said in English as if he had memorized the words.

"No," Jakob shouted, hopeful for the first time because one of the men understood him. "I am not from America, I am Austrian. I come from Europe. I am not a spy. I study old bones, the bones of our ancient ancestors. I am not here to steal from you."

"You are from America. You are going to die. Put on your boots and go. We will give you a quarter of the clock dial to run, and then we will hunt you down." The young Sudanese showed off a cheap watch slung loosely around his wrist. Steiner had fifteen minutes to get into his boots and run.

"But I'm not from—"

"Run!"

Steiner didn't even bother lacing his boots. He merely slipped them on, ignoring the small piles of sand that had already accumulated in the toes, and began sprinting.

It took the terrorists only a half hour to catch their quarry, but they did not move in for the kill. They ran behind Steiner, taunting him, goading him. It went on like this for another hour, an hour of Steiner hearing his own painful breathing tearing through his chest and his sore and swollen feet tripping over the jagged ground. Jakob hadn't run like this in his entire life. His legs were rubbery beneath him, his feet slapping ineffectually against the hardpan. His pudgy arms were pumping slower and slower, like a machine grinding down for want of fuel.

The Sudanese slowed to a walking pace behind the shambling Austrian. Their breath came slow and even, and only a little sweat gleaned against their skin. Sensing that the chase was at an end, the leader came forward and smashed down on the scientist's knee with the butt of his AK-47. The joint crumbled and Jakob fell to the ground, rolling in a thin cloud of chalky dust.

Settled comfortably on their haunches, the Sudanese ringed Steiner, their assault rifles held between their knees. The leader lit a Turkish cigarette and passed it to his men, each taking a long draw before giving it to the next. The cigarette made three complete circles before the leader took one last drag, pinched off the burning tip to shred the remaining leaf, and tucked the filter in the pocket of his uniform blouse.

The hunt had ended in another of the countless dry riverbeds that snaked through the lowlands. The banks were not steep but still radiated the heat like mirrors. Blisters of sweat appeared on the men's faces and exposed arms for the first time. They shuffled their feet in the flaky stones at the bottom of the wash, waiting for their leader to give them the order to dispatch the interloper.

Jakob's chest rose and fell in a rapid cadence. His heart felt like it was breaking his ribs with each beat. Somewhere beyond his pelvis, in the sea of pain that had once been his legs, his shattered knee throbbed with an unholy pounding. Already the joint had swollen to twice its normal size. Each time his heart beat, the sharp bone fragments ground against each other, further mincing the tendons and ligaments. Through cracked and bleeding lips, he muttered long forgotten pieces of scripture, freely quoting the Talmud and the Old and New Testaments, mangling faiths in an attempt to supplicate a god, any god.

"Lo, I walk through the valley of the shadow of death." It sounded more like poetry than prayer.

"Thou shall not kill," he screamed, but the sound was little more than a dry croak.

"You are a spy for America," the young terrorist leader accused again, sliding closer to Jakob. "Only your death has worth to us."

"It's not true," Jakob Steiner cried.

"You were sent here to steal from us, and we were sent to stop you."

"Oh, God, please, I only study the past. I don't care about—"

The cadre leader, a man who called himself Mahdi, crashed the butt of his rifle against Steiner's head just at the hair line. The blow was not enough to kill, and Jakob screamed loudly, curling into a ball in a purely reflexive gesture.

Mahdi stood and swung his weapon down again, missing Steiner's head but breaking his collarbone with the blow.

Like jackals, the others sprang on him, raining blows on the defenseless scientist. Steiner screamed for only a few seconds before being beaten into unconsciousness. Soon Steiner was dead, but Mahdi allowed his men to continue for another minute before calling an end to the assault.

"Enough," he said, and his men backed away from the bloody corpse. "Strip the body and then we'll return to his camp to erase all evidence of his presence."

Mahdi tossed aside his old and worn boots and replaced them with Steiner's before joining his troops for the run back to the base camp. There were a number of items that would fetch good money on the black market in Sudan, and he wanted to make sure his undisciplined men did not ruin them in their frenzy of destruction.

Arlington, Virginia
Four Months Later

Philip Mercer was in the habit of waking just before dawn so he could watch the pearly light seep through the skylight above his bed. These early-morning minutes were an important time for him. It was when he did his best thinking, oftentimes coalescing thoughts that had come to him in his sleep.

The night before, he'd helped his friend, Harry White, celebrate his eightieth birthday. The octogenarian was sleeping off the night's excesses on a downstairs couch. Mercer hadn't indulged nearly as much as Harry, so his head felt reasonably clear, but this morning his mind was troubled. He wanted to stay relaxed, but the muscles in his legs and back began to tense, his fists tightening with unreleased energy. He grunted and rolled out of bed.

Mercer was a mining engineer and consultant who had reached the pinnacle of his profession. Within the hard-rock mining industry, his capabilities were almost legendary. A recent article in a trade publication credited him with saving more than four hundred lives following mining disasters and in the next paragraph detailed the more than three billion dollars in mineral finds he'd made for various mining concerns all over the globe. His fees had made him a wealthy man, and maybe that was part of his problem. He'd become too comfortable.

The thrill of making a new find or the adrenaline rush of delving into the earth to pull out trapped men had begun to pale. Since his struggle against Ivan Kerikov and his eco-terrorist allies in Alaska last October, Mercer was having a hard time returning to his normal life. He felt a hollowness that just wouldn't go away. He wanted to believe he hadn't become addicted to that kind of mortal danger, but it was difficult to convince himself. Pitting his reputation against the normal hazards of his career didn't seem to be enough anymore.

His street was lined with identical three-story townhouses, close enough to the city center to be convenient but far enough away to remain quiet. Unlike the others, Mercer lived in his alone and had done extensive remodeling to turn it into his home. The lion's share of his income went into its mortgage. The front quarter of the building was open from floor to roof with his bedroom overlooking the atrium. An antique spiral staircase connected the levels. He dressed quickly and spun down to retrieve the morning paper from the front step.

The second floor had two small guest rooms and a balconied library with a view of the tiled mezzanine. It also contained what had become Mercer's living room, a reproduction of an English gentleman's club that he and his friends affectionately called *The Bar*. It had two sectional leather couches, several matching chairs, a television, and a large ornate mahogany bar fronted by six dark cane stools. The lump under a blanket on one of the couches was Harry. Behind the bar was a circa 1950s lock-lever refrigerator and shelving for enough liquor to shame most commercial drinking establishments. The automatic coffee maker on the back bar had already brewed a barely potable sludge.

Seated with his coffee and paper, Mercer tried to read through the day's fare. The *Post* led with another story about the fatal bombing at Jerusalem's Western Wall six weeks ago. Defense Minister Chaim Levine, a hard-line candidate for the upcoming elections, said that if he were leading the country, such attacks would never happen, and if they did, the investigation would take days, not weeks. He was calling for a draconian crackdown on all Palestinians and a suspension of the latest peace talks. Mercer read that another victim had died in the hospital, bringing the death toll to one hundred and sixty-seven. The destabilized

Middle East held his attention for only a couple of paragraphs, and he slid the rest of the paper out of reach.

Harry still snored from the couch. His rattling breathing sounded like the explosive grunts of some large animal. He gave a startled snort, and then he was awake, yawning broadly.

Mercer smiled. "Good morning. How do you feel on the first day of the rest of your life?"

"Jesus Christ," Harry rasped "What time is it?"

Mercer looked at his watch. "Six-thirty."

"I liked it better when you and Aggie were together. You never came downstairs until after nine." Harry immediately recognized his gaffe. "Oh, shit, I'm sorry. That was a rotten thing to say."

Aggie Johnston had been gone for four months, and Mercer still felt the ache of her absence. She had been in Alaska with him and had gone through even more than he had. The relationship that followed had been rocky even at its best. Though she came from a wealthy family who controlled a multinational oil company, she was an ardent environmentalist, and the attraction she and Mercer shared was not strong enough to overcome their different views of his profession. He had not wanted it to end, but he couldn't stand the arguments either. All he remembered of the day of their breakup was walking around Washington for nearly ten hours in a total fog, his mind unable to accept what had happened even if the decision had been his.

For the first time in over a decade, since the death of his fiancée, Tory Wilkes, Mercer had let someone into his life only to lose her again. Now, whenever he looked at a woman, he wouldn't allow himself to feel anything. He lived like a monk, and the pain made it easy to ignore the sexual side of his nature. On the rare occasion an attractive woman entered Tiny's, the neighborhood bar he and Harry frequented, his conflicting emotions would leave him sullen and withdrawn.

"Don't worry about it." Mercer tried to smile.

Harry levered himself up from the couch and took a moment to roll up his pant leg to strap on his prosthetic limb. He'd lost his leg so long ago, his walk to the bar was natural and without any trace of a limp.

Mercer had met Harry the night he moved into the renovated townhouse. He had gone to Tiny's as a distraction from the monotony of unpacking while Harry seemed to live in the seedy establishment. Harry was more than twice Mercer's age, but both enjoyed a recluse's solitude and a bachelor's aversion to sobriety. They never analyzed the deep friendship that had grown since then, but others who knew them realized that, in each other, they sought the family neither had. Childless, Harry needed to know that there would be someone who remembered him after he was gone. Mercer wanted the stabilizing force that his friend represented, a responsibility and loyalty to someone other than himself. In many ways, one was an older version of the other, yet they complemented as well. Harry acted as a temper to Mercer and Mercer's vitality reminded the octogenarian what his life had once been. And along the way, they had learned to rely on each other, an act alien to both men. What had started casually had solidified into a bond stronger than any father and son's, for this was an association of choice.

Mercer made a fresh pot of coffee, one not brewed to his masochistic tastes, while Harry smoked through his first of forty daily cigarettes. Harry was quieter than normal, and Mercer sensed something was bothering him. "You okay?"

"Ah, it's nothing." While time may have thinned his frame so that his hands and feet seemed oversized and folds of skin hung from his face, Harry's voice still grated like a rusty machine tool. "How long have we known each other?"

"Going on seven years now. Why?"

"I made the mistake of watching this news show a couple days ago. They had a segment about aging."

"Oh shit."

"Oh shit is right," Harry replied. "Do you know that statistically I've been dead for nearly fifteen years? According to the experts, I have a more dangerous lifestyle than an L.A. gang member. I smoke two packs a day, I down a couple bottles of booze a week, and the last time I got any exercise was World War Two."

Mercer grinned. "Don't worry about it. You're the other end of the spectrum, that's all. You make up for the health-nut Wall Street types who drop dead at forty. When was the last time you were sick?"

"This morning."

"Hangovers don't count."

"Christ, I don't know. It's been years."

"So what's the problem?"

"I don't know. Death, I guess."

"You afraid of dying? Who's not."

"I guess that's it. I'm more afraid of living nowadays," Harry said through the cloud of a fresh cigarette. "Death is starting to sound good to me."

Mercer looked at him sharply. "Don't you talk like that, old man."

Mercer had lost both his parents when he was still a child, and while his grandparents had been wonderful surrogates, they, too, had died while he was a freshmen at Penn State. Death was not unknown to him; he'd seen it in a hundred forms. But to hear Harry talking about it, sounding like he embraced it, was chilling. For Mercer, death was the enemy to be fought at all costs.

"Relax, I'm not dead yet. It just doesn't sound so bad anymore." Harry pulled himself from the sullen mood. "Besides, if I go, Tiny will lose his best customer."

"If you paid your bar tab, maybe."

"I guess it's just post-birthday blues," Harry dismissed easily. "So what are you up to today?"

"Probably start working on my final report to Yukon Coal," Mercer replied.

"You don't sound thrilled by the prospect."

"You have no idea," Mercer breathed. "This is my second contract since Alaska, and I just can't make myself interested anymore. I've changed and I don't know why."

"Yes, you do. You just don't want to admit it." Harry eyed Mercer, judging how much honesty his friend needed and guessed correctly that Mercer wanted it all. "You're lonely. You miss Aggie, but you can't go back to her. I chose bachelorhood and it's a lifestyle that suits me, but you're different. It isn't for you. I stayed single because I just don't want to be bothered with the whole thing, but you're single because you're scared of women."

Mercer was surprised by Harry's statement. It wasn't at all what he'd expected. "I wasn't talking about that, but what in the hell do you mean, I'm scared of women?"

"You are. Ever since Tory's death, you're afraid of losing someone again, so you keep people, especially women, at a distance. When you let Aggie in and your relationship ended in disaster, you stopped letting yourself feel. You've shut yourself off because you're afraid of being hurt again. Hell, right now I'd say you are more afraid of living than I am."

"Bullshit," Mercer said angrily.

"Hit a nerve, didn't I?"

Mercer said nothing. The pain of Tory's death was right under the surface. He could feel it now, but deeper than that, he felt anger, anger at himself for not preventing it. He had been there when she was murdered by an IRA gunman and still blamed himself for not stopping it, even if there had been no chance he could.

"Hey, listen, I'm sorry. Maybe that was out of line."

"No, it really wasn't. I don't think I'm afraid of living, but you're right, I am scared of being hurt."

"Who isn't? That's what it means to be human. Every time you let someone in, you run the risk of pain. I think for a long time you were willing to accept the loneliness, but Aggie reminded you of the actual price you've been paying. You haven't been yourself since you two split."

Mercer considered Harry's words. "I've been thinking it has to do with the danger we went through. It was the excitement I was missing."

"I'm sure that's part of it. I never felt more alive than during the war. There's nothing like being chased by a Japanese sub or surviving a kamikaze attack to tell you what it means to feel. Do you think surviving the oil rig collapse and the tanker fire and all the other stuff in Alaska opened you a little bit and Aggie stepped through your armor?"

"So she caught me at a vulnerable moment?"

"No, she caught you at a time when you were actually feeling for a change. You aren't the hardened recluse you thought you were."

Mercer couldn't deny the charge, but he wasn't ready to admit it was true either. "So what should I do?"

"How the hell should I know?" Harry laughed. "I *am* the hardened recluse I think I am."

"Bastard," Mercer smirked.

"For whatever it's worth, I think just talking like this is good for you. It's the first time you've ever brought it up, which means you're probably ready to start dealing with it. I don't have much in the way of experience to help, but I'm here to listen." Harry struggled into his windbreaker. "Why don't you work on your report and meet me at Tiny's around four?"

Mercer considered for a second. "Yeah, I think I need that."

Mercer was just toweling off when the phone rang. It was twenty minutes until four, and thinking it was Harry telling him to hurry, he answered, "Keep your dentures in. I'll be there in a minute."

"Dr. Philip Mercer?" an unfamiliar female voice asked.

Oops. "Yes, this is Philip Mercer."

"Please hold the line for Undersecretary of State Hyde." The woman put him on hold before he could ask if he'd heard right.

Hyde came on the line an instant later. "Dr. Mercer, this is Prescott Hyde, Undersecretary of State for African Affairs. I hope I'm not disturbing you."

"No sir. Not at all," Mercer replied, naked and still dripping on the carpet next to his bed.

"Good, good." There was an element of the Teddy Roosevelt bluff in Hyde's voice, a collegiate jocularity that might not have been forced but was certainly polished. "I'm surprised to find you home on a Monday afternoon, but Sam Becker said you worked strange hours."

While Mercer did not know Prescott Hyde, he was familiar with Sam Becker, the head of the National Security Agency. The two had worked together on the Vulcan's Forge affair in Hawaii. Mercer knew the use of Becker's name was more than just name-dropping. In just that single sentence, Hyde told Mercer that he'd done some checking into his background and knew of his reputation. Mercer wanted to be incensed, but he found he was more intrigued than anything else.

"What can I do for you, Mr. Undersecretary?"

"Please, call me Bill. Sam tells me people just call you Mercer, is that right?"

"Among other things."

"Excellent. Good to know the boys at the NSA have their information correct," Hyde laughed. "Listen, Mercer, I'll come to the point. We're both busy men, after all."

It had taken only twenty seconds for Mercer to dislike Hyde. Most public officials took at least a full minute. "You called me," he said cautiously, feeling he was walking into a trap. "What can I do for you?"

"Right to business, I like that," Hyde said as if it was Mercer who had instigated the call. "All right, then. I may have a job for you. Something right up your alley, so to speak."

"I didn't know the State Department was into mining these days." Mercer tried to keep the disdain from his voice.

"It's nothing like that. But it is a little hard to explain over the phone, if you know what I mean?" Hyde's bonhomie was wearing on Mercer fast. "Something's come across my desk that is tailor-made for your unique talents. I've asked around town and you've got yourself quite a reputation for getting tough jobs done. I know all about what you did in Hawaii a few years back and what happened in Alaska last year. While not nearly as exciting, what I have represents a similar challenge."

Just hearing the word sent a jolt through Mercer. "What sort of challenge?"

"Let's just say that you alone are qualified to possibly help millions of people. If that doesn't whet your appetite, nothing I say will. I'd like to get together with you. Is tomorrow okay? Shall we say one o'clock at my office?"

"I think not." Mercer was going to meet with Hyde, but in any opening negotiations with someone who wanted something, it was best to quickly establish control. "Shall we say noon at the Willard Hotel? You can buy me lunch while we talk."

Hyde chuckled. "Very good, sir. I knew your price would be high. However, it'll be worth it. For both of us. Tomorrow at noon."

"Tomorrow at noon," Mercer agreed and hung up.

Now, what in the hell was that all about? He finished dressing and left to meet Harry, realizing that the tension he'd felt this morning was gone.

Across town, the listener waited a few seconds for both parties to clear the line, then began tapping at the computer in front of him. Behind him, his superior waited, watching the screen as the listener attempted to track the signal from their bug.

While the living room of the College Park apartment had traditional furniture, the two bedrooms were unlike any other in the high-rise complex a few blocks from the University of Maryland. The first contained desks, computers, and all manner of communications gear with one wall dominated by a large map of the city. The other was furnished with three sets of bunk beds, jammed together so closely that only a narrow walkway separated them. The permanent staff who used the suite slept in shifts to minimize their conspicuousness.

"It's an unlisted number in the Washington area. Give me a second to track it down," the eavesdropper said. The computer whirled frantically, narrowing down through the unlisted numbers until it found the one it wanted. The algorithms used for the search were the most sophisticated in the communications encryption/decryption arena and halved the time normally needed to trace calls.

"Philip Mercer," the listener said to his boss. "I've got an address in Arlington. The computer's about to print out a hard copy of their conversation."

"Do you have anything on him in Archive?"

The listener cleared his screen and brought up their massive database. A moment later, a slim dossier of Philip Mercer appeared. The overseer, a medium-built man in his late thirties with black curling hair and strong dark eyes, read the file as his aide scrolled through it, memorizing nearly everything with just a glimpse. It was a skill he had been taught, not born with.

"I have no doubt why Hyde's calling in this geologist," the leader said, then called to a man in the front room of the apartment. "Come in here, please."

The man wore a plain gray suit, and his skin and features were so ordinary that he almost blended with the walls of the bedroom. If one wasn't actually looking at him, he seemed to have the ability to hide in plain sight, a talent necessary for a field operative.

"Sir, Hyde is making another call," the listener said, pressing the earphones tighter to his skull.

The group leader led the other agent to the kitchen to give the communications officer privacy to do his job. "I want round-the-clock surveillance on a man named Philip Mercer. Hyde may be bringing him in, and we need to know everything about him. I'm going to get a full background check as soon as possible, but I want teams in place immediately."

The man nodded.

"I have a feeling that this may be the one we've been waiting for," the team leader continued. "Use as many men as necessary and for now assume Mercer knows countersurveillance techniques. Understood?"

"Anything else, sir?"

"No. As soon as I get anything from the background check, I'll let you know."

Washington, D.C.

The Willard Hotel has been around for generations and has gone through numerous transformations since the time it was the home away from home for senators and representatives, a time when politics wasn't a full-time profession, merely a yearly calling. Renowned as one of the finest establishments in the city, the hotel's Round Robin Bar exuded an aura of wealth and power and privilege with subdued lighting, heavy woodwork, and a skilled but unobtrusive staff.

Sipping his first vodka gimlet of the day, Mercer debated with himself whether he should have done a Nexis background check on Prescott Hyde. Certainly, the powerful news search system would contain general information on the Undersecretary; however, he hadn't bothered. He had a sneaking suspicion that this meeting was a fool's errand.

The Round Robin was surprisingly busy for a Tuesday. He overheard two men arguing a pending House bill a few stools down on the bar, and clusters of men and women were conferencing around the numerous low tables. Black-tied waitresses laden with trays of drinks and snacks danced around the furniture, their movements appearing choreographed. Mercer liked to see anyone, no matter who, do a job well. He suspected that these women were better waitresses than the people they served were public officials.

"Dr. Mercer?" The maître d' was at Mercer's shoulder. "Your party is here."

"Thank you." Mercer glanced at his aged Tag Heuer watch. To his surprise, Hyde was right on time.

Walking behind the maître d', Mercer felt his stomach

suddenly knot up. It was an old feeling, the sixth sense that had kept him alive countless times. It had saved him while working underground when millions of tons of earth were about to collapse and aboveground as well, when the danger was from men, not nature. It was telling him that something wasn't right. He spun quickly, scanning the patrons in the bar. Nothing was out of the ordinary, but there was a tingle at the base of his neck and he didn't know why. He swung back and followed the retreating maître d' into the dining room.

The watcher was not certain if she had been seen; but her orders were clear. While Mercer's glance had passed right by her as she sat unassumingly in a corner thumbing a Washington guide book, she felt it wasn't worth the chance.

She reached into the pocket of her skirt, making sure her motions were masked by the folds of her sweater and double-clicked the micro-burst transmitter all of the team carried. Seconds later, another member of their detail walked in, alerted by a similar transmission from their cell leader. The woman did not acknowledge her teammate. She simply finished what little remained of her diet soda and signaled the waitress for her bill.

While no surveillance is immune from detection, usually no more than ten people are needed to maintain a twenty-four-hour watch on even the most paranoid target. Such was their interest in Mercer that all twelve operatives stationed in Maryland were assigned to shadow him and report on his every movement. As the woman walked out of the hotel to catch a taxi, she realized she hadn't been told who Philip Mercer was or what the interest in him could be.

"Dr. Mercer, I presume?" Prescott Hyde laughed at his tired joke as he proffered a hand.

Hyde was in his early fifties, almost completely bald, with a fleshiness that showed self-indulgence. His face was dominated by a large chiseled nose that on someone else would have been distinctive but on him simply looked big. His chin was soft and his cheeks were rounded, giving him an open, comforting quality. But as Mercer shook his hand, he noticed that Hyde's eyes were hard behind gold-rimmed glasses.

"A pleasure to meet you, Mr. Undersecretary."

"I thought we dispensed with that yesterday. Please, it's Bill. My middle name is William, thank God. I can't imagine going through life being called Prescott." Hyde flashed another smile. His teeth were perfect. Capped.

Until they ordered, the conversation was dominated by Hyde, who turned out to be a gracious host, talking about the latest scandals within the halls of power with an insider's knowledge and a gossip's love of speculation. Mercer ordered another gimlet while they waited for their food. Hyde drank sparkling water.

"I wanted to make this a leisurely get-together," Hyde said as their drinks were brought. "A sort of familiarization session because I have a feeling we will be working with each other for a while. However, I have a pressing appointment a little later on, so I am afraid our time is short."

Hyde seemed to talk as if his words were thought out in advance, written down and practiced.

"I understand. I'm afraid my afternoon is rather full too." Paul Gordon, the former jockey who owned Tiny's, ran a horseracing book in Arlington. With the Kentucky Derby only two weeks away, he and Mercer had some serious strategizing to do.

"All the better, then." Hyde leaned back in his chair. "Tell me what you know about Africa."

Mercer chuckled. "To begin with, I was born there, in the Congo. My father was a mine manager and my mother was a Belgian national. I've been back probably twenty-five times, and while I don't speak any native languages other than a bit of Swahili, my French is good enough to get me by where English fails. If you want me to describe Africa's history, the current political situation, and economic outlook, we're going to be here for a while."

"I wasn't aware that you were born there, but Sam Becker told me that you're somewhat of an expert."

"Not really. I'm a miner, and Africa happens to be where most of the action is." Mercer didn't tell Hyde that he loved the continent. Despite all the cruelty, pain, and suffering he'd witnessed there and had experienced himself, he truly loved the land and its people. His parents had been killed by Africans in one of the many rampages, but he never once blamed the people for what happened. He smiled remembering the Tutsi woman who had hidden him in her village for nearly six months after her parents' murder. When he recalled how she'd died during the ethnic cleansings in Rwanda in the mid-nineties, his smile faded.

"What do you know about Eritrea?" Hyde asked.

The question surprised him. Eritrea was a backwater even by African standards, and Mercer couldn't guess Hyde's interest.

"Located just north of the Horn of Africa on the Red Sea coast, bordered by Sudan, Ethiopia, and Djibouti. They've been independent from Ethiopia since 1993. Their struggle was a Cold War battleground between the U.S. and the Soviets in terms of arms and aid. Currently, Eritrea has nothing in terms of raw materials, industries, or hope. I've heard the people live on little more than the pride of being independent for the first time in modern history."

"Very true, very true." Hyde nodded at Mercer's assessment. "There's a chance you can change all of that if you're interested."

A waiter took their lunch orders before Hyde continued. "While most Eritreans are agrarian, cattle mostly, there is one major urban center, Asmara, the capital. It was the only city left standing after the war. The country's in shambles. Per capita income hovers around one hundred and forty dollars a year. Still, the land can support the three million people living there, so starvation has yet to become a problem. But there are a quarter of a million Eritreans living in the Sudan, refugees deliberately not allowed to return because the influx of that many people would shatter the struggling economy. It's a sore spot for the government because they want to bring the displaced home. However, they refuse aid, not wanting to become a debtor nation, and unless some miracle economic boom takes place, those people are going to rot in some of the worst refugee camps on the continent."

From his briefcase, Hyde withdrew a thick manila file folder bound with rubber bands. "You have to understand that what I am about to tell you is strictly confidential. In fact, some of this information has only recently been declassified from 'Top Secret' down to 'Eyes Only.' " Hyde slid some photographs from the folder across the table, pulling his hand back quickly as if the images could somehow contaminate him.

Mercer had been to Africa, knew the people, and was not immune to their suffering. He had seen some of the worst hellholes on earth while in Rwanda during their civil war. He could still feel the bony limbs of children he'd carried to aide stations where the struggle for food and medicine was a losing battle. He had seen the ravages of disease—cholera, malaria, and AIDS. He had watched human skeletons shuffle in miles-long lines escaping one war and walking into the teeth of another.

While these images haunted the darkest nightmares his sleep could generate, they could not prepare him for the six photographs before him. One showed an old man lying against a rusted drum, his legs looking like gnarled twigs. A feral dog chewed on one of his feet as the last of the man's blood soaked into the ground. Another was of a young girl, her face peaceful in death, while in the background uniformed men waited in line to rape her corpse. Another showed a child—Mercer couldn't tell the sex—waving at the camera with its body covered in suppurating wounds, dark leaking holes in its flesh that were eating away what little starvation had left behind.

He didn't want to look at the other three. Here were images of the worst humans could do to each other, and he felt the impotency he'd experienced in Rwanda. The tides of misery were endless, and no matter how much he'd thrown himself at the problem, it never went away. He was also enraged that the photographer had stayed behind the anonymity of his camera and not stepped in to help.

"I'm sorry that you had to see those before we ate,"

Hyde said, but there was no apology in his voice. The pictures were designed to provoke a deliberate response and Mercer knew it. He steeled himself for what was to come. "I believe we have the ability to help these people, to give Eritrea hope for the first time.

"In 1989," Hyde continued, "NASA and the U.S. Air Force launched a spy satellite code-named Medusa. It was meant to be the eyes of the Star Wars defense program. But there was an accident, and it crashed before completing a single orbit.

"As it came down, its cameras exposed a series of pictures. Because the area photographed was not deemed strategically important and because the Air Force hadn't been able to calibrate the satellite, the photos lay forgotten for over a decade. Even after they were declassified, no one paid any attention to them. Much of what they show is gibberish even to those who developed the system.

"The clearest Medusa pictures show what is now northern Eritrea and eastern Sudan." Hyde pulled more photos out of the file and placed them before Mercer.

Though familiar with satellite photography, Mercer had never seen pictures like these before. These shots, twenty in total, resembled X rays. It was as if he was looking inside the earth, rock strata showing up in various shades of gray, what he assumed to be underground water appearing as bright white rings and whorls cutting across each shot, all beneath a ghost image of the surface topography.

"These shots are of northern Eritrea, each one representing a deeper level below the surface. As Medusa went down, its onboard computer followed preprogrammed instructions, increasing the power to its photographic element between each picture," Hyde explained as Mercer shuffled through the stack, noting similarities between them. It was like looking at a cutaway model, peeling back successive layers with each photograph.

Mercer was awed by the satellite's capabilities. "What in the hell was this Medusa?"

"It had abilities that go far beyond what you see here. When I first became aware of these pictures, I asked the same question. The Air Force liaison who showed them to me equated Medusa to a medical CAT scanner or an MRI, which make old-style X rays seem like a throwback to the nineteenth century. We're talking about one of the most sophisticated machines man has ever built. If it hadn't crashed, Medusa would have forever put the United States on the forefront of orbital surveillance and intelligence gathering."

"Fascinating." Mercer had no idea where Hyde was heading with all of this, but he couldn't help being intrigued. "But I don't see what this has to do with me."

"Let me show you this and see what you think." Hyde pulled another picture from the file.

Mercer glanced at it quickly; it looked no different from the other Medusa pictures.

"One of the scientists who built the satellite was a geology buff. A rock hound is what he called himself. Anyway, while modeling for the system, he was tasked with developing computer simulations of what Medusa's potential would be. Because so much of South Africa's underground makeup, its geology, has been studied by mining companies, it's one of the best-catalogued regions for what lies under the earth's surface. What you are seeing there is what they believed the area around Kimberley, South Africa, would look like if Medusa were to use its positron camera on it."

Mercer understood and then he saw it.

First known as Colesberg Kopje because of the small hillock on the African veldt that was nothing more than a blister on the open savanna, Kimberley had grown into a boom town before the turn of the twentieth century when diamonds were discovered there. Within a few years, a city had grown up on the plain and germinated the fortunes of such notables as Cecil Rhodes and the DeBeers Corporation. The diamonds had long since run out at Kimberley, but in their wake, the miners had left a mile-wide, mile-deep hole in the earth. It was the mouth of what was known as a kimberlite pipe.

Kimberlite was the name given to a diamond mine's lodestone. In fact, Mercer had a large chunk of it in his home office that acted as his good luck piece. The two minerals went hand in hand, much like gold and quartz. The kimberlite pipes are channels to the earth's heart, openings where molten material, including diamonds, are thrust up toward the surface under tremendous pressure. Born in the planet's liquid interior, diamonds are nothing more than elemental carbon, no different from coal or the graphite found in pencils, except that nature spent a little more time cooking the atoms and compressing them into perfect crystals. From their first discovery on the Indian subcontinent, Mercer knew, diamonds have had the power to captivate men and drive nations to war. Their dazzling beauty is the mirror reflection of our own greed, and their purity is the foil to humanity's ugliness.

Placing the Kimberley computer projection next to one of the actual Medusa pictures, Mercer quickly traced nearly a dozen similar features between the two. Rather than let his imagination run wild, he studied them more closely. But the truth was right there. His heart raced, and his fingers and palms began to sweat as excitement tore into him. Such a discovery was made once in a lifetime, and Hyde was setting it right in front of him. Buried in the wasteland of northern Eritrea was a kimberlite pipe very much like the one discovered accidentally a century and a half ago in South Africa. He looked up at Hyde, his amazed expression verifying Hyde's suspicion.

"Some of our people think so too. If there is a diamond-bearing pipe in Eritrea, it could mean economic prosperity for a nation that has absolutely no other prospects."

Mercer reined in his excitement, forcing neutrality into his voice. "Intriguing, but from what I know of the region, there has never been any indication of diamonds or their marker minerals in the area. I can't say for certain that Eritrea has been gone over with a fine-toothed comb, but it's pretty unlikely that a find like this has gone unnoticed for the past hundred years. Especially since Eritrea fell under British protection after World War Two. The Brits rarely miss things like this."

"But they didn't have Medusa," Hyde said. "Because Medusa was destroyed before it was calibrated, we have no way of knowing the depth of the pipe or exactly where it is on the map. It could be anywhere between the surface and ten thousand feet underground. It's impossible to tell until we get a man on site, stake the area out, so to speak, and assay it for what treasures lie hidden."

Despite himself, Mercer felt drawn to the possibilities. The pragmatic side of him knew the chances that what was on the picture was actually a kimberlite pipe were remote. And even if it were, it was likely it didn't contain diamonds; many pipes had been found to be barren. Or its glittering cache had been washed away by erosion over the eons since the vent first reached the surface if, in fact, it ever had. A team could spend a lifetime scouring the wilderness and never find even a trace of the pipe.

On the other hand . . .

"You can guess why I wanted to talk with you now," Hyde said. "I've got to warn you that the best we can give you from the pictures is a two-hundred-square-mile area for your search in some of the most inhospitable terrain on the planet. But I've every confidence you can find the kimberlite pipe and prove whether or not there are diamonds present."

Hyde paused while a waiter cleared their plates. "I also have to tell you that until independence, that part of Eritrea saw some of the fiercest fighting of the war and is littered with a quarter-million land mines courtesy of Ethiopia's Soviet backers. And bandits from Sudan prey on the region regularly. Just a few months ago, I got word about an Austrian archaeologist who was killed, butchered really, very close to the epicenter of the search area."

"Is this part of your sales pitch?" He should have been turned away by those two admissions, but Mercer's interest increased. He'd talked with Harry about his need for a challenge that went beyond his normal job, and Hyde was laying a big one on him.

"No." Hyde smiled disarmingly. "But I want to tell you everything I know. I don't want there to be any secrets between us. This mission is not without its risks, and I want you to be fully apprised before you make a decision."

"Why don't you just turn this over to the Eritreans?" Mercer asked, circling a finger at the waiter. He didn't know if Hyde was still thirsty, but he wanted another gimlet.

"Good question. And I can answer it very simply. Medusa does not, nor has it ever existed."

Mercer looked at him, puzzled.

Hyde continued. "While the Air Force may have given me these pictures, they're still considered secret. It took a lot of persuasion for them to allow me to bring you into this, but there was no way they would allow us to show them to a foreign power. My armed forces liaison could neither verify nor deny that other satellites with similar capabilities haven't been launched since Medusa was lost. For purposes of national security, these pictures do not exist."

Mercer waited for Hyde to continue, for he knew there was another motive. He had lived in and around official Washington long enough to know that ulterior motives were as common as tourists on the Mall.

"The other reason is strictly a policy decision from my office." Hyde leaned forward conspiratorially. "What I want to do is present the government of Eritrea a fait accompli, not just a suspicion of fabulous wealth, but the exact location of the diamonds, potential worth, and proper means of extraction. I understand this kind of work is your stock and trade. I want you to go to Eritrea, find the kimberlite pipe, then figure out the value of the vent and just how to get the diamonds out of the earth."

Mercer said nothing, but he was certain Prescott Hyde was lying to him. Maybe not directly, but lying through omission. He hadn't liked the Undersecretary on the phone yesterday, and he liked him even less now.

The man from State continued, playing his final hand. "If you're concerned about security, I can tell you that, while not really sanctioned, I did bring in someone from Eritrea's embassy here in Washington. I didn't go into many details, merely hinting at the possibility of a tremendous mineral find, testing the waters for possible opposition if we took the initiative ourselves. As you can guess, our plan was literally jumped on. While not getting full sanction from their government, I've managed to get you the next best thing." Hyde paused and smiled. "If you're willing to go, that is."

"Finding the pipe, if it's even possible, would take months. That's a big chunk of time, and my time doesn't come cheap. I'm going to need to think about this awhile. How about I give you an answer in a week or two?" Something was up here. Hyde still wasn't telling him everything, and no matter how interesting the project, Mercer was getting a bad feeling. He saw his tablemate's stricken expression. "Is that a problem?"

"No, no," Hyde covered. "It's just that I led my Eritrean associate to believe that this could be done quickly. Already plans are in motion, you see."

Suddenly the restaurant became very uncomfortable. That prickly feeling was back with a vengeance. Mercer knew when he was about to be railroaded, and rather than wait to blow Hyde off later, he made his decision. He stood abruptly. "Then I guess I'm the wrong person for the job. Sorry. I'm familiar with how to handle national secrets, I know a few myself, so rest assured what was discussed here will go no further. Please don't try to contact me again."

He wasn't particularly angry about being lied to. From a government employee, he almost expected it, but that didn't mean he was going to waste any more time listening either. There was another agenda in place here, some shadowy plan that either Hyde wouldn't discuss or couldn't. Not that the reason really mattered to Mercer. He might be in a professional rut, but he knew Hyde's proposal wasn't the way out of it.

He didn't pay any attention to the businessman at a table in the bar working from an open briefcase. The case hid a sophisticated unidirectional microphone. The entire conversation had been recorded.

College Park, Maryland

The tape deck had been placed in the center of the small, faux-wood dining table, the four chairs clustered around it occupied by the station chief and the three senior members of his team. All of them had listened to the recording just forty-five minutes after Mercer's exit from the Willard Hotel.

"Comments?" the team leader, Ibriham, invited at last.

"Sounds like a bust," the only woman present stated. "He's not going to jump at the bait."

"I agree," said another.

"I was surprised by the level of detail Hyde went into with this one," the team's most experienced operative noted. "The last two he approached got far less from him than this Philip Mercer."

"True," the leader said. "However, neither of those engineers had Mercer's reputation. I read through his dossier from Archive. His academic and field qualifications are impeccable, and he has a substantial résumé with American covert activities, first during the Gulf War and later during the Hawaii crisis and last year when the Alaska pipeline was threatened. I'm willing to bet that Hyde wanted Mercer all along, but had to try the other two first because he was unavailable."

"What should we do?" the woman asked. "It's obvious Dr. Mercer isn't interested. Do we wait and see who is next on Hyde's list?"

"I don't think so," Ibriham replied. "We need to take the initiative now. We've burned nearly a quarter of our budget already, and the operation hasn't really started yet.

We need to get more actively involved. Without results, we may soon be recalled. And this mission's too important to let that happen."

Already he had a plan in his mind.

"I believe Philip Mercer's the man we want. Hyde failed to recruit him through normal means, so it's up to us to get him with other, harsher tactics. We need to get leverage on this man, something to force him to Eritrea. Not only as Hyde's agent, but ours as well. From the dossier, I know he has no living family, but we have to find a weakness we can exploit, some vulnerability. There is nothing, and I mean nothing, that is off-limits. This takes our highest priority. Mercer must be in Eritrea within two weeks."

"So you're saying our operational perimeters are wide open?"

"Yes. Use any means necessary to compel him into accepting Hyde's offer. We know that bribery won't work—he is too wealthy—but there's something out there that will coerce him. I need you to find it. And use it. Any more questions?" Ibriham received nothing but accepting looks. "Good. Get to work. I'll stay on Archive, but I doubt I'll turn up anything more."

Ibriham dismissed the others and headed into their command room, closing the door behind him. He booted up the main computer terminal and logged on to the Internet, using the World Wide Web as a conduit to the secure Archive database. While his eyes were on the monitor, his mind was elsewhere.

Born into a family who had resided just outside the walls of Jerusalem for the past nine hundred years, he was no stranger to either tradition or sacrifice. In his youth, many of Ibriham's friends had been Christians and Muslims, but his family was part of a small handful of Palestinian Jews who'd lived for generations in the Holy Land. For centuries that distinction made little difference. But then strife came. Since Israel's creation, first Ibriham's neighborhood and later his family had been shattered by divided loyalties, torn between clan and God. He, too, faced the personal dilemma. On one side was the fiery Palestinian in him, raging to see his people free from outsiders for the first time since Saladin's conquest five hundred years earlier. On the other was the desire for a homeland for his displaced fellow Jews, a place where once and for all they would no longer fear pogroms and anti-Semitism.

Much like Americans during their Civil War, his family was ripped asunder. One of Ibriham's uncles had been shot and killed by another during the *Infitata,* the Palestinian uprising that swept the West Bank and Gaza during the 1980s.

Ibriham had tried to stay out of it, but he, too, was swept into the violence. It happened after the murder of a favorite cousin, a young woman of promise who was slain by Israeli security forces for being at the wrong place at the wrong time following a PLO demonstration in 1989. Ibriham changed that day. He took up arms and began a new life of violence. Putting aside the morals that had shaped his youth, Ibriham deliberately became that which all abhorred. He became a terrorist, one driven by the perverse belief that, no matter what, the ends always justified the means.

"Ibriham?" Yosef stood at the door of the office. He was the most experienced member of their team, a veteran who had seen more action than any other team member, including Ibriham.

"Come in, Uncle," Ibriham said. "And save me from thinking too much."

Yosef sat so close to his nephew that their knees almost touched. "What were you thinking about?"

"Violence and its meaning."

"It has no meaning, it's a tool. Like the plow or the tractor or the AK-47."

"I know, but I wonder about its nature."

Yosef smiled indulgently. He'd trained Ibriham since the day after his niece's death and yet the boy continued to ask questions. He was proud that Ibriham wasn't one of the mindless drones that blindly followed orders. "It has no nature. Only people have that. And while the tenets of humanity call for peace, if we are threatened, violence becomes an option. Its nature then becomes ours. We use it for defense and it is virtuous, but if we use it to kill without thought, then our nature is reflected in its wastefulness."

"And using violence against this Mercer?"

"Justified." Yosef didn't even pause to consider the question. "Especially when you hear what I have to tell you. I didn't want to mention this in front of the others until I told you first. While Mercer was meeting with Hyde, I searched his house." Yosef took Ibriham's silence as acceptance of the unauthorized break-in. "I didn't have enough time for a thorough job, but I learned enough to make me a bit leery."

"Go on?"

"Mercer's security system is good, not perfect, but it provides more than enough protection from all but the best trained." Yosef smiled, thick wrinkles enveloping the corners of his dark, deep-set eyes. "I have to admit, I'm getting too old to scale staircases using the handrails alone."

"And what did you find?"

"A cache of weapons in an office closet, a Heckler and Koch machine pistol, a Beretta 92 autoloader, ammunition, smoke and fragmentation grenades, night-vision gear, and several blocks of plastique. The stuff looks like it's been in the bottom of a trunk for a while, but its presence is disturbing."

"Souvenirs from some earlier mission for the U.S. government?"

"I assume, but if he kept the stuff, it means he would probably use it again." A worried scowl crossed Yosef's face. "These weapons, and Mercer's doubtless familiarity with them, raises the stakes considerably when we consider what type of action is necessary to force him to Eritrea."

"But it doesn't stop us from doing it," Ibriham agreed.

"I think we should proceed with a bit more caution than originally thought warranted. My instinct tells me that there is more to Philip Mercer than can be learned from a computer dossier."

Ibriham sat silently absorbing this.

"And one more thing. Mercer's Rolodex contains the direct office and home phone numbers of Richard Henna, the head of the FBI. I think their relationship has a personal element stemming from some past mission."

This revelation rocked Ibriham. "There is nothing I can do about that now. We must proceed. Cautiously, yes, but this mission must go on." His voice intensified as the image of their goal flashed in his mind. "It's there, Uncle, waiting in the African desert, buried for thousands of years and we will get it. A symbol for our people all over the world, a link to God that will make believers out of everyone. Even if he is friends with Henna, do you really think Mercer will stand in our way?"

Yosef was pleased to see the passion in his nephew's eyes. This would be his last mission. He'd only agreed to come in order to help Ibriham on his first command. None of the others even knew they were related. "No, he won't."

Arlington, Virginia

Despite what he'd said to Hyde, Mercer couldn't leave this one alone. No sooner had he gotten home than he found himself at his desk poring through reference books and the volumes of information available on the Internet. Darkness settled heavily, leaving the city washed by the pink glow of streetlamps, but the passage of day to night had gone unnoticed. While many would find such research work tedious, Mercer enjoyed it. Searching for one fact invariably led to countless other avenues of research, and a tug at any of these steered him to even more. It was easy to become lost in such a deluge of information, but Mercer was able to distill what he wanted, his mind sifting through mountains of useless data for the few elements he found important. It was a gift that he exploited to its fullest.

His final report to Yukon Coal lay forgotten on his word processor as he tore through the material searching for a trace of validity in what Prescott Hyde described existed in northern Eritrea.

He turned up nothing. The geology of the region was all wrong for a kimberlite pipe. Eritrea stood at an edge of the Great Rift Valley, and while there had been active volcanism in the region millions of years ago, there was no indication that diamonds were present. None of a diamond's tracer elements had been found, nor had there been any recorded discoveries of alluvial stones, those washed away from a vent by rivers or streams. Nothing he could find pointed to even a hint that Eritrea was the home of a potential strike.

But those satellite pictures suggested otherwise. Mercer

could not deny that the Medusa pictures of Eritrea looked remarkably like the computer projections of the environs around Kimberley. There might be hundreds of reasons for this similarity, most notably an error in the modeling, but he could not let go the possibility that Hyde was right, that an unknown kimberlite pipe lay out there waiting to be discovered.

He was shocked by how much he wanted it to be true. He'd never been to Eritrea, knew no Eritreans, but he wanted this for them badly. He wanted it for himself too. There hadn't been a kimberlite pipe discovered in more than a decade, and he wanted to be the one who found the next. He admitted that his reasons might be more selfish than charitable, but if he could find diamonds, everyone would win.

Mercer spent the rest of the day running down possible leads, but all the evidence pointed to a mistake on Hyde's part. Yet, against all of his scientific training, he found himself searching for evidence to fit Hyde's theory rather than allowing a hypothesis to develop out of the accumulated facts. He couldn't shake the feeling that Hyde was somehow right.

Earlier in the afternoon, he found he *was* correct to turn down Hyde's offer. He had telephoned Dick Henna at the FBI, but the director was in New York, so he'd spoken with Marge Doyle, the deputy director and the real hands-on head of the organization. Mercer didn't know her well, but she knew of him and went out of her way to provide Mercer with an outline of Hyde, his past and his future, which did not look that bright.

Prescott Hyde came from a family whose service to the American government stretched back to the drafting of the Constitution. The Hydes had played significant roles during every major watershed in our history, from the Revolution through the Civil War and Reconstruction to the development of the United States as a superpower during the forties and fifties. Hyde's father had served with Eisenhower when he was Supreme Allied Commander during World War Two and later as President, working closely with Allen

Dulles during the early years of the CIA and with Adelai Stevenson at the United Nations.

Prescott Hyde had turned out to be the only disappointment the family had ever produced. He was barely holding on to his current position as an Undersecretary of State, a job given to him more out of nepotism than individual achievement. He'd already shown a great deal of ineptitude during his brief tenure heading the State Department's Africa section, missing the clues of a coup in Zambia last year and so insulting South Africa's ambassador that the man returned to his homeland for two weeks in protest.

Mercer suspected that if Prescott had not been one of *the* Hydes, he would have been fired months ago. As it stood, Mercer wondered just how much time the man had left. The current President was more interested in foreign relations than domestic issues, and he liked to have the best people leading the charge for him. Mercer guessed that one more screw-up on Hyde's part and he would be out on his ass.

Hence, Eritrea. If Hyde could pull it off, not only would he save his floundering career but could also add himself to the anointed pantheon of his ancestors. Thus Hyde's motivation was more personal than professional, and Mercer was glad he had flatly refused the contract offer. To get involved with someone gambling to save a sinking career would be foolish at best.

At eight, Mercer logged off his system, his eyes gritty with fatigue and his stomach making not so subtle noises. Maybe when he had the time to delve into it again he would, but for now he put Eritrea out of his mind. Tomorrow he would work on his report to Yukon Coal.

He went into the kitchen and pulled a frozen entrée from the packed freezer, set his oven to the prescribed temperature, and slid the stiff meal onto the center rack, confidently ignoring the directions about peeling the film from certain portions. While his meal was transformed from a frozen mass to a gelatinous one, he spiraled up the circular stairs to the master suite and took a long shower.

Precise to the minute, he was back in the ground-floor

kitchen when the oven timer beeped. He ate standing just a few steps from a polished birch table long enough to seat eight, using a plastic fork while one of the countless drawers contained matched silverware for a dozen. Finally he tossed the press-form tray into the garbage, and left his house for the short walk to Tiny's.

Paul "Tiny" Gordon was behind the bar as usual, and the diminutive former jockey had a vodka gimlet poured by the time Mercer crossed the barroom to sit next to a slouched Harry White. Already, Mercer felt the tension in his shoulders ease. There were only a handful of other people in the bar.

"I read somewhere that people who drink on a Tuesday are either drunks or alcoholics," Harry said, looking at Mercer.

"What's the difference?"

"Alcoholics have to go to meetings," Harry deadpanned.

"And this from the guy who thinks booze is the missing link on the food chain," Mercer smiled. "Old joke, Harry."

"What do you want? I'm an old man." In his large hand, Harry's highball glass looked like a thimble.

"Are you still on that?"

"No, not really." Harry sparked a match for a cigarette that had materialized between his lips. "I did a little soul searching and realized that if I'm still alive, despite myself, I should just accept it. Most of the people I've known who made it to eighty never took what time they had left to enjoy themselves. They just sat around nursing homes and griped about how much better they used to feel. Well, I still feel pretty good, and goddamn it, I'm going to make the best of it." He rapped on the bar top. "Tiny, fetch my friend another drink and put it on my tab."

"Oh, Jesus." Paul Gordon threw up his hands theatrically. "You are really dying, aren't you? The only reason you'd ever buy Mercer a drink is if you planned on checking out before you paid your bill."

By the third round, Tiny was drinking with them, and Mercer related the story of his meeting with Prescott Hyde and his own subsequent findings. He summed up by saying the facts indicated that there was no kimberlite pipe buried in northern Eritrea.

"Didn't all the facts once point toward Divine creation until Darwin came up with the theory of evolution?" Tiny asked.

"Yes," Mercer replied cautiously, knowing not to underestimate Paul's intellect.

"Now, creationists are left with faith, which is strong enough, if you believe. You have to ask yourself if your faith in the facts on this pipe thing are strong enough to discount evidence you haven't found yet."

"It's not the same thing, Paul, and you know it."

"You're right, of course, But isn't the word *atom* Greek for 'indivisible'? And haven't we proved that the atom can be split into protons and neutrons and electrons and each of these particles split into countless more 'indivisible' pieces."

"So you're saying I don't know everything yet?"

"What he's saying," Harry interjected, "is that you wouldn't have brought this up if you didn't believe there are diamonds where this guy said there are and you want us to talk you out of looking for them."

"I don't want to look for them, at least not for Prescott Hyde, but something—call it faith, Paul—is telling me that Eritrea sits on a major find."

"Then what are you going to do about it?" Harry asked.

"Drink until I can get a very stupid idea out of my head."

"Well said," Harry agreed, and knocked back the rest of his bourbon.

About a half hour later, a spellbound look suddenly glowed on Paul Gordon's face as he looked toward the bar's front door. Mercer snapped around to see who had come in. A woman stood poised in the doorway. She was nearly six feet tall, reed thin, in loose white slacks and a light gray blouse. A white sweater was knotted around her slender throat to ward off the slight chill in the air. She was neither black nor white, but combined the best features of both races. Her skin was like milky coffee, creamy smooth, and her thick hair flowed freely. Mercer saw it was tinted reddish purple with henna. Her features were thin and sharp, and very dramatic with Nilotic cheekbones and a high forehead. Soft brown eyes dominated her face.

"Oh . . ." Tiny's mouth had gone slack.

"My . . ." Mercer, too, was enraptured.

"God, that was good." Harry finished his drink and settled the empty glass on the bar, paying no heed to the direction of his friends' stares. "Tiny, pour me another and put it on Mercer's tab." It was only then that Harry noticed Tiny was looking past his shoulder. He turned. "Holy shit."

The woman smiled at the attention, though Mercer was sure she was self-conscious.

Maybe it was because Harry had mentioned Aggie yesterday or maybe because Hyde had Mercer thinking about Africa, but he couldn't tear his eyes from her. She was beautiful, with an African's poise and allure. Studying her, Mercer didn't experience the usual gut clench he'd had for the past months. Rather, in its place was a new feeling, something a bit lower than his stomach and eminently more enjoyable.

She strode to the bar, gliding over the scuffed linoleum with a dancer's grace, her narrow hips swiveling to the delight of the three men. "Good evening." Her accent was untraceable, but her voice matched her face, melodious and provocative. "I'm looking for Dr. Philip Mercer. He wasn't at his home and I was told that he sometimes comes here. Have any of you gentlemen seen him?"

Harry was the first to find his voice. "Yes, I'm Philip Mercer. What can I do for you, beautiful lady?"

She thrust out one slim hand to shake Harry's. "Dr. Mercer, I'm Selome Nagast from the Eritrean embassy. I was supposed to be at your meeting today with Prescott Hyde."

"Your presence would have graced a rather fruitless luncheon, I'm sure." Harry leered, coming to his feet and pouring on the charm.

Mercer debated with himself about how long to allow the charade to continue.

"I'm sorry I couldn't make it. Bill told me what happened, and if you don't mind, I'd like this opportunity to state our case once more, this time from the side of the people you can help."

"Miss Nagast," Mercer broke in, sensing that she was becoming uncomfortable with Harry's lustful looks. "I'm Mercer. This is a friend of mine, Harry. He suffers terribly from a multiple personality disorder. Just before you came in, he thought he was Rita Hayworth."

Selome Nagast barely missed a beat. "It's a pleasure to meet you, Ms. Hayworth. I've been a fan ever since seeing *Gilda* on television."

Harry looked as if he could have killed Mercer as he shook the woman's hand once more. "Just a little joke," he chuckled, "one that Mercer ended too quickly and will surely pay for. Can he buy you a drink, miss?"

"A white wine, I think."

"In a place like this?" Tiny said from behind the bar. "You must be adventurous."

A moment later, he set an eight-year-old French chardonnay from his private stock in front of her.

Mercer gathered her drink and a fresh one for himself. "Why don't we take a booth?"

She followed him to a leatherette bench seat just below a smoke-grimed plate-glass window. Rather than analyze Selome Nagast's presence at Tiny's and how Hyde's dossier mentioned he frequented the establishment, Mercer started speaking as soon as they were comfortable.

"I spent most of the afternoon going over Hyde's proposal, and what I said earlier at the Willard still stands. I'm sorry, Miss Nagast, but I must decline your offer. I can neither refute nor prove what those photographs show, but I don't believe there's a diamond-bearing kimberlite pipe in northern Eritrea."

"How can you be so certain?" She arched one narrow eyebrow.

"I can't be certain, but you and Hyde wouldn't have come to me if you didn't value my opinion. I've been in this business for a lot of years, and the little bit of research I did today says there are no diamonds in your country. I'm intrigued by the prospect, but the kind of search Hyde was talking about at lunch just isn't worth it, either to me or to you."

"Is it the money?" Selome accused sharply. "I know that your expertise is expensive, but we are able to pay for at least six weeks of your field time."

Mercer shrugged. "If you're planning on a six-week search, I'll save you the money and disappointment now and tell you that even if there was a pipe with a great big 'X' to mark it and a sign saying 'Dig here,' you're not giving yourselves nearly enough time to find it. The search area is a couple hundred square miles, and it must be gone over inch by inch. No matter who you get to lead the expedition, even with all the luck in the world, don't expect results for months."

"Our timeline may be a bit short, I grant you, but it is our money to spend. And we feel this project is worth the expense."

While he was listening to her words, Mercer found his attention drawn to the movement of her mouth, the way her lips formed each syllable perfectly. She was truly captivating. And he also sensed she may be a lure, what the Russians used to call the "honey trap." He then discounted the idea. A woman as beautiful as Selome Nagast made such a ploy too obvious. "Why six weeks?"

"The photographs show the pipe to be close to our border with Sudan. Even with the best security, six weeks is all we feel we can keep a team safe from marauders. The search area is one of the most dangerous in Africa. You must have heard about the archaeologist and his guide who were killed there several months back."

"Hyde mentioned it," Mercer replied. "Listen, you and he have enough information, without revealing the Medusa pictures, to contact one of the big mining outfits in Canada or Europe. Why not give them a shot at finding your pipe?"

"It was considered. But at this stage, any deal we struck would be disastrous. Mining companies are notorious for making contracts that benefit only themselves and leave little to the countries in which they work. To get one involved at this stage would mean giving away too much.

Look at what happened in South Africa and Namibia. For decades, the money from their mines lined the pockets of Europeans rather than the locals. We will be in a better bargaining position if we can find the pipe ourselves."

"I can't agree with you more. If there are diamonds there, you're in a unique position to learn from the mistakes of other African nations, countries that all but gave away their wealth or saw it plundered by corrupt officials. I have to say again, though, if you are serious about searching for the pipe, give it at least a year and triple whatever budget you've set yourself. That way you can be assured one way or another."

She took his assessment sullenly. "That is just not possible."

"Then abandon the whole idea, use the money you were going to pay me and help your people directly. Bring some of the refugees home from the camps in Sudan, use it to court some industry to locate in Eritrea, hell, give it to the United Nations as a way of getting favors later on. Whatever you decide, it will be better spent than outfitting a poorly conceived geologic expedition almost certain to fail."

Mercer didn't like being so harsh, but he knew he should end this as quickly as possible. He was impressed by Selome and her determination but he also knew she was fooling herself. In fact, he'd fooled himself too. He'd wasted a day looking for the pipe because he too wanted it to be there. He saw a trace of defeat in her eyes and wanted to take her hand as a physical reassurance.

"We are going to pursue this," Selome said, surprising steel in her voice.

"I wish you luck, I really do. I'm sorry I can't help you."

She got up to go, but Mercer could not let her leave on such a sour note. He reached out and touched her wrist. "Listen, I could be wrong. You could be sitting on the biggest diamond strike in history, but you must prepare yourself to be disappointed. No matter what, it's going to take a long time."

"Dr. Mercer, none of us are as naive as you think. Of

course this is going to be difficult, we all expect that, but it does not mean we shouldn't try."

Mercer got up from the booth after she had gone and slumped back at the bar next to Harry. "You heard?"

"Yeah," Harry replied. "Don't you think you were a little tough? Before she came in, you thought there might still be a chance that the diamonds are in Eritrea."

"I know, but I was wrong. Talking to Selome, I realized I was merely hoping, just like she and Hyde. Unless they can get one of the big mining concerns to foot the bill, it's best they forget the whole idea." Mercer demurred Tiny's offer of another drink. "They live in one of the poorest places on earth, and they want to blow possibly millions of dollars on a project with a thousand to one odds. It's wrong and I think even our Miss Nagast recognizes it."

"Why do you say that?"

"This six weeks she mentioned. I don't believe her reason for the rush any more than she does. Eritrea's been an independent country for a couple of years and the diamonds have been there for a couple hundred million, so why the big push now? I don't think they have the money for anything more extensive. And I think there is something more going on here. Prescott Hyde and the lovely Selome Nagast are keeping something from me. I don't know what it is and I don't really care. I'm done with this whole thing."

Mercer had seen it dozens of times, especially in Africa. Money that could really help the people squandered on some glamorous project that usually never gets completed or, if it is, gets abandoned shortly. He hated that type of epidemic waste and wouldn't let himself become part of it. He considered calling some of his contacts in the mining industry to try to blackball the whole thing. It was the best he could do to save Eritrea its money.

"Are you going to continue your research tomorrow anyway?"

"No. I'll finish my report to Yukon Coal like I promised and look for another project. If the diamonds are there, they weren't meant for me to find."

* * *

The next morning, Mercer had already gotten his newspaper and a cup of tar-thick coffee before he noticed a package resting on the polished bar top. It was a plain buff envelope that hadn't been there last night! A sudden adrenaline burst shot through his system. His home had been violated before—indeed, he had killed a potential assassin in the bar less than a year ago—but knowing someone had secretly broken in while he slept was even more disturbing. He ruthlessly crushed down a rising sense of panic.

After checking his entire house to make sure he was alone, he returned to the bar. He approached the package with trepidation. He quickly discounted his first thought, that it was a bomb. If someone had wanted to kill him, they could have done it as he lay in his bed. A silenced bullet was much more efficient than an explosive device. He considered calling the police, but if it wasn't a bomb then it was a message, one meant for him alone. Ignoring the fact he might be destroying crucial evidence, he picked up the packet, recognizing the squishy feel of "bubble wrap." He tore it open and a standard videocassette slid into his hand. His stomach turned to knotted ice. He had a chilling premonition of its contents.

He walked over to the entertainment center and slipped the cassette into his VCR, turning on the television in the same motion. The image that sprang up drained the blood from his face.

Harry White sat naked on a wooden chair with heavy silver tape binding his wrists to the chair's arms and more of it wound around his thin white chest just below his sagging pectoral muscles. Electric wires were clipped to his nipples, and deep bruises surrounded his mouth and blackened both eyes. There was a look of terror on Harry's face. The morning's *Washington Post* lay in his lap. *Jesus, the paper meant that they'd been in his house at most a half hour ago.*

When he finally spoke, Harry's usual rasping voice sounded more like a child's plea. His speech sounded scripted.

"Mercer, I was grabbed last night after leaving the bar.

I don't know who is holding me, but they are serious in their intentions." As if to prove this statement, a hand appeared from off camera and backhanded Harry viciously. It took him a few moments to recover, his chest heaving in fright and pain. "They demand that you go to Eritrea and find the diamond mine or they will kill me. You have no choice. If they find that you are not planning to go, parts of my body will be dumped on your doorstep, culminating in my head in two weeks' time."

Harry stopped speaking, his rheumy eyes focusing beyond the camera's range for a second as if listening to someone. Then Mercer heard another voice, one masked by an electronic synthesizing device. "Dr. Mercer, listen to your friend. We do not wish to kill him, but the discovery of the mine is too important to us to worry about the death of one old man.

"You have six weeks to accomplish the task. If you are not successful, Harry White will be killed. If you attempt to find us, Harry White will be killed. If you tell anyone what has happened, Harry White will die. His life, or his death, are your responsibility."

Two men entered the frame, though Mercer could not see their faces. One wrapped his arms around Harry's torso while the other positioned himself next to the old man's hand.

"We will be in contact with you periodically when you get to Eritrea," the voice droned. "When you find the diamonds, you must tell no one but us, or your friend will be brutally tortured before his execution."

"Mercer, listen to me," Harry shouted at the camera. "I'm not a hero. I don't want to die. I haven't had a cigarette in hours, and I'm already starting to get the shakes from the DTs. For Christ's sake, do whatever they want, kill the fucking President if that's what it'll take. Just get me out of this."

Without warning, the one man grasped Harry's pinkie finger and snapped it so quickly that a look of surprise hung on Harry's face for a few seconds before the waves of pain contorted his features. He screamed, bubbles of saliva dripping from his mouth. The video ended abruptly.

Fear welled up in Mercer and he staggered back against the bar. He saw Tory again on the platform and himself in a train car and he saw her head explode the instant before the gunman ended his own life. He'd done nothing. It didn't matter to him that he'd been forty yards away and the gunman had one arm wrapped around Tory's throat, the pistol screwed into her ear. He'd been paralyzed with fear then, and it slammed into him again now. It pinned him to the bar and he struggled against it. He had been powerless that one time and vowed never again. But in all the times since then, it was he who was in danger, not someone he loved. Not Harry. He felt trapped, out of control, which for him was the worst of all. He couldn't tear his eyes from the dark television, his mind shrinking away from what he'd just seen.

And then came a spark of rage and he grabbed on to it, feeling it grow so he could think again. Rage was something he could control and channel and use. His fists balled at his sides so his knuckles strained against the skin. Harry was in trouble, Harry who had saved his life and who had been a friend for so long, a father in every way that really counted. Seeds of guilt crept on him because had they not been friends, Harry would have awakened this morning in his own bed, bleary-eyed from last night's drinks, but none the worse for wear. Mercer could use the guilt too, because it focused his anger. And if his guilt and his rage were strong enough, they would crush the fear.

Five minutes passed before the rational side of Mercer could finally take over from his emotions and allow him to think of some plan of action. First and foremost was finding who had kidnapped Harry. His first thought was Prescott Hyde. Mercer knew the State Department maintained a covert arm for just such activities. Grabbing an old man from his bed and bypassing Mercer's home security system would be child's play for them. But they didn't need Mercer that badly, not like this. There were dozens of men equally qualified to conduct the search in Eritrea. Selome Nagast, he thought. No, she was on Hyde's side. That left, who?

Mercer didn't know. But he was sure he was in over his head. He had options, namely going to Dick Henna, but he also knew if he was going to get Harry back safely, he would have to go to Africa. There was someone out there with access to expert home breakers capable of kidnap and possibly murder. Harry was his responsibility and he would do whatever it took to bring him home.

He couldn't let himself consider the consequences if the kimberlite pipe didn't exist.

Arlington, Virginia

Because Mercer had no way of knowing if phone lines had been tapped or his home bugged at the same time the tape was delivered, he spent the day in Tiny's cluttered back office, a room just bigger than a phone booth and plastered with horse-racing pictures. While he worked, Paul kept him supplied with coffee and sandwiches. Mercer told Paul everything, and the former jockey agreed that in a situation like Harry's kidnapping, involving the police wasn't the right move.

Mercer did place a call to Dick Henna, and they agreed to meet later that night. Mercer suspected he would be tailed but had a plan for shaking them while not drawing attention to the fact. Much of what he did during the afternoon could have been accomplished at his place, but Mercer hated the idea of working under a microscope, and as he made his preparations for going to Africa, there were a few details he wanted to keep to himself. It was a little past four when he was ready to tell Selome Nagast and Hyde that he would go to Eritrea after all.

"Embassy of Eritrea, how may I direct your call?" The receptionist's accent was thick.

"Selome Nagast, please."

Mercer waited fifteen seconds as the woman checked her directory. "I am sorry, sir, but there is no one here with that name."

"Are you sure?" Mercer realized it was a stupid question.

"Yes, sir."

"Is it possible she works at the embassy but doesn't have

a phone listing?" Mercer asked hopefully but a niggling doubt was forming in the back of his head.

"We have a new voice-mail system," the receptionist explained. "Even temporary employees can receive messages."

"Thank you." Mercer kept the suspicion out of his voice and dialed Prescott Hyde. He wondered if his dismissal of Selome Nagast as Harry's kidnapper had been premature.

"I'm surprised to hear back from you, Dr. Mercer. You made it clear yesterday that you aren't interested in our venture."

"Let's just say I've had a change of heart. I'm on board now one hundred percent and wanted you to be the first to know." Mercer said nothing about Selome. At this point, any information he had was a weapon, and now wasn't the time to use it. "I've already started working on the project. I've got heavy equipment en route from South Africa, three D-11 dozers, a couple of big front loaders, six Terex dump trucks, and a Caterpillar 5130 hydraulic shovel. All of the iron is leased for six months except the 5130, which Eritrea is going to have to buy."

"Hold on there. I'm with Selome right now and you're on a speaker phone. She's shaking her head something fierce."

"Dr. Mercer, I can't authorize any of that. It's just too much money." Selome's voice sounded distant over the speaker connection.

Somehow he'd expected her there. It only deepened his suspicions.

"Listen, you two wanted this project in the first place. If I'm going to get results, it's got to be done my way or not at all," Mercer said sharply. "I didn't set this six-week rule, you did. If I'm expected to find anything, I'm going to need to move a lot of dirt. I've got a pretty good lease package for us, and if need be, I can get a sales contract on the excavator for when we're finished with it. That'll save you a couple million bucks. You're lucky—my first idea was to bring in a walking dragline with a forty-million-dollar price tag, but we'd lose too much time with its on-site assembly. As it is, the 5130 will take two weeks to put together once it's shipped in."

"You don't understand. We just can't do it this way," Selome protested. "I can't guarantee your safety if you present that kind of target."

"By the time the equipment rolls in, I'll have pinpointed the best site, and you'll only have to protect a single camp. From what I understand, nearly every Eritrean over the age of thirty has a military background, so surely you can muster a protective force? When I'm doing the actual prospecting, I'll basically be on my own, so you won't have to worry about me."

"We wanted something much more low-key," Selome said.

"You know what she means," Hyde broke in. "A small team, minimal equipment and maximum secrecy. You're talking about bringing in an army."

"That's what it's going to take," Mercer snapped. "I tried telling both of you that earlier. Selome, you said your government doesn't want to get involved in a mining operation. You just wanted oversight, right? Well, consider this a trial run, but this is going to be my show. I'll bring in the equipment I need and any people I want. If you don't like it, if it isn't what you expected, well, tough shit. This is what you got."

Hyde finally broke the silence. "I guess we caught a tiger by the tail here. You've taken us both a little by surprise. We need some time to digest all of this."

"You've got until Friday. That's when I catch my flight to Eritrea. I plan to be in Asmara on Saturday morning and in the area of the search no later than Monday. I have a lot to go over with both of you before I leave, but that can wait until tomorrow. For now, you need to start working on getting me local support once I'm in country."

"And if we take your earlier advice and abandon the project?"

There was no malice in Mercer's voice when he responded. "Then I call a few friends, and within a month Eritrea will be dug up from one end to the other. I've got the contacts to guarantee your nation will be stripped clean with total impunity, and there is nothing either of you can do about it. I'll talk to you again tomorrow."

Mercer was panting when he hung up. He was gambling with Harry White's life when he just bluffed Hyde and Selome, and it made him tremble. His nerves were fraying. He dialed the phone again.

"The Knight Medical Group," a receptionist chirped.

"Is Terry there?"

"Dr. Knight is with a patient. May I have him call you back?"

"He's playing video games in his office," Mercer said. "Why don't you give him a buzz and see if he'll talk to me. This is Philip Mercer."

A minute later Terrance Knight came on the line. "Great timing, Mercer. I was on the final level of *Doom* and I still have two men left."

"I'm getting better. The last time I called it was coitus interuptus with one of your nurses."

"Yeah. She sued me for sexual harassment a week after she discovered my sperm count is too low to knock her up."

"That's what I love about you, Terry. Your lurid attention to detail." Mercer chuckled for the first time today. Terry Knight had been his personal physician ever since he moved to Washington. "I'm going to Africa again. I need a gamma globulin, a cholera booster, and I think I'm ready for another tetanus. And I'll also need anti-malarial pills for a couple of months."

"God, I love patients who know what they want. I'm going to give you an oral polio booster as well. The CDC in Atlanta posted warning for most of the continent. Since you're headed to Africa, I'll throw in a box of condoms while I'm at it. I doubt you'll get lucky, so give them to a doctor before you come back. Anything else?"

Mercer laughed again. "Yeah, put together a med kit for me, nothing more elaborate than a couple of aspirin and a suture set. Write me a prescription for morphine and antibiotics."

"You sure you don't want a defibrillater and a portable CAT scanner?" Terry joked.

"No, not this time, but maybe later. I'll be in sometime tomorrow for my shots."

"Hey, I'm the doctor, I tell you when you come in, remember?"

"Go back to *Doom*, Terry."

"Knowing you is doom."

Mercer sat back as far as possible in the cramped office, rubbing his eyes. There were a million details to be considered, yet his thoughts kept returning to Harry White. He was a tough old bird, a war veteran, but he was eighty now. Mercer focused on what his friend must be going through and used that anger to shove aside the exhaustion and refocus.

Tiny ducked his head into the room. "How you doing?"

"I've been better."

"I know what you mean. Do you realize today is the first day in twelve years that Harry hasn't come in. God, I never realized how much I loved the bastard until he'd gone."

Mercer straightened quickly. "He's not gone, Paul. I'll get him back. No matter what it takes, I'll get him back." His bravado sounded empty even in his own ears.

After Mercer had hung up on them, Prescott Hyde and Selome Nagast looked at each other, both having similar thoughts. Hyde's office in Foggy Bottom was well appointed, more New York executive than government official, with oil paintings gracing the walls and an antique desk that had been in his family for generations. The carpet was a thicker pile than standard issue, and the matching wingback chairs had been given to Hyde's father by President Kennedy. Selome was sitting in one of the chairs, dressed in a simple business suit.

"Well, what do you think?" she asked, breaking the silence.

"I just don't think we can afford it. He's talking about millions of dollars, and the best we've been able to come up with is three hundred thousand and a lot of that is for Mercer's consulting fee. I never thought about all the equipment we would need." Hyde's voice was dull with defeat. "We should call the whole thing off. It was a long shot at best anyway."

"You call it off, and I'll have a congressional committee knocking down your door within twelve hours. They would love to hear how you really obtained the Medusa pictures from the National Reconnaissance Office," Selome hissed. "We can come up with the money somehow."

"Buying those pictures from Donald Rosen cost me nearly everything I have. If my wife finds out I took a second mortgage on our house, she'll kill me."

"I don't care about your domestic problems. We are going to need more money very soon if this is going to work. I've had expenses on my end, too. Do you hear me complaining about them? Mercer is the best shot we've got. We need to support him, and that means cash. We both have our sources. If need be, we can cut in a few more people. We're talking about a billion-dollar payoff when this is done. That's worth a little more risk."

"This is getting out of control," Hyde complained.

"No, it isn't. We're still in control. We just can't allow ourselves to forget it, that's all."

"I don't know . . ." Hyde's voice trailed off.

"You don't know what?" she accused. "We're about to make a major discovery, one that will lift my country into the twenty-first century and provide jobs for thousands. Both of us will get what we want if we don't lose perspective. We'll get the money, Bill. We have to."

"You're right," Hyde nodded slowly. "I just don't like the fact that Philip Mercer has suddenly decided that he is in charge."

"But that's why we wanted him in the first place. Like he said—what he wants, he gets. It's up to us to make sure it goes smoothly."

"You scare me, Selome," Hyde said suddenly, looking her directly in the eye, seeing beyond the beautiful shell to the person who lay beyond.

"Good." She had Hyde caught between his greed and his fear of exposure. To her, he was inconsequential, a means to an end, but it was reassuring to know how easily he could be dominated. She knew it wouldn't be possible, but she wanted to see what happened when Hyde's wife discovered how her husband had lost their house. The greedy pig would get what he deserved.

Paul Gordon drove, the headlights of his aging Plymouth lancing into the night. Mercer sat next to him, sweating heavily in two bulky sweaters and a leather jacket, a pair of skateboarder's knee pads over his jeans. He fingered the motorcycle helmet on his lap. Both the helmet and the pads had been borrowed from his neighbor's son.

"About another mile." Paul glanced at Mercer in the intimate confines of the car. "You sure you want to do this?"

On this deserted stretch of road deep in the heart of Virginia horse country, it was easy to spot the headlights of the car that had been following them since Arlington. "Yeah, Tiny, I'm sure. It's the only way."

"I'll say some good words at your funeral," the little man said, his eyes barely above the arc of the steering wheel. "We're coming up on it now."

Mercer put on the helmet, cinching it tight beneath his chin. Ahead, the road curved sharply, the turn traced on its outside by a white picket fence belonging to one of the numerous Farquar County farms. Just out of view, Mercer knew there was a thick copse of pines within feet of the uncoiling road.

Easing into the corner, Tiny used the emergency brake to avoid telltale brake lights. Mercer didn't even take the time for a breath. He threw open the car's door and allowed himself to be sucked out by the vehicle's centrifugal force, landing hard on the macadam and tucking into a tight ball as his body began to roll. The darkness swallowed him as Tiny accelerated away, his car vanishing even before Mercer came to a stop. New scuffs marked his battered bomber jacket, and his shoulder ached from the first contact with the road. He scrambled into the woods, ducking into the underbrush as another car passed by. He caught a glimpse of two dark-complected men as the car continued in pursuit of Tiny's Plymouth.

Mercer checked the luminous dial of his stainless watch and found that he only had a few minutes to wait. Standing at the side of the road, he massaged his sore shoulder with his free hand, the helmet dangling negligently from his other. There was a low moon, a pale glow hidden behind tumbling clouds, and the night insects made a steady, soothing rhythm.

Five minutes later, Mercer saw the approach of another set of headlights. He eased back into the woods, watching. The car stopped no more than twenty paces from where he was crouched.

"Come on, I haven't got all night. Fay is pissed enough that I'm out here at all." Dick Henna was behind the wheel of his wife's car, a light blue Ford Taurus that had been brutalized by too many Washington rush hours. "I've been in New York for the past few days, and I'm leaving tomorrow for Los Angeles. I promised her that I'd be home for tonight, at least."

Mercer broke away from the shadows and hopped into the passenger seat. Henna backed the car around and started toward the nation's capital. "You're lucky she likes you or I wouldn't be out in the middle of nowhere playing cloak and dagger. She wanted to talk about buying another dog, a corgi of all things, and she's not too pleased you called. This is worth it, right?"

"Harry's been kidnapped," Mercer said flatly.

"Jesus, Mercer, why didn't you tell me on the phone." Henna had swerved the car dangerously. "What happened?"

Dick Henna wasn't an imposing man, just below average height, with a rounded stomach and a heavily jowled face. While Henna had achieved the highest position in the FBI, he hadn't forgotten what it was like to be a field agent. He'd been on the streets for thirty years before being tapped to head the Bureau. His mind was sharp and he had instincts better than nearly anyone Mercer had ever met. It had been Henna's recommendation during the

Hawaii crisis that allowed Mercer to stop a secret operation code-named Vulcan's Forge. The two had been friends ever since.

Mercer related the whole story, his narrative coming in a rush, for it was the first time he was able to speak about the horror he felt. He'd told Tiny the dry facts, but with Dick, he talked about his own feelings of responsibility.

"Marge Doyle mentioned you'd been in touch about Prescott Hyde," Henna remarked when Mercer was done. "I can tell you right now, his days are numbered. Justice has a file on him about four inches thick. Nothing to indict him on, but certainly enough to get him out of State."

"Pursue that, but I don't think Hyde is behind Harry's kidnapping."

"Christ, Mercer! Of course he's not." Henna was startled that Mercer would so nonchalantly suspect an undersecretary of state. "The guy may be shady, but he's not a violent criminal."

Mercer's voice was hard-edged, his emotions barely contained. "I'm talking about the abduction of my best friend, a total innocent, and right now I suspect everything and everyone. For now, I've got to believe it has a connection to a woman named Selome Nagast. She's lied to me at least once, claiming to be affiliated with the Eritrean embassy when she's not, yet she and Hyde are working together."

"Is she Eritrean?"

"Either Eritrean or Ethiopian. Almost six feet tall, great body and a face that should be on the cover of fashion magazines. I'd like you to check her out. If she isn't with the Eritreans, then who does she belong to?"

"And if that's a blind alley?"

"I don't know," Mercer admitted. "I don't have a Suspect B."

"I'll get a team into Harry's place first thing in the morning, in case whoever grabbed him left physical evidence."

"Don't. The video made it clear that if I went to the authorities, they'd kill Harry immediately. I'm sure his place is being watched for just that reason." There was something else on the tape that bothered Mercer, something either Harry or the kidnappers had said that didn't make sense, but the answer wouldn't come.

"I think we know what we're doing."

Mercer handed the videotape to Henna. He'd made a copy for himself but felt the FBI could do more with the original. "This is the tape. I'm sure I destroyed crucial evidence by handling it."

"Don't sweat it. Today's technology can do wonders."

"Listen, Dick, I'm responsible for what happened to Harry. He's just a tool to get to me, and I'm afraid I'm using you to get him back. I've never tried to presume on our friendship until now. But every day Harry's being held is a day I feel like I've failed. Can you understand that?"

"Yeah, I can. As a field agent, a lot of my cases became more personal than was healthy, and I know Harry too, don't forget. I'll get our A-Team into action for his sake." Henna clasped a hand on Mercer's forearm. "What are you going to do?"

"I called Chuck Lowry. Do you remember him? He used to be the computer archivist at the U.S. Geological Survey." Henna nodded. "I've got him hacking airline reservations. If the group that took Harry are foreign, they'll want out of the country but won't have had the time to make an earlier booking. Chuck's checking on reservations made since yesterday for a flight out of Washington in the next day or two. Long shot at best, but it's something." Mercer had seen Dick bend the laws a few times and didn't worry about his disapproving frown. "And I'm going to Eritrea to find the pipe."

"In these situations, we tell people not to give in to demands," Henna said quietly, expecting an explosion from Mercer.

"These situations," Mercer emphasized the words, "don't usually include eighty-year-old victims and they never include me."

Henna pulled into a gas station just moments before Tiny's Plymouth arrived from the opposite direction. The FBI director promised Mercer that he would call the next evening at Tiny's with any information. Mercer dodged unobserved from Henna's car to Paul Gordon's before the sedan trailing Tiny came into view. Tiny put a couple of gallons into his tank, paid at the pump with a debit card, and the two were on their way quickly.

"Any problems?" Mercer asked as they sped back to Arlington.

"They never got close enough to see I was alone."

"Great," Mercer said with relief. "Thanks, Paul. I owe you big for this."

"If it was for anyone other than Harry, I'd agree. But for him, it's a wash." Tiny kept his eyes on the road as he spoke. "Is Henna going to help?"

"Yeah, he's in. They're going over Harry's place tomorrow. He's going to call me at your bar and tell me if they turned up anything."

"You're still going to go to Africa, aren't you?"

"I'm covering my bets, so yeah, I'm going."

Monastery of Debre Amlak
Northern Eritrea

Morning prayers were long over, but the sun was still an hour from rising. The moon hung shining and fat, three-quarters full and bright enough to wash away the glow from Venus, the morning star. April was rainy season, yet the downpours had not come to the lowlands; the desert stretching into the interior of Africa had not seen a drop. However, the air was chilled with humidity, forcing the twelve monks and their abbot inhabiting the ancient monastery to wear heavy woolen mantles. With their legs bare and their feet in leather sandals, they shivered in the predawn light as they prepared to break evening fast at the long table in the dining hall.

Situated along a razor crest of mountains that cleaved across the desert floor and afforded the monastery some reprieve from the worst of the summer heat, the retreat had a commanding view of the surrounding flats, as if its original builders had an eye for defensive positions rather than the sequestration of its inhabitants. Constructed in the twelfth century as an outpost of Christianity and expanded once during the 1600s, the abbey had enjoyed continuous occupancy until the latter part of the twentieth century, when the intense fighting between Eritrean freedom fighters and the occupying Ethiopian army forced the brothers to evacuate to another monastery in Ethiopia. Contrary to the "scorched earth" policy practiced by the Ethiopians at the close of the conflict, when they returned, they discovered that their abbey had not been molested save for a few stray bullet holes that marred its stone facade.

The monks sat at a wide plank table built five hundred

years earlier by another, nameless brother, the chairs added over the centuries by different hands, both skilled and unskilled. It was a point of pride among those assembled to sit at the most uncomfortable and poorly constructed chair as possible—that bit of added discomfort testified, in a small way, to their fealty.

Their meal was simple, a spongy unleavened bread which they tore into small pieces to dip into the gray/green stew of peas, lentils, and peppers. They all drank black coffee, brewed from beans from their own bushes.

Breakfast was the only time the monks allowed themselves full discourse. All other conversation was restricted to prayers and singing. While not exactly informal, the breakfast meetings contained an air of relaxation not normally associated with men who made their devotion by the selfless sacrifice of monastic life. The ages of the men ran from the mid-teens of the three novice boys to nearly a hundred. The abbot, however, was not the eldest of the group, as was normal practice.

When the monastery was abandoned in 1983, the head abbot at the time had vowed he would never return, feeling shame in breaking the chain of occupation stretching far into the past. He died while they were still in exile, and many of the elder monks refused to return home in honor of their friend. Those that did come back made it clear that they would not take the reins of leadership in order to show deference to their fallen leader. Thus it fell to a younger man, an Ethiopian by birth, who had been part of the monastery since he was a novice.

Not knowing his own age but guessing it to be around sixty, Brother Ephraim (he had used the name for so long he scarcely remembered the one given to him by his parents) sat at the head of the table in the oldest, most dilapidated chair, the pewter plate before him mopped clean with the last of the bread. Small bits of food clung to his mostly silver beard. He spoke Latin, conversationally.

"Did our little friend return last night to harass the chickens? I heard a disturbance about an hour after midnight services. I thought maybe our jackal was back."

"Alas no, brother. He has not returned, and I fear he may not," one of the monks responded sadly, for in this dead land the return of even a single scavenger was seen as a renewing of life. "I saw his body across the valley yesterday. He had been shot."

"God works to return what man has plundered from the earth by the war, and yet we continue to defy Him. I fear the day when He no longer replenishes that which we use up." Brother Ephraim shook his large head with disappointment.

"That day is closer than you think," the eldest of the monastic family muttered, a monk who had lived here for almost nine decades. "Judgment is coming."

"Yes, Brother Dawit. His Day of Atonement is never far away," Ephraim agreed patiently, for the elder monk had lost much of his mind as well as his eyesight. Dawit's body was paper thin, his skin so parched that even candlelight could silhouette the delicate bones in his hands. In recent weeks his health had deteriorated alarmingly, and his thoughts had become scattered and disjointed.

"Not His day, brother, but another's," Dawit cawed. "Before we face God's judgment, we will be questioned by men, and our answers will offend them most grievously. They will take up arms against us and all others who defy them. They know of a secret meant to be kept forever. The sins of our fathers are about to be revealed."

There was a silence for a moment, and Ephraim was about to reassure the aged monk when Dawit sat straighter in his chair, his milky white eyes glaring sightlessly. "My brothers, the time has come for us to accept the shame of the distant past. The deaths of the children will be exposed. The Evil, brought to earth from hell itself, will kill again. Many will die in order that many more will be saved. You know nothing of this, Brother Ephraim, for our chain was broken and secrets were not passed to you by your predecessor. But there are truths within these walls that will pit nation against nation if they are divulged. Judge wisely, brother. The fate of the Lord's battle with Satan rests upon your shoulders. Why do you think none of us wanted your chair when we returned?"

Dawit craned his fleshless neck around the room, his blind eyes falling unerringly on those older members of the brotherhood who, like himself, had refused to take the leadership of the house. "We did not do it to honor the former abbot. We all despised him, though none would make that admission. What he knew made him a hate-filled, bitter man, one concerned more with the decisions of this world than contemplation of man's place in the next. Such was the nature of his position, of yours, young brother."

Ephraim had gone a little pale under his natural dusky complexion. He was stunned by the coherence of Dawit's speech, even if he didn't understand the content. "And what were these truths, brother? Who will question us?"

Dawit's body shook with the effort of his outburst, his narrow chest heaving under the dark cloak. In the eyes of the other clerics, the strain of speaking seemed to age him further. "I do not know. I do not wish to know, and if you had a choice, neither would you. But God's will be done, and it is up to Him to reveal what that is."

Later that day, as the sun slid silently past its zenith, Brother Ephraim went out walking. The heat was ferocious, but he still wore his woolen vestments. It was dangerous where he wandered. After the war, a team sponsored by the United Nations had painstakingly cleared the hundreds of land mines planted in the area around the monastery and the fields the monks used for pasturing their goats. Nearly twelve square miles had been decontaminated, but beyond the little red markers, the land was fouled with can-sized bombs. Ephraim knew he'd stepped over the boundary, but his thoughts were too deep to pay that fact particular attention.

He had spent his life devoted to the Church, and unlike many others who had taken up the calling, his faith had never wavered. But as he walked across the desert, he felt a superstitious dread tingling his spine. He wanted to discount Dawit's ramblings, but he could not. Dawit's tirade had rattled him, not to the core of his faith but at least to the core of his manhood, for what the old brother said sounded more of the work of man than of God.

The role of monks and the monastic system was not the spread of the gospel nor the recruitment of new members to the fold. A monk's single occupation was prayer and contemplation for the salvation of others. It was the most difficult of callings for one never knew, like a parish priest watching his congregation flourish, if their devotion had been successful, if they had really touched the lives of others through their work. Thus Ephraim had had very little contact with the world outside of this valley. Dawit's words had unsettled him. He was well armed to attack questions of faith, but ill equipped to deal with issues between men. It was a world as alien to him as the monastery was to those who lived beyond its cloistered walls.

There were two things he needed to do, two deeds that that would help him put into context what Dawit had said. He had little doubt that the old brother knew something he was unwilling to divulge, so Ephraim felt he had to prepare. The first deed, a guilty pleasure learned at the other retreat in Ethiopia, he looked forward to more than he cared to admit. The other was a mortal sin—the breaking of a confessional trust.

Suddenly, he whirled around so that his long robe danced against his exposed legs, and he started back the way he had come, his stride more determined, his path more direct.

In the cliff below the monastery was a deep cave, its mouth hidden from easy view by a fold-back of the valley wall, a natural sandstone screen. The cave had been used long ago as a resting place for shepherds lost deep in the desert and by primeval men, who had painted the walls with frescoes of their hunts. Before making it his personal sanctuary, Ephraim had watched it for many months to make certain he was not intruding on the solitude of one of the others. He did not know how many of his brothers in the past centuries had used the cave as their own retreat from the house.

Because he had planned for a long walk, he carried a flask of water and a modest meal of dried vegetables and a little salted mutton. Now inside the cave, he removed these items from the pocket of his robe and set them on the carefully swept sand floor. He placed the food against one wall next to the other flasks brought from previous visits and left for those times he came unprepared. He was surprised to realize he had built up quite a cache and wondered if it wasn't time to spread it out into the desert for the small nocturnal creatures and the keen-eyed vultures.

The light in the cave was dim and ill suited for his purposes, and he had forgotten to bring a candle again. As he settled against a smooth wall, the coolness of the stone leaching through his cloak, he knew that part of his pleasure was the suffering afterward, as if the eyestrain was in some small way a penance. His heart pounded with anticipation, and he felt a tightness in his stomach as he did every time he reached for one of the books. The volumes were old, their leather worn by countless hands and the harshness of their African home. They were meant for a fine library in Europe.

Because Ethiopia and Eritrea—Abyssinia as the region was known then—were Italian colonies up until 1940, Ephraim had learned to speak the language as a young boy, and while he was sorely out of practice, he could read it well enough for the books to bring him tremendous pleasure and insight into the workings of the outside world. He had found the five volume set at their temporary home in Ethiopia. Selecting a book at random, Ephraim began to read laboriously. It was prophetic that the passage was from *Othello,* the scene in which the Moor realizes he's been betrayed by his lifelong friend, Casio. Brother Ephraim's love for Shakespeare's plays and sonnets was his most guarded secret and also his only real tool for understanding the outside world.

Only after a few hours with the Bard would he tackle his second task, one that would make the monk realize that life today had become much more complex than even Shakespeare could have imagined.

Arlington, Virginia

In the best of circumstances, Mercer needed a minimum of two months to mount the type of expedition he was planning, but he'd given himself only another three days. Even with full cooperation from Eritrea, which he suspected Selome Nagast could not provide, he would land in Africa poorly equipped, underfunded, and lacking vital information.

Mercer had committed himself, unsure whether his vague hunches were right and with little equipment and even less data to back him up. It was daunting even for him, but every time he felt his commitment wane, he thought about his responsibility to Harry and he could temporarily slough off the exhaustion. Already, Harry had been gone for more than twenty-four hours. Mercer's frustration was mounting. He worked as fast as he could, but still felt he wasn't doing enough.

Since early morning, his fax machine had been buzzing continuously as had the ink jet printer attached to his computer. Both machines were producing reams of text about the geology of Africa's Horn, gathered for him from both local and international contacts. Between phone calls, he'd managed to skim just a tiny portion of the accumulated material. Though his knowledge of Africa's geologic composition was voluminous, he didn't know enough of Eritrea's specific makeup, its formations and history, for what he was about to attempt. He had yet to find even a vague hint as to the whereabouts of the kimberlite pipe.

The top of his desk was buried under two inches of paper, some organized in piles, others spread haphazardly. Somewhere under the clutter lay the plates he'd used for both breakfast and lunch. He hadn't slept since returning from his late-night meeting with Dick Henna, and while the pots of coffee he had consumed kept him awake, a raging headache had formed behind his eyes and spread so that his entire skull throbbed. There was a break in the incoming faxes, so he reached for the phone. Prescott Hyde's number was permanently imprinted on his brain.

"Yes, Dr. Mercer, what is it now?" Hyde was as tired of receiving the calls as Mercer was of making them.

"Bill, I'm probably going to need a blasting license once I'm in Eritrea. I'm faxing over copies of my master's licenses from the U.S., Canada, South Africa, Namibia, and Australia. Whatever functionary issues them in Asmara should be suitably impressed, so I won't need to be tested once I'm there."

"Shouldn't Selome be handling stuff like that? You have her cell phone number."

"She hasn't answered the damn thing all day, so the job is falling on your lap," Mercer explained. Because Selome didn't have a connection to the Eritrean embassy and Mercer didn't know if she was involved with the kidnappers, he didn't want to reveal his misgivings about her. He felt that Selome and Hyde's collusion ran deep. "While we're at it, the explosives I've ordered need an End User's certificate before they can be shipped. You'll need to arrange that. I also want to get some collapsible fuel bladders for filling the equipment at the site. I can order them from a civilian supplier, but the military versions are stronger."

"Why not just use tanker trucks to refuel the equipment?"

"Once we get geared up, I can't afford to have tank trailers laying idle. They'll be making round-the-clock runs to bring in more diesel. You can't imagine how many gallons per hour some of those trucks drink."

"Okay, anything else?"

"Yes, I've got a bill on my desk for two million seven hundred thousand dollars, payment due in thirty days for the heavy equipment leases. My word was enough to get the equipment in transit, but my reputation is on the line here and I need to know that this is going to get paid."

"Don't worry about the money," Hyde said. "Selome and I have that all taken care of. Fax the bill to my office and don't give it another thought."

Mercer didn't like Hyde's snake-oil-salesman's tone, but he let it pass. "All right. How are you two coming with the rest of my requests?"

"Excellent. I spoke with Selome earlier this morning, and she said that the small equipment you wanted is waiting for you in Asmara. It's being loaded onto trucks for shipment closer to the target area. She's found a local who has experience in mining—well, quarry work actually, named Habte Makkonen. He'll be your guide once you're in Eritrea."

"Do you have a number where I can reach him?"

Hyde chuckled. "If you had any idea how horrible the phone service is over there, you wouldn't have asked that question."

"Fine. We'll talk later." Mercer cut the connection, adding two Iridium satellite phones to his long list of necessary equipment.

He had to get to Tiny's office for Henna's call, and he gathered a bundle of papers for the wait. He hated to use the time this way, but he couldn't chanced his phone being tapped or his office bugged, nor could he afford to miss the call. He was almost out the front door when his phone rang again. He raced back into the kitchen and grabbed the extension hanging from the wall, its coiled cord nearly brushing the floor.

"Where are you?" Chuck Lowry asked. He knew more about computers than any of Mercer's other friends.

Much of Lowry's business was legitimate, erecting data protection systems and investigating electronic fraud, but he kept his hand in the illegal side of the Internet and computer networks. Mercer suspected the Vietnam veteran still loved the underworld of the electronic age that he had helped create. He was a bit of a flake who purposely cultivated a computer geek's eccentricity and had made a fortune debugging computers for Y2K compliance.

"At home. Where the hell do you think I am?" Mercer snapped, too tired to care that Lowry was responding to an appeal for help.

"Hey, I didn't know if I dialed your home number or your cell. Doesn't matter. Head to Dulles Airport. I'll call you on your car phone in two minutes." There was an urgency in Lowry's twangy voice. "I found Harry for you."

Mercer slammed the phone in its cradle, dropped the papers to the floor, and sprinted out of his house. His Jag was parked on the street, as he usually left it, the keyless entry system chirping even as he swung open the long door. The Perelli tires left two long greasy marks on the asphalt as he smoked them away from the curb.

He was on the beltway doing eighty, weaving though traffic like a stock car driver when the car phone rang. Needing both hands on the wheel, he activated the speaker mode. "What have you got, Chuck?"

"It may already be too late." Lowry's strident voice filled the Jaguar.

"Tell me." Mercer jinxed his car around a minivan occupied by a startled mother and four equally wide-eyed children. He was pushing ninety miles per hour now, the tension in Lowry's voice transferring to the gas pedal.

"I went through all the major airline reservation databases last night and this morning looking for new bookings out of Reagan National, Dulles, and BWI. The kidnappers more than likely would have drugged him to keep him quiet. Can't have some old man screaming and yelling on an international flight, can they? So I figured they might have requested special assistance. Had to crack into a government computer system to use their juice for the search engine, but that's neither here nor there."

"Come on, Chuck, get on with it!" Mercer's frustration was finding an outlet.

"The search turned up bupkis, but then I got thinking. What about a charter jet service? I started that search just a few minutes ago and got a hit first try. A Gulfstream IV out of Dulles was chartered yesterday morning for a departure in . . ." Lowry paused. ". . . eighteen minutes, according to the flight plan."

"Why suspect this particular charter?" Even as he asked, Mercer felt his excitement swell.

"Ticketing code had a WCHC flag, which is a request for wheelchair assistance to the plane. If they drugged an eighty-year-old man, chances are Harry won't be tap dancing up the boarding stairs. General Aviation at Dulles told me the five passengers are there right now waiting to board, and the old man in the wheelchair hasn't made a peep since they arrived."

Bingo!

Mercer floored the Jag, the speedometer needle arcing past a hundred just as smoothly as the engine builder could make it. The feline-sleek car knifed through the steady afternoon traffic with elegant ease, Mercer deftly passing cars on both the left and the right, dodging dangerously into the breakdown lane when necessary.

There it was. The shot of adrenaline, his drug of choice. Harry had said that the hollow in Mercer's life was loneliness, and he agreed that there was a lot of truth in that statement. But Mercer also missed the danger. He'd become addicted to it in Alaska and craved the feeling of life it gave. The narrow gaps between cars seemed like open chasms as he bulled the Jag toward Dulles. He scarcely noticed a fender bender in his wake, caused by an overagressive move. The honks of protest as he accelerated past commuters sounded like a chorus.

"Thanks, I owe you a big one. I'll call you later."

I've been in New York for the past couple of days and I'm leaving for Los Angeles tomorrow. Mercer could only pray that Henna hadn't left yet. He dialed the director's cell phone number.

"Hello."

"Dick, it's Mercer. I've found Harry White. He's at the General Aviation building at Dulles."

"Holy shit!" Henna shouted. "I'm already on the road, heading to Dulles right now."

"Where exactly are you?" Mercer prayed that he wasn't just leaving his downtown office.

"We passed the first toll booth on the airport's access road about ten seconds ago."

"Thank Christ. How many agents with you?" Mercer decelerated slightly for the Dulles exit.

"Me and Marge Doyle and two agents." Henna understood what Mercer really wanted to know. "The two agents are armed. Wait, so's Marge."

Fortunately for Mercer, traffic heading to Dulles International was light, and he was able to steer his car into an open slot at the first booth. There was a mechanical arm blocking the lane. While every commuter had dreamed of a moment like this, it gave Mercer no pleasure. He shot into the lane, hitting the barrier with the center of the hood, snapping it off cleanly. It flew away like a crippled bird.

Mercer paid no attention to the chaos behind him, knowing it would take time for a patrol car, if one was stationed there, to take up the pursuit. By then he would be two miles down the road and pulling away by the second. He saw a white sedan ahead of him with government plates.

"Dick, are you in a white Crown Victoria?"

"How'd you know?"

"Look out the left side window." Mercer's black Jaguar streaked by the Crown Victoria as thought it were parked. Henna's driver was doing seventy.

"Christ on the cross. Are you out of your mind?" Henna screamed over the cellular phone.

Mercer's hard gray eyes flicked to the rearview mirror, noting with satisfaction that the FBI driver was gamely trying to keep pace. Another toll booth was coming up fast, the Jag eating the distance so quickly that Mercer's vision felt like a camera lens on fast zoom.

Warned by the workers at the first booth, all the mechanical barriers were down and men stood in the lanes trying to block the speeding Jag. Mercer had only seconds to commit himself, but he couldn't chance hitting one of the men. He cursed bitterly and was about to slow.

"Far left!" Henna shouted, seeing an opening at the same instant Mercer did.

Mercer spun the wheel, the rear end of the car twitching dangerously as he eased the brakes with his left foot and applied more power with his right, his feet dancing nimbly. He executed a perfect controlled slide across the tarmac, the Jag lining up with the narrow lane just as its rear tires regained firm traction. He had a clear route all the way to the airport.

Dulles's main terminal, with its arcing columns of brick and concrete and its long slabs of glass, reminded Mercer of some giant animal's rib cage left out in a field to bleach. He fish-tailed the Jag through the grounds, past the terminal, and followed the overhead signs to the newly built General Aviation building. Mercer took his Jag through the maze of parked luxury vehicles before throwing it into a four-wheel drift, rubber smearing from the tires with a protesting scream. The car stopped just a few feet from the automatic glass entry doors. The Crown Victoria was only a few seconds behind.

Mercer dodged into the terminal just as Henna leapt from his car with the two agents, Marge Doyle's .38 snub-nosed revolver in his hand. The agents carried matte-finished automatics that matched their deadly expressions. Though his size and ample stomach made Henna look out of shape, he was almost as quick as Mercer and was on his heels in an instant.

The terminal was well appointed, more like a comfortable hotel lobby than an airport waiting room. It catered to the ultra-rich who could afford their own aircraft or had the money to charter one. Its far side was dominated by plate-glass windows that looked over ranks of Lears, Gulfstreams, Citations, and other corporate aircraft. At the tarmac exit, a group of men were just leaving to board their plane. Mercer immediately recognized the back of Harry White's head as he lolled in a stainless steel wheelchair. A woman waiting for her plane screamed when she saw Henna and the others burst into the terminal with their guns drawn. The four men hovering over Harry whirled at the sound, and when they saw the weapons, they drew guns of their own.

Mercer shoved Henna aside, then dove to the carpet as if he were sliding into home to win the World Series. The kidnappers all carried the AKMS, an updated version of the Soviets' venerable AK-47, built with folding stocks for easier concealment. The guns had been under long coats.

The AKs chattered, and Henna's driver caught half a clip in the chest, his torso nearly ripped apart by the onslaught. The other agent took two slugs in the shoulder and thigh. Three civilians fell in the opening fusillade, their corpses landing close enough to Mercer for him to see the horror frozen on their faces. The terrorists lost track of Henna and Mercer in the exploding panic and turned to bundle Harry out of the building to where their jet waited.

Without thinking, Mercer leapt from the carpet, snatched the driver's fallen Beretta, and took up the chase. From outside, the kidnappers fired back into the building. Bullets slammed into the plate-glass window, sending shards cascading like a waterfall. Mercer lunged for the floor again, raised the Beretta over the mangled windowsill, and started firing, hoping to scatter the kidnappers. He gave no thought to the jets on the apron that were all fully fueled and cost millions of dollars apiece.

Either one round hit a terrorist or the return fire had made them duck because the AKs fell silent. Mercer chanced looking out the ruined window, his knees grinding into the shattered glass. The fleeing men were at the steps of a Gulfstream, bodily lifting Harry through the open door while one of them kept an eye on the terminal. The gunman spotted Mercer and raised his assault rifle, but Mercer ducked before he could fire.

His chest pounding in the brief respite, Mercer felt the fear giving way to immeasurable fury. He mentally counted the rounds he'd fired and figured he had only one shot remaining before the Beretta locked back empty. The range to the aircraft was too far for an accurate shot, and even if he was closer, Mercer couldn't risk hitting Harry.

On the tarmac, the engine noise of the terrorists' chartered plane increased to an earsplitting shriek. Mercer doubted the pilot was part of the terrorist gang, and he could imagine the gun held to his head, compelling him to take off. He looked out again and saw the plane pulling away, the door still open and one terrorist hanging out with his AK pointed at the terminal.

Mercer vaulted through the destroyed window and raced across the open expanse of concrete, poorly aimed bullets from the fleeing Gulfstream raking the tarmac. He could hear distant sirens approaching the airport and Dick Henna's booming voice calling him back, but he ignored the distractions.

He dodged several planes and a towing truck left abandoned by a frightened ground worker. The Gulfstream was accelerating, but its pace was little more than a slow trot and Mercer raced to the gunman's blind side. When he came even with the tail, reeking fumes from the engines engulfed him in a dark cloud. He veered and got the terrorist in his sights. Mercer triggered off his final round at a range of only eight yards. The gunman tumbled from the doorway, his AK clattering behind him. The shot must have alerted the terrorists because suddenly the Gulfstream leaned back on its rear landing gear as the pilot increased power, leaving Mercer in its wake. The Gulfstream turned on to the main taxiway leading to the center of the airport complex and the runways.

Mercer sprinted back toward the terminal and the apron of executive jets, rushing to a Gates Learjet with its tail mounted turbofans already whining on idle.

Mercer closed the Beretta's action and used its butt to wrap on the closed hatch. "Police. Open up!"

A second later, the door sprang upward. Mercer recognized the well-dressed African-American as the anchorman for a CNN news program. Mercer grabbed a fistful of his shirt, jacket, and hand-painted tie, and with one graceful move he tossed him effortlessly to the ground. Mercer was aboard with the door closed in an instant.

The Lear's cabin was small, barely four and a half feet tall and just a bit wider. Had there been other passengers on the plane, Mercer wouldn't have continued, but the ten seats were empty. He could hear the pilots talking from the cockpit.

"You okay back there, Mr. Jackson?" the copilot called.

Mercer shuffled forward until his body was between the pilots' seats and both men could see the gun in his hand. He used it to point at the Gulfstream, now a quarter mile away. "Follow that plane," he said, unable to ignore the absurdity of his order.

The pilots realized Mercer's seriousness and the damage the 9mm could do at such a close range. The copilot sat back in his seat, distancing himself from the controls as the pilot applied power to the turbojets.

"Just stay cool," the pilot pleaded, his voice tight.

"Don't worry about me." Mercer sounded distant even in his own head. "Just don't lose that Gulfstream."

The Lear closed quickly, its tires strained by the aircraft's excess speed. The Gulfstream's hatch was still open, and when one of the gunmen went to close it, he caught sight of the small jet stalking them. Mercer could see the surprised expression on his dusky face and his eyes go wide before the terrorist ducked out of view.

"Brace yourselves," Mercer shouted just as the gunman reappeared, holding the AK out the hatch and firing one-handed, the weapon jerking in his fist.

Lead streaked from the weapon like water from a hose, chunks of concrete exploding from the taxiway. Several rounds pierced the Lear's thin skin, though the engines continued to pour out thrust.

"That's it, pal," the pilot screamed. "Chase is off."

"Keep after them."

"We're hit, man. There's no way I'm flying without assessing the damage."

"You can ram them," Mercer said more coolly than he felt. "Not hard enough to destroy their plane, but enough to prevent them leaving."

"You're out of your fucking mind."

"They just killed four people in the airport and they're

kidnapping a fifth. We're the only ones who can stop them."

The pilots exchanged glances and came to a mutual agreement. The Lear increased speed, careening onto the runway, dipping so hard into the turn that the wing-mounted fuel tank scraped the ground in a shower of sparks. The kidnapper's Gulfstream came to an abrupt halt fifty yards ahead of the Lear to allow a United 747 to loop in for its landing, its shadow racing along the ground to catch the hurtling jumbo jet.

The Lear's pilot saw his opportunity and further increased power. The plane ate the distance to the Gulfstream with the grace of a cheetah on the hunt. From the Gulfstream, a face appeared in the hatch again. Realizing what was about to happen, the terrorist leaped to the tarmac just as his aircraft started rolling again, building up to rotation speed.

"Oh, shit!" the Lear pilot shouted.

The gunman raised his AK as he charged, but either the magazine had been emptied earlier or the weapon had jammed. It did not fire. He tried for a frantic half second to clear the chamber, then realized the gun wouldn't work in the moments before the Lear reached him. He tossed it aside.

"What the hell is he doing?" the copilot asked.

Mercer understood. The dead look in the terrorist's eyes told him exactly what was going to happen. The kidnapper kept running at the low-slung aircraft, judging distances, and at the critical second he leaped. One foot landed on the Lear's left wing, momentum making him tumble, but he had enough coordination to twist as he rebounded, aligning himself with his intended target. His arm went in first, the titanium blades of the Garrett TFE 731 turbofan having little trouble liquefying both muscle and bone, but when his shoulder and head hit the whirling turbine, the engine came apart, blades exploding off the roller-bearing shaft and blowing through the aluminum nacelle.

The Lear's pilot shut down both engines when he realized the gunman's suicide mission and prevented a spontaneous detonation. The Gulfstream lifted off the macadam a mile down the runaway, trails of exhaust marring the air like angry brush strokes. Mercer gave little thought to the pilots or the man who'd allowed himself to be sucked into the jet engine and watched as Harry's kidnappers flew off into the distance.

Because he hadn't done enough, his friend was gone. He'd been so close, but then again, he'd been only forty yards away when Tory was murdered. His hands began to tremble with rage and frustration. And guilt. He could have done more. He could have driven faster or run harder or shot out a tire rather than allow himself the grim satisfaction of using his last bullet to kill one of them. He wanted to believe he'd given it his best effort, but with these high stakes, it was obvious that his best wasn't good enough.

He was sitting on a grassy verge bordering the runway when an airport security car whooped its way to the stationary Lear. There were knotted muscles at the base of his jaw as he tried to keep his mouth firm. Dick Henna jumped from the car and approached slowly. Mercer was as close to breaking down as he had ever seen him, and the sight sent a chill through Henna's guts.

"Are you okay?"

Mercer took a long time to answer, his face blank, but beneath his eyes, rage boiled. "Yeah, I'm fine," he whispered. "You?"

"I lost a man in there and another is already on his way to the hospital. Listen, Mercer, I've got to get you the hell out of here. Marge has already called for an FBI forensics unit, and they'll be here shortly. I can explain away this thing as an arrest gone bad, but as a civilian, you can't be involved." He held out a hand. Mercer used it to hoist himself to his feet.

"What about the Gulfstream?"

"I don't know. I guess someone has it on radar, but I'm not sure."

"What a fuck-up, Dick," Mercer said. "I am so sorry."

They got into the car. "It's not your fault. Neither of us had any idea the men who took Harry are terrorists lugging machine guns. We had no way of knowing." Henna's voice was calm and soothing. "Chances are, that plane's heading outside the country, and that makes this an international incident. I'm going to call Paul Barnes at the CIA, and if we can figure out where they're headed, I'll have him get some agents there to meet it."

"Do you think the CIA can get him back?"

"Frankly, I doubt we'll have the time to learn where they're going to land. A jet with extended tanks can be in Europe, Africa, or South America in just a few hours. But, hey, there's a ton of evidence lying around here and a paper trail for the jet lease, so there is hope of finding them."

Mercer didn't speak until the sedan's driver circled around the terminal and parked next to his Jaguar. Marge Doyle stood next to Mercer's car, making sure the airport police didn't look at it too carefully. Henna forestalled any questions with a sharp look, so Marge gave Mercer's shoulder a pat and went into the building.

Her commiseration shook Mercer back to the present. Harry was beyond his reach, and for the time being, there wasn't a thing he could do about it. "You're right," he said. "Maybe you can find these bastards through the abandoned weapons or the guy I capped on the runway. I have to get to Eritrea and help Harry that way. Have you found anything on that front? Anything on Selome Nagast?"

"You're not going to believe this one. When I was following your lead about her not working at the Eritrean embassy, I got a call from the ambassador himself. He said that she was in the country under his authority and that she was working without the support of his staff. They know nothing of her or her mission here."

"Which is?"

"According to the ambassador, securing private funding for humanitarian programs within Eritrea. He didn't get more specific than that, and before I could press, he'd hung up on me." Henna paused. "I dug a little deeper and things got real interesting. I cross-referenced her name through the CIA database, and within minutes I got an angry call."

"Eritrea's ambassador again?"

"No. Are you ready for this? Paul Barnes."

"What?"

"You heard me. The director of the CIA. Typing her name into the computer sent up all sorts of red flags. Part of our system is indexed with the Mossad's, and when her name came up, alarms must have screamed all over Tel Aviv. Barnes's opposite number in Israel called and read him the riot act about interagency cooperation and a bunch of other shit. The upshot is, Israel did not like me poking into the background of Miss Nagast."

"Why in the hell would the Israelis care if you're researching an Eritrean national?" This was one turn Mercer hadn't expected.

"Because she's not," Henna said. "Selome Nagast holds duel citizenship, Eritrea and Israel, and she has an officer's commission in the Israeli Defense Force as well as a position in their government."

"I don't get it." If Selome was Israeli, that could mean Harry was being held by one of the Jewish state's legions of enemies.

"Neither do I. But ten minutes after getting off the phone with Barnes, Lloyd Easton called."

"The Secretary of State?" This was going far outside Mercer's realm, and the implications were beginning to scare him.

"No other. He told me that he'd just received a call too, this one from Israel's foreign minister. We are to back off Selome Nagast or face serious consequences. She's one of theirs, operating in the United States on a mission—get this—'not detrimental to America and therefore none of our concern.' The guy told us to piss off in our own backyard. He said by investigating her mission, we are jeopardizing our close alliance with his nation."

"What the hell is going on here, Dick?"

"You tell me," Henna shot back. "I thought this would be a routine inquiry, and the next thing I know, I've got shit coming down on me faster than I can shovel. What do you think?"

Mercer thought for a moment, paying little attention to the ambulances and police vehicles around them. "I didn't trust her from the beginning. I thought there was something dirty about her—Prescott Hyde, too, for that matter—but this is unbelievable."

"Why can't you be like the rest of my friends?" Henna wasn't upset, but he was serious. "When they call up for a favor, it's usually to help paint their garage or put together a gas grill. With you, it always has to be something else, doesn't it? And it gets worse every time. Harry's kidnapping has turned into a bloodbath. What is it about you?"

"Lucky, I guess. What'd you find at Harry's?"

"Too early to tell. The team went to his place just as I was heading for the airport. What can you tell me about the night Harry was grabbed? It'll help sift through the evidence the forensic team picks up."

"There's nothing I can tell you that would help. It was a night like any other. We were drinking at Tiny's until Selome arrived. We had a couple more after she left, then Harry took off and I headed home too."

"I guess there's nothing we can do unless we can track that plane." Henna rested an arm on the Jag's open door as Mercer finally swung into his car. "Except wait for the forensics reports."

"When do you think you'll have something from Harry's apartment?"

"A couple hours for a preliminary, I'd think," Henna replied, watching his friend critically. "After this mess, I won't be going to California, so why don't you come over to my place tonight and we'll go over it? We'll have a couple of drinks."

"I know what you're trying to do and I appreciate the gesture, but don't bother. I've got too much work. I know my limitations better than anyone." Mercer fired up the Jag's throaty V-12. "When I reach the end of my rope, I'll stop."

"I just hope the end of your rope isn't a noose, you crazy son of a bitch," Henna muttered at the receding car.

Venice, Italy

Giancarlo Gianelli brooded with his back to the windows in the spacious drawing room of his ancestral home located on the Grand Canal. The windows—huge floor-to-ceiling affairs of leaded glass and wrought iron—were over three hundred years old, made at a time when the glassmaker's art was still being perfected. There was a blister in each of the eight hundred individual panes where the blower's pipe had once been inserted into the molten glass. The sunlight streaming through them cast a grid shadow on the floor that matched its checker pattern of beige and rose carrera marble.

The room's furniture were all antiques, each piece exceptional in its own right but coming alive when blended with the rest of the surroundings. It was a room of extraordinary wealth and was only one of forty-three in the home. Gianelli, too, looked as if he were a furnishing for the house, an elegant addition placed just so. His sports coat had been custom made in Milan, his shirt of Egyptian cotton, and his tie had been given to him personally by the late Gianni Versace. He was the epitome of an Italian merchant prince, comparable with the Renaissance Medicis.

Today, the planet was a small place. Anyone had global accessibility in just a few hours with jet aircraft or instantly with the telephone and the Internet. Thus the days when men with vision could generate wealth in direct accordance to the risk were all but gone. Only a few still retained the kind of independence to function without the constraints of obfuscating lawyers and miserly bankers. Giancarlo Gianelli was just such a person.

As the last male heir in a dynasty that stretched back more than six centuries, Gianelli stood at the apex of all his clan had struggled to achieve. In two months the last of his six daughters would be married, and all that would remain to give him succor as he eased into the second half of his fifties was the fabled history of his family. While he had two sons by two separate mistresses, neither of them could ever assume the Gianelli mantle. It was possible that this lack of an heir gave him the recklessness to draw himself away from the legitimate portions of his businesses and delve deeper into the shadows of what his family had created.

The twentieth century had been good to his family. His grandfather had added not one, but two new fortunes, first at the turn of the century when the manufacturing revolution reached the Italian peninsula and again during the fascist reign of Benito Mussolini, when he switched the Gianelli companies to wartime production under the direct patronage of Il Duce. During the 1930s and early 40s the Gianellis rivaled the Fiat Corporation in size and scope, manufacturing everything from submarines to infantrymen's mess kits.

Giancarlo's father had taken the reins in 1955 and shepherded Gianelli SpA, the principle holding company, through the turbulent but profitable 1960s, the downturn of the 70s, and into the meteoric 1980s. He turned over stewardship to his son, Giancarlo, just weeks before the American stock market crash of October 1987. Though Giancarlo's first years as CEO were trying, the company remained one of Italy's largest and most profitable.

Looking out the windows, Giancarlo could see a few gondolas on the Grand Canal, mostly empty, for the boats were used mainly by the tourists and it was still too early for them. There were several *Vaporetti* plying the wide waterway, the lumbering old boats acting much like public buses would in any other city. Around them dodged sleek, polished water taxis, many of them occupied by businessmen, again like any other city in the world. In the distance, the sixteenth-century Rialto Bridge arced gracefully across the canal.

It was April in Venice, a magic time of year. The sun's rays were warm enough to make strolls along the narrow streets comfortable yet the heat wasn't enough to turn fetid the sewage that tended to choke the canals later in the summer. The shop owners were happy and expectant, eagerly awaiting the tourists' imminent arrival. By July, their smiles would be forced, their bonhomie worn a little thin, and by August they would be downright surly because they had made a year's income and were ready to be rid of the droves.

The phone chimed.

"He's leaving in two days' time, Mr. Gianelli," the caller said without preamble.

"What do you think of his chances?" Giancarlo asked.

"He's good. Some say the best, but I don't believe he can find it."

"Why do you say that?" Gianelli wasn't paying the informer enough to trust his deductions. Raw information was one thing, but Giancarlo would do the interpretations himself.

"Time, Mr. Gianelli." The response was immediate, as if the question had been expected. "Hyde gave Mercer a six-week window for his exploration, and Mercer himself wants to be in Eritrea by this weekend. He's really lit some fires here to get things moving. He may be the best mineral prospector in the business, but with only a week to get organized he won't be able to find his asshole with his hemorrhoid creme."

Gianelli grunted with distaste.

"He's made a lot of progress securing equipment and material, but he can't get started for at least another week once he's in Africa. It'll take him that long to sort out the logistics of it all."

"And then?"

"Well, Eritrea may be a small country when you look at it on a world map, but when you're exploring it on foot or from a vehicle, it's a big, rugged place."

"Are you any closer to getting a copy of the Medusa

photographs?" Gianelli asked. "Those pictures are a sure way of narrowing our own search."

"No," the caller replied. "I explained to you before. Hyde never lets them out of his sight. I've already checked the National Reconnaissance Office's archives, and there was only that one set created, something to do with the material they are made from being impossible to photocopy or scan." He paused. "I'm sorry."

"Will Hyde give them to Mercer?"

"I believe so, yes. But he doesn't have them now. Hyde won't turn them over until Mercer is ready to leave."

"Hyde's reason being security?"

"Or paranoia."

"We should be able to get those photos from Mercer once he's in Eritrea." Gianelli was speaking more for his benefit than his listener's and realized that this discussion went beyond the caller's need to know. He changed tack. "When is Selome Nagast going back to Asmara? Will she be with Mercer?"

"I don't know yet. I'd guess she'll be flying with Mercer. When I find out her travel plans, I'll let you know."

"Anything on your suspicions about her?"

"Nothing. But my intuition tells me that there is more to her than she's saying."

"Your intuition also made you sell those pictures to Hyde for a fraction of what I would have paid," Giancarlo said acidly. "She'll be out of Washington in a few days. If there's anything to discover about her, I will handle it from this end. More than likely your instincts are picking up the fact she's sleeping with Hyde."

"It's possible, but I doubt it. He's a pig and she's a living goddess," Major Donald Rosen of the National Reconnaissance Office said.

"It doesn't matter. Just keep me informed. You may be able to atone for your earlier mistake." Gianelli hung up the phone.

So, he mused, *Hyde has found his expert to dig in the desert for him.* While it was a complication that Gianelli didn't particularly relish, it wasn't totally unexpected and he might be able to make it work for his own needs. He would have preferred getting the Medusa pictures from Major Rosen, but Hyde had beat him to them. Now he had to try and steal them from Mercer in Asmara. He thought about taking both Mercer and the pictures and using the American as his own prospector. Giancarlo currently had people scouring the Eritrean wastelands, but his teams certainly didn't have Mercer's expertise. Taking Mercer alive, however, wasn't the priority, the pictures were. He reached for the phone again to put into motion just such a plan, recalling how it had all started.

Eritrea had been an Italian colony starting at the end of the nineteenth century and had been the major staging point for their conquest of Ethiopia in 1935. That war had been particularly brutal, fought between a modern mechanized army on one side and horse soldiers on the other. The outcome was almost inevitable, especially after the League of Nations imposed an arms embargo on the region that Italy, with her own weapons manufacturers, including the Gianellis, totally ignored.

Soon after taking power and long before the war that preluded World War Two, Mussolini had set about creating a modern nation in the hardscrabble desert. For decades there were fortunes made in Eritrea, and it happened that Gianelli's family made most of them. Such was their interest in Eritrea that Giancarlo's great-uncle, Enrico, had lived in a villa outside Asmara and ran much of the country as a virtual slave state.

Enrico was not as shrewd as his older brother, who ran the entire corporation, but he was a Gianelli and knew how to wring profits from every venture: plantations of fruit trees and coffee, timber, salt production, and the importation of amenities for Eritrea's growing Italian population. However, Enrico did have one interest outside the family's traditional spheres that he pursued vigorously. He was an amateur geologist and spent countless months casting about the countryside in search of raw minerals.

He'd convinced himself, and to a much lesser extent, his older brother, that there was gold in the mountains near the border with Sudan. Enrico spent a fortune digging into nearly every mountain that looked interesting. He kept poor records of his work, and most mines were abandoned and forgotten the day they proved barren. Frustrated, his elder brother finally ordered Enrico to stop wasting money and resources on his foolish hobby, but this just made Enrico redouble his efforts. There was one particular mining venture that he was certain would prove valuable. He believed he had found not gold but diamonds.

Giancarlo had all of the family papers concerning Enrico's Folly, as it was called, and had studied them as a child, captivated by the legend. But none of them ever told where this particular shaft had been sunk. Enrico dutifully recorded legitimate aspects of his business affairs, but withheld information about the mine.

Just after New Year's of 1941, it was found that Enrico had been falsifying the account ledgers to cover up the fact that his fabled diamond mine had cost more than all his other ventures combined and put a severe dent in the Gianellis' profits from the colony. He was recalled to Italy immediately. The family patron even sent a private plane with fighter escort to ensure that Enrico returned.

This happened the same time as the British, under General Platt, were sweeping into Eritrea. Enrico had cabled saying he was looking forward to returning to Venice, not only to get away from the fighting, but also to talk with his brother about the mine.

Giancarlo had read that particular cable many, many times because it was the last anyone ever heard from Enrico. The plane to take him home was shot down over the Mediterranean by British Hurricane fighters, and all knowledge of the mine was lost with it.

As a boy, Giancarlo had promised himself that someday he would return to Eritrea and find Enrico's diamond mine. The dream never left him, but it would be years before he could fulfill it. By the time he was in a position to pursue the legend, he was occupied with the rest of the company and his family. At times during his career, he'd been tempted to mount a search, but Eritrea's war for independence was raging, and the likeliest areas for the exploration were some of the most hotly contested and oft-bombed regions in the country. Also, even decades after Italy's brutal occupation, the name *Gianelli* was still cursed in Eritrea and he doubted they would welcome his investigation.

But with the independence struggle over and his obligations to his family coming to a close with his daughter's wedding, he knew that now was the time. Expense on this venture meant nothing—a billion lira, ten billion? What did it matter? All of his life he had done what was expected of him, but this once, like Enrico, he wanted something for himself. If he was successful, he had a plan to make this a very lucrative venture, though timing would be critical. The diamond syndicate in London had a major meeting in two months, and Gianelli needed to be able to show them a lot of stones, several thousand carats at least, if he was to force them to accept his demands. He had already divested himself of all South African stocks because if he pulled this off, that country would become a financial sinkhole.

If he did not succeed? Gianelli shrugged. A few accountants would scratch their heads and wonder where the money went, but that was it. Giancarlo really couldn't lose.

But he knew he would pull this off, for surely what Hyde's satellite pictures had seen and what Enrico Gianelli had found were one and the same.

Monastery of Debre Amlak
Northern Eritrea

The monastery's closest source of electricity was more than a hundred miles due east, in the city of Nacfa, so any illumination after sundown came from either candles or oil lamps, and both were expensive and hard to obtain. With the exception of Midnight Mass, they were used sparingly, and thus life in the monastery was dictated by the rising and setting of the sun. Other than the late-night service, it was rare to find a monk up and about in the darkness of night.

On the day following Dawit's outburst, another monk only a few years younger than Dawit had spoken privately with Ephraim, verifying what the older brother had said. There were secrets here in the monastery and maybe now the time was at hand for them to be revealed. Since returning from his private retreat, Brother Ephraim spent his nights praying and meditating deep into the dead hours, a single candle burning in his room. He had taken no food since returning from his desert walk and precious little water. His eyes were glazed with exhaustion, and his beard had become wild and unkempt. He did not notice the stale smell of sweat on his body nor the pebbled layer of grime on his normally well-cleaned teeth.

A milky-white shaft of moonlight shone through the single window of Ephraim's cell and fell unerringly on the ancient book set on his rough wooden desk. Ephraim's hands rested next to the book, just out of the circle of light, a string of rosaries twined between his long fingers, almost binding them together. The book was leather-bound, its two covers locked together with a tarnished brass clasp. The pages were so old that they had swollen, giving the book a tattered appearance even though it had been lovingly protected for eight hundred years.

Ephraim had been given the book during the final confession of his predecessor, just hours before the man had died during their exile from Eritrea. Ephraim had sworn to the dying abbot on the sacred vows of the confessional that he would guard the book and turn it over to the next head brother when his time came. Under no circumstances, he promised, would he ever open it. Never would his eyes rest on the handwritten parchment within its covers. Even as Ephraim agreed to these last requests, he read the book's title. It was written in Ge'ez, one of Ethiopia's ancient languages. He translated the arabesque-looking script easily.

The Shame of Kings.

His hands had begun to tremble, and the text had almost slipped from his grasp. He felt like Adam in the Garden holding the ill-gotten apple, the luscious fruit poised at his lips. Ephraim knew immediately that the book contained an evil as deadly as original sin. At that moment, he began to finally understand the man dying before him. He turned his gaze to the frail figure lying on the simple cot so far away from their home, knowing the answer but unable to prevent his eyes from asking the question.

"Yes," came the breathless answer. "I read it and God damned me for it, he damned us all. I could not help myself. At the time, I felt as if it was God's will that I read the words and break the silence. It was only when I finished, on the night of November 13, 1962, that I realized it was Satan himself who seduced me into reading the book."

Ephraim stared at him.

"Don't you recognize the date? The day after I finished the *Shame of Kings,* Ethiopia officially annexed Eritrea. It was the beginning of the end for our country, Ephraim: the Ethiopian occupation, the pogroms, the immeasurable suffering under the Dergue. And it was I who caused the war. My hubris brought about God's wrath! He punished me for reading this book by destroying our homes, laying waste to our lands, and killing hundreds of thousands of our people. All because I could not refuse to read what is written in that accursed book, the dark companion to our greatest religious texts."

Within the faith there were two ancient books, *Kebra Nagast: The Glory of Kings* and *Fetha Nagast: The Justice of Kings*. While largely unknown in the Western world, these two books predated most notable Christian writings by many hundreds of years, coming first from Egyptian Copts at least a thousand years ago. The works chronicled the visit of Makeda, The Queen of the South, to the land of Israel, and the life of her son Menyelek, who was fathered by the King of Israel. They told of Menyelek, spiriting the Tabernacle of the Law of God from Jerusalem, transferring His terrestrial seat to Aksum in what is now northern Ethiopia. The books attested that the rightful kings of Ethiopia from those far-off days until the reign of Haile Selassie were thus the direct descendants of Noah and Abraham and Moses, the chosen Children of God.

Being a Christian, Ephraim possessed a faith grounded in the teachings of Jesus and his Apostles and Disciples, yet his beliefs were based on a much older faith, that of the Jews, the first believers in the one true God, blessed even if they did not see Christ as His son. While unfamiliar with later Jewish works like the Talmud, Ephraim knew well the earlier teachings, believing strongly in the Old Testament and the *Kebra Nagast* and the *Fetha Nagast*.

The validity of what was written in the *Kebra Nagast* had been a point of contention among religious scholars soon after its discovery. But in the nineteenth century, Western missionaries returned from Africa with tales of black-skinned Jews living in Ethiopia who practiced a much older, and some said purer version of the faith. The question of whether these people, called Falashas—*Outsiders*—were really Jewish was answered in 1984 when Israel executed Operation Moses, a secret program run by the Mossad to bring as many Falashas as possible to Israel at a time when the Ethiopian famine was at its worst.

How it came to pass that this unknown third book, *The Shame of Kings*, fell into the hands of the Christian monastery, Ephraim could not say. Yet he sat at the bedside of the dying abbot holding the volume in one hand, his other resting on the withered shoulder of the priest.

"Swear to me, Ephraim, that you will not read it. There are things within those pages that were never meant for man's eyes." The old abbot's voice had the strength of a guttering candle. "I lost my faith that night. It was too much for me to believe that a god, our God, could allow such an outrage, such an abomination."

"I swear it to you," Ephraim readily agreed, wishing he had not even touched the unclean work. "On the sanctity of your confession in the eyes of God, I will never again look at this book."

It now lay just inches from his hands, bathed in eerie moonlight. Ephraim knew he had to read it. A cold wind rattled the fragile windowpane and flickered the nearly spent candle sitting in a pool of its own wax. The weak flame cast bizarre shadows on the raw stone walls, familiar shapes in the room taking on ominous dimensions. He felt a chill run the length of his spine.

Why do you test me so, Lord? Am I to be like Job, forced to endure hardships so you can prove to Lucifer that man's love for you can not be corrupted? I fear that I am not strong enough. Is my test not to read this book? Is it Your will that these words are never again seen by the eyes of man? Or is your mission for me to read it and bring its truths to light?

The night wore on, Ephraim lighting another candle from the embers of the last, filling his room with fresh light. The moon tracked across the sky so that it no longer beamed onto the table but instead rested on the simple crucifix hanging over Ephraim's bed. He stared at the image intently, feeling His suffering on the cross, and for the first time in days, Ephraim felt a lightness in his chest. The answer to his dilemma was before him. Christ had died for our failures and to knowingly fail Him was sinful, but it was still to be forgiven, the deed condemned, not the man.

At almost the same instant he turned back to his desk and undid the book's clasp, Brother Dawit cried out in his sleep and died in his own room. But by the time Ephraim learned of this the following morning, he had read the book, and the death of the aged monk was no longer such a tremendous concern.

Somewhere over the Atlantic

Mercer sprawled across two first-class seats, his mouth agape and his jaw covered by a thin shadow of beard. His flight to Rome, Europe's only major hub with connecting flights to Asmara, had left early, so he'd shaved and showered the night before. He desperately needed to review his work and correlate his findings with the Medusa photographs Prescott Hyde had finally sent him, but his eyes had refused to stay open. He had purchased two adjoining seats, planning on using the extra space to spread the material, but best intentions are just that: intentions. He fell asleep even before the jetliner took off.

Mercer's sleep was troubled, and every once in a while a flight attendant would check on him as he muttered aloud in his dark dreams. There was a sheen of clammy sweat on his forehead. When he woke, his eyes were red-rimmed and gummy, and his mouth tasted awful. He looked around the quietly humming cabin, momentarily dazed, trying to clear the cobwebs of sleep from his brain. He was thankful to be released from his nightmares, but a thought had come to him in his sleep, something buried deep in his mind that vanished when he came awake. Once again he thought there was an inconsistency somewhere, something either Hyde or Selome or the kidnappers had said that didn't make sense. Something, but he didn't know what. *Damn.*

He caught the attention of a stewardess and ordered two black coffees and a glass of orange juice. They were waiting for him when he returned from the rest room, where he'd cleaned himself up. Selome Nagast was waiting for him as well, an enigmatic smile on her face.

"I hope you don't mind?" She batted her eyes playfully. "I don't have your expense account to enjoy myself with. I'm sitting in the back with the rest of the sardines, and I knew from Bill that you have two first-class seats."

Mercer looked at her in shock. "Why didn't you tell me you were taking this flight." Apart from that one meeting at Tiny's, he'd only spoken with her on the phone. "My expense account could have paid for another seat. After all, it's your money I'm spending."

Selome quickly grasped that Mercer was making a joke and not being boorish, and she smiled again. "I have to confess that it's been a fantasy of mine to pay for a coach seat and sneak into the first-class area."

"And I thought diplomats always enjoy the finer amenities."

Selome seemed to take his comment to heart. "They do if they represent a wealthy country. I'm lucky when my government can afford to send me abroad. I pay for many of my missions myself."

Mercer wondered which master she was serving now. Was she on a diplomatic mission for Eritrea, the land of her birth, or a covert assignment for her adopted state of Israel? It was easy to figure out Prescott Hyde's interest in this affair. Under the guise of his undersecretary position and spouting humanitarian platitudes, he would certainly manage to reap personal financial gain as well as political cachet if Mercer found diamonds. But Selome Nagast?

Was her motivation the betterment of some of Africa's poorest people, those who dwelled in what is referred to as the Fourth World? Or was she currently working for the Israeli Defense Force or the Mossad? Was there something darker behind her willingness to help his search?

They had another five hours together on the flight, and maybe, Mercer thought, he could find out.

"Never let it be said that Philip Mercer came between a woman and her secret fantasies," he quipped. "But you must allow me a fantasy of my own. If they ask, tell the attendants that I picked you up on the plane and that you're going to have a romantic tryst with me when we land."

"Deal." She shook his hand. He was surprised again by the strength of her grip and the warm feel of her skin.

"It's nice to see you again." Mercer slid back into his seat, making sure to bundle his papers into his two briefcases. "The last time we spoke face to face wasn't one of my most productive meetings."

"I don't blame you for turning down Bill's offer. It's daunting, to say the least. I was more surprised that you changed your mind." She looked into his eyes as if searching for an answer. "Why did you agree? What made you join us?"

Mercer deflected the question quickly. "Why did you pick me in the first place?"

"That's easy. You're reputed to be one of the best in the world at finding valuable minerals."

"Keep talking like that and we'll need another seat for my ego."

"You didn't answer my question. Why did you change your mind?"

Mercer gave her his most honest look. "I guess you could say that going after the impossible has become one of my trademarks. God, does that sound pretentious. But it is sort of true. After I refused Hyde, I spent that afternoon and most of the night looking for any indication that what he was saying was true," he said, mixing fact with fiction. "While I couldn't find any proof, I walked away with a gut feeling. I've learned to trust them before, and I just couldn't refuse this time."

"Does that mean you believe that the diamonds exist?" There was a breathless quality in her question.

"No, it means I don't mind spending six weeks and a lot of your money searching." Mercer meant to sound harsh. He was not about to get trapped into giving her any false hopes.

The sun coming through the porthole caught the claret highlights in her hair. "You may convince yourself with talk like that, Dr. Mercer, but you don't convince me."

"Well, maybe I believe a little bit. But not much." He grinned. "Tell me about yourself."

Before responding, Selome ordered tea for herself and a croissant. Mercer downed the last of his coffee and ordered a third cup. "My mother is Eritrean and fell hopelessly in love with an American serviceman stationed at Kagnew Base, a U.S. military installation on the outskirts of Asmara that was used to monitor Soviet communications during the Cold War. When my family learned of the affair, my mother was forbidden from ever seeing him again. But they were one night too late, I'm glad to say, or I wouldn't be here now.

"When he learned of her pregnancy, my grandfather sent my mother to Italy, where we have other family, but she snuck back soon after I was born. As I understand the story, when my grandfather saw me for the first time, he took me in his arms and laughed aloud when I peed on him. After that, I became his favorite grandchild. My mother was forgiven."

Selome Nagast smiled again. For the first time Mercer felt she was showing her true self. "I went to school in Italy and spent two years in London studying economics. Afterward, I worked for the Eritrean People's Liberation Front in Europe, raising awareness of what was happening in our country."

"I did some research on your war for independence," Mercer cut in, "and found the parties involved more than a little confusing."

"While they may be fierce fighters, my people are not known for originality," Selome agreed. "At various times during our war with Ethiopia, we were represented by the ELF, the PLF, and eventually the ELF-PLF, none of whom agreed with each other. We wasted years with factional fighting. Believe me, it's confusing for an Eritrean too." There was little pride in her voice. "The war would have ended much earlier if we had left the political squabbling until after victory."

"And after the war ended, how did you get involved in the government?" asked Mercer. "Don't be offended, but

I know it's . . . shall I say, difficult . . . for an African woman to be as highly placed as you."

"Difficult isn't the word," Selome concurred, her tone bitter. "In most African nations, the only prerequisite for leadership is a penis. It really isn't important if there's a brain attached to it. Someday Africans will learn not to allow dictators and despots to rule their lives."

"And until then?"

"We'll blame European colonialism and Western bigotry and continue to slaughter each other wholesale."

"Harsh," Mercer replied.

"But true," Selome rejoined quickly. "You've been to Africa. I know you've seen it."

She went silent for a long time. He had seen her expression a hundred times. It was on the local news nearly every night in D.C. It was the look of a mother whose child lay dead in the streets from drug-related violence she was powerless to stop.

"It's not hopeless," he said softly, seeing tears at the corners of her eyes.

"That will be up to you," Selome replied. "At least for us. We've known peace for only a short time, and already factionalism is starting to pull us apart. Religion will be the curse of Eritrea, not the tribalism that has torn apart a lot of other African nations. But the outcome will be the same. Devastation.

"Muslims and Christians are already rattling their sabers from church and mosque alike, calling for the elimination of the other. Sudan's Muslim government isn't helping, exporting their version of fanaticism. Bandits raid us constantly, killing those who don't believe in Allah. Have you ever been to the Sudan?"

"No."

"Pray you never go. I've been to the refugee camps a number of times. In fact, I was on the trip where those photographs Bill Hyde showed you were taken."

Mercer winced, remembering.

"When we finally ousted the Ethiopians, they practiced a scorched-earth policy during their retreat," Selome explained. "They burned villages, destroyed roads and bridges and irrigation dams. They even cut down nearly every tree in the country in an effort to demoralize us. The trees lining the streets in Asmara are the tallest in Eritrea because all others were hauled back to Ethiopia. No matter how bad off we were when the Ethiopians withdrew, it is nothing compared to the ruin found in the Sudan. There are roving bands of guerrillas, terrorizing everyone, some allied to the government, others to the Sudan People's Liberation Army, and still others that are just mercenaries looking to capitalize on the bloodshed. Slavery is rampant and some say government sanctioned."

"What's the reason for their war?"

"Religion. The government in Khartoum is Islamic and has made life unbearable for those in the south who are mostly Christian and animists. If this war is allowed to spread, we will see the same thing in Eritrea. And you are the key for preventing this from happening. It's an old axiom that hatred is the fuel of the hopeless and peace the progeny of the satisfied."

Watching her face, Mercer felt confident that Selome Nagast's loyalties lay in her native Eritrea. He didn't doubt that she also worked for the Israeli secret police, but for this mission her only goal was the welfare of her people in Africa. Knowing this peeled away only one layer of complication, however. He felt there were still depths here that he didn't know.

Before leaving home, Mercer had spoken extensively with Dick Henna about the preliminary findings of Harry's abduction. The private jet that had spirited him out of Washington had been chartered by a corporation in Delaware, but the company was just a post office box, a front. They had been unable to track the fleeing Gulfstream except for a report that it was seen flying over Maryland's eastern shore low enough to burn leaves off trees. They also had a sighting in Liberia, where it landed to refuel before continuing east. The plane's final destination was Lebanon. A CIA agent arrived at the airport in Beruit just in time to see an older man bundled into a van and taken away. He'd lost the vehicle in traffic near the city's Christian Quarter.

A Mideastern connection was further confirmed by Harry's few neighbors who had heard the abduction. The language they described spoken by the kidnappers sounded like Arabic. The only neighbor to see anything reported that the four men all wore black coats and jeans and had dark complexions and dark hair.

All this matched with what Mercer and Henna had seen at the airport. Henna still didn't have any identification of the one kidnapper's body, but he assured it was only a matter of time. He did, however, have better luck tracing the weapons.

"The U.S. Army maintains the largest database in the world of the ballistic characteristics of various individual weapons," Henna explained. "Each weapon has microscopic differences from its mass-produced counterparts, small flaws that affect the shape of the rounds they fired. Identifying these traits is painstaking, but it's possible to trace a single weapon from just the smallest fragments of expended bullets or shell casing.

"The Army Ballistics Laboratory," Henna said, "has been looking for these weapons for a while. The Kalishnikovs were traced back to our peacekeeping mission in Lebanon in the late eighties. Both recovered weapons had been used against our Marine garrison. One gun, carried by the man who jumped into the jet engine, has claimed an American life before, an Army sergeant sitting in a café in 1984 near the harbor in Old Beruit."

There was that Beruit connection again. "How the hell did they get here?" Mercer asked.

"Good question, but what's got me wondering is: where have they been for the past fifteen years?"

Mercer and Henna had talked about the weapon's significance and that Harry's kidnappers were apparently Islamic fanatics—who but a fanatic would allow himself to be sucked into a jet engine—but neither man could explain how these facts meshed with a potential diamond mine in Africa. Selome's affiliation with Israel only deepened the mess. But having talked with her as the Boeing hurtled across the Atlantic, he felt certain that her interest was with Eritrea, not Israel.

"Are you okay?" Selome placed her hand on his wrist, a reassuring touch. "You faded away for a moment, and it looked like you were in pain."

"I'm all right," Mercer lied. He so wanted to talk with her, with anyone really. Bottling up his concern for Harry was tearing him apart. He noticed Selome's hand on his arm. Her fingernails were as long as stilettos, bloodred from multiple coats of varnish. She saw Mercer staring at her hand and let it lie there a moment longer before withdrawing it. He looked at her with a kind of longing, not of desire, but of the need to express himself. He wanted to trust her so he could release some of what he held inside. He wanted to tell her about Harry and about how it was his fault that he'd been kidnapped and beaten. He needed to talk, but he just looked at her mutely. His pain must have been obvious because she reached over and caressed his cheek. It was an intimate gesture that surprised them both.

"I'm all right," Mercer said again, feeling something new sparked by that touch. He found he couldn't look her in the eye.

This could be a real complication, he thought.

Southern Lebanon

Harry White woke with a raging thirst, not for water, but for bourbon. He'd consumed at least two bottles of Tennessee whiskey a week for years. Though he rarely got drunk—his tolerance having been built up over the years—his body needed liquor as surely as it needed oxygen. His hands trembled, adding a new agony to his broken but splintered finger. For the first few days after his abduction, he'd been sufficiently drugged so he didn't know how long it had been since alcohol had passed his lips, but after a couple of conscious hours in the cell, he knew down to the second.

Every waking moment was a torture crueler than anything he'd ever conceived of. He shivered in the twelve-by-twelve room despite the heat that soaked through the stone walls and beaded his body with perspiration. He kept the ragged blanket he'd been given clutched around his bony shoulders.

His need for a drink was an overpowering craving that was driving his mind beyond the realm of sanity.

He used the blanket not only to ward off the chills, but also to protect him from the flying monkeys that circled the room with the maddening persistence of hornets. He knew they were a DT-created hallucination, but they were terrifying nevertheless.

He'd seen the first one only an hour after waking and had called out in horror. The rational part of his mind told him it wasn't real, but he was too weak to prevent its wheeling attack. A guard had come to check on him, a red and white *kefflaya* headdress covering his features. As

Harry cowered, the man determined that nothing was wrong and left. The monkey clung to the wall near where it joined the ceiling and winked.

Two more appeared to terrorize him. They flew at him without mercy, breaking off their aerial charges just inches from his face. He could feel the air move from their swift passage, and their unearthly screeches were like nails drawn across a chalkboard. They would swoop by briefly and then land on the walls, their sharp little claws digging into the stone.

None of the monkeys had touched him yet, but it was only a matter of time.

"There's no place like Tiny's," he moaned aloud, praying the invocation would transport him away from here.

After three long hours his hallucinations ended, and Harry fell into a nightmarish sleep more haunting than his periods of wakefulness. Demons more cunning than the monkeys were after him, chasing him down an endless hallway. They carried bottles of Jack Daniel's, which they tried to pass to him like relay runners, but the bottles slipped out of Harry's hands.

When he woke, his mind had cleared some. A breakfast tray lay on the floor near the bed, the coffee still steaming. His stomach was too knotted to eat the fruit or the jam-smeared bread, but he drank the coffee quickly. And then his lungs reminded him that he'd smoked a couple packs a day for the past six decades and he wanted a cigarette. Needed one.

"For the love of God, you sadistic sons of bitches, give me a smoke," he yelled.

The guard appeared again, and Harry repeated his request with a little more civility, shouting just a few decibels quieter. The guard didn't seem to understand the words, so the octogenarian pantomimed smoking a cigarette. With a sympathy known by smokers the world over, the guard pulled a half-empty pack from his pocket and tossed them on the floor with a book of matches.

"How about some booze, you bastard," Harry said half-heartedly as he scooped up the rumpled pack. The splint made it difficult to light one of the cigarettes, and it took him several tries.

As the nicotine coursed through his system, he looked at the monkey that had appeared on the wall again, its teeth bared in an aggressive display.

"Screw you, too," Harry said to the apparition, a filterless cigarette hanging from his lips. He knew from experience that the DTs would pass quickly and the monkeys wouldn't bother him much longer.

He sat back on the bed, keeping one eye on the monkey just in case, and massaged his injured hand. He didn't know where he was or who had grabbed him, or even why. He hadn't seen the guard's face, but the colorful headdress made him pretty sure they were Arabs and that his abduction involved Mercer and his search for the diamond vent.

Harry chuckled darkly. He'd seen what Mercer was capable of when he was riled and knew that his kidnappers were going to pay. Still, Harry wasn't the type to sit back and wait to be rescued. He'd gotten himself out of a few tough scrapes before. Former Senator John Glenn was only three years younger when he went into space, he thought. If Glenn could pull that one off, surely he could escape this bunch. The guard had given him cigarettes, and it was only a matter of time before Harry figured a way to get the man to give him his freedom too.

Washington, D.C.

Dick Henna was at his desk when his secretary buzzed his intercom and told him he had a call that should not be ignored.

"Who is it, Susan?" The investigation into the Dulles attack had more than eaten up the time he'd saved by not going to California. The day was just starting and already he felt behind.

"Admiral Morrison. I know you don't want to be disturbed, but I thought you'd want to take this one."

"I guess maybe I do."

Henna knew C. Thomas Morrison, the charismatic chairman of the Joint Chiefs, both professionally and in Washington's social scene and had always liked and respected him. Knowing that Morrison was going to be a strong presidential contender in the next elections, and possibly his boss if he won, Henna adopted a respectful tone. "Admiral, Dick Henna here. What can I do for you?"

"Hello, Dick, how you doing?"

If informality was what the African-American naval officer wanted, Henna was more than happy to comply. "Fine, Tom, fine. How are you?"

"I was doing great until a couple of hours ago," Morrison replied somberly. "A problem's come up that's going to involve your office sooner or later, and I thought it best to bring you in on the ground floor."

"Shoot," Henna invited.

"I'm sitting here with Colonel John Baines from the Air Force's Criminal Investigations Division and he's much better suited to speak legalese with you than I am. I'd like to get the three of us together."

Henna felt the beginnings of political strong-arming. Like the military, the FBI had chains of command, and Henna felt that Morrison was using his clout to go straight to the top. "Listen, Tom, I appreciate that you want to bring this to me directly, but is this something that should be going to Marge Doyle's office or another assistant director's?"

"I know what you're thinking." Morrison's voice took on a brittle edge. "Let's just say even this little chat falls into the 'Ultra Top Secret' category." Henna whistled softly. The government had no higher classification. In fact, several presidents had been denied access to UTS documents, most recently former President Clinton's 1993 request to read the real file on the Roswell, New Mexico, incident. "Dick, you don't know me well enough to know that I don't make idle calls and that I never go outside the military unless absolutely necessary."

Henna looked up at the Seth Thomas clock against the far wall of his office. "All right, I can give you an hour at about eleven."

"This can't wait. I'm calling from my car phone. We'll be at the Hoover building in ten minutes." Morrison hung up before Henna could protest.

Eleven minutes later, Henna's secretary showed the two officers into his office.

Admiral Morrison's black uniform, only a shade darker than his skin, was covered with gold braid, decorations, and a chestful of combat medals. He cut the perfect image of a sailor, hard and straight, with an imperious bearing that cracked into a smile when he strode across the room to shake Henna's hand. Colonel Baines, in his Air Force blues, looked lusterless next to the Admiral, his uniform nearly bereft of commendations. Where Morrison was tall and good-looking, Baines was shrunken, his voice barely above an apologetic whisper. Only his eyes betrayed the shrewd mind beneath the unassuming exterior.

"Won't you both sit down?" Henna decided his irritation

of this intrusion wasn't important. "And tell me what's so secret and urgent."

"Colonel?" Morrison said, indicating that Baines should take point in this conversation.

"Mr. Henna, I, ah," Baines stammered, then paused for a moment as if to collect his thoughts. "Well, it started nearly three years ago when my office was tasked with stemming the flow of classified material streaming out of the National Reconnaissance Office. The NRO is one of the most secret organizations in the government and was allowed to use their own internal security for the protection of sensitive material. They did an exemplary job for years. However, after the collapse of the Soviet Union, secrets began leaking. The Air Force has more personnel seconded to the NRO than any other branch, and we were instructed to put an end to the leaks."

"Are we talking about another Aldrich Ames case here, like what happened at the CIA?" Henna interrupted.

"In a way, though there didn't seem to be any political motivation behind the thefts. Our threat came from opportunistic employees using information for profit."

"What kind of secrets are we talking about?"

"Let me give you an example of an arrest we made two years ago. A secretary for one of the NRO's satellite photograph analysts had a husband who traded futures on the Chicago Mercantile Exchange. Using information from our Keyhole-11 spy bird, she was able to tell him that Argentina was about to suffer a severe loss of their winter wheat crop due to an insect infestation. Using that information, he made something like twenty-seven million dollars selling wheat futures short before the knowledge was made generally available."

"So, we're talking stock fraud?" Henna settled back in his seat. He'd been thinking that this had to do with Mercer and Harry White and was relieved that apparently it didn't.

"In that case, yes. We brought in the Securities and Exchange Commission to handle the public side of the investigation. They made the arrest, keeping NRO's involvement a secret. Both husband and wife will be out of prison sometime at the end of the next century." Baines spoke more confidently now. "Anyway, that's just one example. Other cases we found were perpetrated by military personnel, and arrests were handled through the Judge Advocate General's office."

Baines paused again and the FBI director knew that the colonel was getting to the heart of the matter. "Six weeks ago, a case came across our desk, one that took us until the day before yesterday to crack. We made an arrest and learned the case has much wider implications than any previous. I felt it prudent to include civilian authorities, notably your office, as soon as possible. My commanding officer agreed and subsequently briefed Admiral Morrison. It was the Admiral's idea that you and I meet before I continue with my investigations."

Morrison interrupted the younger man. "Some material was stolen from an archive at the NRO. The Air Force major who perpetrated the theft, Donald Rosen, was arrested last night and is looking at about five hundred years in prison for his crime. The materials were photographs that had been sent to his office by mistake. He recognized their 'Ultra Top Secret' classification and stole them. Heads have already rolled for the screw-up that put the pictures on his desk in the first place, but that's an internal matter."

Baines took up the story again. "He held on to the pictures for only a week before finding a buyer, selling them for a mere five hundred thousand dollars. You have to realize we're talking about military secrets that could compromise a very delicate ongoing program. Their potential value is incalculable."

Henna suddenly knew precisely where the conversation was headed. "Let me guess. You want us to handle the investigation into Undersecretary of State Prescott Hyde and determine exactly what he did with the Medusa photographs?"

He could have thrown a live cobra on the floor and gotten a more relaxed reaction from the two men.

"How much more do you know?" Morrison was the first

to find his voice, though he could not hide his astonishment. He had jumped to his feet.

"Tom, sit down, for Christ's sake," Henna said. "Your secret is still safe. As far as I know, only a handful of people are aware of the Medusa pictures."

"You don't understand. There are three Medusas orbiting the earth as we speak. Do you think a nation like China would sit idle knowing the capabilities of our newest-generation spy satellite? Shit, the pictures Hyde bought were from the first prototype, and that thing was a dinosaur compared to the latest ones. There's a lot more at stake than a handful of photographs of the Sahara Desert!"

"Yeah, there is." Henna saw that the conspiracy around Harry's kidnapping was taking another turn for the worse. *Stolen pictures from the NRO, Jesus!* "We'll get to that in a minute. Tell me what happened next."

"Rosen must have realized his asking price was too low after selling them to Hyde," Baines continued. "Between the sale and his apprehension, he contacted someone in Europe; we have no way of knowing exactly who because the calls went to an encryption exchange, but we narrowed the field to Italy, Greece, Yugoslavia or Albania."

"I'll be damned," Henna interrupted, thinking about the religious wars raging in Albania and the former Yugoslav states. Was this another connection to Islamic terrorists, like the charter flight to Beruit?

"What?"

"Finish your story and I'll tell you mine."

"There were a dozen calls of various durations, the final one only hours before Rosen was arrested," Morrison said. "That is one side of the investigation that we'll handle ourselves, possibly using the CIA and INTERPOL if anything shows promise, but we wanted to come to you with Prescott Hyde. He works for the government, but he's a civilian so we're going to need your office to spearhead the investigation."

"The investigation is already underway," Henna snorted. "In fact, I think we've got enough to bring the son of a bitch in for formal questioning. Do you remember Philip Mercer?"

"The guy who handled the crisis in Hawaii?"

"And the one in Alaska too. He has the pictures and is on his way to Africa with them, Eritrea specifically. He left early this morning."

Henna spent the next half hour detailing Mercer's involvement with Prescott Hyde, from the initial approach to search for the diamonds, through Harry White's kidnapping and the subsequent shoot-out at Dulles. "Did anyone from NRO do a hard analysis of the pictures?" he asked in conclusion.

"No, not really," Morrison admitted. "The bird hadn't been calibrated when we lost her. The pics looked like a bunch of junk to our people."

"Well, they're not junk to the group who perpetrated that attack at Dulles."

"We need to get that material back. Not only is it highly classified, but it's also evidence," Baines said.

"No. What we need to do is haul in Prescott Hyde, I mean today, right now and then let Mercer figure out just what the hell is going on."

"Dick, we can help Eritrea later. Dig up the diamonds in a few months or something. We have to get those pictures back." Morrison's voice was backed with every ounce of command in his body but Henna didn't even blink.

"Tom, if you want to pick up Hyde on your own authority and have this make the six o'clock news tonight, be my guest. But if you want the help of this office, then we do it my way."

A tense minute passed, the gleaming pendulum of the wall clock knifing through the time, carving the seconds away.

"All right," Morrison relented. "If we do it your way, what happens now?"

"I get an arrest warrant from Justice and we all go over to pay Hyde the worst visit of his life."

Morrison looked over at the still quiet Baines. "What do you think, counselor?"

"Once we have Hyde, we can send someone to Africa to get the photographs from the man Mercer."

"Ass covering, Tom?"

"Mine's on the line. Goddamn right I'm going to cover it. Let's get it over with."

Henna rode with Morrison in the back of a Bureau car, Baines sitting in the front with the driver. Three other dark sedans followed them in convoy as they headed toward Fairfax, Virginia. Before leaving FBI headquarters, Henna phoned Hyde's office and determined the undersecretary wasn't at work and hadn't shown up all morning. He then called Hyde's home but the line was disconnected. Fearing that Hyde had already fled, Henna fast-tracked a warrant through the Justice Department and put together a small team to make the arrest.

As they drove, he sorted details in his head, mentally writing items on note cards and shuffling them randomly, searching for patterns. It was an old trick that served him well. On the first card was Rosen with the stolen Medusa photographs followed by their purchase by Hyde. After that, everything could fit together any number of ways. He wondered if, after Rosen sold them, he was approached by a group in Europe who also wanted them, someone from the Balkans, for example. It was possible that Harry's neighbors heard one of those languages and not Arabic. When Mercer refused Hyde's offer, the terrorists had kidnapped Harry to force him to go to Africa to find the diamonds for them. From security briefings, Henna knew that Iran supported Muslim groups in Albania and Serbia and also had ties to the factions in Beruit. The tie-in was circumstantial at best, but it was a good lead.

That still left Hyde and his motivation. Money was the most obvious answer. He was using his position at the State Department to deal himself in on any potential wealth, Henna thought. He bought the pictures himself, then hired Mercer for the expedition. But where, Henna wondered, would he get that kind of money? And then he realized Israel, through Selome Nagast, was footing the bill. Hyde paid for the photographs and they were paying for everything else. The reasons were obvious when he considered the Iranian connection. Israel was trying to prevent some terrorist group from securing a new font of untraceable wealth, an unknown diamond mine.

He was thinking about his upcoming interview with Hyde and knew he could use any information he got from the undersecretary to get the Mossad to open up about their operation. He'd always felt that America's security arrangement with the Jewish state was too one-sided. This was a perfect opportunity to level the playing field.

Henna's first inkling of a disaster in the making came in the form of a police siren's rising Doppler screaming behind the convoy. An instant later, a cruiser rocketed passed the FBI vehicles in a bejeweled blur, its bubble lights flashing sapphire and ruby. They were on the Little River Turnpike, just beyond the Beltway, and the police car raced through traffic lights with little more than a tap on its brakes. Another siren was approaching fast.

Because of traffic, it took them a further twenty minutes to get to the residential neighborhood where Hyde had his home. It was an affluent subdivision, each four- and five-bedroom house built on more than an acre of land with plenty of old trees to shield neighbor from neighbor. The newly macadamed streets were spotlessly clean, and the telephone poles had yet to darken with the patina of age.

The closer they got to Hyde's street, the darker the sky became and the thicker became the awful stench of burned wood and melted plastic.

Beginning ten houses from Hyde's, the street looked like a riot scene. The police had established a cordon behind which the curious gathered anxiously. Henna's credentials got him through with only a moment's delay and they drove on, the car weaving around police cruisers, fire engines, and idling ambulances in a slow slalom. When the breeze tugged at the clouds of smoke, they could see the bright inferno that had been Prescott Hyde's slice of the good life.

Henna's self-satisfaction disappeared. He was no arson specialist, but he knew enough to realize that an accelerant, no doubt gasoline, had been used to start the fire and was still burning. Hyde's house would have been soaked through to create a conflagration of this size. Given the number of emergency vehicles on the scene, the fire must have been called in half an hour ago or earlier.

The driver eased the sedan to a stop two hundred feet from the fire, close enough for them to feel the heat from the blaze as they stepped from the vehicle. Even as Henna watched, a section of roof collapsed into the churning guts of the building, sending up a fireworks display of popping sparks and burning bits of paper and fabric. The air was laced with the petrochemical stench of melting roof shingles, making Henna close his eyes when the wind shifted into his face. Two pumper trucks siphoned water from separate hydrants and showered the house with ballooning arcs, but still the place burned. Heat washed off the building in visible waves.

The structure was a total loss. The siding had burned through in places to reveal the skeletal fingers of the house's framing. On the far side of the house had stood a chimney, but all that remained was a seven-foot stump. The rest of it lay across the charred lawn in an elongated pile of debris.

Henna saw his theories burning in the fire. Without Hyde, there was no case and all the theorizing in the world wouldn't change that fact. He had no doubt that when the house cooled, they would discover the undersecretary's body amid the ruins.

"You're Henna?" The question came from a fireman much older than those fighting the blaze. His face was weathered like tree bark, and when he pulled off his helmet, his hair was pure white. "The cop at the barricade radioed me you were here. Mind telling me why the director of the Federal Bureau of Investigation is here with the chairman of the Joint Chiefs?"

Henna figured the man was the commander of Fairfax's fire department. He put out his hand. "I can't tell you the particulars right now, I'm sorry." The fireman had a tight grip, his hands deeply callused. "Anyone in there?"

"Not alive, if that's what you're asking." The fireman turned to look at the fire over his broad shoulder. "Judging by the two cars smoldering in the driveway, I'd say the house was occupied. The forensic teams may be able to scrape a few bits of bone and some goo into a bag, but don't expect much."

"What's your read?" Henna asked.

"Some squirrel killed the occupants, then torched the house to cover his tracks or delay the investigation. It'll take a while, but we'll find it's a case of murder."

Henna nodded, his eyes naturally drawn to the walls of fire that erupted from the house. He'd known it at the first police siren, but hadn't wanted it to be true. Whoever was responsible, Middle Eastern terrorists or Balkan extremists, it was clear they were one step ahead. And with Hyde out of the way, their tracks were well covered. Until he could contact Mercer, he could only hope his friend knew what he was doing because right now Henna certainly didn't.

"When do you think you can get some men in there to verify?" Colonel Baines asked.

The chief looked back at the fire just in time to see a wall fall outward to the lawn, an explosion of flame and wood that drove his men back half a dozen yards. "We may not get a team in there until after midnight."

"Anything we can do to help?"

"Yeah, make it rain." The chief turned away to rejoin his men, leaving Henna and Morrison and Baines alone with their questions.

Leonardo da Vinci Airport
Rome, Italy

Mercer and Selome walked side by side toward the Ethiopian Airline gate for their flight to Asmara. Mercer carried his two matching briefcases while Selome sported a slender leather valise hanging from a shoulder strap. Her long legs matched Mercer's pace, both of them striding through the crowds in an effort to stretch their cramped muscles. They joked easily, regaling each other with horror stories from past flights.

At the Ethiopian Airlines counter, Selome switched from English to Amharic when she addressed the willowy ticket agent. Mercer listened in for several seconds before realizing he couldn't understand a word. She turned to him, asking for his ticket, which he quickly produced. Selome and the agent spoke again, their voices rising before Selome seemed satisfied.

Selome was scowling when she led him away from the counter. Over half of the two hundred waiting room seats were occupied, all the passengers either Eritrean or Ethiopian. Looking at their faces, Mercer realized that Selome's exquisite beauty and her thick hair were more the norm that the exception. There were a number of older women, wrinkled and bowed by life, but the younger ones were all attractive. On the other hand, the men were slight, too delicate to be considered handsome.

"Be thankful I was here," Selome said as she and Mercer took seats. "They had you as a standby passenger for coach. You might have been bumped from the flight if I hadn't checked you in. I doubt that witch at the counter"—

she tossed her head—"was going to tell you until you tried to board the plane."

"You sound like you're not coming with me."

Selome nodded, her hair cascading over her face. She tamed it with a flick of her wrist. "I've got a meeting in London tomorrow. I'll meet up with you in Asmara the day after. I never asked—where are you staying?"

Mercer took this news in stride. "The Hotel Ambassoira."

"Good choice, one of our country's finest. But don't expect too much," she cautioned. "The Ambasoira was built during the occupation."

"Ethiopia's?"

"No, Italy's. The hotel dates back to the twenties," she grinned. "And unless you're a masochist, avoid their coffee, and never take the plumbing for granted. I believe that Habte Makkonen is going to meet you at the airport. I don't know him, but I'm sure you'll be fine."

She slung her bag over her shoulder and stood, extending her hand to Mercer. He felt he was being dismissed. The rapport they had built during the transatlantic flight was gone, replaced by a brusque professionalism he hadn't seen from her before.

"Well then," Mercer stood formally. "I guess I'll see you in a couple of days."

Unexpectedly, Selome stepped close to him and kissed him on the cheek. "Don't think this was my idea. I'll see you at the Ambasoira the day after next." She was gone in a flash.

"Not if I don't see you first," Mercer said under his breath, his gray eyes hardening as he watched her cut a swath through the terminal. He returned to the same agent at the ticket counter.

"I'm terribly sorry about all that." His smile was disarming as he laid his ticket on the counter. "I'm afraid there was a slight language problem. I called the airline this morning to say that I wanted to take a later flight and I'm afraid my traveling partner didn't understand. I want to be on tonight's flight which, I believe arrives at 9:00 P.M. local time."

In fact, Mercer had been booked on this flight, but had changed his reservations with a call from the Air Italia plane when Selome had gone to the rest room. He'd had a lingering suspicion that she might ditch him once they got to Rome and he needed the time to track her movements. He had an idea where she was really going. Just because he believed her motivation didn't necessarily mean he believed her.

"I understand." The agent pouted, enjoying a singular female delight in the discredit of another. "These sorts of things happen all the time." Her nails clicked on the computer keys for a moment before handing Mercer a new ticket. "There you are, tonight's flight, departing at 7:20 and arriving at 9:15 P.M. I even managed to get you a first-class upgrade at no additional cost. Our night flight isn't nearly as booked as this afternoon's."

"Thank you so much," Mercer said. "One more question. Where does El Al have their waiting area?"

"At the end of this concourse, to your right, I believe."

Mercer thanked her again and took off down the hallway, his stride purposeful. There was no need for him to hurry. He was certain Selome would be in the Israeli national airline's waiting room, but he felt an anger building that needed an outlet.

Nearing his destination, he slowed, blending in with the crowd so that he walked past the El Al waiting room shielded by a half-dozen people. He scanned the room once and then looked again. Selome wasn't there! A flight was boarding and Mercer cursed himself for being too late, but then saw the flight's destination was Lisbon. He was sure she wasn't going to Portugal.

He continued down the corridor until he came to a cluster of television monitors. Directing his attention at the ones displaying departures, he saw that El Al had a flight to Tel Aviv's Ben Gurion Airport in ninety minutes. He spent the time in a crowded, smoky bar at the other end of the terminal, as far from the El Al departure lounge as possible, in case Selome was waiting in a similar fashion. The two gimlets he drank cost twelve dollars each and he was thankful that European bartenders didn't expect tips because he wasn't in the mood to show his gratitude.

He wasn't really in the mood for the drinks either, but he needed something to dilute the bitterness that scalded the back of his throat. He'd been lied to by some of the best, but Selome Nagast was world-class. He had fallen for her story from the moment she sat next to him on the plane, and all along he should have known it was a setup.

"Bitch," he muttered, more angry at himself than at her. He grabbed his two cases and started back down the concourse.

If he couldn't trust Selome or Prescott "Call me Bill" Hyde, he was totally alone. For all he knew, the man sent to meet him in Africa, Habte Makkonen, was being paid to put a knife between his ribs at the arrival gate.

Nearing the departure area again, Mercer studied the crowd. Selome sat with her back to him, her face in a one-quarter profile, looking out the windows at the white and blue jetliner waiting to take her to Israel and her shadowy masters. Knowing that his earliest suspicions were correct deepened his black mood. He took up a position where he could watch her while shielded from her view.

He considered the connection between Harry's abduction by Beruit-linked terrorists with an Israeli agent trying to gain his trust. Mercer knew the Israelis were interested in all aspects of terrorism that might affect their country, but how did Harry—and for that matter, himself—fit into the mix? Whatever the relation, he knew the consequences were potentially deadly. In the Middle East, being caught between Arab and Israeli could be a death sentence. When threatened, both sides tended to shoot first and apologize for the innocents caught in the cross fire later. If ever.

How did a generations-long war between Muslim and Jew affect what he was trying to accomplish in Eritrea? he wondered. There was the possibility of billions of dollars if he could find a diamond-bearing pipe, but how could Israel or a Muslim extremist group benefit from such wealth when it was located a thousand miles away from the Mideast? His answer slipped away with Selome as she walked down the embarkation tunnel.

Mercer jerked his head upward at a ceiling-mounted speaker when he thought he heard his name. The message was repeated, translated from Italian to English in the same female monotone. "Passenger Dr. Philip Mercer, please pick up a white phone for a message."

There was a bank of phones a few paces away.

"This is Philip Mercer."

"Uno momento, per favore." A male voice came on the line, one that Mercer didn't recognize. "We have some things to discuss, Dr. Mercer. Some items that if not addressed now will mean an increased level of discomfort for a friend of yours."

Oh, Jesus! His stomach tightened, and an adrenal surge made his limbs tingle. "Is Harry okay?"

"What happened at Dulles will not go unpunished, but you will not suffer the consequences. Harry White will pay. Consider that I'm not going to kill him outright as your final warning. If you make any attempt to find him or assault us, he will die more horribly than you can imagine."

Th call had come just seconds after Selome had left the waiting area, Mercer realized, and that couldn't be a coincidence. Two ideas sprang to his mind. Harry's kidnappers didn't want Selome to know that Mercer was still in the airport following her and . . .

Mercer started looking around the concourse, searching for someone on one of the countless pay phones or speaking into a cellular model.

"Well done, Dr. Mercer. You are being watched. I am nearby and if you continue to look for me, I promise that Harry White won't live to see the sun set tonight."

Mercer froze. The kidnapper was only a few paces away. He could almost feel eyes on the back of his neck, and unconsciously he slouched, trying to present as small a target as possible. He knew they weren't after his life—it was an instinctive gesture.

"Since I didn't want her around when I contacted you,

you've probably guessed that I also have a warning about the nubile Miss Nagast. All I have to say is that if she is harmed in any way, if you confront her with your discovery about her Israeli connection, or if you try to back out on your deal with her and Prescott Hyde, Harry White will die.

"You may not believe this, but she is the only person you can trust right now. You and she share the same goal, Dr. Mercer. And that is my goal as well. We can all work together to find that diamond mine or I can work alone and you and Selome Nagast and Harry White will be cast aside like so much garbage. The choice is yours. Nod your head if you understand."

Mercer did as ordered, though he really didn't understand at all.

"You will be contacted again at the Ambasoira Hotel in two days. A protocol will be established at that time for us to receive updates on your progress. And remember, Miss Nagast is your strongest ally.

"After I hang up, you are to remain where you are. Do not turn around. Another member of my team is watching you as well. If he sees you twitch, you will not leave this airport alive."

The phone went dead and Mercer stood unmoving for a few moments, waiting for the caller to get out of visual range. He didn't believe that there was another watcher, but he wasn't about to test it.

Ibriham was fifty yards away, watching Mercer through a camera's zoom lens, the cellular phone already in his jacket pocket. Mercer waited as ordered. The leader of the College Park operation grunted with satisfaction and casually turned away, merging with the ebb and flow of the crowds.

He had remained in America following the disastrous extraction of Harry White to sever any possible connections between his team and the airport shoot-out. Still, it was only a matter of time before their presence and their identifications were made by the FBI. The men who lost their lives and the weapons they'd left behind would certainly betray them. Ibriham could only hope the carefully laid false clues, the guns and the languages they'd intentionally used when taking White, would lead the Federal Bureau down a long tangent.

Ibriham had stayed at a Washington area hotel, keeping a rough watch on Mercer following the Dulles fiasco. It took a little work to catch the same flight to Rome on such short notice, but he had a crack staff backing him at home.

Like any experienced field operative, he knew that even the best plans fell apart soon after the opening gambit. One can anticipate the initial moves of an opponent, plan contingencies a dozen moves in advance, but when the counter finally comes, and from an unexpected quarter, the game must be rethought immediately, an entirely new strategy developed and executed without delay.

When he had started, he was an entire game ahead of Philip Mercer but the American was catching up fast. Ibriham still had the advantage, but he no longer knew how long he could keep it. Extending his protection to Selome Nagast was a calculated risk, one that could backfire all too easily. Ibriham and his team were walking a fine line—he'd known that since accepting this mission—and every day and with every new development it got more perilous.

Yet if Mercer found the mine, Ibriham couldn't calculate how much it would mean to his people. Certainly it would redouble their commitment to their God, not just in the Middle East, but all over the world—to actually possess a relic from the past, lost for thousands of years, a piece of history that had been fabled for eons. The Prophet of the one true God had heard His words and took them to his people and it was just possible that Ibriham could get the exact text handed to man through divine locution.

He heard a disturbance behind him and turned to see the source. As he did, a scream tore across the general hum of conversation on the concourse. Behind him, a man had pulled a short-nosed machine pistol from under his jacket. Ibriham had no time to react before the man pulled the trigger, firing indiscriminately.

Unknown to him, the watcher of Philip Mercer had himself been watched.

The ferocity and surprise of the attack startled him for less than a second. His training took over as his brain went on automatic. The first few rounds went wild, tearing into the floor and the wall to Ibriham's right, a television monitor exploding in a shower of glass and sparks. Ibriham dove to his left, hitting the carpet and rolling away from the spray of bullets, but he was too exposed to make it to cover alive. And without a weapon of his own, he had no defense. He saw the gunman adjust his aim, zeroing in. One woman took two slugs in the chest that punched her backward as though she'd been a puppet on a string.

Two more people went down, slick blood splashing the floor in obscene stains. Ibriham rolled again, catching a moment's respite behind the fallen body of an overweight man in a tan trench coat. Four quick rounds pounded the corpse. Another shot caught him in the calf, and despite his years of combat experience, Ibriham shifted himself slightly to take pressure off the wounded leg. His movement forced his torso off the floor for a just an instant, and the next burst from the automatic caught him high in the chest, lead penetrating deep into his body, searing what little tissue remained intact. It was a race between shock and blood loss to see what would kill him first.

His heart stopped when there was no fluid left in his body to pump.

The gunman, a tall African dressed as a worker for an airline catering service, twisted toward the window facing the apron and fired the last of his clip, the machine pistol buzzing like a chain saw until the bolt crashed against an empty chamber. The huge slab of double-plated glass exploded, blasted onto the taxiway below in an avalanche. Four and a half seconds had elapsed from the moment the gunman revealed his weapon until the glass wall disintegrated.

Amid the pandemonium, the gunman leapt through the shattered window, dropping twenty feet to the asphalt below. No one had the courage to look out and see him running before he dodged out of sight under the low belly of a Boeing 737. Moments after the attack, he stripped out of the food service uniform. Underneath he wore the coveralls of a janitor. He became anonymous and melted away, another immigrant performing the menial labor that few Europeans were willing to do.

Mercer reached the bloody scene only a few seconds after the gunman had made his escape. His heart was pumping. At first he'd thought the gunfire had been directed at him. He hardened himself to the death around him and examined each of the victims closely. Of the five dead, his gaze concentrated on one in particular—the body of the only man who fit the description of those who had kidnapped Harry. He found a cell phone in the dead man's jacket.

He looked at the phone and then at the man's blood-smeared face, committing it to memory. "We'll meet in hell," Mercer said under his breath. "and then you'll really wish you'd never died." He was gone before airport security and the *carabinieri* arrived.

Asmara, Eritrea

If asked, Habte Makkonen said he was a carpenter by trade. If pressed, he acknowledged that he had done some work in the open-pit copper mine the Japanese had run in southern Eritrea during the Ethiopian occupation. It wasn't in his nature to conceal the truth from people, but it was his practice to maintain his privacy.

It was a survivor's mentality and Habte was a survivor. It was a skill learned in his youth, and a trait that continued to shape him into adulthood. There was a quiet reserve about him that kept him permanently and intentionally separated from everyone he met.

Few people knew his record during the war of liberation, and they were all on the Eritrean side. Of the Ethiopian, Cuban, and Russian soldiers he'd faced during his fifteen years under arms, few were alive to talk about him, one of the greatest soldiers to come out of the war. That he had survived the war unscathed, physically, was a miracle.

Habte had devoted himself to securing a life of freedom for his people, but it seemed he himself had no place in the world he had helped create. He kept himself aloof purposely, believing that one day the fragile peace would come crashing back down around him. He would not allow himself to share in the postwar calm, for he knew too well its price and also its frailty.

At five foot eight inches, thin under his black leather coat, he did not look like one of the most dangerous men in Africa, though he had a confirmed record of seventy-five kills. He smoked nervously, his fingers in constant motion bringing cigarette after cigarette to his thin lips. His hands were too long for his body, alien appendages probing outward from the sleeves of his coat. Under his sharp nose was a thin wisp of mustache, little more than a carefully groomed five o'clock shadow.

Habte was not handsome in the traditional Western sense, but there was something compelling about him, which caught the attention of those waiting for the flight from Rome with him. He held himself apart from the crowd even while he was in the thick of it. He'd been told once by a comrade that his eyes possessed a gaze that made a thousand-yard stare seem shortsighted. He'd scoffed at the notion, but anyone paying him attention would have agreed. The crowd perceived that he was someone of importance and left him alone, an island amid the press of humanity waiting for the Ethiopian Airlines flight.

Asmara's airport was an ambitious building, constructed several years before with an optimism for Eritrea's future that had yet to come to pass. It could handle four times the volume of traffic that currently used the facility. The one-story terminal was built with cement, yet still it shook as the Rome flight powered over the runway. A cheer went up among the waiting crowd because the flight had been delayed in Europe. Some instinct made Habte tense as people surged toward the windows in anticipation of rejoining loved ones.

A group of Sudanese refugees waited at the back of the crowd. It wasn't unusual that they were all men. In their society, women were rarely allowed in public. What caught Habte's attention was their grim expressions and the fact they were all well dressed; slacks and open-collared shirts. Their appearance was incongruous enough to alert him, and as he looked carefully, he realized they were *shifta,* Sudanese bandits. Habte had spent enough time as a soldier to recognize them as combatants.

He casually drifted back into the crowd until he stood behind and just to the left of the four Sudanese. At this range, he could see that one of them held a piece of paper in his hand, a fax sheet imprinted with a photograph of a Caucasian male. He recognized the face from Selome Nagast's description of Philip Mercer. He could also see the bulge of a weapon under the untucked tail of the man's shirt.

As passengers began streaming into the terminal, the Sudanese guerrilla scanned each face, eyes darting from the travelers to the picture. A single white man entered from the tarmac, the last passenger to deplane. The Sudanese and Habte recognized the face at the same instant. Of the two hundred and fifty people packed into the crowed room, only he felt the tension that fouled the air.

Habte felt powerless. He was not armed, for guns were outlawed in Eritrea, and he did not have enough faith in the two bored soldiers watching the debarkation to help him when Mercer came within the reach of the *shifta*. The war had been over for too long; Habte had become soft. Just a few years ago, he could have come up with a tactical plan instantly. Now, he found himself standing idly as Mercer came closer to the head of the customs line, briefcases hanging from both hands. The leader of the Sudanese terrorists bunched the picture in one fist. His other hand rested on the pistol tucked into his belt.

Thinking that he could reach Mercer before the *shifta* made their move, Habte launched himself across the terminal floor, shouldering aside families still in the rapture of reunion. No sooner had he made his move than the leader of the bandits also started forward, not quite as moderate in thrusting away those who stood in his way. He did not appear to notice that Habte shared his interest in the white passenger. His three comrades followed suit, unknowingly vectoring to cut off Habte's advance.

Mercer stood at the customs deck, his cases at his feet and his passport spread before him, the distinctive pale pink Eritrean visa sticker prominently displayed on the page awaiting an official stamp. Habte increased his pace to get ahead of the bandits and stole a quick glance behind him to see that the *shifta*'s pistol was still out of view. So these men did not want to see the American killed, he thought. That gave him latitude he hadn't realized he possessed.

Habte turned sharply, but the crowd slowed his momentum. He raised one fist and punched with all the force of his spin. It was enough to send the nearest Sudanese to the floor, his jaw either broken or severely dislocated. Several women screamed. Habte took advantage of the confusion, twisting so he was in range of another of the *shifta,* still keeping himself away from the armed leader. He let his wristwatch slide down to his hand so its face stretched across his knuckles, then pounded it into the Sudanese's face. Three rapid blows dropped the man, his mouth and cheeks bloodied and deeply scarred by the watch's sharp bezel.

The two Eritrean soldiers guarding the arrivals lounge came alive, shouting over the din and racing across the room, weapons held low to better push aside the people who were in their way. Mercer came through the gate oblivious to the tumult. Before the *shifta* leader could react, Habte grabbed Mercer by the wrist. A shot rang out, a concussive explosion that echoed painfully. Towing his charge, Habte ducked and dashed out the doors of the terminal. He owned a Fiat sedan and Mercer was just barely in the rear passenger seat when Habte gunned the engine, kicking up twin spirals of dust from the unpaved road.

"Welcome to Eritrea, Dr. Mercer. My name is Habte Makkonen," Habte said, relieved and amazed to be away from the airport. It would take hours for the authorities to sort out what had just happened if they even bothered to try.

"Je ne comprend pas. Je m'appelle Claude Quesnel." Habte's passenger was near hysterics as he spoke in rapid-fire French. *"Qu'est-ce que se passe maintenant? Et qui est Docteur Mercier?"*

Rome, Italy

The dark rain came in wind-driven sheets that shrouded a set of warehouses near the airport. It pelted the metal roofs and sides of the huge buildings like hail, so loudly that even the shriek of distant jets was reduced to a background whine. The air was cold, too cold for April. The storm had come in from the north, an unusual phenomenon, ripping the icy layer of air off the Alps like a katabatic wind so that sleet mixed with the rain. The weather made the hour around midnight particularly black and ominous.

The warehouses were owned by one of Giancarlo Gianelli's many companies, as was the limousine that glided to one of them. They were bonded buildings, meaning the warehouses' contents had already passed customs and were thus to be kept secure. Customs officials guarded the warehouses, as they did similar trans-shipment points all over Europe and abroad, but the right amount of lire in the right pockets ensured laxity in tonight's vigil.

Diesel trucks were lined up outside the building, many with trailers ready for loading. In the darkness, they looked like prehistoric beasts slumbering through the night. The multiple warehouse doors were designed to admit the behemoths, gaping holes that could be opened with a signal from a transmitter. The guard riding in the Mercedes' front seat held such a device and one door clattered upward.

Only when the door was closed again did the driver step from the vehicle and open the rear door for his important charge. As if choreographed, the instant Gianelli's feet touched the floor, a hundred lights snapped on. They buzzed for a moment before coming to full illumination, bathing the warehouse in harsh white light.

Gianelli straightened the drape of his floor-length overcoat, making certain that the four-thousand-dollar garment did not touch the oily stains on the concrete. His suit underneath cost an equal amount. Despite his rough surroundings, Gianelli looked as elegant as usual—not a hair out of place or a wrinkle on his clothing.

Rows of boxes and crates were stacked twenty feet high, lining the walls of the warehouse and creating parallel aisles just wide enough to maneuver one of the yellow forklifts parked near the loading doors. The packing crates ran all the way to the back of the warehouse. In one section, special containers designed to maximize cargo space aboard commercial air freighters waited to be loaded or unloaded. The building smelled of the storm raging outside, of machinery, and of the hundreds of men who usually worked here.

Gianelli idly scanned the pallet of boxes nearest him, reading the listed manifest in its protective plastic sheath. Within one crate were twenty million doses of anti-malaria medication destined for the Congo. Gianelli smiled tightly as he looked at the stack of identical boxes. He'd not known this particular pallet would be nearest him and took its presence as a good omen. There actually were pills within the cases, hermetically sealed in white plastic containers ready for distribution by the medical authorities of one of Africa's most populous nations. He recalled that there were even some active ingredients in the tablets but just enough to pass an inspection if the Africans ever bothered to check. However, most of the medication was composed of inert material. The pills were worthless.

Gianelli was selling twenty thousand dollars' worth of placebos for an even million, and he knew there were twenty identical loads ready for shipment. Twenty million dollars of profit and the only victims of his swindle were a bunch of ignorant blacks who, if given the real medicine, would die of something else anyway. Gianelli was new to the counterfeit medication trade, but he was quickly working his way to its forefront.

An area beyond the first rows of shipping containers had been specifically cleared of crates for the night. In the open space, two of the powerful forklifts were parked so closely their steel tines overlapped like meshed fingers. Several men were standing near them, obviously waiting for Gianelli's arrival. Between the forklifts was the Sundanese terrorist who had fired the murderous volley in the terminal earlier in the day. He had been stripped naked, his bare chest glistening with sweat despite the frigid air. It was the sweat of mortal fear. Heavy cables secured his feet to one set of forks while more wire under his arms tied him to the other.

Gianelli moved into the circle of men with a bored expression, loath to be bothered with such a trivial task. Without preamble, he gestured to one of his henchmen, and the man hoisted a camcorder to his eye and began videoing first the Sudanese guerrilla and then Giancarlo.

With the camera on him, Gianelli began speaking, his tone as uninterested as his demeanor. "Over the past years we have had a very successful business association, and you have been well paid for your services, enough so that your revolutionary movement is beginning to enjoy success in overthrowing the government of Sudan." He was speaking to the man standing before him, but the words were meant for whoever listened to the tape. "Until today you have done well by me. This afternoon's disaster though, forces me to remind you who is in charge of this operation. This fool in front of me was supposed to keep Philip Mercer under observation and determine if he was being followed or contacted. Firing an automatic weapon in a crowded airport was not part of my instructions. We'll never know who contacted Mercer because of you, not to mention that your actions could have cost Mercer his life."

Gianelli's voice suddenly exploded. "You stupid fucking monkey. We may miss Mercer in Asmara because he was delayed here by your action. Security has been tightened in Eritrea, making a snatch when he lands impossible. I won't ask what you were thinking because I know you are incapable of thought." He stared at the camera's cyclops eye. "Let this be a lesson to the rest of you godless cattle fuckers."

He gestured to the forklift operators, and the machines rumbled to life. The cameraman swung to the Sudanese shackled between the two vehicles. His eyes were huge and his mouth worked silently. It was impossible to determine if he was praying or begging for forgiveness.

With a nod from Gianelli, the two sets of forks lifted simultaneously, hoisting the terrorist off the ground. His voice became audible then, a piercing scream that carried over the noise of the diesels. One operator halted the upward motion of the lifting carriage while the other continued to rise. In seconds, the African was stretched in a modern version of the medieval rack. There was just enough pressure on his body to drain the blood from his face and raise the volume of his screams, but he was not yet in any pain. The camera turned back to Gianelli.

"Watch well, Mahdi," he said to his intended audience. "You have failed me once by sending this idiot on such a delicate job. If you fail me again, a worse fate awaits you."

One operator pumped his machine's throttle and the forks began to draw apart, one raising and the other lowering back to the ground. Caught in the relentless mechanical pull, the Sudanese's screams worsened as the pressure on his body increased. Stretched to the very limit, his skin turned an unnatural gray and his body looked like some carnival oddity.

And still the forks drew apart. The cords wrapped under his arms and around his legs turned crimson, and blood began to course down his body as the steel sliced into him. The small give offered by his flesh was quickly exhausted as the wires dug even deeper, drawing taut against bone. Then they began to pull his skeleton apart.

Gianelli was in a distracted conversation with one of his lieutenants when the torture came to its inevitable conclusion. The man's screams were choked off by a wet tearing sound, and the contents of his chest cavity splashed unevenly to the concrete. The dismemberment happened so quickly that Giancarlo didn't have time to step away from the blood that erupted from the corpse. Startled and angry, he stripped off his soiled overcoat and threw it into the puddle of gore under the dangling remains.

"Turn that camera off and let's get out of here," he snarled at his driver. "Call my pilot. We'll be staying in Rome tonight. After what happened this afternoon, I'm sure it will be a while before airport operations resume. Tell him to refile the flight plan for tomorrow."

He sat back into the padded seat of his limousine. While not bothered by the actual murder, he was disturbed that it had been necessary in the first place. His Sudanese mercenaries had been incredibly loyal, fulfilling his orders without question or fault. He thought back to the archaeologist a couple months ago as an example of their efficiency, but he couldn't allow laxity now. As the operation got into full swing, he would be relying on them more and more. Tonight's grisly demonstration was a just reminder.

More disturbing than the blunders in Rome and Asmara was the fact that Gianelli had no idea who had contacted Mercer at da Vinci. There *were* other forces at work, another group that he had no knowledge of or control over. Speculating over their identity was a fool's task, yet he could not help pondering their existence or how they knew about the lost mine. His lost mine.

Unknown Location in the Middle East

News of Ibriham's death in Rome reached Yosef a full day after the machine-gun attack because the team had been on the move during the night, traveling with their prisoner from their previous location in Lebanon to a more secure site. They were now ensconced in an urban safe house near the bustling city center, but cut off from it by the house's ancient stone walls. The house was attached to its neighbors in the time-honored way of Middle Eastern cities, yet it had been vacant for several years.

The neighborhood was full of those sympathetic to their cause and would not report that the previously unoccupied house suddenly had ten people inhabiting it, eleven if one knew about Harry White held captive in the windowless cellar. This location did afford more amenities, but it was still much too dangerous to use for the remainder of their mission. Discovery by the police or special investigative services would mean either a shoot-out or execution after a quick, one-sided military trial. Apart from everything else, Yosef also had to consider the team's next relocation, no more than a week away if he wanted to maintain the hard-and-fast rule about safe houses.

Yosef betrayed no reaction when he'd learned of the death of his nephew. But the few team members who'd worked with him before knew he was taking the killing very badly. He had a new hardness, a new layer of armor that shielded him from the loss and continuing pain of his life's work.

Several of the team sat at the dining room table with pitchers of water and carafes of rich coffee. It was morning, the first minutes they had been able to relax. The remainder of the group were either on sleep rotation or out purchasing supplies. The dining room was heavy with both quiet grief and the coolness of the morning that soaked through the plastered walls.

Yosef had never used this particular safe house, but it was like so many others he had slept in, worked in, and killed in before. He had willingly given up his life to live like this, and while he felt no regrets for that decision, its toll was becoming too heavy. Losing Ibriham could very well be the last blow he would take.

No one at the table had spoken. Each was waiting for Yosef, the team's new leader, to take up his mantle of command. He remained silent, inhaling cigarettes until the small astray before his chair brimmed. This morning had aged him a further ten years.

"What is the state of our prisoner?" Yosef finally asked, avoiding the real issue by addressing other details first.

"Settled as well as can be expected," one of the team replied. "He's much quieter and more cooperative since we started giving him cigarettes."

"His injuries?"

"For an old man, he heals remarkably well. His hand's doing fine." This from a nurse who had been with the organization for a year.

Yosef lit another cigarette, watching the blue-gray smoke coil to the wood beams that trussed the high ceiling. He didn't bother to blink away the smoke that scalded his eyes. The inquiring stares of his people galled to the point where he wanted to escape the room, the house, the entire organization. But not before Philip Mercer paid for his nephew's death.

He forced himself from his reverie. "There is no point in going over what has happened. We all know that Ibriham is dead and this places me in command. It's a job I don't want, but that doesn't matter." If they wanted a morale-boosting speech, they could get it elsewhere, he thought. "We will continue as before. The only significant change of plans is that I will be heading to Eritrea to keep track of Mercer with those already scheduled to go. Also, when this operation's done, I want our prisoner executed and I personally will deal with the American."

The most junior member of the group spoke. "I am not questioning you, Yosef, but aggravating the situation with two more deaths won't help our cause. According to our information, Mercer had nothing to do with Ibriham's murder. Killing him will only draw more attention to our presence."

Again nothing showed on Yosef's face, but his voice was deadly. "Killing Mercer has nothing to do with our cause. It's a personal matter. And no one will be aware of it. Eritrea's a big country, full of danger. One more corpse buried in the desert will make no difference."

He looked around the table to see if anyone else would question his decision, but none would meet his gaze. He had to keep the team focused for just a few more weeks, until the election. After that, he no longer cared what happened to them or himself, or God forbid, Israel.

Yosef thought back to the murder of his niece, Ibriham's cousin, so many years ago. She'd been shot by an Israeli soldier who was so shaken by the accident that he'd been unable to return to active service. Ibriham had taken her death particularly hard, and Yosef had feared that he would join a Palestinian splinter group to reap his revenge. But days later, a bomb at a bus stop in Tel Aviv had killed eleven Israelis. Television reports showed cheering crowds of students in Gaza celebrating the martyrdom of the suicide bomber. That evening, Ibriham approached his uncle and asked to join him in the Mossad. Ibriham had been so impressed by the compassion the soldier had shown following the fatal shooting and so sickened by the crowds that the internal conflict that had torn him since childhood had cleared. He had said he was a Jew first and foremost and wanted to be like his uncle, dedicated to the preservation of the Jewish homeland.

From that time, Ibriham's uncertainty gave way to a zeal that forced him to work tirelessly within the ranks of the Mossad. In just a couple of years, he'd topped the list of field operatives. This brought him to the attention of Israel's current defense minister Chaim Levine, who was forming a secret team from within the ranks of Israel's military and intelligence community for a shadowy program of his own. Ibriham quickly accepted Levine's offer to join and eventually lead his cadre in pursuit of the minister's dream. It had been Levine who drew Ibriham in, but now the responsibility fell on Yosef's shoulders. The team watched him quietly.

"I know what you're thinking: the old man has gone mad. You think I might jeopardize the mission with a vendetta against a man who's actually helping us. I assure you, nothing will happen to Mercer until after he discovers the mine and we retrieve what we lost so long ago." Yosef paused to fill a glass with water. "Ibriham's death has been a devastating blow, not only to me personally, but also to you. But it doesn't mean that we're going to stop. In just a few weeks, if we are successful, we'll rejuvenate our nation and will lay the foundation to ensure that *never again* will Jews feel that we do not have a rightful place on this planet.

"It's true we have our land, bought with blood and defended with yet more. But since the founding of our state, we have lacked a soul. We've existed, lived, and died but never have we truly felt our place. Many thought taking Jerusalem in 1967 would give us that soul—the Western Wall, for generations known as the Wailing Wall because it stood inside Jordan's borders. It was the wall built by King David himself when he erected the Temple. It's a tangible piece of what we once had.

"We have it now," Yosef scowled. "A towering wall of sandstone blocks that sits in the shadow of a mosque. I have been to the wall just once, back in '67, as a soldier. I had killed to take those slabs of rock, killed joyfully. Since then, I find the area an abomination. There are more tourists there gawking than Jews praying. It sickens me.

"I fought and killed and nearly got killed for a symbol. The Western Wall was a first step but it was never meant to be the end of what we wanted to achieve in our promised land. It wasn't until the Scud missiles slammed into Jerusalem and Tel Aviv during the Gulf War that a select group remembered that there was more work before Israel was complete.

"In a few weeks Defense Minister Chaim Levine will be Prime Minister. He's going to nullify the peace accords and outlaw the PLO again. He'll close our borders to the West Bank and Gaza, keeping the hordes in the slums they themselves have created. There will be no more suicide bombers because when he's finished with the Palestinians, any of them willing to die for their cause will already be dead. In a short time, the Third Temple will rise on the foundation of its predecessors, and it will be the sacred heart of Jewry. It's our mission to see that when the Temple is complete, God's words will reside within its walls. That is our covenant with Him.

"Ibriham gave his life to this belief. And his death has not weakened my resolve, nor should it yours. We are closer than any have come in two thousand years. Because I want the geologist Mercer dead does not mean that I have abandoned our cause."

Yosef finished what was the longest speech of his life, feeling bitter and empty inside. He cared nothing for the cause nor Chaim Levine. He'd only come out of retirement to help Ibriham. But his death gave Yosef a mission, a crusade more important to him than anything in the world. He wanted Philip Mercer to die.

"I'll be leaving tonight with the rest of the Eritrea team. Before I go, I'll speak with Minister Levine about finding a more suitable safe house. We can't stay here for very long. Both Mossad and Shin Bet are looking for us, and Levine can't risk our capture. He'll have to find a more secure place than this, preferably on a military base, perhaps the secret weapons research facility in the Negev. I know he wants to distance himself from us in case we're captured, plausible deniability, but we need his protection now that Ibriham is gone."

Yosef knew that Levine would sacrifice everyone in the room if he felt it threatened his chances to become Prime

Minister. Israeli politics was becoming as dangerous as those in some third world autocracy.

"Before I call Levine, Moshe, check on Mr. White and see if there's anything we need when we move him again." Yosef lit another cigarette, blowing a mushrooming jet of smoke across the table. "Remember this will be the last time he's transferred so if he makes any special requests, grant them. In case we need him for another video for Mercer, we want him in good humor."

"Yes, sir," the young sabra said, getting up from the table to descend into the cellar.

The cellar walls were undressed stone, and the floor was heavily packed dirt hardened to an almost cement shine. The air was cool and damp, smelling of mold and neglect. Off a central hallway, a door led to Harry White's cell.

There was no window in the wooden door, so Moshe had his pistol in hand when he threw back the dead bolts and kicked it open. By the murky light of the two dim bulbs strung along the ceiling, he could see the prisoner lying quietly on an army surplus cot. They had given him his clothes back for the move and allowed him this one measure of decency.

Harry looked at the teenager with the gun in his hand, and if he felt intimidated by the weapon, his attitude didn't show it. He recognized him from the earlier cell and took the fact that the guard's face was now uncovered as a very bad sign. "How about some food, you bastard. I haven't eaten in days."

In fact, it had been less than twelve hours but without natural light, Harry White's circadian clock was fouled. Moshe looked at Harry blankly.

"Oh, for Christ's sake," Harry nearly shouted. "You know, food. Breakfast, lunch, dinner, I don't give a shit." He pantomimed eating.

"You want to eat?" Having been born in Israel, English for Moshe was a second language and a particularly difficult one at that.

"Fucking camel jockey. Yes, I want to eat." Harry sat up. He had taken off his prosthetic leg and Moshe stared morbidly at the empty trouser cuff that dangled off the bed. "And how about some hooch while you're at it? My hand is killing me."

Again Moshe stared without comprehension.

"You know, booze, swill, liquor, alcohol. Nectar of the gods, man! Bourbon, gin, vodka, scotch. Hell, I'd give anything for a Pink Lady right now." Harry was getting nowhere and knew it. He lay back onto the bed, cradling his head in the cup of his hands for there was no pillow. "Ah, forget it. I may not know much, but I know Allah forbids you bastards from enjoying life's last pleasure so just piss off."

Moshe turned to go, but Harry stopped him with a shout. "But don't forget some food, you stupid son of a bitch."

Once again Harry was alone. There was a finality to the bolt slamming home that echoed. He heaved himself back up again, recovering his fake leg from under the bed and strapping it back into place under his pants.

They had drugged him late that night—that he did remember. Three men held him down while a woman slid a hypodermic needle into his arm. Of the trip to this new place, he recalled nothing. The room wasn't any better or worse than his last cell except for the blessed relief that the DTs had not followed him. He had wakened, slowly, fearfully, but after twenty minutes realized that the flying monkeys weren't going to bother him again. *What a nightmare that had been.*

As far as Harry was concerned, they could take detox and shove it up their collective camel-riding asses. He had spent the best part of forty years avoiding sobriety, and he wasn't appreciative when it was forced down his throat. Apart from getting over the DTs, he was thankful they had left him his clothes.

Even to him, the sight of a naked, eighty-year-old man with one leg was pretty depressing, especially trying to piss into the little pot they had given him. His hands shook more than he ever realized, throwing off an already notoriously bad aim. *God, will Tiny get a kick out of this story when I tell him.*

For ten minutes he lay still, thinking. He had an advantage, two really, that his kidnapers didn't know. One was that he didn't fear death. He was too old for that. If they expected him to remain submissive, they'd made a big mistake. Thirty years ago, he knew, he'd be blubbering like a baby, but not now. That, he thought, was the one great thing about age. No one could hold death over you any longer. The fear just wasn't there. His second advantage was his unshakable faith that if he couldn't escape, he was sure that Mercer would come for him, someway, somehow. It was only a matter of time.

The locks barring his cell slid open again, and the door slammed back with a crash. The guard had his pistol in its holster, his hands occupied with a huge hunk of dark bread and a wedge of cheese twice the size of a pizza slice. And blessings of all possible blessings, he held a bottle nearly filled with a clear liquid. Even at the sight of it, Harry's mouth flooded with saliva and his hands steadied. He looked longingly at the bottle. He wanted a drink so badly that Moshe was startled when Harry crossed the room with the speed of a man one quarter his age.

"I'll give you a hand there," he said, plucking the bottle from Moshe's arms. He ignored the food the young Israeli had brought him.

Harry didn't recognize the bottle's blue label. With or without his glasses, the writing was an illegible scrawl, but he knew the smell as soon as he twisted off the cap and held its open neck beneath his alcohol-attuned nose.

"I have to say, I'm not much of a gin man myself, but under the present circumstances . . ." He tilted the bottle skyward, his throat bobbing rhythmically, gulping down three heavy swallows as if the harsh liquor had been mother's milk. That first sip was the most pleasurable moment in Harry's life and that included returning home after World War II. He sighed as the alcohol burned his throat and brought tears to his eyes. "I don't suppose you'd want a snort?" He offered the bottle to Moshe.

Harry was shocked and more than a little intrigued when the dark-haired guard, no more than a boy with wide clear eyes and a face that had only recently seen a razor, took the bottle and took a long pull from it.

"I haven't slept in two days," Moshe said, proffering the bottle back to Harry. "Thank you."

"Don't thank me." Harry was all charm. "It's your booze. Take another pull, lad, you look like you could use it."

"No, that is not permitted." Moshe shook his head and left.

Harry sat back on the bed, the gin cradled in his lap. *Damn.* He'd hoped to get the kid drunk and escape but the little prick wasn't going to fall for it. "Okay, Harry, old boy," he said to himself, "what the hell is Plan B?"

Eritrea

Africa lolled tiredly below Europe, looking like the bowed head of some exhausted horse curled against itself as if struggling to draw life's last breaths. Even its very shape was sorrowful, as bereft as the place itself. The red and white Ethiopian Airlines Boeing jet arced in off the Red Sea, taking an indirect route to avoid flying over Sudan. Even at twenty-nine thousand feet, the Boeing 737 was not safe from an errant missile from one of the world's longest and bloodiest civil wars.

The eastern escarpment of the Great Rift Valley rose nearly vertically from the coast in a solid wall of rock that stretched over a thousand miles, a buttress that had protected Africa's interior for millennia. Mercer was looking out the ovoid window of the plane when it crossed this threshold; one moment the aircraft was a mile above the dry scrubby desert that meandered along the coast and the next, they were barely a hundred feet above the ground, the jetliner bucking in the thermal updrafts created by the hot winds lofting up the sheer cliffs.

Though hammerheads of black clouds had gathered at the coast, lashing the shore with torrential rains, inland the air was clear. The sky was a particular shade of clear blue found only in nature; man's pallet lacked the subtlety of light needed to create the effect. The African sky, Mercer felt, had an intimacy found nowhere else on earth.

The last minutes of the flight seemed to be a battle between gravity and the pilot's desire to see his plane land where he intended. Even as the Boeing recovered from a last whimsical twist of wind, the aircraft lined up for its approach. The plane landed right-side heavy, stripping rubber from the starboard tires in a rancid puff of smoke before it settled onto an even keel, slamming the remaining tires to the earth with enough force to ensure they stayed.

Knowing he wouldn't be able to enjoy ice until leaving Africa because it carried the same microbes as the water tourists were invariably told to avoid, Mercer swallowed the last cubes from his drink. He tucked the empty glass in the expandable magazine pouch on the seat in front of him and stood with the rest of the passengers to await his turn to deplane.

Because of the gunfire in Rome the day before, da Vinci Airport had been temporarily closed, canceling last night's flight. Good to her word, the ticket agent had secured him a first-class seat on this morning's, which was the next available. He carried only the two matching briefcases. The remainder of his clothes and nearly four hundred pounds of essential equipment had been express-shipped to Asmara and was waiting for him at his hotel. He was through customs in a few minutes.

Mercer noticed security in the terminal was high. No less than ten soldiers watched those stepping through customs and the people waiting to greet them. He hadn't expected Habte Makkonen to meet him because of the delay, but a dusky youth leaning against one of the few cars outside the building approached as soon as Mercer exited.

"Dr. Mercer?"

"Yes." There was a wary edge to his voice. "Are you Habte?"

The boy grinned. "Habte's cousin. Habte wait for you at hotel. Much trouble yesterday. He tell you."

On guard but with little option, Mercer shrugged. "Let's go, then, Habte's cousin."

Three miles separated the airport from downtown, and the road was lined with a sprawling, ill-kept housing project built by the Chinese during the Ethiopian occupation. The air blowing into the car's open windows was dry and pleasantly cool, spiced with the desert scent and the cleanliness of a city without industry. Asmara itself, a city of half a million, was not what Mercer had expected.

It was spotless. Old women meandered the hilly streets with brooms and rickety wheelbarrows, cleaning any rubbish from the gutters. The architecture was mostly Italianesque and because the capital had been spared during the war, the buildings were in excellent repair. Few were over four stories. The tallest structure was the brick bell tower of the Catholic church. If he could ignore the distinctive dome of a mosque nearby and the darker skin of the people, Mercer felt as if he had been transported to a Tuscan village rather than the capital of one of Africa's poorest nations. Because there was little vehicular traffic, the roads had been turned over to a great many donkey carts.

Mercer kept one eye out for possible tails, but they made it to his hotel without incident. Mercer had images of a classical colonial structure with columns and gardens, much like the British had left dotted all over the globe. The Ambasoira, however, was only four stories tall and located in a residential neighborhood. The "best" hotel in Asmara was boxy and uninspiring, and the lobby's furnishings were hard-used and tired.

Habte's cousin chatted with the hotel's manager while Mercer checked in, making certain that the crates he'd shipped from home had arrived. Then the young man led Mercer to the small bar in a back of the lobby, tucked behind the curving stairs leading up to the rooms. The alcove could seat no more than a dozen people, and Mercer counted only eight different types of liquor behind the bartender. A couple of European businessmen conferred at one table, and a lone Eritrean was seated at another. The local watched Mercer critically, as if weighing a decision, before he stood.

"Dr. Mercer, I am Habte Makkonen." Habte's handshake was brief but firm. "Welcome to Eritrea. I am sorry I could not meet you at the airport, but there was trouble yesterday and I could not risk being recognized."

"Your cousin mentioned something." Mercer noticed the

young man had vanished. "Do you mind telling me what happened?"

Mercer had already decided to trust Habte. If the Eritrean wanted him dead, he could have easily been killed on his way to town and left for the wild dogs. The fact that they were having a conversation lent credibility to Habte's intentions. And on a deeper level, Mercer recognized a world-weary competence in the slim African that seemed to elevate him above the political machinations and dangers that Mercer had faced in Washington and Rome.

Habte Makkonen smoked through several cigarettes while recounting the fight at the airport. He had already learned that Claude Quesnel, a medical supply salesman from Paris, had left Asmara, taking the first flight out of the country early this morning. When Habte had finished, Mercer told him about the gunman in Rome and the kidnapping of Harry White.

"I think if they wanted you dead in Rome, you would not be here today," Habte deduced. "You did not see who shot the man in Italy, but I am sure that he was part of the same group responsible for the attempted kidnapping here in Asmara. They apparently are opposed to the people who captured your friend."

"I agree." Mercer rubbed the rough beard he hadn't had the chance to shave. "Who are they and what do they want?"

"They were no ordinary Sudanese rebels. They were too well dressed, too far out of their element, even for Asmara. And to operate like they did in Rome, they must have outside contacts and help. Perhaps they have been bought to act as mercenaries."

"Then, who's paying them?"

"That is something we will have to find out for ourselves."

"We don't have the time to play detective." There was an urgency to Mercer's voice. "If I'm to get Harry back, I need to be in the bush no later than Monday. That gives us only five weeks to find the kimberlite pipe."

"There is nothing I can add to what you know of the

region in terms of its geology. I know of no diamonds ever found there. But I do know the area. I have buried many friends in those desert mountains during the war." A dark shadow passed behind Habte's eyes.

"We'll get to that in a minute." Mercer changed the subject. "Do you know Selome Nagast?"

"I know of her family. But I do not know her," Habte admitted. "They are wealthy by Eritrean standards, an old and honored family from here in Asmara. I only spoke with her on the phone when she hired me to be your guide."

"She's not who she appears to be. You should watch her carefully."

"Why is that?"

Mercer told the former freedom fighter about Selome's connection to Israel and Prescott Hyde and how she'd lied to him from the beginning.

"Is she coming with us when we head north?"

"I'm not going to let her out of my sight until this is over."

Mercer and Habte spent the rest of the day at the bar discussing the upcoming expedition. Habte had secured a newer Toyota Land Cruiser for their transportation and had hired two locals as laborers. From Mercer's earlier request to Selome, he had also rented an old Caterpillar tracked excavator and transporter that were waiting in Nacfa, the closest town to their target area. The other heavy equipment Mercer had leased was still en route and wouldn't arrive in Eritrea for weeks.

After a meal of overcooked pasta with a watery sauce and an unidentifiable slab of meat, Mercer retrieved some of his luggage from storage, made arrangements to meet Habte the next morning, and retired to his room. The shower produced only a thin trickle of cool water and Mercer had wisely brought his own soap. He was on the small balcony admiring the dark city below when the satellite phone still in his luggage chirped quietly. Mercer cursed himself. He'd accidentally left the phone on receive mode, and when he snapped it open, the LOW BATTERY light glared back at him. *Shit.* Expecting Dick Henna, he didn't recognize the voice on the other end, though the accent matched that of the man killed in Rome.

"Harry White has suffered terribly because of what happened to our comrade in Italy," the voice said. "That is the second time you have tried to foil us. If you attempt a third, White will be executed and his body buried forever."

Mercer absorbed the news like a body blow. Harry was tough, but he didn't know how much his friend could take. His sense of failure deepened.

"I had nothing to do with that," he protested quickly. "I never saw who shot him, but it wasn't me."

"That doesn't matter," the caller said with menace. "Your friend has paid for the murder. We will be calling you on this phone every three days at midnight for an update on your search for the mine."

"Save yourself the trouble." Mercer couldn't contain his anger. "It'll take at least a week just to get started, and I don't need you sons-of-bitches breathing down my neck every couple of days." He didn't want to consider how they had gotten the number to the satellite phone. "Contact me two weeks from Monday at midnight and every Monday after that. I may have something for you by then."

It was a small point of negotiation, Mercer knew, but he hoped it would open the way for more when the time came.

"That sounds reasonable," the kidnapper conceded. "Remember that you will be under observation at all times."

Mercer knew there was no way they could watch him once he was in the mountains. "I understand. I don't want anything to happen to Harry. I guarantee that I will uphold my end of the bargain." He nearly choked on the last words.

"Two weeks, Dr. Mercer." The phone went dead.

Three rooms down the hallway from Mercer's, Yosef snapped off his own sat-phone and turned to the other "European businessman" who'd been with him in the bar recording Mercer's conversation with Habte Makkonen. The other Israeli, younger than Yosef by thirty years, was cleaning a pair of Desert Eagle .50-caliber Action Express automatic pistols. The heavy weapons were perhaps the most powerful handguns in the world. A bullet anywhere in the body would take a man down permanently. A head shot would decapitate. Their other weapons and the remainder of their equipment was with the rest of the team at another hotel.

"I'm still concerned about Ibriham's true assassin," Yosef said with hatred. White hadn't been harmed, but he liked to hear the pain in Mercer's voice thinking that he had.

"We'll find him," the other man replied, filled with the confidence of youth.

"That's not my concern. The gunman wasn't acting alone, and we don't know who was behind the murder. We also don't know their connection to Mercer and our own plans." Yosef sat back on his bed, his eyes focusing into middle distance. "It's inconceivable that anyone knows about us, our security is too tight. Yet Ibriham is dead, and we have a threat we've yet to identify."

"Is it possible we've been betrayed by our own people?"

Yosef knew what the younger man was intimating, but he shook his head quickly. "No, it's too soon for Shin Bet or Mossad to learn that much of our operation. Informants have reported on Selome Nagast's meeting with her control in Israel. She hasn't made any move that leads me to believe she knows who we are."

His companion said nothing.

"She'll be here tomorrow anyway, totally cut off from her superiors. On her own, she can't pose a serious threat to us."

"She'll be with Mercer."

"As long as we hold Harry White, he's not a threat either." Yosef accepted one of the Desert Eagles from his partner, slipping it under his pillow for the night.

It was well past midnight when Mercer awoke. The room was cool and dark, but his body was bathed in sweat, his blankets and sheets twisted around him as if he'd been in the throes of a nightmare. In fact, for the first time since

Harry had been taken, his sleep had been dream-free. And in the depths of unconsciousness an inconsistency that had been nagging him for days came clear. The realization jerked his mind so sharply he swung himself out of bed, his chest heaving.

Since the time he had been first approached by Prescott Hyde, Mercer had felt there were diamonds in Eritrea. Hyde had spoken of, and indeed the Medusa photographs showed, a kimberlite pipe in the northern wastelands, naturally formed millions of yeas ago. Selome, too, had talked about what the pipe's discovery would mean to her people. But not the kidnappers. The men who'd taken Harry talked about Mercer's search for a *mine,* something built by human hands, not the earth's fiery heart. On three separate occasions—the original tape of Harry left in his house, the call in Rome's airport, and tonight's call—they spoke as if they knew the pipe had once been discovered, opened, and actively worked. They weren't after an unknown kimberlite pipe; they wanted a long-forgotten mine. They *knew* the diamonds were there, and now so did Mercer.

The game had changed once again, he thought. He was still at a severe disadvantage, but knowing he was looking for an old excavation gave him his first spark of something he'd lost the moment he saw Harry's image on his VCR. Hope. He pushed aside his self-doubt, buried his self-recriminations. He was ready to face whatever might come.

Khartoum, Sudan

In Arabic, the name *Sudan* means "black," but those in control of the country were not black Africans but people of more Arabian descent. Millions had been slaughtered through warfare, disease, and famine to maintain the subjugation of Sudan's more ethnically African citizens in the south by their northern government. All in all, Africa's largest nation was a hate-filled sewer that claimed a thousand more victims every day.

Sudan was thus a perfect arena for Giancarlo Gianelli to add to his wealth by preying on the misfortunes of others.

People with the kind of money Gianelli had existed in a supra-national elite class who travelled on private jets, stayed in opulent villas or exclusive hotels, and rarely bothered with the formality of customs when abroad. Only moments after landing in Khartoum, he was whisked to a house he owned in the hills overlooking the city, an enclave reserved for Sudan's few wealthy citizens and the rulers of the military government. Though it was his least favorite city in the world, Gianelli did enough business in Khartoum to warrant the expense of a twenty-room house and a full-time staff of eighteen.

Gianelli's majordomo in Venice had alerted his African counterpart to prepare for the visit. The staff was lined up when the limo eased through the gate and up the long drive. The headlights flashed into their faces as the car swept under the covered portico, stopping so that the head butler could simply bend at the waist to open Gianelli's door.

"*Grazie,* Ali," Gianelli said to the majordomo. "How have you been?"

"Very well, sir," the elderly Sudanese replied gravely in Italian. "I was not told how long you would be here, sir. Should we prepare for an extended stay?"

"No, Ali, I won't be here long at all." Gianelli eyed his staff. Not recognizing two girls dressed neatly as maids, he asked Ali about them.

"I bought them about a month ago from a slaver selling off the last of his stock. They were expensive, but they have already been well trained," Ali said proudly.

Sudan was one of a handful of countries that maintained a slave trade. The practice was illegal but more than tolerated by the government. Slaves, usually young girls, were routinely captured during raids in the south by either the army or regular slavers and brought to Khartoum for the pleasures of the city's elite or sold off to Arab countries across the Red Sea. Ever open to possible business opportunities, Gianelli had considered entering the trade, but the big markets had already been exploited and he found it wouldn't be worth his time or effort to open up a new conduit to move girls from Sudan to the Middle East.

He turned his gaze away from the girls and addressed Ali again. "Has he arrived yet?"

"Your guest arrived an hour ago." Ali couldn't keep the contempt out of his voice. "He is in your study. There is a guard waiting with him to make sure he does not move."

Giancarlo chuckled at his man's foresight. He himself wouldn't leave Mahdi alone for a second. Gianelli entered the house, enjoying the sweet coolness provided by the air conditioners. The house was stucco on the outside, but much of the interior was marble, built in the Mediterranean style with a large open foyer. He hadn't dared to bring any of his European artwork to Khartoum, so the decorations were all native pieces bought for him from all over the continent by a professional collector. Ashante masks and Ndebele shields mixed with woven Dinka wall hangings and displays of ancient gold jewelry from every corner of Africa.

The study was at the end of one wing of the great house. Gianelli strode in, ignoring the shelves of books and the tall elephant tusks that flanked the native stone fireplace, their butter patina glowing in the room's subdued lighting. Instead, he kept his eyes on the young Sudanese lying on one of the leather couches, his feet indolently resting on the glass top of a coffee table. The guard standing next to a stinkwood desk came to attention. "Leave us," Gianelli barked at the guard, then stared at his guest.

"Make yourself at home," he sneered, switching to fluent Arabic.

Mahdi wore Western clothes, black jeans and a baggy T-shirt under a loose-fitting leather jacket. His head was covered with a brightly colored *keffleye* like a Palestinian freedom fighter, though he was a Christian and a member of Sudan's rebel movement. "Have I offended you in some way, *effendi*?"

"Yes." Gianelli lowered himself into his chair and slid the video cassette from the outside pocket of his suit coat. "That fool you sent to Rome nearly got Philip Mercer killed. He was ordered to tell me if anyone approached Mercer, not open fire with an automatic weapon in the international departure area. You'd better pray the *carabinieri* never learn of my involvement with this."

"Why did he start shooting?"

"How should I know?" Gianelli's face darkened with anger. "He killed four people."

"He must have had a good reason. Abdula's my cousin, I trust him completely," Mahdi said. "He was with me when we tracked and killed that European scientist a few months ago. Remember, he was exploring near where you thought your mine might be. You questioned Abdula afterward, yes?"

Giancarlo laughed. "I wouldn't call it questioning exactly." He slid the tape into the VCR sitting on a credenza behind him and turned on the attached television.

He watched Mahdi's expression change when he recognized his cousin pinioned between the forklifts. The Sudanese couldn't tear his eyes from the gruesome scene as it played out.

Gianelli shut off the machine when the recording ended. "That is the price of disobeying me," he said mildly. "Your cousin made a mistake that you can learn from, Mahdi, and I think now you see how serious I am."

He stood and went to the small bar near the fireplace, filling two crystal goblets with a fortified wine. He had no way of knowing how Mahdi would react, so one hand didn't stray from the small Beretta automatic in his coat pocket. Mahdi took the offered glass and knocked it back with a quick swallow. Gianelli took a seat opposite the killer, his drink dangling from his long fingers. He filled Mahdi's shocked silence with words.

"Our association has been very profitable in the past. There is no need for this unfortunate incident"—he waved his free hand at the darkened television—"to interfere with that. I've given your cause billions of lire over the years, and I've asked for very little in return. I simply want your continued friendship when you eventually succeed in splitting the Sudan into two separate countries.

"I've supported your cause for years. Still, I believe I am entitled to a simple favor for my efforts, a goodwill token to prove that my money hasn't been wasted on a lost cause headed by a group of fools."

Mahdi wasn't a diplomat or a politician, which was exactly why Gianelli chose him as his liaison with the rebel movement. Mahdi was a soldier experienced in the field of warfare, not words. It was this fact that made him easy to manipulate. Giancarlo suspected Mahdi's superiors knew this too but allowed it to continue as long as the money poured in. If they had any opposition to Giancarlo Gianelli using some of their people as a mercenary army for his own personal reasons, they never voiced it.

Mahdi stood slowly and Giancarlo tensed, his finger tightening around the Beretta's trigger, but the young rebel went to fix himself another, heavier drink. "Before you tell me what you require of me, I must admit that the team sent to meet Mercer in Asmara lost him after a disturbance at the terminal."

Giancarlo hid his satisfaction at being able to read the other man so well. Mahdi was sociopathic enough to see his cousin's death as another casualty in their long-standing revolt and harbored little in the way of anger at who had actually killed him.

"Mercer missed yesterday's flight from Rome," Gianelli said without rancor. "He didn't arrive until this morning. We'll take him in Asmara. It's a small city, and there's only so many places he can hide. I want a team of your best men dispatched at once. We'll get those satellite pictures and leave him in an unmarked grave. He's meddled in my affairs enough and I won't tolerate it."

"I will lead the team myself."

"No," Gianelli said sharply. "We are going to the Eritrean border, near where I think the mine must be. We'll be in position to use the photographs as soon as your men have them."

"Isn't that a risk?" Mahdi's tone was respectful.

"It is, but we don't have the luxury of time." He noted the confusion on the killer's face. "There's something you must know about one of the men your cousin killed in Rome. I learned through my contacts in the *carabinieri* early this morning that one of them was carrying a forged passport. His being near Philip Mercer was hardly a coincidence. There is someone else out there shadowing him, someone else who wants my diamonds."

"Who?"

"It doesn't matter." Gianelli dismissed this threat. "We'll get the photos and whoever it was will give up the chase. How many men can you assemble on the Eritrean border within the next week or two?"

"That will depend on the Revolutionary Council, but I estimate at least fifty."

"That should be enough. We'll need to round up at least another hundred men as laborers. I have South African mining specialists ready to go, but they need workers."

"How long do you think we will be able to hold the mine once we find it?"

"It's remained hidden for seventy years, which means it's in an extremely remote location. The country in the far north of Eritrea is deserted once you get off the refugee routes. Your men will take care of any nomads or shepherds who might stumble on our camp. I suspect we won't be detected for a couple of months. Which is all the time I need."

Gianelli had heard last night from an agent in London that the diamond syndicate was already hearing rumors about a previously unknown mine in Africa. The rumors had been planted by Gianelli himself to subvert the powerful group and it was working perfectly. His agent told him the syndicate was nervous about a possible source of diamonds not in their control. Gianelli knew they would pay him billions if he could prove he had the mine, either for its location or for his assurance that he would never work it. Five thousand carats, Gianelli estimated, was all the proof he would need to get them to pay him off.

"You can count on me, *effendi,*" Mahdi boasted.

Gianelli looked pointedly at the mute television. "I know I can."

Asmara, Eritrea

Selome arrived at the hotel while Mercer and Habte were having breakfast. Her dark skin and thick hair marked her as a native. Her clothes, however, were Fifth Avenue elegant and she wore them with the comfortable neglect of a fashion model. Again, there was the enigmatic confidence about her that Mercer found interesting and more than a little dangerous. He'd thought that her going to Israel would have extinguished that delicate spark he'd felt on the flight from Washington, but looking at her, he knew it hadn't. Whether it was Mercer's earlier warning or some sexist cultural attitude, Habte Makkonen greeted her coolly. Mercer noticed the slight, but if Selome had too, she didn't show it. She gave Mercer a dry kiss on his cheek and sat.

"I see you're heeding my warning about the coffee here." She nodded to the half-empty cups of cappuccino on the table.

"I tried their regular stuff," Mercer grinned. "Crude oil."

She gave him an I-told-you-so smile. "The meals here are safe enough, if a little uninspired. Like most hotels in town, they only serve Italian food, a holdover from the occupation. If we have time, I'll take you to a traditional Eritrean restaurant. If you think our coffee curls your toes, wait until you try our stew called *zigini*. The peppers in it are tiny but pack the fire of a volcano."

"Thank you for your offer but it'll have to wait until after we return here," Mercer said gravely. "Habte's cousin is getting our Land Cruiser right now. This morning I want to load it up, get some fresh provisions here in Asmara, and be on the road north by this afternoon. We'll sleep in Keren tonight and continue on to Nacfa and the open country at sunup tomorrow."

"Why the rush?"

"Because we're not safe here." Mercer wondered how much to tell her about what had happened since seeing her off in Rome. Discretion was still his best ally, he thought. Harry's kidnapper said she was the only person he could trust, but what kind of assurance was that? He wanted to trust her, but until he knew more, he would keep her at arm's length. Sad, he mused, the first woman to attract him in a long time turned out to be a secretive liar with an agenda of her own.

Like his optimism about the pipe having been discovered before, he kept what happened in Rome to himself. He did tell her about the incident at Asmara's airport when Habte was awaiting his arrival. "It was my good luck that I missed the afternoon flight," he lied, "and had to take one the next morning. Otherwise, I would've been captured by the Sudanese."

He watched her reaction carefully. Her surprise and concern were genuine. "Nothing's happened to you since? My God, I can't believe it. It's only a matter of time before Sudan's war destroys us as well."

"Selome, you're missing the point. They were waiting for me, specifically. That means someone else knows about our mission." Her eyes went wide with the realization. Mercer continued. "We're vulnerable in the city. That's why I want to be as far from Asmara as soon as possible. That means all of us. You included."

"I wanted to come with you anyway," Selome admitted. "But this is certainly a good motivation. Our police forces and military leave a lot to be desired. After the war, it seemed few of our people wanted to remain under arms. We'd seen enough fighting. The authorities will be powerless against guerrillas."

"She's right," Habte added. "Our best chance is to get into the northern lowlands quickly."

"Then it's settled." Mercer finished the last of his cappuccino. "Habte, when your cousin gets back with the Land Cruiser, load up the gear I've got in storage and pack anything you'll need. Selome, how much time do you need to get ready?"

"I can be back here in an hour with my luggage. My apartment's close by."

"I don't need to warn you to pack light," Mercer reminded gently. "This won't be a luxury tour."

Less than an hour later, Selome met Mercer back at the hotel, and they walked to the market square to buy water and fresh food for their trek. Habte's cousin, whose name Mercer learned was Gebre but who preferred to be called Gibby, would come with the Toyota to carry their purchases to the hotel when he finished loading the four-wheel drive.

Mercer had Selome lead them first to the post office, where he spent twenty frustrating minutes trying to contact Dick Henna so he could tell the FBI director what had happened in Rome and at Asmara's airport. However, Eritrea's notorious communications problems made any overseas call impossible. He didn't want to use a sat-phone, having discovered last night that both of them had been left on receive mode and had only a finite amount of battery time remaining. His spares were all uncharged. And the charger, he recalled, was sitting on his kitchen counter next to the anti-malaria pills Terry Knight had given him.

There was no discernible pattern to Asmara's paved streets. They followed the terrain haphazardly, once being footpaths when the city was four separate villages. The city's name comes from the word *united* and stems from the time when the small towns were joined into one to protect the people from the hyenas that once populated the highlands. Beyond palm-lined Liberty Street, Asmara's main boulevard, lay a jumble of meandering lanes, some paved but most just narrow sandy tracks flanked by one-story buildings. The streets were bustling. While Saturday was the traditional market day in Asmara, the proximity to the Easter holiday meant everyone was doing a brisk business on Sunday as well.

The city's principal market was a long, open-sided warehouse roofed with sheets of corrugated steel. The aroma of the spices was palpable more than a block away. Old American and Russian trucks sat quietly on the streets nearby as their owners hawked their goods. The roads were mined with the dung of countless donkeys. From behind the market came the strong smell of an open-air cattle stockade. The lowing of the herds punctuated the sounds of the busy shopping district. Despite Eritrea's poverty, there was a vitality that surprised Mercer.

Selome had changed into more traditional clothing, a flowing cotton wrap over a gaily colored dress. Unlike the sandaled feet of the other women in the market, hers sported Western-style boots, and beneath the dress he could see a pair of jeans. Her hair was pulled back, accentuating her broad forehead and her dark liquid eyes. She blended well with the crowd, and while Mercer's clothes weren't incongruent, his white skin certainly was. In the minutes it took to walk to the market, he didn't see one other Caucasian. Yet he knew Africa well enough to be comfortable with the racial differences.

"How often do you get back here?" Mercer asked as Selome finished the negotiations for a five-kilo bag of tomatoes.

"To Eritrea?"

"Yes."

"Not very often, I'm sorry to say." Selome linked her arm into his as they continued shopping. "During the war, I was in Europe. When I came back, I felt some animosity from the people who put their lives in danger for our independence. Perhaps you noticed it from your friend Habte." She gestured to a man guiding a camel. He had only one arm, and part of his face had been shot away. "These people suffered cruelly while I was abroad, and they can tell I didn't fight. Only a few know that we in Europe were doing an important job making our plight known to the rest of the world."

Mercer scanned the street as Selome continued. He was stunned by the number of cripples.

"More than half the people you see are freedom fighters, men and women alike. They are bonded by that shared experience. It is the cult of the warrior, and no matter what I did for them, I will never really be part of them."

"Is that why finding the diamonds is so important to you? Are you trying to make up to them?"

"Yes," Selome replied without hesitation. She stopped and turned to him. Their faces were only inches apart. "Your country has been independent for so long you've forgotten the sacrifice. You take your freedom for granted while we are just discovering ours. I don't feel I did enough, Mercer. I don't feel that I've given anything near what the rest of my people have. I want to give something back so badly. I want to be accepted by them again. Can you understand that?"

As on the first night he'd met her, Mercer was mesmerized by her mouth, the way it moved, its sensuality. She was an accomplished woman, and he cursed himself for the weakness of noticing her physical charms more than her intellectual strengths. It was chauvinistic, he admitted, but he couldn't help it. He knew, too, she was the type of woman who attracted him, someone who was willing to risk herself for what she believed. It was a trait more rare than it should be.

"I think I can understand," he said finally. "I just hope I don't disappoint you."

"You haven't yet." Selome gave his arm a squeeze.

Behind the fresh-food market was a ramshackle collection of shacks with feeble metal walls that leaned against their neighbors so they all wouldn't topple. They were stalls erected to sell merchandise in an African version of a permanent flea market. In the meandering warren, everything conceivable was on sale, from antique furniture left over from the Italian occupation, to brass piping made from reconditioned artillery shell casings. As in much of the third world, items in Eritrea were used and reused until they were all used up. Mercer and Selome quickly became lost in the maze. Selome chatted with the stall owners and answered questions about Mercer's presence. A flock of children followed in their wake, shouting out words in English when Selome told them Mercer was an American.

"They should never know war," Selome said fondly, watching the children watching them. "We fought so they won't have to, and now we must fight again to provide for them. Fully one sixth of our population are refugees in Sudan because we can't afford to bring them home."

Caught in the infectious curiosity of the Eritrean children surrounding them, Mercer hunched down to shake hands with a little boy no more than four who regarded him through solemn eyes and a mouth full of his own thumb.

The whine of the ricochet and the tumbling crash of a body falling against a pile of metal pots came at the same instant. Still on his haunches, Mercer twisted. Had he been standing, the shot would have taken his head off. He rolled to the ground, kicking out one leg to sweep Selome so she crashed against him. One of the children began screaming. Another shot passed over Mercer's head, hitting the bottom of a large cooking pot and blowing through it like a cannon shot.

The market area erupted, men and women running for cover, sweeping up children and clogging the main alleyways between the stalls in an attempt to flee. Mercer shook off his shock, grabbed Selome, and tossed her under a trestle table groaning with the weight of disassembled machine parts. He took a second to calculate the angle of fire before heaving against the table. It crashed to the ground, forming a barrier between them and the unseen gunman just as half a dozen shots pounded into it, several exploding through the wood in a shower of shards, the rest harmlessly absorbed by the metal scrap. Mercer kicked in the back of the flimsy stall, forcing an opening that he dragged Selome through.

The adjoining alley was filled with the panicked crowd. A woman went down and was nearly trampled before Mercer bulled his way to her side, and hoisted her to her feet. Forcing Selome ahead of him so his body shielded hers, they knifed through the throng. Though they couldn't hear the silenced shots, both could feel their supersonic passage as they ducked into the gap between two stalls.

The next lane had already emptied of people, making it too exposed to risk a dash to freedom. Mercer needed to create a diversion. He told Selome to remain tucked in the crawl space and dashed across the narrow tract, entering a low-ceilinged stall that was as dark and forbidding as all the others and as equally loaded with merchandise. The vendor had disappeared but left a small brazier burning next to his overturned chair, a traditional coffeepot set to boil on its grill. The shop sold all types of lighting fixtures, mostly electric and mostly in various stages of disrepair. There was also a selection of oil lamps and on a shelf were several metal cans of what Mercer fervently hoped was lamp oil. He punctured two cans with a screwdriver lying on the cluttered work bench.

"Mercer!" Selome screamed from across the alley.

He spun as a figure turned the corner into the shop preceded by the barrel of a silenced pistol. Even before the assassin had fully revealed himself, Mercer threw one of the cans at him. Clear streams of volatile fuel sprinkled out as it flew into the man's chest. In the same motion Mercer hooked his left foot under the smoldering brazier and lofted it into the air. Sparks and cinders cascaded from it like a fireworks bomb. Mercer dropped to the ground and rolled to the back corner of the stall just as the flaming grill hit the gunman.

Drenched in fuel, the Sudanese erupted in flame. His immolation sucked the air from the stall while fire twisted into the air above him. As he burned alive, his screams were the worst sounds Mercer could imagine. The air filled with the smell of his roasting flesh.

Mercer hefted the other can of fuel. "Selome, come on."

She leaped from her hiding place to join him as he tipped fuel from the one gallon jerry can onto the fire. An errant tongue of flame ignited the lamp oil, and it began burning like a fuse toward the can still in his hand. A bullet passed close to Mercer's head, and he saw two men boldly running down the alley toward them. He screamed for Selome to duck and spun in place, burning fuel spraying behind him, just inches from reaching the container. Like an Olympic hammer thrower, he released the can at the gunmen. It sailed at them like a comet, its tail blooming in a billow of flame.

He and Selome were running in the opposite direction when the container hit the ground just in front of the two assassins. It split open an instant before the flame reached it, and the narrow street caught fire, blocking the Sudanese from their intended targets.

Fighting for breath, Mercer and Selome reached the end of the alley and burst into the snarl of streets that fronted the cattle enclosure. The dirt roads were sprinkled with fallen hay from piles mounded against the stockade's high brick walls. Usually, the crowds moved with purpose, leading cows, sheep, and goats to and from the pen, but everyone was standing still, watching the flames already rising above the market.

Trucks and buses clogged the side streets, making it impossible for Mercer to lead Selome out of the area. Knowing the fire would slow the Sudanese for just a few moments, and with only one avenue of escape opened to them, they raced into the cattle stockade. It was only after they were a quarter way across the circular plaza that Selome stopped, bending double to catch her breath. Cows and men had cleared a path for their mad charge, both equally upset by the intrusion.

"Mercer," she panted and pointed over her shoulder. "That's the only way out of here."

"Oh shit," he wheezed, realizing they were trapped. If they turned back now, they would run straight into the assassins.

The cows weren't like those Mercer had seen in the United States. These were *Bovus indicus,* called Brahmans in America, a heartier breed better suited to hotter climates. Because of Eritrea's sour grazing, they were not prime specimens but all weighed over a ton, with heavily humped backs, sweeping dewlaps, and wickedly curved horns that could pull a man apart with one toss of the head.

To Mercer's left, a female had just dropped a calf. The young heifer was still wet and stood on shaky legs as it tried to get under its dam to suckle. The mother was more interested in protecting the calf than feeding it. She had formed a clearing around them both, jealously charging man and animal alike when she felt they got too close.

Mercer grabbed a wooden staff from a farmer standing close by and dodged through the lowing herd toward the new mother. She watched his movement with tired, angry eyes, keeping her body between her baby and this new threat. He ignored her first halfhearted charges, angling the brahman with the finesse of a matador, forcing her around so her calf was behind her.

She came forward again, her horns like scythes as she lowered them to Mercer's waist. He timed his lunge perfectly and rushed to meet her charge. Dropping to the ground, he rolled as one great horn slit the air just above him, regaining his feet as the brahman turned to follow. The calf was in front of him—unprotected for a fraction of a second. He gave the tottering animal a sharp crack on its rump with the staff.

It squealed more out of fright than pain and began running in a weaving gait that took it in the direction of the exit. Mercer could feel its mother right behind him and dove to the side, missing a fatal goring by inches. He landed on a small flock of sheep, cushioning his fall in the woolly, bleating mass. The new mother ignored him and chased after its child, but the young cow was too panicked to be calmed. Quickly, the alarm spread to the other nervous members of the herd, and suddenly they were stampeding. The peasants were powerless to stop it and wisely concentrated on staying out of the way of the maddened rush.

The two Sudanese had just passed through the entrance when the leading edge of the charge reached them. Their reactions were lightning fast, and cows went down under scathing fire from their weapons. Yet the herd paid no attention to their fallen brethren. When a huge bull was felled by a double tap from one of the silenced pistols, two more filled the gap in the solid wall of fleeing animals.

The gates to the stockade were roughly ten feet wide and three hundred and fifty tons of terrified cattle raced through, their hooves kicking up gouts of dust. The two gunmen never stood a chance. Their screams were lost in the thunderous din. Even their guns were so damaged by the herd they would never fire again. Of the men themselves, two purple/red stains in the churned dirt marked their graves.

Mercer used the flank of a sheep to wipe the worst of the filth from his clothes and hands and went to Selome's side. "We've got to get out of here. After these farmers retrieve their cattle, they're coming back for a little retribution."

Selome peeled off her wrap, placing it over Mercer's head and tucking it around his shoulders so it formed a cowl around his face. Apart from his superior height, the cloak made it difficult to discern him from the angry men milling about the pen. They made their way to the exit and gained the street a moment later.

No sooner had they begun back to the hotel than a white truck turned the corner behind them, its wheels kicking up a spray of gravel and its driver leaning heavily on the horn.

"Trouble at hotel. We leave now," Habte shouted out the open window. His cousin was in the backseat, throwing open the door even before Habte slid the Toyota SUV to a stop.

Selome reacted even quicker than Mercer and jumped into the truck ahead of him. Mercer had just got the door closed when Habte stomped on the accelerator, using the horn again to scatter a group of men trying to calm a dappled bull. A donkey was almost caught by the fender, forcing Habte to crank the wheel to avoid it. Despite the danger surrounding them, his cousin laughed delightedly "Habte hit a donkey. Habte hit a donkey."

"I did not," Habte replied sharply, taking a second to glare at the young man. Because of their plodding predictability, it was an insult to say an Eritrean driver hit a donkey. Habte wasn't going to allow his cousin to get away with even a suggestion of such a gaff.

Mercer extracted himself from the tangle of limbs in the backseat and crawled over to the front of the Toyota, cinching his seat belt as they accelerated over the rough roads. His heart was just now slowing. "What happened?"

"Gunfight in the hotel. A maid caught two Sudanese in your room. When she screamed, two Westerners who were in the bar went up to investigate. I heard shots and the body of one of the Europeans fell from the second-floor balcony. I didn't wait to see if any more followed. I had to leave much of your clothes and equipment behind."

Mercer pulled the folded Medusa photographs from the map pocket sown into the back of his khaki photographer's vest. "Doesn't matter. They didn't get what they wanted."

"You had them with you the whole time?" Selome asked.

"Can't imagine a safer place," he chuckled, coming down from the adrenaline high.

"That was one hell of a risk," she admonished.

"The bigger risk is the Europeans."

"What do you mean?"

"Habte just said he *heard* the shots." Mercer received a nod from the former soldier. "If the men who broke into my room were connected to the Sudanese who just tried for us, they would have had silencers on their weapons. Yet Habte heard unsilenced shots, return fire by the Europeans, not the Sudanese."

"Who are these Europeans?"

"I don't know." Mercer hid his suspicions. "Do you?"

Selome looked right at him when she replied in the negative, though he could see the shadow of a lie behind her eyes.

No one followed them out of the city and traffic was light, only a few lumbering trucks loaded with cotton grinding across the arid landscape. There were signs of the war along the road's verges, the rusted hulks of military equipment slowly disintegrating back into the soil. Soviet trucks and T–55 tanks, badly damaged by mines or missiles, littered the highway like the decomposing bodies of mechanical dinosaurs.

Mercer had read that the highlands were Eritrea's most fertile region, yet the land was rocky and nearly barren, wiped clean by scouring winds and left to bake in the unrelenting sun. The little vegetation was predominantly low scrubs, sage, and cactus. He spotted a farmer working behind two draft oxen, his plow not much more advanced than those developed in Egypt at the time of the Pharaohs. The plow dug deep runnels in his field, turning back the soil that was as parched as the surface. It seemed futile, but with a peasant's patience, he continued on.

They passed through small villages, rough clutches of adobe and brick roofed with thatch or metal. Many of the buildings were round, cone-topped structures called *agdos.* The few people on the dusty streets were thin and drawn, dressed in long plain shifts similar to Egyptian *galabia.*

Two hours later, they reached Keren, a city smaller than Asmara but possessing the same colonial charm with low bungalows and palm-lined streets. The majority of the population was Muslim, so many of the women were draped in long black *chadors* that absorbed the heat brutally. Habte parked the Toyota behind the Keren Hotel, a rambling building with a covered verandah screened by bougainvillea. "We need to get food and fuel here before continuing north."

"Okay, but I don't want to be here long." Mercer unlimbered himself from the truck.

"Agreed," Habte nodded. "Gibby and I will get what we need in the market. I have a lot of friends here. It shouldn't take too long."

Selome turned to Mercer. "No offense, but we'd better keep you out of sight. Whites don't make it to Keren very often, and it's best if no one sees you."

The cargo rack atop the Land Cruiser was loaded with boxes and jerry cans by the time Selome led Mercer back to the steps of the hotel. They'd waited in a nearby alley. Gibby was sitting in the backseat, but there was no sign of Habte. Mercer leapt into the vehicle and asked Gibby to duck into the Keren Hotel's bar to make a few purchases. Habte was in the driver's seat when the lad returned.

"I spoke to some people." Habte cranked the engine. "If any Sudanese come through here from Asmara in the next few days, they're going to find it difficult to continue." There was a smirk on his face.

Mercer pulled a map from the glove compartment. "That takes care of one interested party and now it's time to throw off the other. According to this, there's an airport in Nacfa and I bet the Europeans may try to leapfrog us and meet us there. Why don't we swing west?" Mercer pointed to the map for Habte to see. "This road here bypasses Nacfa and meets up with the main tract again at Itaro."

"The rains haven't come yet, so it should be passable," Habte agreed. "But what about the excavator waiting in Nacfa?"

"We won't need it for a while. Once we're in open country, no one will be able to find us. If I can pinpoint the pipe's location in the next few weeks, Selome can use her contacts in the government to get us some proper protection and then we'll call for the excavator."

Habte's military experience made him leery of an enemy who still posed a danger. "It would be wiser to eliminate the Europeans first."

"Wiser, yes. But not possible. We don't have any weapons. We're going to have to trust that the desert that hid your armies during the war can hide us for a few weeks."

Still unconvinced, Habte agreed, and when the road forked ten miles north of Keren, he steered them westward.

Nacfa, Eritrea

For three days they waited in Nacfa, roughly sixty miles south of the Sudanese border, before accepting that Mercer had slipped by them. When the refugee buses stopped passing through following Sudan's border closure, activity in the town came to a halt. There was little to do except drink endless cups of coffee and watch work crews repairing the roads. For Yosef's team, boredom was the most difficult problem they faced while waiting for Mercer and Selome.

Yosef had the added distraction of thinking about what had happened in Asmara. He remembered the maid's scream while he and one of his men were sitting in the lobby reading a week-old issue of the *Profile,* Asmara's only English-language newspaper. Both of them threw aside the meager papers and charged up the stairs. Yosef caught a glimpse of a tall African in Mercer's room holding a silenced automatic while his partner tore apart one of Mercer's suitcases. Instinct and training took control, and Yosef jumped aside a fraction of a second before the Sudanese fired. The younger Israeli caught two rounds high in the chest, propelling his lifeless body over the second-floor balcony to the lobby below. Yosef unholstered the big Desert Eagle from under his coat, paused for half a heartbeat, and rolled across the threshold of Mercer's room, the gun booming three times in a continuous thundering crash. Both Sudanese went down, their bodies leeching blood from massive wounds.

Yosef had scooped up his partner's weapon before fleeing, meeting up with the rest of his team where they waited in a different hotel. By the time they got reorganized and scouted the Ambasoira again, Mercer's Toyota Land Cruiser was gone. Yosef had lost him.

In an effort to get ahead of the geologist, the Israelis had chartered a plane in Asmara and flown to the rough strip just outside of Nacfa. He had one of his men drive northward on the off chance he could spot Mercer and his party. But now, three days had passed and still nothing. Mercer had taken a different route than Yosef had suspected. The Israelis had little choice but to return to Asmara and cultivate some contacts to gather information.

Yosef didn't like relying on second-party information, but their failure to follow Mercer made it necessary. He felt control of the operation slipping. His men were still loyal and eager; the failure was with him only. He cursed and turned to the two men with him. The other agent was outside watching the southern approach to the town.

"We're getting out of this shithole," he said angrily. "Get Avi and bring the car around. I want to be out of here in ten minutes."

He had underestimated Mercer for the last time. The next chance he got, Yosef would torture the mine's location from the American and dump his body far in the wasteland. As for the Sudanese, who he realized must be responsible for Ibriham's murder in Rome, that would be another battle for another time.

Northern Eritrea
South of the Hajer Plateau

For ten long days and equally long nights they slowly roamed across the desert with nothing to show for their efforts except a dangerously low fuel gauge. The attitude of the team was going sour with frustration and tedium. They were feeling the effects of the Land Cruiser's bone-jarring suspension, the molten air that beat down with the intensity of a blast furnace, and the swarms of stinging insects that found them the moment they stopped. Habte and Selome rarely spoke to each other, and since Gibby idolized his older cousin, he too had gone quiet around her. The silences in the stifling truck were draining.

Only Mercer seemed not to notice any of this. He was in his element and had managed to put everything out of his mind except the geology and geography of the area. Using the Medusa photographs, Habte's recollections, and his own sense of the earth, he guided them almost randomly, never losing his good spirits.

Even after ten days of fruitless searching, his dedication hadn't faltered. In fact, he seemed to move with ever greater assurance as the days passed. But the task was still daunting. He felt like a grizzled Forty-niner who had opened California's gold rush with little more than a pick and high hopes. Used to being part of a well-financed expedition, he had only his years of experience and his innate intuition to rely on.

At least twenty times a day since reaching the Barka Province, Mercer ordered Habte to stop the truck so he could race across the hardpan, a pointed geologist's hammer in his fist. He would scramble up some nameless hill, chip away at the stone, examine it for up to half an hour, using his tongue to moisten some samples to change their reflective properties. Sometimes he asked Gibby to join him with two shovels, and for an hour or more, they dug trenches in the scaly soil. Wordlessly, they returned to the Land-Cruiser. Mercer would point in a new direction, and off they would go again.

They established primitive camps at night. Habte had managed to pack only two tents before their flight from Asmara. He and Gibby shared one, Mercer had the other to himself, and Selome slept on the Toyota's rear bench seat. Their meals were equally crude: millet cakes, turnips or potatoes, and canned meat. The highlight of every day was the seemingly endless bottles of brandy Mercer produced from his luggage, some brought from the United States and a couple purchased for him by Gibby at the Keren Hotel. The three Eritreans usually fell into a death-like sleep soon after their meal, but Mercer worked deep into the night. A hurricane lantern hissed in his tent as he scribbled in a thick notebook, the satellite pictures spread on his knees.

Mercer had intended to use the truck for about a week of exploratory sorties and then return to Asmara to charter a plane and study the terrain from the air, cross-referencing the aerial view with his ground observations and the Medusa pictures. That was now, of course, impossible. It would be suicide for any of them to return to the capital. He was limited to what he could see from the ground and forced to match it to the surface topography from the photos.

At dawn on the eleventh day, the sun was diffused by banks of clouds. Far to the east, the rains had come. The sunrise cast a rose hue on the desert, rouging the sand and casting bizarre shadows on the western mountains. Mercer emerged from his tent before the others awoke, enjoying the solitude of the early morning. They were camped on the bank of one of the rare streams. For the first time in days, water was readily available. Mercer took a few minutes to strip and wash the sweat and grit from his body, dressing again in the same clothes but changing into a fresh pair of socks and boxer shorts. His skin cooled quickly in the dawn chill, and goose flesh rose along his arms and chest. The sensation was wonderful.

Habte emerged from his shared tent with a cigarette already smoldering between his thin lips. He kicked life back into the embers of their fire and heated a pot of water for coffee.

Mercer accepted a mug gratefully, cupping his hands around the warm container. They drank in contented silence. Gibby and Selome awoke a short time later, she going off to perform her morning ablutions and Gibby and Habte falling into a conversation in Tigrinyan, leaving Mercer to watch the grotesque shapes of distant outcrops materialize from the gloom.

"We must return to Badn today," Habte said when Gibby went off into the desert to relieve himself.

They had negotiated with a group of nomads staying around the village of Badn to travel to Nacfa and purchase gasoline. Their camel caravan would have returned by now, and even with extended tanks, the Toyota would just make it to town.

"I know," Mercer replied absently, watching Selome's sinuous return to the camp. Despite the harsh conditions, each morning she managed to look fresh and beautiful. She wore ballooning jodhpurs and a man's large overshirt. Her hair formed a dense halo from under the wide brim of a straw hat, its fuchsia band adding a touch of feminine color to the ensemble. Her lightweight clothes were better suited to the desert than the jeans she had started out wearing.

She curled into a cross-legged position on the ground across the fire from Mercer. There was a trace of blush on her cheeks. She'd been aware of his gaze.

"We're heading back to Badn this morning," Mercer announced, and he could see relief in her eyes. The pace he had set for the past days had been brutal, and they all anticipated at least a small break in the tiny hamlet. "I want to hire those nomads again to return to Nacfa and have them guide the excavator here."

Both Habte and Selome gaped at him. It was Selome who found her voice first. "You found the mine?"

Mercer looked at her sharply, then dashed her hopes with a quick shake of his head. "No, not yet, but the rains are coming soon, and if we don't get the excavator across the Adohba River now, we may never be able to. There aren't any bridges across it strong enough to take the weight of the tractor trailer and crawler." Disappointment made her face collapse. "However, I do have good news."

He went to his tent and returned with his notebook and the now dog-eared photographs. He spread the material on the ground, anchoring the corners of a rolled-up map with fist-size rocks. Habte and Selome clustered over his shoulder while Gibby made himself busy breaking down their camp. "Since my Global Positioning Satellite receiver was left in Asmara, all the reference marks on the map are just estimates. They could be off as much as a mile or two, and a margin of error that big doesn't help our cause."

He pointed at a spot twenty miles north of Badn. "We're roughly here now. The asterisks on the map represent sites where I've taken samples." There were dozens of such notations. Despite the seemingly random route Mercer had taken, the marks were laid out in perfect symmetry, each about half a mile from its neighbor in every direction. Habte and Selome were impressed by his orienteering skills. "The marks in red show where I discovered traces of garnet and ilmenites that may or may not mean the presence of diamonds. The problem is their quantity. There doesn't seem to be enough for me to believe the kimberlite pipe ever reached the surface to be eroded down and its contents spread by these ancient water courses." He pointed at several twisting lines he'd drawn on the map, certain the others hadn't been aware that they'd traveled in any streambeds, such were the changes wrought in the millions of years since they'd been carved. "If the pipe's still buried under the surface, we may never find it."

"So what is our next move?" Habte asked.

Mercer thumbed through his notebook until he came to a pencil sketch of a buttress of rock bisected by a deep valley. Through the valley's sheer aperture, an open plain beyond was revealed in detail. The drawing was harsh in its economy of line, but there was a depth of skill and just a bit of evocative emotion in its composition. "This is the best I can deduce from the surface details revealed by the Medusa pictures. They weren't calibrated when the shots were taken, and the above-ground features suffered the most from this. But this is what the area around the kimberlite pipe should look like from ground level. I wanted to have this drawing finished a while ago, but it wasn't until last night that I was finally satisfied with the results. If the pipe exists, it's going to be behind these ramparts in the valley. Habte, do you recognize any features like this?"

Habte would have easily remembered because the drawing's detail made it very recognizable. But he had never seen the sheer mountain wall with such a narrow ax-stroke cut in its face. "No, but we can show it to the nomads in Badn; they may know of it. I'm guessing this is farther north, near the Hajer Plateau."

"Do you know the region?"

"Bad country up there. *Shifta* control much of the area. The government doesn't even bother to patrol that far north. During the war the whole area was heavily mined by the Ethiopians to prevent us from using Sudan as a safe haven. It is not safe to leave the road that passes through Itaro to the east. The nomads and shepherds avoid the area, but still a few are killed or maimed by mines every year."

Mercer cursed because of the added danger. Military planners called them "perfect soldiers." Once planted, landmines sat silently, effective for decades, waiting long after the wars were over. It took only a few pounds of pressure to set one off, detonating a measure of high explosive that caught its victim unaware. Children usually found and triggered the devices as they played far from their villages.

"Is there anything else up there?"

"There's a monastery. It was abandoned during the war, but I think the monks have come back."

The mines would never be deactivated, Mercer knew, for the cost was astronomical. Northern Eritrea would be contaminated for decades, as lifeless and unsafe as the environs around Chernobyl. "We don't have a choice. If any of you want to abandon the search, I'll understand, but I am going on."

"We're with you," Selome said quickly, and Habte and Gibby nodded.

"Thank you." The two men were risking their lives for him, and Mercer was deeply touched by their dedication. They barely knew him, yet were willing to make the ultimate sacrifice. Selome, on the other hand, was on her own mission, and her willingness to continue gave him a glimpse of her commitment. "I'm going to take a chance and ignore the desert between us and the Hajer Plateau. To get the excavator up here, we can use the main road as far north as Itaro, and the nomads can guide it to this point here." He used his pencil to circle the village of Ila Babu on the Adobha River. "Now, let's get going."

The Toyota was sputtering when they entered Badn, its body so dusty it looked as if it had been painted with a desert camouflage pattern. There were only a couple of permanent structures in the village. The rest of Badn was mostly mounded tents of coarse fabric stretched over wooden frames. On the open plain, they resembled loaves of bread with the sun setting behind them. The town's naturally fed well was its only *raison d'être.* Nomads from all over the Barka Province used the waters for their camels and goats.

Habte recognized the tent of the family he had hired to fetch gasoline from Nacfa and steered the Land Cruiser to the rude compound. Bundles of firewood stood a little way off from the central tent, and in the shimmering distance a caravan of camels was returning from a foray with more. From this range, their misshapen bodies appeared to float in the chimera of rising heat. Several of the bawling beasts were pegged near the camp, their soft eyes regarding the truck with ill-disguised contempt. Behind the faggots of desiccated wood sat a pile of plastic jerry cans filled with their gasoline.

Their return was seen as an opportunity for the nomad headman to throw a party. He was in his sixties with a booming voice and a backslapping greeting that, had Mercer not been prepared, would have driven him to the ground. "Fuck, fuck," he smiled, demonstrating his command of English. "Fuck."

"And fuck to you too." Mercer grinned.

The chieftain turned to Habte and spoke in rapid fire, motioning for a translation for Mercer's benefit. "He says you are welcome back to his humble home and hopes that our travels have been profitable. He also hopes you have brought him his money to cement his friendship."

Mercer reached into one of his vest pockets for a sheath of ten-dollar bills and handed the entire roll across. The money represented more cash than the family saw in a year. The nomad smiled again, slapping Mercer soundly on the shoulder. The few teeth remaining in his smile were jagged yellow stumps that had been filed to points so their sharpness made up for their diminished numbers. "Fuck."

"Fuck, fuck," Mercer rejoined.

Habte translated when the headman spoke. "We must spend the night as his guests. He says he will not allow us to leave until he has shown us his hospitality."

"Tell him we would be honored. If it's permitted, I have a bottle of brandy to bring to his table."

The old headman's eyes lit up with delight. "Fuck, yes."

Two hours later, having bathed, Mercer ducked into the headman's tent with Habte, Selome, and Gibby in tow. He was stopped by the rank odor of the tent and the smoke coiling up through the chimney slit from the small fire. Oil lamps lit the center of the tent, revealing an expanse of beautifully woven rugs on the bare floor. The headman sat amid a circular ring of men, a space opened at his right for Mercer and his party. Inside the circle was a huge hammered brass plate with several matching pots surrounding it. Next to each man was a platter of *injera,* the unleavened bread that was the staple of most Eritreans' diets. There were at least fifteen children in the tent, laughing and squealing with some noisy game, their play adding to the din of the twenty adults. Incongruously, a Michael Jackson tape played on a portable radio. The King of Pop sounded like a baritone because the tape deck's batteries were nearly dead. Selome took Mercer's hand, giving it a reassuring squeeze. "Looks like you're going to get that traditional meal after all." From around the cooking fire the heady aroma of their meal wafted across the room, and even at this distance the spiciness made Mercer's eyes swim.

The headman indicated that Mercer was to sit beside him, and Selome slid into a place on Mercer's other side. The Eritrean thrust a brass cup into Mercer's hand and toasted him with a drink of his own. Mercer recognized the smell of *tej,* a delightful honey wine made only in Ethiopia and Eritrea, and he drank down the tumbler in one quick toss. Unlike the polished, sweet wine he'd enjoyed in Washington's Ethiopian restaurants, this fiery brew was as smooth as sandpaper, with the subtlety of a stick of dynamite and twice the kick. It took all of his will not to cry out as the liquor exploded in his stomach. He finally caught his breath. "Oh, fuck."

It took four more shots of *tej* for Mercer to get into the spirit of the party. He took the bottle of brandy Gibby had been holding for him and handed it ceremoniously to the chieftain. The nomad prince opened it gleefully and tossed the cap over his shoulder, where it landed unerringly in one of the cooking pots. Disdaining his cup in his desire to drink such a delicacy, he tilted the bottle to his lips, his throat pumping. He handed the bottle to Mercer. Hoping the brandy would kill whatever swam in the Eritrean's mouth, he, too, took a long gulp. "Oh, fuck," he muttered again. It was going to be a long night.

The women finished preparing the meal and tipped the cooking pots directly into the three brass bowls around the giant platter. The assembled tribesmen went at the food like a pack of wild dogs. They tore off slabs of *injera,* dunking them into the bowls so their hands came away smeared to the wrist with stew, clots of meat, and vegetables dripping onto the huge plate as they bent forward to cram the mass down their throats. Habte and Gibby ate with equal gusto, though Selome showed a bit more decorum with the size of the bites she took. The *wat* in the bowl closest to Mercer was made of lentils, chickpeas, and oily mutton. The bread helped absorb some of the grease, but he could feel his arteries hardening with every bite. The only thing that cut through the food's spicy edge was the *tej* that the women encouragingly refilled every time his cup was only half emptied.

Unbelievably, the huge amount of food was eaten in just a few minutes, and no sooner had the last of the three bowls been emptied than the women approached and poured fresh *wat* for the men and replenished their stacks of *injera.*

"How are you doing?" Selome asked, wiping her hands on her pant leg. Her eyes were bright and glassy with wine, and the food had brought a flush to her perfect skin.

Mercer could see she was enjoying herself as much as he. He wondered what this was like for her, to sit with her people after so many years of isolation and enjoy the simple pleasure of a communal meal. "A few more cups of *tej* and I'll forget that my stomach lining has been burned away."

Selome suddenly leaned across and kissed him full on the mouth, catching Mercer by surprise. He could feel the spicy heat from the *wat* on her lips and felt a deeper warmth that had nothing to do with the food. The uncharacteristic intimacy shocked her as much as it did him, and she turned away, flustered.

Again the three huge bowls were emptied and again they were refilled, fresh steam rising up in dangerous tendrils that burned like acid. The headman dipped a piece of *injera* into the fresh stew and palmed a chunk of meat the size of his fist. He handed it to Mercer with another grin. "Fuck?"

"Oh, no problem." Mercer emptied his *tej* and jammed the fatty hunk into his mouth with the relish of a native.

Four more times the pots were emptied and recharged. The communal eating platter was mounded with the food the men hadn't been quick enough to get to their mouths before it dropped. The few die-hards still eating were making a significant dent in these leavings. The Eritreans were doused with grease from their mouths to the tips of their ubiquitous beards and from their fingernails to their forearms. The meal was finally winding down, and Mercer thought it a good time to ask his host a favor. He had kept his notebook with him, sitting on it during the banquet to keep it from either being ruined by grease or accidentally eaten by one of the clansmen. He opened the book to his sketch of the valley and mountain around the kimberlite pipe and asked Selome to translate.

"Do you recognize this place?"

"Yes, of course." The headman tried to draw himself straight, but the prodigious amount of alcohol made his spine rebel and he slumped against his neighbor. "My father's mother was born near that place. It is on the western flank of Hajer. We call it the Valley of Dead Children."

"Why is that?"

"Because that is its name," the old man pointed out logically.

"But why that name?" Mercer persisted.

"Who knows? That's what it's been called since long before time was recorded." He was starting to fade away from the conversation, his eyes rolling back into his skull and his lips going rubbery around the last few words. "Even before the war, no one went to this place. Evil spirits live in the hills. My father told me that even animals refuse to enter the valley. They could feel the ghosts. Now the area around the Valley of Dead Children is full of mines. A cousin lost his eldest son there two rains ago when the boy went looking for a young goat that wandered away from his herd."

"Have you been to this valley?"

"No." And the headman started to snore.

Years of friendship with Harry White should have prepared Mercer for the next morning's hangover, but his previous experiences couldn't have possibly readied him for the pounding in his skull or the maelstrom that churned his gut. Everyone was still in the tent, most snoring loudly where they'd passed out the night before. One clansmen lying in the platter was dangerously close to drowning in the grease pooled at its bottom. Mercer came awake in slow, painful stages, dimly aware that it was still dark outside and the tent was lit with only a single guttering oil lamp.

Selome was curled up in the crook of his arm, her head resting lightly on the pads of muscle. Her face was toward him, her mouth parted and her lips shining in the murky light. Mercer recalled the surprising kiss she had given him the night before and passed it off as alcohol-induced affection. He kissed her forehead and carefully disentangled her limbs from his.

By the luminous dial of his watch, dawn was half an hour away. The moon hung near the horizon in its own bright corona. Mercer shuffled unsteadily to the Toyota. He retrieved a bundle from under the truck and returned to the low stools placed just outside the tent's entrance. Mercer recalled that the headman's name was Negga, and he was already sitting, his head hanging limply between his hands. Mercer tapped him on the shoulder and offered one of the Milotti beers he had left overnight in a sodden towel. The beer was refreshingly cold.

"Little hair of the hyena for you." If Mercer was going to make it through the day, he'd need a beer to push back the effects of the *tej.* Harry called it the "deferred hangover plan. Party now and pay later."

Habte and Gibby joined them after Mercer had passed a second beer to Negga.

"Habte, ask our host if he would give us a man to guide us to the Valley of Dead Children."

"I am taking my family farther east to catch the rains," Habte translated for the nomad leader. "My herds and flocks have been months without good pasturage. I want to help you, but I can't delay. But heed my words. You don't want to go up there. Not only do you have to worry about the mines, but I've heard there's an army stationed on the Sudan side of the border. They arrived about six days ago."

"Who are they?"

"I don't know. They're not regular soldiers, and it was said that there are at least fifty of them, all well armed. A force that size is too big for one of the *shifta* gangs." The chieftain shrugged his shoulders. "Their presence is a mystery."

Mercer retrieved his topographical map of Eritrea and spread it on the ground in front of Negga. "Can you at least show me where on the Hajer Plateau the valley lies?"

Negga stared at the map with incomprehension. Like most nomads, he relied on the accumulated knowledge of generations of wanderers to know his territory. Even after Mercer pointed to the Adobha River as a reference, Negga still couldn't understand how the compressed lines on the flat projection represented the rugged northern mountains. "I don't know what this paper means. The valley is on the west flank of the plateau, a long day's ride on a swift camel from Ila Babu. That is all I can tell you."

"Would you at least guide my people to Nacfa so they can get another truck I have waiting and then take them to Ila Babu?" There were no roads connecting the two towns.

"We have drunk from the same bottle. Of course, I will do this thing for you. But I will not permit my people to go beyond Ila Babu. I won't lose any of my family for your search."

"Fair enough."

Negga's expression brightened. "It will cost you only two hundred American dollars."

In their debilitated state, it took Habte and Gibby a half hour to transfer the fuel from the jerry cans into the Toyota, lashing the spares onto the cargo rack under the stores already there. Mercer went to talk to Negga's son, who spoke passable English, shook hands when they came to an agreement, and passed over some money.

"It sounds like we are not going with you," Habte said when Mercer returned to the truck.

"You're not. I don't want Selome with us if I run into any trouble, and I can't trust her alone with Negga's guides." Mercer paused. "There's something else. Yesterday when we were talking about returning here, Selome asked if I thought I had discovered the mine's location. Do you remember?"

Habte nodded slowly.

"As far as I know, she thinks we're only looking for a kimberlite *pipe,* not a mine. It's the same thing the kidnappers said. Unless she has outside knowledge, she shouldn't know anything about the mine. I haven't told her."

Habte accepted this without a change of expression. "I'll keep my eye on her, see if she tries to contact anyone in Nacfa."

"Good. Thank you."

"What about Gibby?"

"He stays with me." Mercer secured the last corner of a cargo net. "I can use the help, and I'll send him to meet you in Ila Babu to direct you to the mine site if I find it."

"What were you talking to Negga's son about?" Habte asked.

"Contingency plan B," Mercer said and handed over his spare sat-phone with instructions on how and when to use it.

At last they were ready. Negga assured Mercer that two of his sons would take Selome and Habte to Nacfa the following morning. Selome was still asleep, and while Mercer felt a twinge of guilt leaving her without an explanation, he didn't let it show. He swallowed three ibuprofin tablets, drank a full liter of purified water, then mounted the truck. Gibby was already strapped into the passenger seat, his head lolling as if its weight was too great a burden for his neck.

"Selome won't be happy that you are leaving her behind," Habte teased.

Mercer ignored the jibe. "I'll call you after my next contact from the kidnappers. If I haven't located the mine by then, plan on coming to meet us anyway and we can continue the search together." When he saw Selome again, Mercer promised himself that they would have a long talk about what she already knew. The men holding Harry White were playing for keeps, and it was time for Mercer to do likewise.

Fairfax, Virginia

The first break in solving the murders of Prescott Hyde and his wife came about through sheer persistence.

On the day of the fire, the Fairfax police had canvassed Hyde's neighborhood for anyone who may have seen the arsonist, but they came up empty. The only glimmer of hope remaining for the investigation were a certain Dr. and Mrs. Grady, who lived adjacent to the Hydes. They had left town only an hour before the fire was first noticed. Dr. Grady was an oral surgeon who donated two weeks of his time and skills every year to a charity clinic in Peru. Despite repeated attempts to contact them at the remote clinic, they had not responded.

Dick Henna himself was waiting in a government car when the Gradys finally returned to the country, arriving from the airport in a boxy Mercury Mountaineer. Normally, the director of the FBI wouldn't have been involved with an individual case, but there were two factors that demanded his personal attention. One was the president's interest in the murder of one of his appointed sub–Cabinet level officials and the implications for the missing Medusa photographs. Henna had briefed the chief executive soon after Admiral Morrison dumped the entire mess on his lap. While much of the evidence was destroyed by the fire, the twin bullet holes in the charred skulls of both Prescott Hyde and his wife, Jacqueline, had galvanized the Administration. Henna's other reason was his friendship with Mercer.

Soon after the story of the fire and execution-style murders reached the press, the *Washington Post* had reported the details of the Justice Department's investigation into

Hyde's life, including rumors of a sale of highly classified documents to unknown parties. The *Post* didn't have anything concrete on this last piece of information, but they were leaning heavily on their sources and it was only a matter of time before someone disclosed the existence of the Medusa satellite and the missing pictures.

The president wanted this solved quickly, faces put on the unknown killers and names to go with the faces. If the scandal broke, the president had already primed his pointing finger and wanted a direction in which to aim it. His Administration was still reeling over last year's Alaska debacle, and was not yet strong enough to handle another embarrassment. The president told Henna to sew the murders up tight, deflect any inquiries away from his African Affairs secretary, and make certain this scandal wouldn't return to bite them all on the ass.

The candy-apple red sport utility vehicle eased up the Gradys' driveway. Both appeared to be in their late forties or early fifties. His gray hair was thinning while hers was dyed blonde. They were tanned and appeared worn by their work in South America. Henna gave them a minute to gape at the blackened pit that had been the Hydes' house before approaching the couple.

"It was arson," Henna said bluntly. Both Gradys turned in unison and looked at him blankly. "And I'm sorry to tell you this, but Prescott and Jacqueline were shot in the head before the arsonist torched their house." Now that he had their full attention, he introduced himself. "I'm Dick Henna, the director of the FBI, and I have a couple of questions for you."

Five minutes later, they were seated in the Gradys' living room. There were dozens of mementos on the walls from their children's lives, culminating in framed diplomas from Georgetown set on a baby grand piano. Meredeth Grady was still weeping, for she and Jacqueline Hyde had been friends and golfing partners. John Grady had taken the news much more calmly, certainly not immune from the horrors of death, but as a doctor better able to hide it.

"As you can understand," Henna said when he gauged

Meredith ready to handle his questions, "the president is very interested in solving this case. He and Prescott had been close, as I'm sure Undersecretary Hyde had told you."

"Oh, yes, Jackie was so excited when they were invited to the Inaugural Ball. I remember she talked of nothing else for months before and after."

Henna had gone to one of the Inaugural Balls himself. He and Fay had decided after only an hour that they couldn't tolerate the pretension and had gone to Tiny's Bar on a lark, still in their evening wear. He remembered Harry White dancing gallantly with Fay to the tuneless music squawking from the jukebox's blown speakers.

"The FBI and the Fairfax police have talked to everyone in the neighborhood except the two of you. We're hoping you can shed some light on what happened." Ballistics had come up empty on the slugs recovered with the bodies. "Did either of you see or hear anything the morning you left for your trip?"

Meredith leaned forward. "I saw a woman go into the Hydes' house shortly before I left. I had never seen her before, but Jackie and Bill knew so many people I couldn't keep track."

"Could you describe her?"

"It was very early, still dark, but I remember she was young, early thirties I would say, and very pretty, dressed casually. I don't remember what kind of car she was driving. She drove right up to the house, knocked at the door, and went in immediately. She left after just a few minutes. You don't think she was the one? She didn't look like a killer."

Thank God for curious neighbors. "Would you recognize her again if I showed you some pictures?"

Meredith hesitated, and Henna knew why. In the age of political correctness, people felt obligated not to mention one thing when they described another person. "Was she black?"

"Yes, she was," Meredith Grady breathed. "It's not all that unusual. African-Americans showed up at the Hydes' house all the time, you know, with his job and all."

"Not all blacks are Americans. She could have been a real African," Henna said. Meredith looked as if she'd never even considered a difference. "Would you recognize her?"

"I don't know, maybe." Meredith Grady didn't have to say that most blacks looked the same to her. It was evident in her uncomfortable expression.

"Dr. Grady, did you see this woman?"

"No, I was at the airport already, clearing medical supplies through customs. Meredith met me just before our flight."

Henna turned back to Mrs. Grady, "Well?"

"Maybe. I'd have to see a good picture of her. The only thing I remember distinctly was her hair. I saw it under the porch light before she entered the house. It wasn't like most African-American women's. It was longer and not extensions either; I can tell the difference. And it was tinted with henna to give it red highlights. Hey, your name and the dye, it's the same word."

Dick smiled. "Fortunately, the kids I knew growing up weren't smart enough to make the connection." From his briefcase he withdrew a file crammed with pictures. "I want you to take a look through these and tell me if you recognize anyone."

Meredith took the thick stack and started going through them with a decisive flick, snapping each one facedown on the coffee table. The pictures were of female Mossad agents who had worked in the United States. A few were dark-skinned, and Henna hoped for a hit. She handed them back. "I'm sorry, but none of these women look even close."

"That's okay," Henna gave her a smaller set of photographs. "How about these."

"That's her," Meredith Grady cried, holding the picture for Henna to see. The photos were mostly of light-skinned black FBI employees he'd had taken to fill out the file, but one was something else entirely.

"Are you absolutely sure?" Henna pressed.

She studied the picture again. "Positive. She was the person I saw going into Jackie and Bill's house."

Henna's gut gave an oily slide. Suddenly it was imperative that he reach Mercer. The picture was a blow-up from a State Department security camera. Even with poor resolution, it was unmistakably Selome Nagast.

Eritrea

After leaving Badn, Mercer and Gibby made good time on their drive north to the foot of the Hajer Plateau. Mercer drove aggressively, racing across the desert like a professional rally driver. After recovering from his hangover, Gibby enjoyed the breakneck pace as only the young can. He would ululate when the heavy truck became airborne as Mercer rocketed out of shallow defiles, the deeply lugged tires spinning off plumes of dust when they came free of the earth.

Despite Mercer's best efforts, they managed to cover only sixty miles in their intended direction, though the odometer showed they had traveled close to a hundred and fifteen. The terrain was too difficult for a more direct route. Also, Mercer did not take Negga's warning about landmines lightly and steered the vehicle over only the worst of the ground—that which would have naturally slowed an advancing army and was thus less likely to be booby-trapped.

Even with Negga's directions that the Valley of Dead Children was on the western side of the plateau, Mercer and Gibby still had over a hundred square miles to investigate. According to Mercer's map, the area resembled a huge maze with hundreds of tall, isolated hills, box canyons, and meandering valleys that crisscrossed each other in complex patterns. He tried to match the map features to what was actually outside the four-wheel drive and quickly discovered the cartographer had simply drawn a representation of the region. No time had been taken to accurately depict every geographical landmark. For all practical purposes, the map was worthless. Instead, he taped the drawing he had done of the valley entrance to the dashboard and used it to guide him.

The territory had been carved by wind and water over the past few million years, the mountains worn down to stubs of harder rock. Having no idea into which mountain the valley was cut, Mercer and Gibby drove around each of them completely, checking the terrain against the drawing and coming up blank every time. They spent three days doing this before Mercer decided to attempt a desperate shortcut.

"This isn't going to work," Mercer told Gibby around noon on the third day.

In frustration, he powered the Land Cruiser up the slope of one of the taller hills, a seven-hundred-foot ascent in low range that loaded down the engine so badly that they reached the summit at a walking pace and the motor was on the verge of an explosive overheat. He twisted the key angrily, and in the sudden silence he could hear engine fluids boiling like a cauldron.

He snatched a pair of binoculars from the backseat and jumped onto the precarious load strapped to the Toyota's roof. He turned slowly in place, the powerful Zeiss lenses pressed to his eyes.

"There's a valley about two miles to the east that looks like it was once the major waterway through this area. If the kimberlite pipe broke through the surface, erosion would have spilled some stones or at least trace elements into the streambed." Gibby didn't have Habte's command of English, so he looked at Mercer blankly. "Don't worry, my friend. We may be on to something."

It was just possible he could jump-start their search, he thought as he leapt back to the ground. He felt that same stirring of hope he'd experienced when the kidnappers mistakenly told him he was searching for a mine.

Surface topography had changed so much over the eons that the ancient river now appeared as if it had flowed uphill, but Mercer had no trouble telling in which direction the waters had once poured. He drove northward for nearly a mile and kept the Toyota canted at an angle as he guided it on one of the banks, suspecting that the streambed might be mined. They reached a sharp bend in the stream in the shadow of yet another mountain, a beige sandstone monument that offered little shade from the murderous sun. Gibby threw open his door as soon as Mercer braked.

"Don't!" Mercer shouted just seconds before the boy stepped onto the dusty soil.

Jesus, he thought and opened his own door, his heart hammering from Gibby's near fatal mistake. He studied the ground intently, looking for a telltale depression that might indicate the presence of a landmine. Seeing nothing, he told Gibby to break off the Toyota's radio antenna and pass it over. He used it as a probe, pushing it firmly but gently into the friable dirt, twisting and working until it sank down about eight inches. Nothing.

The temperature in the vehicle skyrocketed past a hundred degrees. Sweat flowed freely from Mercer's pores, stinging his eyes and making his vision swim. Yet his concentration was total as he continued with the antenna probe. It took twenty minutes before he felt confident enough to step out of the truck and a further two long hours to ensure that the immediate area around the Land Cruiser was unspoiled.

"Get the shovels. It's time to work." He threw the antenna into the truck and stripped off his shirt. His torso gleamed like bronze, and the bunched muscles in his arms moved like oiled machinery.

They attacked the bank where the water's fury would have smashed into it, forcing the ancient river to give up some of the debris it carried. Miners coveted spots like this when panning for gold. Rivers would disgorge pockets of the precious metal in similar curves when the currents eddied and could no longer support the weight of the raw nuggets. Alluvial diamonds were also ensnared in such natural traps, their specific gravity being greater than most other suspended material caught in the flow.

For hours they dug in silence. Occasionally, Mercer would dump a shovelful of gravel onto a plastic tarpaulin and pour water over it from their diminishing stores. Apart from their legendary properties of defraction, diffusion, and hardness, one of diamond's lesser known attributes is its inability to remain wet. Pour water on it, spray it, or douse it and its surface will bead and dry instantly. He used his finger to stir the dirt, wetting it all, picking though it carefully, examining the minute chips of stone that showed brightly in the mud. Satisfied, he would scrape the mess off to the side and continue digging.

The hole was over eight feet wide and nearly six deep when it got too dark for Mercer to accurately study the samples. The sun was a distant red disk painting the desert in thousands of hues—from deepest black to the rich vermilion of a rose petal. He had known when they started digging that they might come up with nothing this close to the surface. Northern Eritrea's bedrock, formed during the Archean era, was some of the oldest anywhere on the planet. Its depth below the surface could be a mile or more, and in the millions of years since its creation, thousands of types of soils had been deposited on it. What Mercer needed was a core driller, a machine that could probe miles below the surface and return with samples. Bitterly, he realized hand-digging a few feet into the earth was a waste of time. His earlier hope evaporated.

"If there is a pipe around here and if it reached the surface and if it was worn down by erosion, there's no guarantee it followed this watershed, and even if it did, any evidence might be buried two thousand feet or more," Mercer told Gibby. "We're going to have to keep driving around and find the valley the hard way."

Mercer tossed one more shovel load of dirt onto the rim of the hole. He heaved himself out of the pit, extending his hand to Gibby and hauling the slender Eritrean to ground level. He looked at the spilled dirt on the plastic sheet and hunkered down to inspect the muddy pile, spreading it around, crushing a hard lump of ancient clay with his fingers. He began picking through it as he had fifty times that day with fifty other samples, his body mechanically going through the motions while his mind was already preparing for sleep. One small lump of rock had not been wetted when he dumped water on the pile. He reached over and shook the canteen over it. A few drops landed on the stone, beaded instantly, and trickled off.

"Gibby, get the flashlight!" Mercer almost choked as he spoke. His mouth had gone dry. He shook the canteen over the stone again, but it was empty. "And more water!"

The lad caught Mercer's urgency and scrambled to get the required items. He was at Mercer's shoulder an instant later. Night had come swiftly, and Mercer shone the flashlight on the kidney bean–sized stone between his fingers. The pebble was dark, cracked, and scarred, but there was a translucency to it, similar to pure quartz. Shaking slightly, Mercer tipped a liter bottle of water over his hands, washing away the accumulated grit from his skin, but no matter how much he poured over the stone, it remained perfectly dry.

"Is it?" Gibby breathed, his eyes fever bright as he looked at the stone.

Mercer didn't respond. He strode to the Toyota, pressed a sharp corner of the octahedral crystal to the front windshield, and drew the stone across the glass. The screech set his teeth on edge. There was a deep white scar on the safety glass.

He was grinning when he spun back to Gibby, tossing the stone to the startled young man.

"It's too rough to ever sit in an engagement ring, but you're holding about twelve carats of industrial diamond, my friend." Mercer whooped. Gibby looked at the stone, understanding at last, and added his own cries.

Mercer wanted to start backtracking down the old streambed to its source right away, but they had to wait until morning. He lay down in the Toyota, knowing sleep wouldn't come. This was it. He'd done it. The men holding Harry would be calling again tomorrow at midnight, and he thought about what he would tell them. He didn't want to disclose this find, but he had to give them something, just enough so they believed he was close. Finding diamonds this quickly was a huge advantage. He had four weeks left on his deadline and wanted that time to figure some way to end-run the kidnappers. If he had to, he would just give them the location, but he'd regained enough confidence to try and stop them first. They were going to pay for what they'd done.

He finally did sleep, and when he woke the next morning, his body had stiffened. Even the most minor movement brought a groan to his lips. "I'm getting too old for this shit."

He roused Gibby, and soon they were driving again. The streambed meandered in long, lazy bends, forming a huge oxbow once and rising up a cliff that had been a waterfall at some point in history. They needed the tow winch to clear the former falls. Mercer took the time to scout the area with his antenna probe, losing several hours in the process.

The river led more or less in a direct north-south course. It appeared they were heading toward the main bulk of the Hajer Plateau, a huge up-thrust that overshadowed everything in the region. Mercer thought about abandoning the serpentine streambed and driving straight for the mountain, but he knew caution was his only ally here and stayed with the winding path.

"Effendi!" Gibby tore the pencil drawing from the dashboard, waving it like a talisman, and pointed to their immediate left.

Mercer's drawing was nearly perfect. The Valley of Dead Children was there, cut into the side of a three-hundred-foot mountain, looking exactly as he had envisioned it, right down to a tumbling rock slide that had torn away one side of the steep valley wall near its entrance, partially filling the near vertical chasm. The mountain, with its inviting cleft, was about half a mile away.

The land between it and the riverbed was an open expanse pocked severely by impact craters, most likely from Ethiopian artillery. The churned-up ground near some of the scars was still blackened by explosives.

"Jesus," Mercer breathed. The devastated area looked

like the pictures he had seen of No-Man's-Land during World War I.

He didn't want to think about the men who had probably been caught in the open when the big guns began to rain death on them. He looked around for a makeshift cemetery but recognized the gesture was pointless. There wouldn't be enough left of the men caught in the barrage to bury. Gibby was also affected by the sight. Too young to have seen the worst of the fighting, he could still comprehend the suffering that had made his nation free.

"We're about to make it all worthwhile," Mercer promised him.

He felt a degree of sacrilege as he drove across the killing field, knowing the tires were likely disturbing the bones of brave men. He wondered if the battlefield had served as a deterrent to others wanting to explore this area. Perhaps that was why no one had been to this region in so many years.

The Valley of Dead Children was roughly two hundred feet wide at its base and only twice that width at its top, a steep V-shaped notch in a nameless mountain. Mercer had to use low-range again to power the Land Cruiser over the loose scree that had tumbled into the valley's entrance, racing the engine until it sounded like a turbine. The valley ran almost straight into the mountain for a half mile. Its sides weren't solid rock but layers of sedimentary sandstone that had built up over the millennia. They were unstable; bits of rock and dirt pelted the roof of the four-wheel drive as he eased them through.

"No wonder the diamonds were never discovered before," he said as the Land Cruiser broke into a huge open bowl of land at the valley's end. "The geology is all wrong. This should be rhyolite or basalt."

Once through the valley, they broke into an open pan roughly five miles across, the distant ring of mountains lost in shimmering waves of heat. Mercer could begin to understand why the nomads avoided this place. While vegetation was always scarce in the country, the bowl was devoid of even the hearty sage or cacti. The land was as lifeless as the surface of the moon. Gibby looked stricken as they drove deeper into the dead zone, his hands clutched in front of his chest as if in prayer.

"I do not like it here," he muttered.

"Me either." Mercer couldn't shake his own feelings of disquiet.

They were halfway across when Mercer spotted something. About a mile away. Near where the protective ramparts rose off the bowl's floor, stood a man-made structure of some sort. "What the hell is that?"

He recognized it when they were a quarter mile off. "I'll be damned! It's a head gear, a mine's hoisting derrick."

The structure resembled an oil well drill tower, a tall spiderweb of rusted steel girders supporting a large flywheel forty feet above the ground. Next to the tower was a cluster of crumbling wood buildings, one of which, Mercer knew, would contain the head gear's machinery. The tower worked as the elevator mechanism for a mine. It would lower men into the bowels of the earth and haul mineral-rich material back to the surface in giant containers called skips.

After finding the diamond yesterday, he'd expected this discovery to be anticlimactic, but it wasn't. Every step that took him closer to Harry was better than the last. He was grinning at the old mine when a sudden thought struck him.

There were diamonds here. The Medusa pictures were a strong indication, and the stone rattling in a dashboard cup holder was the proof. Why, then, had the mine been abandoned? Mercer guessed the buildings were at least fifty years old, and that age made him understand. Most likely, this had been an Italian operation built during their occupation of Eritrea and abandoned when British forces ousted them in 1941. It was possible that the Brits didn't know about the mine site. Its location was remote enough to ensure its secrecy, and if Negga was any indication, the nomads avoided this valley. It was quite plausible that the mine had never been rediscovered, and if it had, during the revolutionary war maybe, the men who found it had been pounded into the earth by the long-distance artillery barrage.

Another question tickled the back of his mind. Eritrea's civil war had been over for a few years. Why hadn't the Italians returned and resumed their work? It was possible they hadn't struck the diamondiferous kimberlite, but they had to know of its presence. Surely they would have come back. And then he wondered if the kidnappers were Italian and not Middle Eastern—a complication that he hadn't even considered. This discovery was changing everything. Again.

Mercer braked next to the head gear, throwing open his door. Since this was a "lost mine," he felt confident that the ground had not been sown with explosives. The head gear tower straddled a twenty-foot square opening in the earth, an ominous black pit that dropped into the stygian underworld like the mouth of Hades. At its edge, Mercer tossed a stone into the hole, his eyes glued to the second hand of his watch. His wait was longer than expected. Finally, there was a faint click from deep below. He calculated the drop: one hundred and sixty feet. "Jesus."

"Effendi." Gibby stood in the doorway of one of the larger buildings.

The building looked like something out of an old Western, rough planking and a shallow roof covered with rusted metal. Mercer peered through the doorway over Gibby's shoulder, forcing himself to remain calm after he recognized the object on the floor. A mummy sat propped against one wall, the body of an Eritrean soldier left here by his comrades when they made their suicidal race out of the valley and into the waiting guns. The body had been so dried by the desert air that the skin on his face looked like a tight leather mask and his hands resembled claws. A dark stain blotted the front of his battle jacket. Obviously he had been wounded in a previous engagement and had either died here or was abandoned because of his injuries. The eye sockets were empty holes, the ragged teeth exposed in a gruesome rictus. Gibby dashed off and returned with the tarp, draping it reverently over the corpse, crossing himself repeatedly.

There were other reminders of the men who had camped here: empty shell casings, the mangled clip spring from a broken ammunition magazine, a blackened circle of stones that had been a fire pit, a heap of trash in one corner.

"We'll bury the body before sundown and use this building as our base," Mercer said. "It's too late to explore the mine shaft."

It was dark by the time Mercer and Gibby finished their grim task. Gibby fashioned a cross from a tent pole he'd snapped in two, thrusting it into the ground, praying over it silently. An hour later, the young man was snoring softly. Mercer rested with his back against the bungalow's wall. Though he was tired, it was still easy for him to stay awake. The kidnappers would be calling at midnight. Because he had given Habte the sat-phone with the stronger battery, he would power the device moments before the appointed contact time. He had plenty of thinking to do before then, about the mine, the kimberlite, and about Harry. As midnight approached, he felt his palms get sweaty and his heart race. There was a knot in his stomach that cramped his breathing.

He feared for the retribution Harry would suffer for the death of the European at the Ambasoira Hotel. Mercer knew it would be bad.

Washington, D.C.

Dick Henna had tried unsuccessfully to contact Mercer as soon as he left the Gradys, and when he couldn't reach the geologist, he called the White House. The president was in Alabama consoling the victims of a recent tornado and unavailable despite his desire for continuous updates. The man spent the night in Huntsville, returning to the White House more than twenty-four hours after Henna had made his discovery. He finally got the president on the phone shortly after seven in the evening.

"Yes, Dick, what can I do for you?"

"Sir, I'm calling about Prescott Hyde."

"What have you got?"

"I'd rather not say over the phone, Mr. President. I'm in my car right now heading into town. I should be at the White House in another twenty minutes."

"We're throwing a party here tonight for last year's Super Bowl champion Seahawks." The president was from Cincinnati, but he had met his wife while attending Washington State. He'd waited half a lifetime for this occasion. "I'll be in the main ballroom."

"After you hear what I've got to say, you won't be in the mood for a party."

Traffic was snarled crossing the Potomac, delaying Henna by an hour. The guard at the south gate checked him through quickly, and he parked in the underground garage. The main ballroom was filled to capacity, men in tuxedos and women attired in glittering gowns. There was the usual coterie of film stars and Washington elite as well as about a hundred of the biggest men Henna had ever seen. Despite the relaxed atmosphere, the largest men, the team's offensive line, still mustered around their handsome young quarterback, protecting him as effectively as they did on the field. The young superstar seemed grateful for the phalanx of teammates shielding him from the predatory advances of some of the city's more infamous man-eaters.

The president was at the head of the room, chatting with the team's coach. The First Lady stood stiffly at his side, bored with the whole affair. For Administration insiders, it was no longer a secret that their marriage would end as soon as his term in office was over. The president was just a few years older than Henna, but didn't look anywhere near his age. His body was trim despite a legendary appetite, and his hair was thick, gray just at the temples and along the edge of a boyish cowlick.

Henna ignored the introduction to the team's coach and took the president by the arm. He spoke only when they were out of earshot of the other guests. "Prescott Hyde was killed by the Israeli government, probably the Mossad."

In less than a minute, they were seated at the sofa cluster in the Oval Office. The president fixed each of them a scotch and listened to Henna's description of his time with the Gradys and about Selome Nagast and her connection to Israel. "Call Lloyd Easton at State if you want verification of his phone call from the Israeli Prime Minister," Henna concluded.

"I'm doing one better." The President's outrage was contained behind a calm expression, but it poisoned his voice. He roused a White House operator and had an international connection a moment later.

In Jerusalem, it was after two o'clock in the morning but David Litvinoff, the Israeli prime minister, was wakened by an aide as soon as it was learned that the President of the United States was calling.

"Mr. President, this is an unexpected surprise," the Russian-born Jewish leader said.

"Does the name *Selome Nagast* mean anything to you, David?"

There was a weighty pause on the secure phone line. "Yes, it does," the Israeli admitted. "Is she okay?"

The question took the president off guard, but he was too angry to consider why it had been asked. "She's going to be put in the Virginia gas chamber if we get our hands on her. She murdered a top State Department official and his wife, burning their house to cover her tracks. Do you know anything about this?"

"Damn," Litvinoff muttered. The president could hear him swing himself out of bed, mumbling something to his wife. "Mr. President, I am going to my study. I will call you back in just a few minutes. I can clear this up for you, but it'll open a whole new set of problems."

"Well?" Henna asked when the president put down the phone.

"He's calling me back, but it sounds as though he'd been expecting me to call."

"He knows Selome Nagast?"

"Apparently. He said he would explain everything, but it's going to cause us trouble."

"Any idea what he means?"

The phone rang before Henna received his answer. The President put the phone on speaker mode. "David, Dick Henna of the FBI is with me, and we both want an explanation why one of your Mossad agents is going around killing members of my administration."

"It is fitting that he is there," Litvinoff replied. "Selome Nagast does not work for Mossad. She's a member of Shin Bet, our version of your Federal Bureau of Investigation, and she did not kill Prescott Hyde."

"How do you know I was talking about Hyde? I doubt his death made the Jerusalem newspapers."

"Mr. President, if you'll permit, I will explain," Litvinoff said. "This is going to take a few minutes, so please bear with me.

"You know that I am facing a vote of no-confidence in the Knesset that will dissolve my government and call for general elections. If this happens, Chaim Levine, my current defense minister, will probably become our new P.M.

I don't need to remind you of his facist views and his plans to tear up the peace accords with our Arab neighbors. He also has this ridiculous idea about destroying the Dome of the Rock and rebuilding Solomon's Temple in its place. He has tremendous support since the Wailing Wall massacre two months ago. Even our moderate majority is leaning toward his camp."

"I don't need the political lesson, David. I have my own sources. Our prediction is that he'll defeat you by a five-to-three margin. We don't want to see it happen any more than you; the guy is a lunatic."

There was a new gravity to Litvinoff's voice. "What I'm about to tell you will damage relations between our two countries for many years to come. I would have rather not admit this, but I see no other way. The greater good must be considered." Henna and the president exchanged glances. "The Mossad has cultivated an asset in your National Reconnaissance Office, a highly placed photo interpreter. I would rather not reveal his name at this point. To do so would put his life in danger. However, he has been feeding us information gathered from your spy satellites, including the latest-generation Medusas."

Henna hated the idea of allies spying in the United States. Enemies he could understand, but Israelis using the U.S. in this way infuriated him. His hands clenched. He wondered if Admiral Morrison or Colonel Baines knew about this conduit and doubted they did.

"He started with the NRO two years after the first of those spy craft was launched and discovered a forgotten set of pictures taken during the ill-fated 1989 flight of the first Medusa. Because of security restrictions, he couldn't pass them to us through his normal channels, nor could he steal them directly. They could not be copied either. I understand it has something to do with the type of paper used in the printing process. However, he devised a plan to get them out of the NRO involving an Air Force officer as an unwitting courier. Our agent expected to meet up with the officer later that evening, but Major Rosen, the courier, discovered that he had them, realized their value, and made his own plans for disposing of them. As you know, they ended up with Prescott Hyde.

"Realizing he'd lost the images, our agent contacted his superiors, outlining what was on the pictures. Their contents came to the attention of Chaim Levine."

"I thought the Mossad was a civilian agency. Doesn't the military have its own intelligence arm?" Henna spoke for the first time. He recalled Rosen was the guy that the CID investigator said they'd already arrested. That meant the Israelis still had a spy operating in the NRO. He made a mental note to pass this new piece of information to Baines.

"It does, but Levine has many supporters in the upper echelons of Mossad. You are aware that the pictures show the northern sections of Eritrea and southwestern Sudan and may or may not reveal the presence of a diamond vent in the earth's crust. They may also reveal something else, something that I will get to in a moment, but trust me when I say Levine became very interested in getting the actual pictures.

"For some time, he's been building a private army from the ranks of our military, intelligence services, and anywhere else he could find useful people. These are men and women who share his beliefs and are willing to die for Levine's vision of Israel's future. Shortly after learning of the Medusa images, Levine sent one of them to Eritrea posing as an Austrian archaeologist. His name was Jakob Steiner, and his real job, of course, was to search for the kimberlite vent. He had been recruited by Levine from the geology department of Tel Aviv University. He was killed by bandits before he could find the vent." The Prime Minister paused, as though considering how much more he should say.

"Go on, David," the President prompted, his face suffused with the dark blood of fury at Litvinoff's disclosure. If anything, he was angrier than Henna.

"Levine had to get those pictures, so he ordered a team to Washington under the leadership of Ibriham Bein, a brilliant field operative who is both Palestinian and Jewish. Bein had turned his back on his Palestinian heritage and became a vehement Zionist. His orders were to get the Medusa pictures at any cost."

"Are you saying that Selome Nagast was working for this Bein?" the President asked.

"No, she's actually one of my people ordered to stop Ibriham and his team. We found out about Rosen's sale of the Medusa pictures to Prescott Hyde and sent Selome to Washington, putting her in contact with Hyde. Her Eritrean nationality convinced him that she could help discover the kimberlite pipe."

Things were clarifying for Henna. "That must be where Mercer comes in."

"I'm sorry, but I don't know anyone by that name." Litvinoff was clearly confused.

"He's an American mining engineer currently in Eritrea looking for that vent," Henna explained. "Selome Nagast and Prescott Hyde approached him to make the search." Suddenly Henna stiffened. "Oh Jesus, it's Israelis holding Harry White, not Arabs!"

"What?" the President asked.

"It's this bastard Bein who kidnapped Mercer's friend, Harry White." It took a physical effort for Henna to calm himself. "Mercer didn't want anything to do with Hyde, but shortly after their first meeting, Harry was taken from his home. His ransom is Mercer's participation in the search. Harry was spirited out of Washington on a private jet destined for Beiruit, which led Mercer and I to believe the kidnappers were Arab terrorists. Neither one of us considered there could be Jewish ones."

"I did not know about this kidnapping and apparently neither did Selome, but you have my word that if Harry White is in Israel, I'll do everything in my power to rescue him," Litvinoff promised. "And Mr. Henna, fanaticism and terrorism are not just the province of our Muslim friends. We Jews also have a long history of terrorist activities, less publicized, but no less brutal. Ask any British soldier stationed here after the Second World War."

"Then it was this Ibriham Bein who murdered Hyde and

his wife?" Henna realized Selome must have gone there right after Bein had shot them.

"Yes. He had probably tried to acquire the Medusa images through nonviolent methods, but when that didn't work, he resorted to intimidation or torture to get what he wanted."

Henna was putting the pieces in place. "Mercer must have been in possession of the pictures by then. Hyde was killed when the Israelis realized he was no longer an asset, was now, in fact, a liability because he knew about the diamonds."

"Correct! Selome Nagast showed up at their house after they were killed. She set the fire to delay an investigation and protect us and then got out of Washington. She returned to Israel right after that to brief me personally about what had happened. I'm surprised she never mentioned that mining engineer you just told me about, but she has an independent streak that tends to protect her friends if she feels our knowledge of them may pose a threat to their lives."

"So where is Ibriham Bein now and what can we do about him?" Henna asked.

"He's dead, which leaves us with a much bigger problem. It's now time to tell you why Levine is so interested in that kimberlite pipe and introduce an entire new faction, Italian and Sudanese, that complicates this mess even further."

It took an hour. Both Henna and the President were held spellbound by the story David Litvinoff told. It bordered on the unbelievable, but there was so much supporting evidence in the past weeks that neither doubted what was really at stake. When he had finished, the President had just one question. "Do you believe it's buried in that abandoned mine, David?"

"I don't know. It's possible. We're talking about an artifact my people have coveted for thousands of years, and Lord knows we've looked everywhere else. I guess it's a question of faith, Mr. President, which is a force of immeasurable power. Mine gave me the strength to survive labor camps in Russia and build a life here in Israel. However, it doesn't matter whether I believe it. Our concern is that Chaim Levine does, and no amount of bloodshed is going to stop him from proving he's right. If it is in Eritrea and Levine recovers it, he'll use it to rally Jews from all over the world to his cause. After that, you can forget about there ever being peace in the Mideast again."

Dick Henna grabbed the phone the instant the President hung up. Dialing quickly, he looked at the President when the connection was being made. "I've got to warn Mercer. He's got no idea he's sitting in the middle of a three-thousand-year-old battle."

"Calm down, Dick," the President said in a reassuring voice. "You know him better than I do, but Mercer has proven more than once that he can take care of himself."

"Yeah, but not when he's facing an ambush from two different fronts by people who have a very old score to settle." The phone was pressed tightly to his head, his knuckles whitening with the pressure.

Valley of Dead Children
Northern Eritrea

Mercer fell asleep a few times during his vigil, jerking himself awake only seconds after nodding off. His eyes were red-rimmed and scratchy from the fine particles of dust that invaded the dilapidated camp building. At eleven, knowing that if he drifted off again he wouldn't wake until dawn, he walked out onto the lonely plain, taking the sat-phone with him. The temperature dipped only slightly as night smothered Africa. The Milky Way was like a great smear across the sky. Wind moved silently across the landscape. The loudest noise he heard was the sound of his own footfalls on the cracked desert floor.

With about ten minutes before his appointed contact time, he activated the satellite phone and it rang almost immediately. Startled and wondering why the contact had come early, he pressed the button for the receive mode. "Mercer."

"Dr. Mercer, it's good to hear your voice again." It was the man who'd spoken to him in Asmara. Mercer hoped he'd been killed in the Sudanese attack on the Ambasoira Hotel.

"Can't say the same," he replied bitterly.

The caller ignored Mercer's quip. "I've tried calling several times, but your phone was deactivated. We have a great deal to discuss. Much has happened since our last conversation."

Maybe it was that he was standing near the mine's entrance and had already done what was demanded of him or maybe it was because he'd been pushed too far, but Mercer couldn't hold back his anger, couching it only slightly in sarcasm when he spoke. "Yeah, like you getting your ass kicked by a couple of amateurs trying to steal my underwear. They'd tried the night before. Fortunately, the maid scared them off with her mop. Looks like kidnapping defenseless old men is about the limit of your abilities. Maybe you ought to practice a bit more. Try taking candy from babies for a while—I hear it's tougher than it sounds."

"Your humor is strained," the voice said. "Perhaps this will dry it up entirely. Listen very carefully."

There was a short pause and Mercer heard a new voice. Harry! He sounded distant, as though he had been recorded and the tape played into the phone. Through the distortion, Mercer could still feel the terror in the old man's voice. He sounded as if he'd been through hell.

"Mercer, you've got to find that diamond mine. They've told me that if you don't reach it in the next two weeks, they're going to start cutting me." Harry's voice quavered. "They're keeping me in a rat hole with some shit that's worse than Boodles. I don't know how much of this I can take." Harry was cut off and the terrorist returned to the phone. "That should satisfy you that your friend is still alive. I'm maintaining our end of the bargain, how about you?"

"What did Harry mean about two weeks? I thought I still had four."

"Not anymore. You will give us the mine's location in two weeks or Harry White will be killed."

"I'm not even close yet," Mercer lied, looking at the black silhouette of the mine's head gear in the moon glow. Two weeks? That wasn't enough time to come up with any sort of workable plan and he knew it. *Shit.*

"That is your and Mr. White's problem, not mine."

"I have a lead," Mercer offered, adding a pleading note to his voice. "From a nomad family I met a couple of days ago, but I need more time. For Christ's sake, this is a big country! You've been reasonable until now. Give me an additional week. In three weeks I'll have the mine's location, I swear."

"You have two." There was a finality in the reply. "Now,

there's the problem of what happened in Asmara that we have to discuss."

"I didn't kill your man."

"I know that, Dr. Mercer. As we both now realize, there is another party interested in our activities, and it may become necessary for me to protect you and your team. You will tell me where you are right now."

"Do you really think I am going to trust your sudden concern in our well-being?"

"Our interest in your welfare is well documented. Hence the two dead Africans I left in your hotel room," the caller said placidly. "I consider you an employee and I want you to succeed. Tell me where you are."

"No. You want that mine and I want Harry White. That's our agreement, and you're going to leave me alone until I find it." Mercer's voice hardened.

"And the Sudanese?"

"I'll worry about them myself."

"You know I can't make you tell me," the other man conceded. "But when we next speak, I will have another tape recording and you'll hear Harry White losing his left hand." The phone went dead.

"Shit!" Mercer punched off and then dialed the satellite phone he'd given to Habte.

"Selam?" Habte answered immediately. As discussed before they separated, he'd been waiting for Mercer's call.

"Habte, it's me. I think I just screwed up with the kidnappers. They're making some threats and I believe them." Mercer was replaying the conversation in his head when he considered something odd Harry had said. *Some shit worse than Boodles.* What the hell was the old bastard talking about? "Listen, I'm not going to say too much, but I'm going to need that excavator sooner than planned. Can you start at first light?"

"Yes, the vehicle's owner has been working here repairing roads, but he told the city's council that he would have to leave at a moment's notice."

"Making a little money on the side?"

"I don't see anything wrong with that. Nacfa is in disrepair and excavating equipment is rare in Eritrea."

"As long as he's got full tanks when you get here," Mercer cautioned.

"He will. We also have the other equipment you had me pick up before you arrived in Eritrea."

"Good. We're going to need that generator and the portable floodlights." While the sat-phones were not secure from eavesdropping, Mercer felt sure that no one was listening to this particular frequency at this particular time. However, he wasn't going to take any unnecessary risks by broadcasting their location in clear. He gave Habte map coordinates roughly ten miles from the Valley of Dead Children, planning to send Gibby to guide them in the last few miles. "What's your ETA?"

"It will take us at least a day. That's rough country and the Adobha River may already be flooded. It would be best if Gibby met us at noon the day after tomorrow to be certain."

"Understood," Mercer said, still thinking about Harry White. Boodles was a brand name of gin. What was he doing with gin if his captors were Muslim and thus forbidden alcohol? Obviously, Harry was trying to tell him something, but Mercer was too tired to put it together.

Mercer woke Gibby as soon as it was light enough to see. He'd gotten just enough sleep to satisfy his body's immediate needs, but he felt slow and lethargic in the mounting heat of the dawn. Gibby agreed that he could stay in the valley assisting Mercer until the following morning and still make the rendezvous with Habte, Selome, and the bulk of their equipment.

After a quick breakfast, Mercer inspected the head gear's framework while Gibby unpacked all the rope they had brought with them. The rust on the steel struts was only surface accumulation; the metal underneath still appeared strong. There were only three fifty-foot lengths of rope in the Toyota, but if they attached them to the tow cable on the Land Cruiser, they would have enough to get Mercer to the bottom of the shaft.

He rigged a series of pulleys using the metal frame, wrapping the struts with wads of tape and smearing them with oil drained from the Toyota's sump to prevent the sharp metal from fraying the rope. He showed Gibby how to belay the harness Mercer had fashioned and devised a quick series of verbal and tugging signals for communication.

"Remember, Gibby, you're all that's keeping me from a quick drop to hell," Mercer warned, standing at the threshold of the old mine opening. Gibby had proved to be an able assistant, but Mercer still didn't like the idea of trusting his life to the teenager. The black pit seemed to want to suck him into its depths.

Mercer took several breaths and stepped off the crumbling edge, hanging above the hundred-and-sixty-foot void. Gibby struggled for a moment, shifting his grip, so Mercer dropped a few quick inches. "You okay?" Mercer gasped, a sickly smile on his face.

"Yes, *effendi,*" Gibby grinned. "Your rope tangle makes you weigh just a little bit."

The pulley system made it so Gibby was supporting only about fifty pounds of actual weight, but Mercer made sure the rope was still secured to the Land Cruiser's winch. When the time came to haul him out, Gibby would need the power of the Toyota to pull him to safety.

"All right, lower away."

Mercer dropped into a black world, the square of light over his head receding almost too fast. He switched on a six-cell flashlight and made certain his mining helmet was planted securely on his head. Bits of debris rained around him, pinging against the helmet and plunging down the vertical shaft. "Slower," he yelled, bracing his feet against the irregular wall to give him just a little slack in the line. He gave two quick tugs to reinforce his verbal command, and his progress slowed dramatically.

Down he went, the makeshift bosun's chair digging painfully into the back of his legs, the flashlight casting a white spot before his eyes. He trained it below his swaying perch, but the light could penetrate only a few feet. There should have been a steel guide rail bolted into the rock face to stabilize the skips and cages but there wasn't, and Mercer could see no evidence that one had ever been installed. It made him wonder just how far the earlier attempt at digging out the diamonds had progressed.

There had been no evidence of a crushing mill or separation facilities at the surface camp. Since they hadn't even installed a proper hoist system, it was possible the mine hadn't been worked for very long. Yet a shaft this deep would have taken a year or more to dig, considering its age and the quality of equipment available a half century ago.

He came to the first drift roughly eighty feet down. This was a horizontal working passageway the miners had dug off the central shaft in order to tunnel into the mineral-laden ore. From this depth, the shaft's surface opening appeared to be no larger than a storm drain. Mercer twisted himself across the open shaft until his boots landed firmly on the shelf that led off into the living rock. Whoever had opened the mine knew enough not to bore the main shaft straight into the volcanic vent, but rather sink a hole next to it and from there tunnel into the kimberlite ore. Mercer gave the signal for Gibby to hold the line where it was and unhooked himself from his sling, tying it to a wooden support beam so it wouldn't dangle back over the void.

The flashlight cut into the gloom, revealing a long tunnel that was roughly twelve feet wide, six high, and God alone knew how long. Mercer played the light along the ceiling, surprised not to see any bats. In fact, he hadn't noticed the guano smell so typical to abandoned mines. Like the Valley of Dead Children, the mine too was devoid of life. A chill ran up his spine that had nothing to do with the coolness of the subterranean passage.

He walked fifty yards down the drift before coming to the first cross cut, a right-angle passage roughly the same height as the drift by only half the width. For a moment Mercer considered taking this branch, but thought it better to keep to the main drive. Another cross cut appeared on his left after only a few more yards and then a third shortly after that. As he kept exploring, he again played the beam of the flashlight on the hanging wall—the ceiling, in mining parlance—and saw that bolts hadn't been driven into it to help its stability. The rock was mostly rhyolite and probably didn't need the bolts, but it deepened his concern. There was something very wrong about this mine.

He discovered a winze after two hundred yards, an open hole in the floor that dropped directly to the next level down. Such small vertical shafts connected two mining levels and frequently dumped into a haulage, a passage used for the removal of mined material. The wooden railing around the winze was dry and broken, and a descending ladder bolted to one side looked so weak it wouldn't support a mouse, let alone a man. He continued on. By the time he reached the working face of the drift, fifteen hundred feet from the main shaft, he'd passed a total of eight cross cuts, two winzes, and a raise, an aperture in the hanging wall over his head that meant there was another level above him, one not directly joined to the principal shaft.

His original estimate of the size of the workings was way off the mark. Without exploring the cross cuts, he could only guess that they at least doubled the amount of mined tunnels from just this one drift. There was still a further hundred-foot drop to the bottom of the shaft, and there was no telling how many more drifts there were. Depending on the stability of the rock and the way in which the drifts were driven, there could be several more miles of tunnels shooting off the original bore.

Mercer spent fifteen minutes at the working face minutely examining the rocks. The ore from the last explosive shot hadn't been cleared when the miners were pulled from the stopes, evidence that they had left in a hurry. Miners never, ever, left unprocessed ore in a mine. He sifted through the debris on the foot wall—the term for the floor—using brute strength to lever aside some of the larger chunks so he could scrutinize the rock face. No matter how he held his light, he could see no evidence of the opaque blue ground, the kimberlite, that would yield the diamonds.

He figured about a year had been wasted here with nothing to show for it. This drift had been a bust, worthless.

Back at the main shaft, he tugged on the bosun's chair, signaling Gibby, and slipped into the harness, cinching it tight around his legs and across his waist. He jerked twice more and stepped out into the void, spinning like a dervish as the rope took up the strain and unkinked itself. His descent was dizzying, but Mercer had done this before and felt no ill effects as Gibby lowered him farther into the earth.

He ignored the next three drifts, knowing he could explore them if necessary on his way back to the surface. As he expected, at the bottom of the shaft lay a twisted pile of machinery and hundreds of feet of braided steel cable. When the mine had been abandoned, the men working it had dumped their equipment into the hole rather than allow it to be taken by their enemies, probably the advancing English army. Mercer landed on a coil of hoist cable, the strands rusted together by Eritrea's seasonal rains into a solid mass of metal that looked like a modern sculpture. Below it, his flashlight revealed the top of the cage used to haul men out of the mine, and farther into the tangled gear, he saw a large ore skip. He played the light across the debris and saw that the equipment had not actually fallen all the way to the bottom of the shaft; it had jammed together about fifteen feet from the ground. Shining the light around the perimeter walls of the mine's sump, he jumped back dangerously when the beam flashed across a twisted corpse. It took several seconds for his heart to slow.

He picked his way across the pile of junk to get a closer look, the metal scraping against itself as his weight shifted its precarious balance. The body was in a similar state of decomposition as the Eritrean soldier he and Gibby had buried the day before, and his uniform looked about the same too. Mercer guessed that a curious soldier had stepped too close to the open pit, lost his footing, and plummeted to a quick death. Unhooking himself from the rope again, he signaled Gibby to hold his position—not that the lad would have much of a choice. With Mercer this deep, the line was at full stretch.

There were gaps between some of the equipment, a tangled warren of openings that Mercer could possibly edge his way through, gaining access to the mine's deepest drift, whose entrance was buried by the abandoned mining gear. Yet even in the best circumstances, making the attempt was dangerous. The scrap could shift, crushing him or trapping him without any hope of rescue. If he became stuck, there wouldn't be any way to signal Gibby, and even if he could, there wasn't anything one person could do to set him free.

But he didn't have a choice. Mercer took a moment to work his muscles, limbering himself for the challenge. He dropped to his knees, peering down into the shadowed jumble, picking his first moves with his eyes before committing his body. Like a contortionist, he twisted through the equipment, torquing and shifting constantly, lowering himself across the scaly steel, cutting his hands on the sharp edges, smearing skin off his legs and back. His clothes were reduced to rags. It was like moving through a huge knot of barbed wire. If he found a passage to the drift, it would be easy to retrace the trail of blood back to the top of the debris.

Eight feet into the pile, he maneuvered himself into a head-down position, flashing the light under the elevator cage where it had wedged against the wall of the shaft. The beam was swallowed by the darkness of another drift, the last one. His position put him at the inky tunnel's ceiling. Wriggling like a landed fish, he worked his body under the cage, holding his breath when a section of ruined equipment settled, grinding like a huge pair of steel jaws. He felt the pile was ready to collapse. Ignoring the pain as a piece of metal ripped across his back, he forced himself those last feet, tumbling into the drift as the junk gave out. The tons of machinery, precariously balanced for half a century, collapsed deeper into the mine's sump with an echoing crash, kicking up a choking cloud of dust. Had Mercer been a second slower, his body would have been cut in two as the cage sheared across the entrance to the drift like the blade of a guillotine.

His breathing raged despite his efforts to slow it, drawing in rancid dust with each inhalation. He took a second to check the worst of his bloody injuries. Once he'd recovered, he cast the light toward the clogged shaft. The drift's rectangular opening was completely blocked with an impassable wall of debris packed so tightly now that Mercer couldn't get his arm more than a few inches into it. He gripped a steel I-beam and heaved at it until stars and pinwheels flared behind his closed eyes. Yet the beam didn't move more than a fraction of an inch. When it collapsed, the cables, hoists, cages, skips, and all the other equipment thrown into the shaft had keyed into itself, locking together like puzzle pieces, plugging his exit. It would take explosives to dislodge any of it.

Mercer was trapped.

"Well, this is an unexpected wrinkle," he said aloud.

Mercer knew panic resulted from fear of the unfamiliar, and for better or worse, he had been trapped in mines before. He kept his fear firmly in check. As calmly as a man walking to his office, he turned and started down the dark passage. After only a couple of yards, he stopped short. Blood drained from his face, and his gorge rose acidly in his throat.

The long tunnel was a crypt with hundreds of bodies laid out like cordwood. Ranks of them lined both walls for as far as Mercer's flashlight could penetrate. He first thought they had been trapped down here like himself, but he realized that their postures were too orderly. These men would have struggled until the last possible second to get themselves out of the chamber. They would have been clustered at the shaft, not resting in these peaceful poses. He inspected the man lying closest to him, and understood. In the parched skin of his forehead, a neat hole had been drilled through his skull. Judging by their clothes, these men were the miners who had excavated the tunnels. They had been shot when the Italians had fled, their bodies abandoned here, the secret of the mine kept by their eternal silence.

"Jesus." Mercer was reminded of the slave labor gangs used by the Nazis to dig the clandestine underground factories for their rockets and jet fighters.

Walking by the grisly ranks, he judged there were more than four hundred bodies in the drift. Even as he fought his pity for them, he considered just what this meant and had no answer.

Delaying his search for a way out of the drift, Mercer took the time to walk all the way to its end. It ran for more than a mile, branching numerous times to both left and right. The hanging wall was just inches from the top of his miner's helmet. This tunnel alone doubled again his estimates of the size of the mine and the time taken to create it. Like the first drift he'd explored, the working face had been abandoned shortly after a shot. A mechanical scraper hulked just before the face, and the cables that maneuvered the plow-shaped machine ran back to a four-cylinder donkey engine. The miners had even left their picks, shovels, and pry bars a little way off, the metal kept pristine by the dry air.

A number of questions were answered for Mercer as he studied the rock face itself and examined the ore that had broken away from the stope. He turned away sadly. "Oh, you poor bastards, you never had a chance, did you?"

There was a whole other set of questions Mercer needed to think through, but first he had to get back to the surface. Having spent much of his professional career in the subterranean realm, he had developed the ability to map these three-dimensional mazes as he walked, part of his brain counting distances and angles without really being conscious of it. It was a skill honed with years of practice and allowed him to move underground with relative ease. He backtracked to the first raise he'd come across on this level. Peering up the black hole, he sensed that it wouldn't lead to the level above but would branch off into a subdrift. He searched for a cross cut that led to another drift, shorter than the main one and angled downward. A short distance down this tunnel, he came to another raise and inspected the ladder that ran upward. The wood had grayed through the years and was so riddled with dry rot that it felt chalky to the touch. Mercer tested the bottom rung, and his foot snapped the strut with only a tiny amount of pressure.

"Okay, we'll do this the hard way."

Instinct told him that at the top of this vertical raise would be a tunnel to the main shaft above the pile of ruined machinery. And his rope to safety. There was enough loose stone on the floor for him to build a mounded pyramid below the aperture. He hummed to himself as he worked, often switching off the flashlight to conserve the batteries, working in a darkness more total than the deepest night. After twenty minutes, the pile was high enough. With a ceiling height of just over six feet, he'd needed a platform of stones three feet tall and had built one nearly four. He aimed the light up the raise, but its ray vanished in the gloom.

The rubble was loose under his boots as he climbed to the top of the pile, ducking into the opening so the rim brushed against his thighs. Just to be certain, he tested another section of the ladder, tugging it gently, but the wood splintered in his hand. Mercer took a deep breath and jammed one foot against the side of the three-foot square vertical shaft. He levered his shoulder against the rock, kicked upward, and swung his other foot against the stone, lifting himself off the pile of gravel and bits of rock. Standing in the chimney with his legs akimbo, he would need both hands to steady himself as he continued the ascent, so he tucked the Maglite into his belt, shifted his weight to his left foot, raised his right a few inches, and rammed it against the wall again.

It took him fifteen minutes to shimmy twenty feet up the shaft because he could take only six-inch steps safely and had to force his palms against the rock face to help distribute his weight. He thought the raise would have ended by now, landing him in another drift, but still it rose into the darkness. To his horror, Mercer realized the shaft was widening; his legs were now spread more than four feet and the strain on his groin muscles and upper thighs was becoming unbearable. For the first time since the collapse of the machinery in the sump, he was starting to have doubts about getting out. He shifted positions, pressing both feet against one wall and forcing his shoulders against the opposite so that his body spanned the void.

Rolling his shoulders alternately and walking up the far wall, Mercer resumed his climb, blood soaking his shirt and running into his khaki pants. The shaft continued to widen as he climbed, making it necessary to exert more pressure against the walls to maintain his perch. If it opened much farther, Mercer knew he wouldn't have the leverage to bridge the opening and still be able to climb. He shut his mind to that possibility, but he was becoming desperate, his body aching in areas he didn't know existed. He was running out of strength, his muscles cramping, and knew he would never be able to control his descent if it became necessary. A fall from even thirty feet against the stone floor below would break bones. And in his position, he knew the most likely were his neck and back. Mercer climbed doggedly.

He realized he'd made it to the top of the raise when he could no longer hear stone scratching against his metal miner's helmet. Levering himself upward another six inches, he was able to kick with both legs and torque his body to the side, rolling himself onto the floor of the upper drift. He lay there panting, his cheek pressed to the cold stone, blood dripping from the cuts in his back and from the scrapes on his hands.

Five minutes ticked by before he could move again. He stood shakily, brushed himself off, and flipped on the flashlight. Ignoring the passage to his left, he moved off to the right, knowing he was in a main artery because of its size. After two hundred yards he could see shadows in the darkness cast from light spilling down from the surface. He looked at the luminous dots on his watch. It was not yet noon, but he felt as if he'd been in the mine for a day or more.

The rope was dangling just out of his reach at the drift

entrance, and he had to use his belt to snag it and draw it to him. In the gloom below he could see the abandoned machinery that had nearly trapped him forever. He gave the rope a sharp tug. Immediately, Gibby started hauling. When the bosun's chair reached this level, Mercer jerked the line again to signal Gibby to stop. It was only when he had stepped into the harness and secured himself that he pulled a flare from his pocket and sparked the igniter off the stone wall. This was Gibby's signal to start the Toyota and back the vehicle away from the head gear. The chair rose like a silent elevator.

The sun was a blessed relief after so many hours of darkness, and had Mercer's eyes not possessed a feline quickness to adjust, the brightness would have left him blinded. He shucked the harness and was leaning against the head gear's struts when Gibby drove back. Mercer felt an exhaustion that had nothing to do with his morning's work. Gibby had the foresight to retrieve Mercer's last beer and hand it over. Mercer downed the warm, gassy brew with several heavy swallows, belching so loudly it brought a startled guffaw from the Eritrean.

"Well, *effendi*?" The boy couldn't contain his excitement. "Show me more of the stones that will make our nation rich."

Mercer looked up at him, squinting against the blazing sun. Gibby looked like the image of a black Jesus Christ, a halo of sacred light cast around his head. Mercer dug something out of his breast pocket, a small misshapen lump. He tossed it to the eager teen, bowing his head.

Gibby stared at the bit of metal for a long time, his expression that of total confusion.

"It ain't riches, kid. It's lead from a bullet fired into the head of a man at the bottom of the mine, just like the four hundred other men who'd worked with him," Mercer said.

He'd discovered the body slumped over the controls of the scraper at the end of the lowest drift. He'd been murdered like all the others, executed not only to preserve the mine's secret location, but also to hide the fact that the entire project had been a failure. They had never hit the fabled blue ground, the kimberlite that held the diamonds. They had tunneled for years with their blood and their sweat, yet turned up nothing. And their reward? Their reward had been a summary shot to the head.

There were diamonds here, someplace, Mercer was sure. And with a couple of years, a few thousand men, and a couple hundred million dollars, he would be able to find them and bring them up. None of which he had, none of which would save Harry. The men holding him had said they wanted Mercer to find a mine, which he had, but he knew they would never accept this bust-out. They wanted diamonds, not a big hole in the ground, and they could set deadlines from now until doomsday and there was nothing Mercer could do to satisfy them.

"Son of a bitch," he muttered, dammed-up tears of frustration and grief and pain finally spilling onto his cheeks.

The Eritrea-Sudan Border

There were two rugged gravel roads that crossed the lonely border, both of them traversing a deep gorge bridged with rickety wooden structures that dated back decades. Near both crossings, roughly forty kilometers apart, refugee camps had grown out of the scrub plain, tens of thousands of miserable people huddling together in tents that offered little protection from the wind or the brutal sun. The tent cities housed Eritreans who could not return to their homeland. Since the intensification of Sudan's civil war, Sudanese natives too were seeking shelter here, hoping for the chance of a better life in Eritrea. Such was their desperation, they saw their impoverished neighbor as a promised land.

Situated close to the border and thus easier to reach, these camps were in much better condition than the reservations in Sudan's interior. The people here received regular visits from United Nations and EC trucks carrying food, medicine, and clothing transshipped through Eritrea.

At the bottom of the gorge, a thin trickle of water passed the camps, and each camp had a continuous chain of girls making the trip down and back, heavy pots of water balanced on their heads. Washing and latrines were situated a short way from where they took their drinking water, but by the time the stream reached the downstream camp, it was fouled by its neighbor. Diseases such as dysentery and other bacterial infections raged.

A farther ten miles south from the second camp was a third, one occupied by soldiers rather than refugees. A compound had been carved out of a rare grove of camel thorn trees, tents erected in their meager shade. A generator hummed a short distance from the camp, and a pump drew water from the gorge through a two-inch hose. A team of three men tended the fires for boiling the water, purifying it with heat before it was further chemically treated.

Despite the efforts to maintain a sanitary encampment, the fetid smell from the refugee camp wafted on the breeze, carrying with it the stink of sewage. That and the constant buzzing of metallic green flies were the two biggest drawbacks to the soldiers' camp, in Giancarlo Gianelli's opinion. He found everything else to his liking. His tent was large and air-conditioned, and the cooking was surprisingly good. One of Mahdi's rebel troopers had been a chef in Khartoum before taking up arms, and he delighted in the equipment Gianelli had brought into the bush. If he could ignore the armed troopers bivouacked around him, with their continuous arms practice and parade formations, Gianelli would have likened this to one of the elegant "Hemingway" camps run by the big safari companies in Kenya or South Africa.

Gianelli sat in the shade of his tent's awning, his view of the world beyond made indistinct by gauzy mosquito netting. His desk was mahogany, but cleverly constructed so it could be folded flat and easily moved. The matching chair was covered with zebra hide. A glass of sparkling water, blistered with condensation, rested in easy reach next to a laptop computer, allowing him to keep in contact with the many branches of Gianelli SpA through a satellite link.

Had the country been more interesting, filled with game, for example, he would have resented the intrusions of his business life here, but the desert was dry, featureless, and empty of all life save the stinking humanity farther north. So Gianelli filled his days of waiting with the tasks of running his multinational corporation.

As promised, Mahdi had secured enough soldiers for the mission. When the Sudanese Liberation Army's Revolutionary Council learned that the request had come from their biggest European supporter, they dispatched fifty men to the

Eritrean border under Mahdi's command, but Gianelli's control. The men were the best of the SLA, combat-toughened veterans who all had at least ten years of experience in the bloody bush war. With Gianelli's help, they were equipped with the latest NATO field gear, though they refused to use the new assault rifles, preferring to keep their venerable AK-47s.

"Mr. Gianelli, sir?" One of his white miners was standing outside the tent fly.

"Yes, Joppi? Come in, come in." The miners Gianelli had hired were expatriate South Africans who'd fled their country after the ANC took power in 1994. He had found them in Australia like so many other countrymen who feared living in the new black-run nation. Gianelli imagined many of them might return to their native country when his plan so destabilized South Africa's economy that the people would scream for the relative prosperity they'd had under the white regime.

The rangy Boer ducked through the mosquito netting and took a camp chair opposite Gianelli. "We've finished going over the mining gear you brought. Damn impressive stuff."

Gianelli had secured the services of five white mine supervisors, all of them master explosives experts and former shift bosses. They were to lead the hundred-strong gang of laborers Mahdi had promised. He had also brought five large diesel trucks loaded with mining equipment, big pneumatic drills called drifters, explosives, and several small utility trucks specifically designed to work in underground conditions. The equipment had been shipped to Africa over many months and stored at a Gianelli SpA facility in Khartoum, waiting until Giancarlo found the location of the mine his uncle had started so long ago.

Joppi Hofmyer lit a cigarette, leaving it between his lips so it jumped and danced as he talked, smoke coiling around his head, slitting his heavy-browed eyes. "Those fookin' *kaffirs* keep wanting to get to the stores of plastique, and I've had to crack a few skulls to teach them a lesson."

Gianelli smiled. "Nothing too rough, I trust. Those soldiers may save your life one day."

"Your typical *kaffir* has a skull like a boulder. A little beating may chip it some, but don't hurt it at all," Hofmyer grunted. "On the Rand, management never understood that a good whipping will get more work out of a black than extra meat rations or a fookin' dental program."

"Joppi, those men aren't going to work for you," Gianelli said irritably. "They are guards in my employ."

"*Ja*, and you expect us to work with the dregs from the camps? Mahdi's been bringing us a couple dozen at a time to check 'em out, you know? *Gott*, if we can use one out of fifty, we're doing well. Mining's tough work, and half those *kaffirs* can't even stand. And they're about as stupid as sheep."

Giancarlo logged off his computer to concentrate on his conversation with the South African. If they were going to reopen the mine, they were going to need labor. Mahdi had suggested, and Gianelli agreed, that recruiting able-bodied men from the camps was their best option. These men were desperate for work. They would do anything asked of them, grateful for the first job many of them had ever had. Most of them were second- or third-generation refugees. "How many have you gotten so far?"

"Forty." Hofmyer didn't catch the edge of anxiety in his superior's voice. "Once we get to work, I bet half of them will either take off when they get a taste of real work or die in the mine. The northern, fuzzier, *kaffir* is a delicate creature and can die on you without any warning."

"You've worked with Sudanese and Eritreans before?"

"*Ja*, in the Zambia copper mines when the country was still Northern Rhodesia. A few hundred of 'em came down to work the pits, but in five months they were gone again, half of 'em dead and the others willing to starve to death in the big famines up here."

"I hadn't realized," Gianelli remarked, sensing a serious problem.

"Don't worry about it. When it's time to go into Eritrea,

we'll have enough of the bastards to take up the slack of those that drop or take off. Any word on when we're heading in?"

"Nothing yet." No sooner had he said this than Mahdi appeared at the tent. He was layered with sweat, and his chest heaved in the hot air. "Yes, what is it?"

"Sir," Mahdi panted, "I was just at the refugee camp. About fifty men and their families crossed the border last night with a nomad who came here to recruit them. The rumor is that a great mine has been opened in Eritrea and men are needed to work it. Many other families are packing now to join them. I've learned that the nomad was sent here by a white man."

"That's it!" Gianelli bolted to his feet. "Mercer has found it!"

"Yes, sir, they are talking about a white overseer who knows how to talk to rock."

Emotion filled Gianelli in waves. The Medusa pictures had shown that Enrico had been right all along, and Mercer had used them to find the mine. There was a kimberlite pipe in northern Eritrea, one of the rarest geological features on the planet, and Enrico had found it decades ago without any modern aids. Enrico's Folly was now within Giancarlo's grasp.

Of course, Giancarlo had never known his great-uncle, but a large part of him admired the elder Gianelli for the independent streak that had driven him. Giancarlo had it too, that ceaseless desire to prove the impossible, to follow a belief to its only conclusion. He thought about his plan that followed the diamonds' recovery and smiled wickedly. While restoring Enrico's name was a noble goal, Gianelli had also made provisions to profit handsomely from this adventure. He debated making the call to London now, then decided it was better to wait and see just how many diamonds they could find before the Central Selling System's next meeting. His target was five thousand carats and, getting a sense of Joppi Hofmyer's brutality, he had little doubt they'd reach that goal.

"Mahdi, alert your men. We must move out quickly."

Gianelli's emotions raised his voice to a shout. "The refugees have a head start on us that we'll make up in the trucks, but I don't want them getting too far ahead. Joppi, I think our friend Mercer has gotten the rest of the men you needed to work the mine. Those Eritreans will supplement the men you've already recruited. Is everything packed on the trucks?"

"Ja." The Africaaner grinned. He was plainly relieved to escape the boredom of the camp. "We repacked them after checking each load."

"Mahdi, how fast can that refugee caravan walk through the desert?"

"If they left their women and children behind, twenty or more miles a day, but they are bringing their families. That would cut their progress in half."

"Good." The refugees moving so slowly tempered Gianelli's haste and changed his plans slightly. "Send out scouts to track them. It shouldn't be too difficult. We'll remain in camp until they get a few days ahead of us. That way we won't trip over them when we leave. That also gives us more time to get another fuel truck from Khartoum."

"Mr. Gianelli, if there are that many people at the mine, we're going to need more water too," Joppi remarked.

Giancarlo opened his laptop again and began a list. "Water, fuel, what else?"

The three of them worked for an hour, refining the list. By the time they had finished, they had the provisions to sustain the camp for several weeks without resupply. After that, they would start to bring stores from Sudan, which wasn't a problem given Gianelli's influence. In addition to his support to the rebels, he also maintained contacts with the government in Khartoum, working both sides of the civil war.

Gianelli concluded their meeting. "Mahdi, send out those scouts now, have them take a hand radio to report their progress. I'm going to order the rest of the equipment and supplies from Khartoum and make the necessary security arrangements. Joppi, you just make damned sure your men are ready to go."

"Yes, sir," both men said in unison. In the bizarre twist of Joppi Hofmyer's racism that made him hate the group but not the individuals, he held the tent fly open for Mahdi as they left the screened enclosure.

Valley of Dead Children

It was just before dusk when Habte, Selome, and Gibby arrived in the Valley of Dead Children on the half-loaded tractor trailer. Five minutes after the rig had crossed the secret bowl of land and trundled to the head gear, a bright yellow excavator tracked onto the plain, its hydraulic arm coiled to the boxy, rotatable cab. The operator had been forced to clear away part of the ancient landslide at the valley's entrance to allow the truck access to the mine site. Rather than reload the cumbersome machine, he'd driven it to the former Italian installation.

Wind whipped the dust of their progress across the landscape, eddies and gyres forming and collapsing in their wake. At the camp, both vehicles were shut down, and silence rushed in on them. Habte quickly followed Selome out of the truck, and he dodged into the main bunkhouse. Returning outdoors, he shielded his eyes against the red sun nestled on the western rim of the bowl and scanned for Mercer. The Toyota Land Cruiser was gone and there was no sign of him.

"Gibby," he called, and the boy scrambled off the trailer. "This is the right place. Where's Mercer?"

"I don't know," Gibby admitted. "He said he was going to wait here for us. He was upset that the mine was empty and seemed eager to talk to us. I can't guess where he went."

Habte ignored a creeping sense of alarm when Selome and the two hired drivers joined them. "What's wrong?" she asked.

"Mercer should have met us. But I don't see him." They

walked over to the head gear, both peering into the inky depth of the abandoned mine.

"Could he have been that upset?" Selome put to words the fear both were thinking.

"No," Habte replied sharply. "I just wanted to see down there for myself." He turned away from the pit. "It'll be dark soon. We should make camp."

"Where's the Toyota?"

"Mercer must have gone off exploring. He took the camping gear from the bunk house. I doubt we'll see him tonight."

"Will he be okay?" There was something deeper than friendly concern in Selome's question.

Habte recognized it even if she did not. "He knows Africa. He'll be fine."

An hour passed while they removed their camping gear from the tractor trailer. Selome spent more time looking across the horizon for a telltale plume of dust than helping Habte and the others. They ate dinner in the old bunkhouse by the hissing light of hurricane lamps, but there was little conversation. The men fell sleep long before Selome. She lay awake, her ears straining for the first hint of an engine's beat. But eventually she, too, dozed off.

Mercer swept into the cabin after midnight, waking everybody. His face and clothing were filthy, his hair matted with so much dust it looked like he wore a sand-colored skull cap. He was exhausted, his eyes closed to near slits, and he slumped gratefully to the ground near the camping stove. Lamps were quickly lit, and in their glow Mecer spooned the remains of their dinner onto the plate, avoiding the questioning looks they all gave him.

"Where have you been?" Selome finally asked, her voice full of emotion.

Mercer smiled at her. She was still a mystery, but he could feel her concern was genuine.

"If at first you don't succeed . . ." He grinned, then turned to Habte. "Any problems getting the gear?"

"We had to use the excavator to build a temporary ford over the Adohba River. It was flooding and we won't get the vehicles back across until it loses its swell. The good news is, we saw no signs of trouble in town. It is possible the Europeans have given up."

"No. They just don't know where we are." Mercer sopped up the last of his food with a piece of *injera* bread. "Damn, I needed that. I haven't had anything since breakfast."

"Gibby tells me you went down into the mine." Habte's statement invited an explanation.

"Yeah, it's a bust. They never hit the kimberlite, and Lord knows, they dug enough tunnels." Mercer accepted a cup of thermos coffee from Selome.

"This is the mine everyone is interested in?" Habte asked. It was obvious to them all that Mercer wasn't as upset as Gibby had led them to believe.

Mercer rested his back against the wall, struggling to keep his eyes open, an enigmatic smile on his face. "Oh, someone's interested, all right. I just don't know who."

"What do you mean?"

"There are two groups after us, right? And considering what Habte saw in Asmara and what I saw in Rome, they don't play well together. I think one group is after this mine, and the other wants something else entirely."

"Like what?" Selome asked quickly.

"Like another mine," he said, enjoying the astonished looks. He'd figured it out yesterday and had spent today testing his theory. "I'll explain everything in the morning," he sighed. "It's been one hell of a day, and right now I need some sleep." He was snoring softly before Habte could extinguish the lamps.

Mercer roused them at dawn and hustled them to get moving. He'd already made coffee and laid out bread and butter for breakfast. "We've got a full day ahead of us and sunshine is wasting." He offered no explanation to his good mood.

The owner of the excavator was the first Eritrean out of the old camp building, and when he saw Mercer seated in the cab of his machine, he started yelling, windmilling his arms to get him back off the vehicle.

"What's he saying?" Mercer asked Habte, who had come outside, drawn by the angry shouts.

"He says you are not qualified to operate his excavator. He must work it at all times." Habte was fumbling with a pack of wooden matches to light his first cigarette.

"Ask him if I can give him a demonstration of my qualifications," Mercer laughed.

The driver agreed to the request, and Mercer remounted the tracked excavator. The engine gauge showed the machine had been worked for several thousand hours and he doubted it had seen much maintenance in its long life, but it fired at the first turn of the key. He dismounted as the engine warmed, and he took the matches from Habte.

"I'll give them right back," he promised. He secured one of the wooden matches to the longest steel tooth on the excavator's bucket with some tape he'd found in the cab. He eyed the ground for a second before asking Habte to move a few feet closer to the excavator.

Back in the cab, Mercer tested the vehicle's hydraulics, rotating the entire body, extending the arm, flexing its three joints, and tilting the bucket through its ten degrees of play. Satisfied he could gauge the lag between his wrist movements on the joysticks and the machine's response, he glanced at his audience, a devilish grin on his face. *Damn, it feels good to be on some iron again,* he thought.

Selome, Gibby, and the two drivers watched, guessing at Mercer's intentions but none of them believing he could actually do it. The owner of the rig had a particular smirk on his face when Mercer accidentally overrevved the engine.

"Trust me, Habte, and don't move," Mercer warned.

He lowered the bucket to the ground, the sulfurous tip of the match almost, but not quite, touching the hard soil. His hands were feather light on the joysticks. He lowered the bucket that fraction of an inch more, twisting the cab on its gimble. The match flared against a rough stone, and as it burned, he rotated the cab, extending the boom so it swung dangerously through the air, the match nearly flaring out by the movement. Habte closed his eyes as the huge bucket swept at his head.

Mercer's feet and hands danced over the controls. He had judged perfectly. An instant before the wind extinguished the match, he touched it to the tip of the cigarette in Habte's mouth. The Eritrean took a nervous drag and laughed delightedly, a jet of smoke blowing from his mouth and nose. Mercer gave a mock salute to the applause from the others.

"How did you do that?" Selome's question was filled with awe.

He grinned like a boy. "I grew up on machines like this. My grandfather taught me when I was ten or twelve. Habte, ask the driver if I'm qualified to use his machine, then let's get the excavator reloaded. We're going for a little drive."

At the far end of the bowl, under the looming rock face of the northern ridge, Mercer slowed the Land Cruiser. He drove hunched to the windshield so he could study the cliff over their heads, using its irregularities for reference. Finally he stopped and the tractor trailer pulled up behind them. Mercer was on the ground in a minute, running up a long talus slope in the mountain. "Come on," he called down.

At fifty feet above the plain, he paused to allow Selome, Habte, and the others to reach a wide sandstone plateau. "What do you see?" Mercer invited, pointing out over the bowl.

"Nothing," Selome breathed.

"I thought the same thing when I first got up here yesterday." Mercer lowered himself onto his haunches.

"Okay, explanation time. After exploring the mine—which was dug during the Italian occupation, by the way—I had a hard time believing that there could be two different groups of people looking for the same defunct property. They didn't seem know about each other until the gun fight in Rome, and yet they are playing for the same high stakes. The chances that they were after the same thing without knowing about the other seemed pretty remote. So I started thinking that maybe both groups are after a diamond mine, but not necessarily the same one."

"What are you suggesting?" As Mercer suspected, there was something besides curiosity in Selome's tone.

"That there are two mines here, one dug before World War II and one worked a lot longer ago. I'm guessing those Europeans in Asmara must be representatives of the Italian company which built that head gear out there and sank the shaft. The Sudanese are coming at us from a different angle. They must know of the older, earlier mine in this valley but aren't sure of its precise location." Selome appeared to accept his explanation, but he noticed a discomfort that hadn't been there a second ago. In his scenario, however, he had no idea where Harry's kidnappers fit in. He considered that if Harry's captors had given him gin and might not be from an Arab terror group, he couldn't begin to guess at her and the Mossad's interested in this whole thing.

"Go on," Habte prompted.

"The older mine must have been lost long before the Italians came here or they would have discovered it themselves when they surveyed the valley. They sank their shaft a couple miles off the mark."

"Why do you say that?"

"They dug three miles from the kimberlite vent. It was an understandable mistake. Their geologist must have assumed the vent was in the center of this circular depression and drove the shaft accordingly. He didn't realize that erosion by wind and rain had shifted the surface topography in the past billion years, distorting the rim of mountains so they no longer surrounded the vent, but sat atop it instead. Now, assuming the vent had been mined by someone else before the Italians came, all I had to do was find the ancient workings."

"And did you?"

"I'm pretty sure," Mercer replied. "One of the keys to mining is ventilation, moving air into the underground workings to blow out the dust and provide oxygen to the miners. In the big mines in South Africa, they pump about sixteen tons of air into the shafts for every ton of ore they remove. Now, the problems of ventilation for an older mine, say one dug before modern machinery, are even tougher. I jury-rigged an anometer yesterday out of a metal can and a shovel handle after Gibby went to get you, then drove around the bowl, testing wind speed and direction until I found this spot. The wind whips over the northern wall of the depression, curls back on itself in a vortex that can gust to about twenty miles an hour." Mercer used his finger to draw a crude sketch in the soil. The drawing showed the side of the mountain with a V-shaped symbol pointing at its flank.

"The tricky part comes when you need to channel the air into the shaft, concentrating the flow exactly where you want it. Now, look again on the desert floor right below us."

It was Gibby, with his younger, sharper eyes who saw it first. "There," he pointed. "I see what you drew."

There were two faint lines in the dirt, just a shade darker than the rest of the desert. They were two hundred feet long, angling toward each other so they nearly met below where the party stood. They were too geometrical for nature to be their creator. They were the work of man.

"What are they?"

"All that remains of the foundations of two huge walls. Judging by their width, I'd guess they were at least seventy feet tall, more than enough to catch the wind blowing off the mountains and channel it into a mine entrance. I'm sure there are some vents driven into the mountain to allow an escape outlet for the wind, but I'm not too concerned with those quite yet."

"You mean, we are standing on top of another mine?"

"That's right." Mercer tempered his excitement with difficulty. "A horizontal drift tunneled into the mountain."

"When was this excavated?" asked Habte.

"I don't know. We can check the foundations to get an idea, but it's not really important."

"The question I want answered is, who dug this in the first place?" Selomė said.

Mercer glanced at her, feeling she already knew the answer. "We'll find that when we open her up."

An hour later, the excavator was ripping into the side of the hill, clearing away the dirt that had piled against the stone face. Mercer stood next to where the bucket clawed into the ground, using hand gestures to guide the operator. He kept a shovel with him, and every ten minutes or so would descend into the trench dug by the machine. The temperature was again hovering around a hundred degrees, and Mercer worked stripped to the waist. Every trip into the trench was more dangerous than the last. It was already fifteen feet deep and twice as long, its sides loose and crumbling. He used the hand shovel to dig a bit farther into the soil, exposing earth that hadn't seen daylight in who knew how many years. Carrying samples out of the trench, he examined each minutely before motioning for the excavator to continue.

"What are you looking for?" Selome asked when he emerged after the sixth time. Habte, Gibby, and the truck driver were busy unbundling the pallets of equipment secured to the tractor trailer.

"Overburden, the mine's waste rock." Mercer wiped the sweat from his forehead with a saturated bandanna. "When it was first excavated, they would have piled the worthless material at the entrance. It should be easy to detect it from the accumulated surface material."

"But if the mine's at the point of the two walls, why don't we dig into the mountain there?"

"Because I want to know what's in there before we reopen the shaft. It's a question of safety," Mercer explained. "And I'm hoping to discover the mine tailings, the kimberlite that has already been broken down and picked through."

"Why? We know the diamonds are here."

Mercer just grunted and watched her walk off. She knew there was something here, he was sure, but he wasn't banking on her interest being diamonds. He decided that when they found the mine's entrance, he would have his talk with her.

By noon there was a fifty-foot scar in the hillside. The side of the mountain had tumbled in small avalanches as its support was torn away, and the laborious process of digging had to be repeated. Mercer was at the controls of the excavator, and the Eritrean operator, named Abebe, was standing in the pit when the teeth of the machine bit into the first of the kimberlite tailings.

Mercer shut down the engine, bounding from his perch. Abebe was already on his hands and knees examining the pulverized bluish stones in the bucket. The kimberlite had been crushed into a fine aggregate, the biggest piece no larger than the first joint of Mercer's thumb. The men who had originally worked the mine had been very thorough in the processing of the ore, nearly powdering it to find even the smallest diamonds. To warrant this kind of extra work, Mercer knew, meant the mine's assay value was high. It also told him that this had been a massive operation, with hundreds or perhaps thousands of workers. Kimberlite was notoriously tough, and it would take days to hand-crush even a small amount to this consistency.

He took the shovel from Abebe and dug into the exposed vein of kimberlite waste. The digging was slow, for the rock had been cemented together by the weight of the mountain above it and the countless rains that had percolated through it. The shovel hit a particularly tough spot and Mercer tossed it aside, dropping to his belly to peer into the hole he'd created. He thrust both arms into the earth, wrestling something out of the ground. It was another type of stone, white and badly chipped, roughly the size of his fist. Mercer held it to the light with reverence.

"I'll be a son of a bitch." As he studied it, his estimate of the mine's age was pushed back several thousand years.

Abebe didn't understand Mercer's fascination with the lump of worked stone and ignored him when Mercer retrieved his leather kit bag from the excavator and placed the rock inside.

Selome and the others joined them a short while later. Gibby had made lunch, and Habte had found beer in the village of Ila Babu. They ate and drank in companionable silence. Selome sat close to Mercer, her knee almost touching his.

Habte translated a question from the truck driver. "Do you want us to work through the day? It is going to get hotter."

" 'Fraid so," Mercer replied. "I don't know how long our presence here will remain a secret. The mountains contain most of the noise from the excavator's engine, but people on the other side will be able to hear us."

The driver nodded at the response, but it was apparent he wasn't too happy about it.

"We're just about ready to open the mine entrance," Mercer said to lighten their mood. "We hit the kimberlite tailings just before lunch, and I'm satisfied that we can open the mine without any danger."

"What do you think we'll find?"

"I have a theory," Mercer said, then looked at the youngest member of their party. "Gibby, Habte mentioned there's an old monastery near here. Do you know where it is?"

"I can show you," Habte replied. "It's about sixty miles away."

"No, I need you here to start opening the mine, but I want to go up there and talk to the priests. Gibby, do you know it?"

"Yes. I think I can find it from here, but it is far." The teenager didn't sound sure.

"Talk to Habte about it. We won't be leaving for a day or two anyway."

"Why do you want to talk to the priests?"

"That monastery has been here for a thousand years. And I'm willing to bet they already know about this mine and the people who opened it."

"But what do you wish to learn?" Selome pressed.

"If I knew that, I wouldn't need to talk to them, now would I?" Mercer stood and brushed off the back of his pants. He was sure that Selome had detected a change in his attitude toward her. She'd been playing him for a fool, and it pissed him off. She knew what this was all about, had known since the beginning, but still was asking questions she knew the answers to. Mercer had some questions of his own, and it was getting time for the answers.

They worked for three straight days, each of them settling into a routine that left them wasted when the sun finally set. Habte and the truck driver rigged a plow on the front of the ten-wheeled rig to use it as a bulldozer. They worked in unison with the excavator, pushing aside the piles of debris that the big Caterpillar stripped from the side of the mountain. Mercer and Abebe took turns running the excavator while Gibby stood in the excavated sections, guiding the bucket to maximize the bite it took with every scoop. Only Selome, who didn't have a specific task related to the digging, balked at the traditional female role of housekeeper and chef.

Late afternoon on the third day, there was still no sign of the mine entrance. The team was gathered at the excavation. The ground had been compressed by the movement of the excavator until it felt like concrete. They had opened up a chasm nearly sixty feet wide and over twice that deep. The mountain towered above them. It hung precariously. From the bottom of the chasm, the sky was just a narrow blue band between the two sides. Habte and Abebe were smoking cigarettes while Mercer pulled from a bottle of beer. They were all frustrated by the amount of work and the lack of results.

Mercer broke the tired silence. "I'm going to have to blast the mountain. We've dug so deep, I'm afraid that lot over our heads is going to come down pretty soon. We have to cause our own avalanche, and that'll mean at least another full day to clear the debris before we can continue to dig for the mine entrance."

"No other way," Habte agreed. "We did the same thing when I worked in the quarries."

"Did you get the fertilizer I requested?" Mercer asked as he finished the last of the beer.

"Ammonium nitrite, two hundred pounds' worth. And I got five thousand feet of detonator cord." The explosives

Mercer had requested when still in Washington had been abandoned in Asmara so he was forced to improvise.

"Good. We'll use the diesel from the truck's auxiliary tank. We won't need that much punch—the mountain will collapse with just a good swift kick." He looked at the hill, gauging where he would place the amfo. "After I make the shot, Selome, Gibby, and I are going to the monastery and have a chat with the good fathers."

"Why do you need me?" Selome didn't sound like she minded the trip, but she was curious.

"No offense to Gibby, but his English isn't much better than my Tigrinyan. Congratulations, you've been promoted from scullery wench to interpreter."

Selome smiled. "Give me another week and I'll be running this operation."

"That's the spirit." Mercer matched her smile for the first time in days. They'd have a chance to talk on the ride to the monastery.

Asmara, Eritrea

Night was his element. Yosef had the ability to blend with the shadows so he was like a wraith on the nearly deserted streets, easing around the puddles of light cast by an occasional street lamp. His motions were deliberate, his pace deceptively quick though he did not hurry himself.

After eleven in the evening, Asmara virtually shut down. Even the busiest streets were devoid of cars, and there was little chance of running into pedestrians. In all his previous nocturnal meetings, the rogue Mossad agent had yet to see a police patrol.

Since their return from Nacfa, he and his team had holed up in a rundown hotel near the old Soviet-style parade ground. The hotel's owner, though harboring suspicions, had been paid enough not to ask questions about his guests. Asmara's police were on the alert for a European in connection with the shootings at the Ambasoira Hotel, and while they did not have a good description of Yosef, he maintained constant vigilance. According to *Profile,* the authorities were more interested in the two Sudanese terrorists and the others responsible for a disturbance at the old market and cattle stockade. The newspaper's editorial was calling for a crackdown on all Sudanese in the city, many of whom were there illegally, and barely mentioned the white man who had killed the two rebels.

This apparent lack of interest gave Yosef the time he needed to cultivate a contact in the city. Because of his nationality, he already had an established support network nearly everywhere in the world. After returning to Asmara, he had needed only a few hours to find it.

Asmara boasted a very small Jewish community, just a few families, and only a couple of them had the resources he could use. Of course, there was Selome Nagast's family, who would certainly be able to get the information he needed, but it would be impossible to go to them for obvious reasons.

Though there were no formal synagogues in the city, there was a rabbi who taught and held services in his home, a man in his late thirties with a pretty wife and two children. His father had been a rabbinical student in the United States during the fifties who had trained his son so he too could shepherd Eritrea's Jews. Hoping for a better life for his own children, the ersatz rabbi wanted his children to go to university in Israel when they were old enough, and Yosef used the leverage to make him an accomplice.

Aharon Yadid had welcomed Yosef that first night with something akin to worship. Not only was the secret agent from the fabled Holy Land, but he was also a member of the Mossad, the agency most responsible for protecting the Jewish state. The young rabbi had never been to Israel himself and felt disconnected by his isolation from the rest of world Jewry, especially since Operation Moses had airlifted thousands of Ethiopian Jews to the homeland.

Aharon met Yosef at the door of his one-story bungalow, having observed the Israeli agent through the curtained front window. *"Shalom, shalom,"* he greeted eagerly, showing off his only word of Hebrew.

"Hello, Rabbi. I hope this night finds you and your family well?" Yosef spoke in English, the only language both men could use.

"Yes, we are well, come in, please. The children are already asleep and my wife has gone to a friend's. She won't be back for a while, so we can be alone."

"Good."

Aharon turned on a single lamp. The interior of the house was Spartan. The Yadids were not wealthy, although the furniture was well cared for and the feminine touches of flowers and colorful prints on the scrubbed walls made it cheerful. Yosef demurred an offer for refreshment and both men sat quickly.

"I know I have said this at all of our meetings," Aharon gushed, "but I want to tell you again how much it means to me to help you and to help our beloved Israel."

Yosef regarded Aharon's open face, saw the innocence in his eyes. He wondered how many years had passed since he too had believed so strongly in what he did. "It's the duty of every Jew to help our homeland, and it's refreshing to find a man who knows this and embraces it. Jews in America just give money as long as it isn't too much of a sacrifice."

"My father spoke of that often," Aharon agreed.

"So, my friend, what have you found out for me?"

"You were wise to come to me, but not for why you think. There is only one Jewish family living in the north, and when I reached them, they knew of nothing unusual taking place near the border. But the brother of my wife's closest childhood friend owns a small shop in Nacfa, and he said there was a truck there for many days working on the roads."

"Yes, I remember seeing it, an excavator of some kind. I assumed it was owned by the government."

"It wasn't. This friend of a friend spoke often with the machine's owner and learned that he was waiting to take his equipment up near the Hajar Plateau for another job, a secret job." Aharon was gladdened by the look of interest in Yosef's eyes. "I learned just today that the excavating machine has left Nacfa and headed for Hajar, or more accurately, a place the nomads call the Valley of Dead Children."

"Do you know this valley?"

"I've heard it is a bad place. There was a massacre there during the war, several hundred Eritrean soldiers were killed in a surprise artillery attack, but even before that, it was a place that people avoided. Eritrea is riddled with superstition, and I've learned that the Valley of Dead Children is one of the most feared places in the country."

"Do you know why?"

"No. I don't believe in superstitions. They are the providence of the ignorant and unenlightened. Many of the nomad clans are still animists. They worship their ancestors and hold pagan rituals. Their petty fears are of no interest to a learned man like me."

Yosef struggled to keep the smirk off his face. Even this man, with secondhand knowledge of his faith, was a snob. "How can I find this valley?"

Aharon handed a folded piece of paper to the Israeli. "This is an old military map that shows the location of the valley. It is marked with a red cross denoting a site of a battle in which Eriteans were killed. There are no roads leading to it that I could see, and you must cross the Adobha River, which the friend told me is now in full flood."

Yosef glanced at the map. They still had the rented plane they had used earlier to leapfrog ahead of Mercer when the engineer had fled Asmara. They would simply fly over the natural barrier of the river. Judging by what he'd seen of the northern desert from their drive back from Nacfa, there would be no problem finding a level place on which to land the aircraft near the valley. He forced a smile. "You have done very well, and when I return to Israel, I promise that I will make certain your children will be sponsored to study at Tel Aviv University."

Before Aharon could show his gratitude, his wife stepped through the front door. Aharon told her of Yosef's offer, and she rushed across the room to throw her arms around the Israeli, tears of happiness streaming down her cheeks. She spoke to him in excited Tigrinyan, her emotions transcending language.

Yosef barely acknowledged her joy. His mind was planning out the next and perhaps final phase of the operation. Mercer must have been at the mine when he had been contacted earlier and had lied about his location. The American had bluffed, and Yosef found his anger rising at such an insult. The Israeli agent had told Mercer that Harry White was going to lose a hand, though Yosef hadn't intended to carry out the threat. But now? Yes, he would order it done. He would record the sounds with the microcassette he carried, as he had done for White's previous message.

He considered that if Mercer had found the mine and was working to reopen it, there would be no reason for his team to return to Asmara after reaching the valley. And after tonight Yosef could not afford to be seen anywhere in the country.

"Yosef?" Aharon broke into his silent musings.

"Yes?"

"My wife wants to do something for you to show our thanks, perhaps a meal in your honor."

Yosef gave him a sad smile, "That won't be necessary. Tell her another hug is thanks enough." He stood, his right hand hidden behind his back.

The woman's arms came around his neck, her cheek pressed to his chest. *"Yekanyelay,"* she sobbed. *Thank you.*

"I am sorry," Yosef said quietly in Hebrew.

He used his knife. Normal procedure dictated he kill Aharon first. As a man, he posed more of a physical threat. But Yosef decided that watching his wife die would stun the rabbi enough for him to dispatch the Eritrean before he recovered. Further, a woman's reactions are quicker than a man's, and her scream would likely have alerted the children asleep in their beds.

Yosef was across the room, plunging the bloody blade into Aharon's chest before the body of his wife hit the rug covering the wooden floor. The rabbi stood still as the knife came at him, his eyes fixed on a horror beyond his comprehension. In seconds it was over, and Yosef was back on the street, heading toward his hotel.

For security reasons, he had no choice but to kill them. Someday, Aharon Yadid would have told a friend about the Israeli agent he had helped, and that was a leak Yosef could not afford.

There was a great deal to accomplish before he and his team left for the Valley of Dead Children. He had to contact the team members in Jerusalem guarding Harry White and order his mutilation, a task he would enjoy for the pain it would cause Mercer. He also had to reach Defense Minister Levine and order the helicopter for when the mission was over. The Israeli Defense Force had CH-53 Super Stallion helicopters that could make the flight with their upgraded inflight refueling capability and safely return with their precious cargo. It would take some coordination to have flying tankers standing by to support one of these choppers, and only Levine could clandestinely order all the necessary equipment.

Even through the churning ideas that flooded his brain, Yosef still found a few seconds to consider what he would find at the mine. The idea was staggering. Not only would it ensure Levine's election, there was something even larger at stake than a political victory. Out in the desert lay hidden a tangible link to the founding of Judaism, a talisman unlike any other religious artifact ever unearthed. If they could bring it to light, it would make the great Dead Sea Scrolls pale in comparison. A piece of living history was within his reach now, something stolen from Israel hundreds of generations ago that had become his destiny to bring home.

He shook himself of these feelings and refocused on his job. Things were coming into place. First was the location of the mine. And now he finally had an idea who was behind the Sudanese attacks in Rome and at Mercer's hotel. Yosef had learned from Archive, their secret tap into the Mossad computer system, that Italian industrialist Giancarlo Gianelli was under investigation by the FBI and Interopol in conjunction with documents stolen from the United States. Yosef harbored the suspicion that they were talking about the Medusa pictures. Taking into consideration Italy's colonial presence in Eritrea, it seemed likely that Gianelli was after the pictures and the mine. He guessed that the Italian was behind the Sudanese, perhaps using them as a mercenary army to thwart Mercer's and indirectly Yosef's own efforts.

What he didn't know was how close the Italian was and if he knew about what really lay hidden out in the northern wastelands.

Jerusalem

Security all over Israel was still on a heightened alert even after two incident-free months had passed since the deadly bombing at the Western Wall. Nowhere was this more apparent than within the towering ramparts surrounding Jerusalem's Old City. Armed patrols walked the narrow, twisting streets in even greater numbers than during the *Infitata.* While every Israeli citizen had to perform two years of active military service, it appeared that the IDF was using only the toughest veterans to patrol the sacred city. Uniforms and machine pistols were a common sight all over the country, but the grim faces of these shock troops chilled even the most impassive residents.

The streets and meandering alleys were eerily quiet this night except for the low mutterings of the patrols and the occasional rustle of feral cats picking through garbage. The shops were boarded up for the night, and little light escaped from the shuttered windows of the houses. The gibbous moon shone on the cobbled roads, its milky, otherworldly light only adding to the haunted feeling of the city.

Beyond the crusader walls, the new city of Jerusalem, too, was quiet. The presence of so many armed soldiers patrolling the streets and neighborhoods, harassing both Jew and Arab alike in their search for terrorists, had strained the patience of the inhabitants to the point where they no longer ventured out unless absolutely necessary.

In the safe house within the old city, the strain of maintaining vigilance was also telling on the remainder of Yosef's team, those charged with guarding Harry White. These soldiers were the group's lowest ranks, those with minimal combat experience. The best of the organization had gone to Eritrea with Yosef, leaving the younger, less-trained zealots to hold their prisoner. Without Yosef's direct control, discipline had started falling and was now at its lowest ebb. While their belief in their cause and in Defense Minister Levine had not wavered, they'd lost interest in babysitting a cantankerous old man.

The younger members chafed at the forced inactivity. Arguments had become a problem. Rachel Goldstein, the nurse who was the ranking member in Yosef's absence and now team leader, found herself treating cuts and abrasions from the fights that broke out with increased regularity. Her authority was all but gone, and she realized that if they didn't receive new orders soon, they would murder the old man and leave for their homes.

Fervency, like flame, needs fuel to burn brightly. Untended, it can quickly die.

Then, finally, direction had come. Minister Levine had called earlier in the evening with word that he wanted them out of the city. He promised them a new safe house at a secure military base in the Negev desert, adjacent to the Demona nuclear research facility. This was welcome news, but Levine had not specified how they were to get past the security patrols in Jerusalem. Rachel had asked him about safe passage out of the city and Levine had responded that he could not issue such orders without rousing suspicion. He explained that the curfew in effect all over Jerusalem could not be broken for any reason without direct orders from Prime Minister Litvinoff, no exception. She had argued with him fiercely, but the Defense Minister didn't budge.

Because vehicles were not allowed in most parts of the Old City, Rachel realized they would have to walk Harry White to a van they had waiting in the new city, making their task that much more difficult.

Rachel had already sent one man to get the van and wait for them outside the Zion Gate on Eziyyoni Street. He had a cellular phone and would call when he was in position. She sat at the kitchen table with the rest of her people, discussing ideas that would make their evacuation easier, but so far they had come up with nothing inspired. Their lack of training and experience showed.

"I guess we will have to go with the idea of a diversion," Rachel surmised after thirty minutes of wasted conversation. "Jacob and Lev will leave here when David calls from the van." The two agents nodded. "I want you at least a half kilometer from the safe house before starting anything. What you do for a diversion is at your discretion—a burst of automatic fire into the side of a building should be sufficient. I needn't remind you that you can not be apprehended."

She noted the excitement in the young men's faces. They didn't understand her completely, so she spelled it out for them. "If it appears that you'll be captured by a security patrol, your only option is suicide. We can't take the risk of your capture exposing us. There is no way you would ever be able to stand up under a physical and pharmacological interrogation."

"Yes, ma'am."

"Moshe?" She looked at the youngest member of the team, the man most responsible for watching Harry White. "Get our prisoner ready. We should be leaving within ten minutes."

"Okay," the boy said smartly.

Harry knew something was up as soon as Moshe entered his cell. As the days of his captivity ran into each other, their interest in him, and thus their attention, had slackened. It was unusual for his guards to check on him unless it was meal time. Not being harassed gave him some comfort, but it didn't offer any better chance of escape. They had guns and he did not.

Always a thin man, Harry had lost weight during his captivity. His cheeks hung like empty pouches off his face, and his bright blue eyes had sunk behind wrinkled folds of skin so they almost disappeared in his head. Despite his ragged appearance, he felt better than he had in years. He'd drunk sparingly of the bottle of gin Moshe had given him and still had nearly half left. At first it had been difficult not to polish off the bottle in one drunken sitting, but after getting over the physical craving, Harry's discipline surprised even him. Back home, he drank more out of routine than any deep-seated emotional problem, and with the tension he'd experienced in the past weeks, boredom was no longer a problem.

Once this ordeal was over, however, he promised himself a week-long bender. But until then, he had to keep sharp. Knowing his life depended on his actions, he allowed himself only a few small sips before falling asleep after his dinner. Three weeks of near sobriety had done wonders to clear his mind of fifty years of accumulated hangovers. He was a bit more liberal with the cigarettes but he still smoked less than half a pack a day. A few more weeks of this, he joked to himself, would leave him feeling like he wasn't a day over seventy-five.

"What's going on?" Harry greeted the young Israeli when the boy nudged him gently awake.

"We are leaving, Harry. Get dressed."

Harry sat up, swinging his foot to the floor. His prosthetic leg leaned against the wall like a little-used umbrella. "Time for another bogus call to Mercer?" Harry could only hope that his friend had understood the reference to Boodles during their last communication. Of course, the brand Moshe had given him wasn't Boodles, but he was sure the men holding him wouldn't recognize the brand while Mercer should. Even Harry knew that if Moshe drank, he couldn't be a Muslim as he had first guessed.

"No, Harry, we are leaving this house," Moshe replied while his prisoner strapped on his leg and began to dress.

Excitement tickled the back of Harry's brain. He'd thought that if they ever moved him again, and they didn't drug him as they'd done the last time, he might find a way to escape. He kept his voice neutral. "Where we headed?"

Moshe gave a small laugh. "You know I can't tell you that."

"Yeah, yeah, yeah." He finished with his shirt and reached into the bundle of blankets to retrieve the gin still cached there. "Can I at least bring this along? Nothing makes time pass quicker than a drop or two of liquor."

Moshe's expression brightened. "We will share it on the drive. We'll have a few hours together. But you must cooperate with us when we walk to a vehicle we have waiting."

"Come on, my boy, look at me," Harry chuckled. "Does it look as if I have a choice?"

Moshe laughed. Harry was as threatening as a toothless tomcat.

Their driver, David, called twenty minutes later. He was waiting at the Dormition Abbey just outside the Zion Gate. Lev and Jacob left the safe house immediately, their Uzis hidden under long dark coats.

"All right, people, get ready. They should be in position in a couple minutes. As soon as we hear the gunfire, I want us moving," Rachel ordered.

The wait was only seven minutes.

The sound of gunfire was muted by the distance. Still it echoed throughout the old city. Rachel's face remained impassive as they paused at the door. Seconds later, the night was filled with running feet and police whistles. She could imagine the people in the neighborhood cowering in their beds, quietly asking each other what was happening.

"Okay, let's go."

There were only four of them including Harry White. Moshe kept a tight grip on the old man's arm as they eased out the door. Rachel took the lead, an automatic pistol held discreetly against her thigh. They had to cover about three-quarters of a mile through the Jewish Quarter to reach the waiting van, and while she didn't like the exposure, she had no choice.

Harry's mind worked furiously. He tried to recognize any landmark that might look familiar as they moved, but nothing came to him. He was in the Middle East, of that he was sure, but had no idea where. The one clue he had—Moshe drinking the gin with him—gave him nothing. And then he realized that a woman was now leading the team. A woman! Not in an Arab country. In a rush everything came clear. His kidnappers were Jewish! Some Israeli extremist group, no doubt.

He should have seen it all along. Moshe was a Jewish

name, the name of a former Israeli leader. "Shit," he cursed himself under his breath.

But how to make this work to his advantage? This was his best opportunity to escape, and still he had no ideas. Muslim or Jew, it didn't matter as long as they were armed. He did sense the group's tension and wisely decided not to delay them by intentionally slowing his pace. He could tell they were all in danger.

Rachel stiffened when she heard a group of men running toward them. She hid the pistol behind her leg just as a dozen soldiers rounded a corner a half block away, their equipment slapping against their uniforms. As soon as the security patrol spotted the four people breaking the curfew order, their weapons came up, twelve fingers tightening on the triggers.

"No, please, wait!" Rachel cried in Hebrew. "We are Israeli citizens!"

"What are you doing on the street?" the ranking soldier called back, his weapon centered on Rachel's head.

"There was a shooting close to our apartment, my grandfather was frightened," Rachel improvised, pointing at Harry. "He demanded we leave immediately. He is very ill. The strain is bad for his heart."

"Return to your home at once," the soldier ordered. "You should not be out here."

"I know, but we cannot calm him." She lowered her voice to draw on the soldier's natural compassion. "His wife, my grandmother, was killed in the bombing at the Wall. He has not been himself."

At that revelation, the leader of the patrol lowered his weapon, and his troops followed suit. The soldier looked at the group critically, deciding that a woman, two boys barely out of their teens, and a man who looked as though he would die at any moment did not pose a threat. The radio on his belt squawked, and he shifted his attention from Rachel to it.

"A patrol has made contact," he said to his group. "Two men armed with automatic weapons. They've split up. I think one of the bastards is heading our way." He looked at Rachel again, but already his concentration was on the hunt for the renegades. "Clear the street as quickly as you can. There are two of them out here tonight."

Harry watched the exchange, realized that the patrol was about to leave, and got a sickening inspiration. It was now or never. *God forgive me for what I'm about to do.* Then as loud as he could, he screamed, "Heil Hitler!"

His shocking outburst had the desired effect. The patrol swung back toward the group of kidnappers, and in the split second of indecision, one of the young Israelis with Rachel was startled and drew his weapon. Harry dropped to the ground as the patrol's Galil assault rifles chattered, the street dancing with the fire of the muzzle flashes. Rachel dove out of the way, bringing her pistol up. She dropped one of the soldiers with a double tap, the trooper's throat exploding with the impact of the two rounds. Another soldier was taken out before the patrol managed to direct their aim with more accuracy. Moshe was dead from a dozen bullet wounds before his corpse hit the ground.

Rolling on the cobbled street, Harry maneuvered himself around a corner and out of the battle as gunfire whined over his head. In the gloom ahead, he saw a dark figure running toward him, a machine pistol at the ready. He guessed that it was one of Rachel's diversionary troops, and he slunk into a darkened store entrance to let the kidnapper pass, knowing he would add to the confusion behind him.

Lev's Uzi had a sharper sound than the patrol's Galils, and a full magazine exploded into the ranks of soldiers, scything down four of them and wounding three more. His burst gave Rachel the covering fire she needed to race from the confined street, firing behind her as she managed her escape, limping badly from a bullet lodged in her upper thigh.

Harry didn't wait to listen for the patrol's return fire. He got to his feet and started running, keeping to the shadows, cutting through any alley he came to in an effort to lose himself in the ancient city.

The only thing that saved him from being picked up was the patrol's diminished number and the fact that they tracked the fleeing kidnappers slowly, fearing an ambush. In ten minutes, Harry felt he had put enough distance between himself and the firefight to rest for a few minutes and consider his next move. Savoring freedom for the first time in weeks, he was still cut off and alone. He realized that a curfew must be in effect and he would have to wait before trying to find help.

He had to find Americans, embassy staffers or someone, if he hoped to get out of the country alive. That would be his best option. But how? Where could he find countrymen in a nation he knew virtually nothing about? Harry looked around and saw a church across the street. In the milky glow of spotlights washing up the building's facade he saw that there was an English translation to the announcements on their bulletin board. Reading the list of regular services the church provided, Harry saw his opportunity and smiled.

David was waiting exactly as planned, the engine of the windowless van idling quietly. Rachel ran up to the vehicle, her face tight with the pain in her leg. Without a word she threw open the passenger door and eased herself into the seat. "Drive."

"What about the others?"

"No one else made it. We were hit by a security patrol. Everyone else is dead." Her voice was weak and exhausted.

Her cell phone chirped. *Now what?*

"Rachel, it's Yosef."

"We were hit, Yosef. The team was wiped out, and White's gone."

"At the safe house?"

"We ran into a patrol while leaving the city, and Harry White managed to escape in the confusion. Levine said he couldn't compromise himself by giving us a military escort or ordering troops to let us break curfew. He left us on our own, and it turned into a massacre."

"That prick," Yosef spat. "He wants the prime minister's office, and now that it's within his reach, I think he wants to cut us loose. I spoke with him about a helicopter extraction, and while he agreed to it, it sounded as though he's not too enthusiastic."

"I've been reading the papers. It looks like he's going to win the election in a landslide," Rachel said. "He really doesn't need us any longer." The enormity of her situation crashed in on her. "Do you think he'll have us killed?"

"No, he still wants what's at the mine, but afterward? I don't know." Yosef paused as he reconsidered. "Levine is an ambitious bastard, but we know enough to force him to honor his commitment. If he kills us, he'll never be sure we haven't told what we've done to others. Besides, when we're successful, his position within the government will be secure forever. Our involvement and our actions couldn't hurt him. There would be no need to kill us."

"But White will talk."

"He doesn't know anything, and when I kill Mercer, there will be no witnesses."

"That still leaves Selome Nagast," Rachel reminded.

"I know. She'll have to die too. I didn't want to do that. The fallout from Shin Bet will be enormous, but Levine will have to handle it."

"Yosef, are we right?" Rachel asked. "Is our job important enough for all of these killings?"

"No *job* is important enough to kill for, but our quest is. Not because of Levine, but because of what it will mean to the rest of Israel."

He told her about Mercer's discovery of the Valley of Dead Children and his plans to reach the site the following day. He also told her about Giancarlo Gianelli's operation and how it likely overlapped with theirs. Yosef had a suspicion that he would find the industrialist had already beaten him to the mine, which forced the Israeli agent to modify his plan. He decided they would approach the valley cautiously and keep it under observation before making their own play. He refocused his attention on Rachel and her plight. "You have to find someplace to hide until after the election and let us worry about what to do next. Don't contact Levine, I'll handle him. We've got just a few weeks left, and then it will be over. For all of us." Yosef cut the connection.

Northern Eritrea

The Toyota was a speck in the vastness of the desert, moving just ahead of the billowing dust of its wake. The twin scars of its tire prints ran off to the infinity of the horizon. Other than the truck, nothing moved in the desert—no animal or bird, no lizard or crawling insect ventured out into the torturous heat. While rain fell on the eastern part of the country and angry masses of clouds were visible in the distance, the storms had not yet come to the Hajar region. The desert floor was cracked, split open in a natural process that tripled its surface area and would allow a greater amount of water to be absorbed when it finally did rain. It was as if the soil itself needed the precious water to survive.

Mercer drove recklessly, trusting his own reactions and the vehicle's speed in case they drove over any of the antipersonnel mines sown on the open plain. If they hit a larger antitank mine, nothing he could do would save their lives. Gibby sat next to him, his hand braced against the dash while Selome grimly gripped a ceiling strap in the back, her eyes riveted out the rear window.

"Do you see them yet?" Mercer shouted over the engine's roar.

"No, not yet," Selome replied hoarsely. "Oh shit, I see them now."

Mercer shifted his gaze to the rearview mirror for a second and spied the pursuing four-wheel drive. At this distance, it was only a sparkling reflection, a jewel pinned to the desert by dust blowing up behind it.

"Sorry, guys," he called darkly. "I don't think we're going to make it."

They had started their drive from the camp two hours after dawn. Mercer and Habte, with the help of Abebe, had laid the explosive charges Mercer had fashioned during the night by premixing the ammonium nitrate and fuel oil in a dozen one-gallon metal cans. At dawn, the three of them had dug holes into the mountain according to a plan Mercer had devised to maximize the shots and tumble the overhanging walls of their excavation.

Once the holes had been dug and the charges buried, they scrambled back to ground level, moved the vehicles to a safe distance, and waited while Mercer made the final connections to the battery-driven detonator. He called the countdown but gave Gibby the honor of shooting the amfo. The boy had practically begged. The fuses burned at twelve thousand feet per second, so it seemed the detonations were instantaneous, but a cascade compression wave had been created in the rock that built steadily in fractions of seconds.

If Gibby was disappointed by the small geysers of dirt thrown up by the detonation, he was delighted by their final results. The man-made chasm they had laboriously dug into the mountain collapsed inward at the same instant the bulk of material above let go, creating a long-slide avalanche that carried tons of dirt nearly four hundred yards from the slope. Gibby let out a whoop that echoed even as the rumble subsided. Abebe, Habte, and the other driver took up the cry, and even Mercer gave a victorious shout. The blast had been better than even he had anticipated.

"Okay, boys, you know what to do," Mercer said.

It would take two days to remove the rubble from the blast, but when the arduous task was finished, they could continue to chip away at the mountain to expose the mine entrance without fear of a cave-in. Mercer had set the charges high enough on the hillside to ensure that the blast went outward rather than into the mountain, so he was not concerned with damaging the ancient workings below.

Selome and Gibby had left the Valley of Dead Children with Mercer while Habte and the others tore into the heaps of debris. They had packed for a couple of days in case it took them longer to find the monastery, but Gibby assured Mercer that he could locate it quickly.

It was Selome who had first spotted the other vehicle. She had noticed it when they were no more than half an hour away from the entrance to the valley and immediately alerted Mercer. "This can't be good," he said.

"It could be another survey team looking for minerals that just happen to be in the same area," Selome suggested lamely.

Mercer didn't waste the time to respond. As soon as he saw the truck cresting a hill behind them, he'd started to accelerate. Immediately, the other vehicle took up the chase. Once, when the other truck had gained enough ground for them to recognize it as a Fiat, a winking light appeared in the passenger-side window. An instant later, feathers of dust exploded in the wake of the fleeing Toyota; mid-caliber machine-gun fire. No matter how hard Mercer pushed their battered Toyota, the pursuing truck was quicker. It was only Mercer's driving skills and his ability to read the terrain that had kept them out of weapon's range again.

But now, out in the open, the Fiat was rapidly closing.

"What do you mean, we're not going to make it?" Selome asked.

"They've got a newer, faster four-wheel drive." A gust of wind nearly tore the steering wheel from his grip. When he was back in control, he continued. "There's no place to lose them out here because our tire prints and the dust this pig is kicking up are going to give us away."

Neither Selome nor Gibby could argue.

"Another happy fact," Mercer said after a minute of silence, "is the land mines. If this region is covered with them, which everyone tells me it is, we're going to hit one. It's just a matter of time." Even an anti-personnel variant would stop the Toyota dead.

"Maybe those guys behind us will hit one first."

"Not if they drive in our tracks."

Another blast of wind hit the Toyota. On a horizon that was rushing toward them, the storm clouds piled into towering walls that blocked the distance like dark curtains. It was frightening, an awesome display of natural fury.

"How long before it hits?" Mercer asked quickly.

"I don't know," Gibby shouted over the wind whipping through the Toyota's open windows. "I have seen storms like that stay over one area for days and not move at all."

"Are you kidding me?"

"It's true," Selome yelled from the backseat. "These storms usually hug the ground and can't get over the mountains. Often, rain won't fall from them for days, even weeks."

"That means the air in front of them compresses against the hills and springs back, creating—" Mercer's voice was choked off as the air around the truck came alive.

The sandstorm blew up so suddenly and violently that the trio was coughing before they could close the windows. The Land Cruiser filled with a dark amber light that shifted constantly as the storm raged over them. The sky screamed as sand was stripped off the surface of the desert and blown thousands of feet into the air. Mercer slowed the Toyota, his visibility down to zero.

"Jesus," he muttered as the storm unbelievably intensified. Already the windshield was opaque. Selome gave a little cry from the backseat and Gibby stared goggle-eyed into the maelstrom. The wind shoved the Toyota so hard it felt as if they were still speeding over the broken ground.

"Selome, how far behind was the other truck?" Mercer shouted.

"I don't remember."

"Come on," he prompted. He could see the terror in her eyes when he twisted around to look at her. "Just give me your best guess."

"Half a mile, maybe."

"All right. The storm's going to erase our tire tracks, but we're still too close to the Fiat. When this mess blows over, they're going to spot us in a second."

"What can we do?" Gibby asked.

"We're going to continue on." Mercer's jaw clenched with determination.

"But you can't see," Selome cried.

"Sure I can. I just can't see outside of the truck." The joke felt flat to Mercer's ears too.

He replayed the last image of the desert he'd seen before the dust had obscured it, studied it in his mind, and engaged the transmission, gambling that the driver of the other truck wouldn't budge until after the storm had passed. The Toyota crept forward, Mercer driving from memory. The desert floor had been relatively flat before the storm had hit, so he wasn't overly worried about any sudden drops or dips, but as the wind pummeled the side of the Land Cruiser, keeping them on a straight course was next to impossible.

Ten minutes trickled by, the Land Cruiser crawling blindly through the twisting slashes of wind and sand, Mercer's hand slick on the steering wheel, his body attuned to any attitude shifts that would signal a hill or a valley. Then as suddenly as it had started, the storm blew over them and they were in the clear. Even before his eyes could adjust to the sudden burst of sunlight, Mercer floored the accelerator, flinging Gibby and Selome back in their seats. They had a precious few minutes before the sand settled around their pursuers.

"Selome, keep your eye out for that Fiat and tell me the instant you see it."

There was a series of low hills a half mile ahead, and Mercer was hoping that they would be behind them before she saw the other vehicle. If the three of them were spotted first, it would all be over.

"Anything?"

"No, the storm is still hanging on back there. I can't see them. I think—"

The Toyota catapulted in the air, throwing off smoking hunks of body work and bits of its undercarriage. The thunder of the explosion drowned out the screams of the passengers. Crashing on its three remaining tires, the Land Cruiser flipped on its side, its front fender plowing a deep furrow into the soil.

A "perfect soldier" had waited decades to strike its

deadly blow. Designed as an antipersonnel weapon, the Soviet-built landmine did not have the power to destroy the Toyota, and because of the vehicle's speed, much of the detonative force was released under the engine rather than below the wheel that had activated its primer. With most of its energy absorbed by the engine block, only a tenth of the charge blasted into the cab. It was more than enough.

The last thing Mercer remembered clearly was the sound of Selome's voice. Then he was assaulted by a jumbled whirl of images, screams, and pain, the earth erupting under the Land Cruiser and the jarring crush as it slammed into the ground again.

His ears ringing, Mercer wiped his face, and his trembling hand came away covered with blood. His whole body ached as his senses slowly returned. He couldn't feel the pain that would indicate a wound capable of producing the amount of blood splattered on his clothes. His first thought was Selome. He tried to turn and check on her, but he couldn't move from where he was wedged under the steering wheel. A heavy weight pressed on him, and he recognized it was Gibby. Or what was left of him.

The explosion had been channeled into the passenger-side foot well, shredding the boy's legs so badly that only a few stringy bits of flesh kept them attached to his body. Massive tissue trauma had killed him immediately, but ropes of blood still drooled from the ragged wounds, pouring onto Mercer, saturating him. Seeing the dead Eritrean sharpened Mercer's mind, and vomit flooded his mouth. He choked it back painfully.

"Selome?" he called.

She was sobbing. *Thank God!* Slowly, he eased Gibby's body off him. When he stood on the smashed-in door, a wave of nausea nearly dropped him back on top of the corpse. He ignored any injuries he might have and concentrated on Selome. She lay curled on the driver's-side rear door, her face cupped in her hands, her shoulders heaving. Mercer called her name again and finally she looked up. Her face was filthy, her hair bushed around her head, but he saw no blood, and while her eyes were made enormous by fear, she didn't appear to be in shock.

"Give me your hand." He hadn't forgotten the Fiat still behind them. "We have to get out of here."

She reached for him tentatively, and as soon as her fingers laced with his, Mercer pulled her to her feet. She winced when her weight pressed against her right foot, the one closest to the explosion. "Are you okay?"

"I don't know." Her voice was small and frail.

"We have to get moving. That other truck will be on us in no time." Mercer looked beyond the shattered rear window and saw a plume of dust speeding out of the shifting sandstorm like some questing tentacle. The Fiat was too distant to see yet, but Mercer knew he only had minutes before it reached them.

"Give me your gun," he demanded quickly.

"What?"

"Your gun, Selome, give it to me."

"What are you talking about?"

Her acting job was unconvincing. "We have about five minutes before they reach us, and if you want to live beyond then, give me your goddamned gun."

She stared at him, her face a mixture of fear and confusion, then she reached into her knapsack to retrieve a big automatic. "How did you know?"

Even in this situation, Mercer felt relief that the wall of secrecy between them was starting to come down.

"I'll tell you later. You know, we could have used this in the cattle pens in Asmara." Mercer took the Heckler and Koch. Selome shrugged but couldn't meet his eye. Mercer levered himself out of the destroyed four-wheel drive, twisted on his perch, and lowered his hand back to Selome. "Climb up to me. I'll help you, but don't look in the front seat. Gibby didn't make it."

The Fiat's trail of dust no longer merged with the storm dying behind it. Mercer jumped to the ground, held up his arms, and Selome leaped to him. "Stay here."

At the back of the Toyota, a five-gallon jerry can of gasoline was clamped tightly in a special bracket. Mercer unclipped it from its mounts, grabbed a pair of knapsacks that had been tossed from the roof storage rack, and returned to Selome's side. The crater left by the landmine looked like a tiny, smoking volcano. He judged that the Land Cruiser had been thrown nearly fifteen feet by the blast.

"What are we going to do? We're in the middle of a mine field."

Mercer didn't answer her question, nor could he ignore it either. The desert here was loose and sandy, the surface raked smooth by the storm. However, there was a rocky outcrop about fifty yards away that would be free of mines. The trick was to get from the stranded Toyota to the rocks without blowing themselves up and doing it quickly enough so the pursuing Fiat didn't discover their escape. He twisted the lid off the gas can and began dumping its contents onto the Land Cruiser.

"Mercer, I need to get—"

He cut her off. "No time. I'm sorry."

The Fiat was about a half mile away; its roof was visible as it drove in a shallow depression. Mercer scanned the ground as he worked, hoping to see the imprints of mines, but praying he'd never see another one again. Finished dousing the vehicle, he led her a few yards away, using its battered hulk to cover their escape. Whenever he was working in the field, Mercer carried half a dozen cigarette lighters with him. It was a safety precaution that went way beyond the Boy Scout motto, but he'd been in situations where he'd needed all of them.

Using his left hand, he sparked open a Zippo and tossed it underhand into the pool of gasoline beneath the Toyota. In a continuous motion, he began shooting into the ground as a whooshing explosion engulfed the four-wheel-drive, masking the sharp cracks of the H&K. A wall of heat overwhelmed them as they stood in the open. Selome tried to move away from the raging flames, but Mercer held her wrist tightly. He fired off the entire magazine, walking his shots toward the boulders a short way off, each bullet plowing a small crater in the dirt roughly five feet beyond the previous one. Had a round hit a mine, it would have carried the power to detonate the charge, but there was no secondary explosion.

Mercer released Selome's hand and jumped into the first pock created by the 9mm bullets.

"Land where I step," he cautioned and jumped again, leaping into the next shallow depression.

It took every bit of his balance to land in the tiny craters, teetering on one foot for breathless seconds, his arms windmilling until he could center himself again. Then he would leap to the next, Selome at his heels. Unencumbered by the two knapsacks Mercer carried, Selome bounded easily, her long legs covering the distance with the grace of a gymnast. If her foot was bothering her, she didn't let it show.

"Give me another clip," Mercer said when he reached the last impact hole.

"That's what I wanted to go back for," Selome answered. "The rest of my ammo was in the Toyota. I don't have any more."

Mercer's eyes went wide as he stared at the seventy-five feet of open space separating them from the safety of the rocks; seventy-five feet of mine-sown no-man's land with only one way across. He couldn't hear the engine noise of the approaching Fiat over the fiery eruption behind them, but he knew only a few seconds remained before the vehicle rumbled into view. Mercer took the deep, final breath of a man bent on suicide.

Fighting an instinct to yell and vent some of the pent-up emotion, he started running. It took his entire will not to stretch his gait to its fullest. He had to leave footprints close enough for Selome to use as stepping stones.

With every step, Mercer expected the detonation that would come like a sledgehammer at full swing; a shearing pain that at best would kill him and at worst would immobilize him for the pursuers to finish the job. He covered the first half of the distance without incident, but took no solace from this. The law of averages was working against him, and with every step, the ratio tipped more and more out of his favor. With just ten more feet to cover, he moaned aloud in frustration for not being able to leap those last few yards. He could have done it in a flying dive, but again he thought of Selome and took a step that cut the distance in half and made it safe for her.

Click.

He felt the dusty ground give just a tiny fraction of an inch. The sound was like a distant finger snap, muted by his own weight on the mine. It was the primer, and in the millimetric sliver of time before main charge blew, he could only hope that Selome would get clear.

Working on instinct, with his weight barely pressing on the can-sized bomb, he shifted his body in mid-stride, heaving himself forward in an awkward lurch. But his desperate leap wasn't necessary. After lying dormant for fifteen years, the mine had been fouled by dirt and corrosion. The primer could not detonate the principal explosive. Mercer smashed into the rock with his shoulder, too stunned at being alive to roll with the impact. In his shock, he almost slid back off the tor and into the dirt. Scrambling, he turned and planted his heels on the stone, arresting his slide.

"Selome, come on," he shouted.

Like a sprinter in the blocks who reacts even as the gun fires, she was in motion, her face scrunched in concentration. She bounded from print to print, her arms pumping in perfect synch, and even in his wasted emotional state, Mercer appreciated the shifting play of her breasts as she moved. In seconds she was at his side.

"Are you okay?" she panted.

"Later." Mercer was on his feet again, leading her over the hill and across a flat table of stone toward the foothills of one of the region's numerous mountains.

A quarter mile and five minutes after clearing the mine field, they heard a muffled explosion behind them. Mercer turned. A Fiat half-ton truck was parked directly behind their four-wheel drive. Two Africans, Sudanese no doubt, stood in its open rear bed, and he could just make out the shadow of two more in the cab. They were all looking at the rumpled figure lying doll-like a few dozen feet from the vehicles. There was a new crater in the desert, wisps of gray smoke blowing from it on the gentle breeze. The body leaked blood from the stump of his left leg, the severed member bleeding into the soil a few feet away. Mercer guessed that one of their pursuers had tried to chase on foot, trying to duplicate their feat, and paid the ultimate price for failure. He and Selome continued on without comment. Soon afterward, they had lost themselves in the rugged terrain, and Mercer slowed their pace, no longer concerned about being followed.

Selome called a halt hours later, her face blistered with sweat and dark patches appearing beneath her arms. She lowered herself to a stone plateau, lying flat and stretching her arms luxuriously over her head. Mercer flopped next to her, his attention riveted to the cache of goods in the two knapsacks he'd taken from the Land Cruiser. One of them had been Selome's, and he dumped out the cosmetics and extra clothing. Selome ignored him and stared up into the hazy sky.

"Selome?"

She looked at him and her eyes widened. He held another full magazine for her Heckler and Koch. "Oops."

"Oops is right." Mercer shook his head. He combined and consolidated the useful items into one pack, discarding stuff that had no value for the trek to come. Those things he did keep were pathetically few in number, some rope, a hammer, several lengths of fuse. He took the Medusa pictures from his vest and stuffed them in with the rest of the gear.

"I feel so terrible about Gibby," she said after a few minutes. "Not only about his death, but the disrespect we showed his body. That wasn't right. He deserved a Christian burial."

Gibby's death was one more on Mercer's conscience. The Fiat proved the Sudanese were in the area, and they would find the mine long before Mercer could warn away the refugees he'd asked Negga's son to bring to the valley. They would be arriving soon, and their plight was his responsibility too. "Please don't talk about religion for a while. I'm not in the mood."

She was about to respond when Mercer leaned over and reached a hand to the wedge of skin showing between the collars of her bush shirt. A thin gold chain rested against her glossy skin and disappeared between her breasts. Mercer tugged it from its resting place, keeping his eyes locked with Selome's even as the necklace popped free, revealing a golden Star of David.

"Mossad?" he asked quietly.

"No. Shin Bet." There was a defiance in her voice. "It's like your FBI."

Relief flooded through Mercer. He knew there would be no more lies. "I've heard of it. Are you going to tell me what's going on?"

"I guess I owe you."

"That's putting it mildly."

She blew out a long breath. "A few months ago, the Medusa photographs came to the attention of an Israeli fanatic group."

It was an answer Mercer was unprepared for. "Israeli? I thought Muslims were behind this."

Selome shook her head. "Those Europeans Habte saw in Asmara are Jewish extremists headed by Defense Minister Chaim Levine. We've known about them for a while, but we didn't realize until recently how powerful they'd become."

Mercer realized they'd all been duped. Dick Henna must have followed carefully placed false clues leading both of them to believe it was Arabs who had masterminded Harry's abduction. He was both stunned and impressed by how cleverly this had been worked out.

So many things came clear as he studied her. That's what Harry had been trying to tell him when he said his captors had given him Boodles gin or something. Harry must have known that he'd been abducted to the Mideast, but recognized that his abductors weren't Muslims. Mercer should have made the connection, and that oversight rekindled his anger at himself. He wondered how many more mistakes he'd made and how much others had paid for them.

Selome continued. "Levine and his followers want to

make Israel a totalitarian theocracy. He recognized what the Medusa photos revealed and knew such a discovery, accredited to him, would ensure him the prime ministership. He tried to have them stolen from your National Reconnaissance Office, but instead they were sold to Prescott Hyde. Hyde, too, saw something in them, something that would bolster his shaky position within the State Department. We learned about all of this shortly after Hyde bought them, and I was sent to the United States to work with him. Shin Bet paid off a member of the Eritrean mission in Washington to vouch for me so Hyde never knew of my connection to Israel. My mission was to gather intelligence, especially if Levine's people tried to contact Hyde directly.

"Unfortunately for Hyde, he called you soon after I arrived in D.C. and you joined his search for the mine, shutting down that option for Levine's agents. Hyde and his wife were killed the morning you and I left for Africa."

Hyde dead too? Jesus, where was this going to end? "You left me in Rome to report your findings about Hyde to your control in Israel?"

"Is that how you figured out I was Israeli?"

"I was told by Dick Henna before we left Washington. Also, the night you came to Tiny's Bar, my best friend, Harry, was kidnapped to Beruit."

It was obvious from her expression that this was new information. "The old guy who introduced himself as you?"

"The same," Mercer replied. "The abductors appeared to have Middle Eastern connections, so I figured Israel would fit in eventually." He told her the whole story about Harry's kidnapping and about the assassination at da Vinci Airport. "I didn't know if you were on my side or not. Remember, you were working with Hyde when we met."

"It must be Levine's people holding your friend. After you turned down Hyde, they must have grabbed him to compel you to come to Africa and find the mine. The man killed in Rome was undoubtedly Ibriham Bein, Levine's top agent."

Mercer guessed Bein's warning in Rome about not harming Selome was because the Israeli feared a problem if Levine's plot had caused the death of a Shin Bet agent. They were already planning for the day they had Israel in their grasp.

"Levine's a fascist," Selome said bitterly. "I know that sounds strange for one Jew to call another that, but he is. He believes in the purity of the Jewish people and wants all others out of Israel. He wants to build concentration camps and corral the Palestinians in fenced stockades.

"He's been planning this for years. I don't know if you remember the airlift of Ethiopian Jews to Israel in the eighties, but he was a major supporter of the operation. He said it was for humanitarian reasons, but even then he wanted to do away with the Palestinians who perform many of the menial jobs in Israel and replace them with African refugees."

So, Mercer thought, he and Harry had gotten in the middle of an internal Israeli problem and not some international terrorist plot. Selome was trying to stop Levine from using the Medusa photographs to give himself unfair advantage in the elections. All of his suspicions about her ebbed away. For the first time he felt that he could trust her. A dam was breaking inside of him. He'd been on his own for too long and now he had an ally. He felt like hugging her. "So your job was to keep an eye on this group and report their activities?"

"And to stop them if I could. But we came to Eritrea before I got close."

Suddenly something didn't make sense. "I understand Levine is a maniac, but I also read that his election was all but guaranteed even before we left Washington. Why is he willing to ruin his chances by going after a worthless fifty-year-old diamond mine?"

"He's not." Selome laughed for the first time in a long time. "You already know we have no interest in the Italian facility. I think the Sudanese and their backers are looking for that one. That's how they stumbled on us. Our two missions come from different directions but end at the same location."

Mercer matched her smile, the horrors of the morning sloughing off at least for a few seconds. "Before you'd arrived in the valley, when I was exploring for the older workings, I'd already guessed that you were aware of another mine in the area."

Mercer's expression suddenly changed as a new thought struck him. The white rock he'd found in the kimberlite tailings was a stone-aged tool, a hammer used thousands of years ago to crush the ore to get at the precious gems. Suddenly everything tied together: Jews, ancient mines, religious fanatics. He finally realized why the stakes were so high, and it had nothing to do with diamonds. *Oh, my God!* He tried to repress the wild thought but couldn't. "Is that mine what I think it is?" He could barely speak.

"We're on our way to talk to some priests who will confirm it, but yes, it is." Selome smiled at his breathless wonderment. "It'll be the greatest find of your life. The stuff of legend."

When he said it, it came out as a whisper. "King Solomon's Mine."

The Eritrea-Sudan Border

Gianelli felt like a conquering Caesar as his trucks rumbled into Eritrea. He sat in the passenger seat of the lead vehicle, the windows rolled down so he could smell the dry desert and hear the bellowing of the big twelve-cylinder turbo-diesels. Chuckling, he realized that the heavy-duty transporters loaded with mining gear and provisions weighed twice as much as the CV.35 light battle tanks Mussolini had used to invade Abyssinia. Kitted out in de rigueur khaki, with a bush hat clamped on his head and sunglasses protecting his eyes from the worst of the driving sun, Gianelli was at the very pinnacle of his life. Everything up to this moment, every deal and every decision, had led to this instant. Leading the trucks back to the mine that his uncle had opened decades before was the culmination of his existence. Let others wonder at his wealth and power—they were nothing, merely an extension of what had been handed to him through his family, a quirk of genetics. This was what he saw as his destiny.

Soon after the Eritrean refugees had left their camps in Sudan under the leadership of a nomad prince, Mahdi had approached Gianelli with his idea of searching ahead of the column so they could reach the mine more quickly. The refugees were covering only a couple of miles a day, and the lethargic pace rankled the Italian. Gianelli agreed and sent out a scout truck. Three days later the radio call had come saying they had found the mine in a bowl of land at the end of a narrow valley after hearing an explosion. Gianelli ordered the main convoy to bypass the refugees and speed to where the advance scouts waited. A short time after, another call from them reported a Toyota Land Cruiser driven by a white man was attempting to flee the valley. Gianelli's first thought was the fools had given away their presence to Mercer, but realized that Mahdi's people wouldn't have made such a blunder.

He instructed the Sudanese rebels to stop the Toyota and made it clear that Mercer was not to be harmed. He learned a few hours later that Mercer had escaped through a mine field at the cost of one of Mahdi's men. Gianelli cursed the whole team over the radio until his fist nearly crushed the microphone. Mahdi listened to the exchange as he sat on the back bench seat of the ten-wheeled Fiat truck. When his turn came, he took Gianelli's wrath without comment. His employer was fully in his right. Mercer never should have escaped. His men's failure was inexcusable, and their punishment, when the cargo trucks reached the valley, would be more severe than Gianelli's verbal tirade.

The radio crackled again, and he snatched up the handset. "Yes?"

"We are back at the valley now and have it secured. The American left only three people here, Eritreans. They have some excavating equipment but are not working at the mine."

"What are they doing?" Gianelli asked the leader of the advance detachment he had sent out to leapfrog the meandering refugee column.

"They were just digging into the side of one of the mountains. They haven't said yet what they were looking for."

"They knew about my uncle's mine, right?"

"Yes, sir," the soldier replied, then lowered his tone, knowing his next statement would not please his superior. "The man left in charge here said that there were no minerals in the mine. He told us the American explored the shaft and said there was nothing in it of any value."

"That can't be right," Gianelli stammered, the buoyant mood that had carried him across the frontier evaporating quickly.

Despite their increased speed, it took eight hours before the convoy eased between the ramparts that guarded the bowl of land called the Valley of Dead Children. Listening to the chatter of the men in the backseat with Mahdi, Gianelli learned that they knew of this place and held it in superstitious dread. He asked Mahdi about it, and the soldier couldn't give him a definitive answer. He told his employer that the region's taboo went back many generations, but no one knew its origins. The myths surrounding it had spread as far as Sudan and Ethiopia.

"Rubbish," Giancarlo said dismissively.

His expression was fevered with anticipation, a sense of history weighing on his shoulders. The valley looked nothing like what he'd thought as a child, but now that he was here, he could imagine it no other way.

Across the open pan, he saw the skeleton of the head gear rising out of a watery heat mirage, recognized the support buildings next to it, and after a few minutes, saw the open Fiat his advance scouts had driven. His heart pounded with eagerness.

The trucks lumbered to the abandoned mine, wheezing as their overworked engines spooled to silence, air brakes hissing. Gianelli launched himself from the cab, running across the desert to the rim of the open shaft.

Joppi Hofmyer was the first to join him.

"This is it," Giancarlo gasped. "Two lifetimes of work, mine and my uncle's, and here it is." He gave no consideration to the earlier news that the mine was empty. It was a possibility he would not allow.

There was no way the mine could be worthless, he thought. Enrico had been sure there were diamonds in the area, had died believing it. Gianelli had always felt that if his uncle's plane hadn't been shot down during the war, he would have given the family proof. Mercer hadn't taken enough time to properly explore the subterranean tunnels, he told himself, nor did he have the proper equipment for a thorough search. The diamonds were here.

"Yes, sir," the South African replied uneasily. "Ah, Mr. Gianelli, I'd like to know how you want to handle this?"

"What do you mean?"

"Now that we're here, do you want me to take charge of the men, or are you going to be issuing the orders?"

Gianelli's laugh was a quick barking sound. "Joppi, my friend, I am one of those people who knows how to hire others for their knowledge and abilities. I'm paying you because you know how to extract minerals from the ground, an art that I know nothing about. From now on, you are in complete control. However you want to handle this operation, whatever steps you feel necessary, are fine. Consider me nothing more than an interested observer."

Hofmyer turned away, more disturbed by Gianelli's sudden bonhomie than he cared to admit. "Okay, you fookin' *kaffirs*," he bellowed at the Sudanese troopers clustered near the trucks. "Until those refugees get here, you bastards are going to be miners. You take orders from Mahdi, and as of this moment Mahdi takes orders from me. Once I get the checklist, I want ten men unloading the camp stores and setting up the tents.

"I want the rest of you unloading the mining gear, separating underground equipment from surface stuff. If you don't know what something is, ask either me or one of the other white miners and don't forget to call him *Baas*." The four other South Africans grinned at this. "You boys," he said to the whites, "I want the explosives off-loaded and placed in a protective redoubtment no closer than five hundred yards from the mine or the camp. Now, someone bring me the three *kaffirs* who were already here when the scouts arrived."

Habte sat handcuffed in the shade of the scout's Fiat with the two Eritrean equipment operators. Neither of the hired workers understood what was happening. Their fear was palpable, but ever since Asmara, Habte had been expecting something like this. He figured that these men were allied to the ones who had attacked Mercer and Selome in the market square. As of yet, the Caucasians he had seen at the Ambasoira Hotel had not made their appearance. When they did, he knew that he could expect little help from them. This time the enemy of his enemy was not his friend.

Two Sudanese rebels approached and gestured with their rifles for the trio to follow. Led back to the open mine shaft, Abebe began praying aloud. Habte had faced death many, many times before, and he would not let his own fear show.

Joppi sauntered over a few moments later, his gut sagging over his belt. With an expert eye he looked over the three captives, fixing his gaze on Habte, recognizing him as their leader. With a casualness that belied the brutality of the act, he stepped forward, planted his hands on Abebe's shoulders, and shoved him into the pit.

Abebe's scream echoed up from the shaft, diminishing like a siren until it was cut off with an undeniable finality. Habte didn't so much as blink when Joppi's eyes bored into his, waiting for a reaction that the Eritream refused to give. They were locked in this frozen tableau for several breaths.

"Oh, you're an uppity nigger, aren't you?" Hofmyer finally said. "You want me to push your other friend in as well, or do you want to start answering some questions?"

Habte willed himself not to say that the South African hadn't asked any, knowing such a retort would cause the murder of the other equipment operator. He allowed his eyes to drop in a pose of submission that Joppi interpreted as a victory. Like many others from his country who hadn't taken the time to understand traditional African ways, Joppi believed Habte's silence connoted acceptance. "That's better, now. Why don't you tell me what you were doing at the far end of the valley?"

Balancing his desire to defy the Boer and his realization that the longer he was alive the better his chances were for escape, Habte told Hofmyer everything.

An hour later, the trucks rumbled away from the Italian mine so they could set up their camp a short distance from the ancient one.

The Open Desert

In hindsight, Mercer felt he should have chanced the mine field again after the Sudanese had withdrawn in order to recover any useful equipment from the burned-out Land Cruiser, especially canteens. Or his sat-phone. Though he continued to carry the single backpack, everything in it was worthless for the ordeal to come. With nightfall only an hour away and their bodies ravaged by thirst, those short few yards through the mines could have made the difference between survival or perishing in the desert.

Without food, they could last for a couple of weeks, but a lack of water would kill them long before starvation. Mercer's mouth was beyond dry. His tongue felt like the scaly body of some desert reptile. The last time he was able to swallow, hours ago it seemed, his throat screamed in desiccated protest, as if lined with ground glass. While a woman's body was better suited to survival situations, Selome wasn't faring well either as they trudged under the unrelenting African sun. Inventorying their condition, Mercer judged that they would be dead in twenty-four to thirty-six hours if they couldn't find water. Selome's revelations, about herself, her mission, and the King Solomon mine had buoyed him for a while, but now his mind focused only on the miles.

With the setting sun at their backs, the desert bloomed crimson, painted in shades and shadows that made the steep mountains look like fairy-tale castles, heavily turreted and remote. The sight would have made them pause under normal circumstances, but as night deepened, they simply continued to walk, their pace slowing with each footfall.

Selome and Mercer used scraps from their clothing to fashion rudimentary sun protection for their heads and breathed through their noses to reduce fluid loss. They tried every survival trick either had ever learned, and still their efforts were falling far short. Had either of them carried a compass or knew celestial navigation, they could have walked in the coolness of the night. As it was, they were forced to march in the daylight, the sun as their only guide. And after just one day, with an unknown number more to go, it was clear that they would die.

"The sun's almost behind the horizon." Mercer spoke for the first time in nearly six hours. "It'll be cooler in just a little while."

"And I'll be dead in just a little while, too." Selome managed a smile, though her voice scratched like an old phonograph record.

"That's the spirit," Mercer rasped. "Nothing like a positive attitude."

His grin cracked his dry lips and a tiny bead of blood quivered at the corner of his mouth. He surveyed the terrain around them. The landscape was spiked by mountainous ramparts that grew from the desert floor with brutal regularity, forcing them to follow a meandering route as they tracked eastward toward the Adobha River.

They continued on, their steps less sure, fatigue and dehydration taking their toll. Just before total darkness set in, Mercer steered Selome to one of the countless kopjes, rocky hillocks similar to the buttes that dot the American Southwest, and led her into one of the hundreds of caves that pocked the cliff, riven out of the stone by eons of erosion. Too exhausted to speak, they tumbled to the floor and soaked up the cave's chilled air. A full half hour passed before Mercer felt he had the energy to sit up and press his aching back against the rock wall. He tried to use his pack as a pillow but its contents were even harder and more jagged than the stone.

Neither dared remove their boots. Their feet would have swollen immediately and they wouldn't be able to don them again in the morning. Mercer did loosen his laces to ease the pressure against his tender skin.

"Try it," he prompted Selome. "It feels better than sex."

"You must not be very good," she teased. "How far do you think we've come?"

"I'd guess about twenty-five to thirty miles."

"Then we're halfway to the Adobha River."

"Unfortunately no. Because of the terrain and our need to go around these damned hills, I estimate we've only walked about fifteen miles due east." Though he wanted to protect her from their reality, she had a right to know.

"So the river is . . ."

"Another forty-five miles. If the ground doesn't flatten out soon, we'll actually have to cover seventy. And our bodies are going to weaken even more during the night. Our pace will be slower tomorrow, and every second we're out in the sun, we're going to dehydrate further. I'm sorry to tell you this, but these are the facts."

Selome's body slumped in defeat. "Can we go back and take our chances with the Sudanese?"

"I don't think we'd make it half the distance to the mine. Remember, we were driving for a couple of hours before the attack."

"We're going to die, aren't we?"

"Sure we are. In about fifty years, when old age catches up to us." Mercer straightened. "We're not dead yet, Selome, and I've gotten out of worse messes than this."

Mercer couldn't specifically recall facing a more desperate situation but Selome took comfort from his words. She crawled to him, laying her head on the hard pads of his stomach muscles. He stroked her hair softly and she mewed before drifting into an exhausted sleep. For Mercer, the respite of oblivion was a long time in coming.

He was almost too tired and sore to sleep. Something about what Selome had told him nagged at the back of his mind, something about Levine's quest to find King Solomon's mine. It was an archaeological treasure, the find of the century, but Mercer couldn't figure out how the Israeli minister planned to use it to gain power or to help him hold it once he'd won the elections. Something didn't fit. There was another piece to this puzzle that Selome hadn't mentioned.

Had he not been so exhausted and his mind tortured by the dry thirst, he would have demanded an explanation, but until they were safe again, neither could afford to waste the energy talking about something that was, for the moment, out of their control. Just before sleep claimed him, Mercer had one more thought: the Eritrean refugees he had sent for from Sudan. They were leaving one hell and heading straight into another. He knew their labor would be eagerly accepted by the rebel soldiers who were undoubtedly at the mine at this very moment. Mercer realized that his and Selome's struggle for survival was also a race against time.

At dawn the next day, Selome woke before Mercer and her feeble stirrings brought him awake. They had snuggled together during the night, their legs twined. It was a position of intimate trust, the nocturnal pose of lovers, and for several seconds they silently enjoyed the touch. It was only when Selome tried to lift herself that they realized how much their muscles had stiffened. She whimpered, her face screwed up with pain.

"Oh, Christ," Mercer said, his voice barely a hoarse croak.

Moving like arthritics, Mercer followed Selome's lead as she began stretching her tensed limbs. His joints popped and creaked in the confines of the cave and he knew intimately how Harry White felt every morning of every day.

Thinking of his old friend brought a burst of adrenaline to Mercer's heart, the natural drug giving him just enough strength to motion for Selome that it was time to continue. It was almost six in the morning, and they would have a couple of hours before the sun's heat began searing the desert floor.

"Last one in the swimming pool is a rotten egg," Mercer tried to joke. Selome was too exhausted to respond.

The vastness of the wasteland made their progress seem like that of insects crawling across a huge table. Yet for them, every step was a personal triumph against the ravages of thirst and exhaustion. Selome called for a break after two hours, but Mercer urged her on with just a touch of her shoulder. She moved like an automaton, her gait mechanical, her arms no longer swinging because the effort was too great. After two more hours, Mercer could not dissuade her from stopping, and she plopped to the ground in the shade of a small granite outcropping. Mercer slumped next to her, watching fifteen minutes ratchet by on his Tag Heuer before staggering to his feet and extending his hand. Gamely, she reached up and allowed him to haul her up.

Trying to maintain some sort of steady pace, Mercer began counting footsteps, planning on calling for a halt after two thousand, guessing that they would have covered another mile, but when he reached the number, he knew they had walked half that distance. He abandoned the counting and continued to put one foot before the other, thinking their next rest would come when Selome could go no farther. Yet it was he who needed the break first.

Just after noon, at the edge of one more nameless mountain, Mercer saw a cave similar to the one in which they had spent the previous night and he led Selome to it, intending to wait out the hottest part of the day. The remorseless sun gave him a headache like a thousand migraines, an all-consuming agony that left him dizzy and nauseous. "We'll get moving again at three," he managed to say before drifting into an empty torpor that was neither sleep nor wakefulness, but a vacant zone somewhere in between.

Neither was able to stir at their three o'clock goal, so they didn't start out again until it was nearly dark, their pace so slow that they would have trouble making it to the next sheltering mountain before their strength gave out completely. Death by dehydration would still be another torturous day away. But no amount of determination or will could lessen the possibility that when they stopped for the night, they might never rise again.

"Do you think you can keep going after sunset?"

Selome nodded, then asked after a pause, "Won't we get lost?"

"We already are," Mercer admitted, and they walked on in silence. They could cover more ground in the dark, regardless of direction. He had to keep them moving—simply sitting and waiting for the end just was not an option. An hour elapsed before Mercer continued their exchange, not realizing so much time had passed. "We can rest again tomorrow and maybe make it a few more miles the next night, but that'll be our last."

Selome's half-hour delay in her reply went unnoticed in their misery. "Isn't the monastery on this side of the river?"

A quarter mile later. "That's what Habte and Gibby said. I don't know how much closer it is."

Twenty minutes: "Let's hope it's a lot closer."

Darkness came swiftly, sucking the heat from the desert with a welcome suddenness. When the stars showed, they shone with a cold, indifferent brilliance. With the temperature down twenty degrees, Mercer and Selome found they could cover a greater distance between rest stops, and even those stops were shorter. For the first part of the night, they felt a small degree of hope.

But by midnight what little strength they'd managed to hold in reserve had burned away, and as suddenly as night had stolen the day, exhaustion stole their will. From a starting average of two miles per hour, they were down to just half and every hour slowed them even further. Their thirst was no longer a simple agonizing craving. Every second brought greater and greater damage to their bodies. Another twelve hours would lead to severe and possible irreversible kidney damage. After that, death would be quick.

The sun approached at five, rouging the sky. Amazingly, Mercer and Selome had traveled nearly twenty miles, their route eastward more direct as the gaps between mountains widened. Still there were untold miles remaining, and as Mercer began searching for another cave in which to hole up, he knew they would never see the end of their journey. When the sun went down again, they might cover a few more miles, but most likely, this stop would be their last.

In desperation, Mercer sucked at the blood that dripped from his cracked lips.

His eyes were nearly closed by dehydration and the fast-approaching sunrise. Beyond a few feet, everything was a dazzling white. The gritty pain in his eyes was nothing compared to the thirst that blistered the back of his tongue. The pebble he kept in his mouth could no longer trick his salivary glands into producing, so it lay like a boulder. His body screamed for water, and his mind was beginning to drift into fantasy. He could hear a stream just a few hundred yards ahead, and even the breeze carried its sharp clean smell. But as they approached, the illusion moved ahead, establishing another goal that he slogged toward mechanically.

He had forgotten about Selome until he felt her collapse against his legs. He was too weak to break his own fall, and his head rebounded against the sand. It took him several long minutes to realize she had lapsed into unconsciousness. He looked into the murk ahead of them and saw they had come to the side of yet another mountain, a solid wall of rock that stretched beyond his vision. He blinked hard, but he could see nothing that would lead them around this latest obstacle.

Wriggling slowly, like a snake shedding its skin, he slid out of his pack. Had he given any thought to what he was about to do, he wouldn't have attempted it, but he and Selome were beyond the point of choice. Mercer's arms had been darkened by the sun until his skin was the color of leather. He drew a pocket knife from his pants, fumbled until he could get the smaller, sharper blade open, and without pause drew it across his arm.

He half expected dust to blow out from the wound, but a steady line of blood welled up and quickly, so as not to lose even a drop, he pressed the gash to Selome's mouth. Consciously, she never would have broken mankind's oldest taboo, but her body craved the liquid and her throat gently pumped as the life-giving fluid eased her agony. Even as he continued to hold his arm to her lips, Mercer could see her regaining awareness. Before she could realize what he'd done, he drew his arm away, binding it with a cloth and wiping her face clean. He was leaning over her when her eyes fluttered open.

"What happened?"

"You passed out. You hit pretty hard and gave yourself a split lip. Are you okay?"

"I think so." He could see her tongue moving around experimentally, feeling for the source of the taste in her mouth.

"Sun'll be up in a few minutes. We need to find shelter. Can you walk?"

Selome nodded, but when she tried to stand, she fell back. She shot him a pleading, frightened look.

"By now you can't weigh much more than the backpack." He tried to smile, but his face wouldn't cooperate. "I'll carry you."

He ignored her unbelieving expression and tucked her into his arms, lifting her off the ground so easily she was stunned. He set her on her feet, turned to present his back, and stooped to make it easier for her to climb onto him. "This will be the final boarding call for the Mercer Limited. Those waiting for another train should remain on the platform."

Selome was slender under normal conditions and had lost several pounds in the past forty-eight hours, but her weight was staggering. Mercer closed his mind to the pain and started out again, Selome's chin resting against his shoulder so he could feel her steady breathing in his ear. He had no illusions of carrying her all the way to the Adohba River. He'd be lucky to find a cave in the next few minutes. Once the sun erupted over the mountains, his strength would leave him for the last time.

"Selome, I can't really see anymore. You have to keep an eye out for another cave." His legs were shaking after only a few dozen yards.

Another agonizing hour went by, Mercer carrying Selome northward along the cliff face. He was numbed to the pain, using the last scraps of energy left within him like a flame flaring brightest before it's extinguished. The sun was a brutal weight that tried to pound him like a hammer against the anvil of the desert floor. He thought that Selome had slipped into unconsciousness once again, but suddenly she cried out, a choking caw like a startled bird. Mercer could see the tip of her hand aiming ahead of them. He couldn't distinguish what she had spotted so, like a donkey following the carrot at the end of a stick, he dogged her slender finger. Glare had become a constant gauzy curtain, and it wasn't until they were almost at the entrance to a cave that he saw its shadow emerge from the haze.

Selome slid from his back, falling. Mercer didn't even notice. He was beyond the farthest point he had ever pushed himself. Like any mortally wounded animal, he wanted to find a sheltered place in which to die. He dropped to his hands and knees and crawled blindly into the cool cave, stopping only when his head hit the stone wall. Selome entered moments later, collapsing next to Mercer's facedown, immobile form.

He knew he would never rise again. His head pounded fiercely, and he felt it would split at just the slightest touch. He reached over to touch Selome's arm. Her skin felt like a dried-out parchment. Every fiber of his body craved water, but the last remnants of his rational mind knew it would never come.

"This is where we die," Mercer mumbled into the dusty floor of the cavern. "I'm sorry."

Selome rolled Mercer so she could study his face. Under the days of beard, his skin was gray and cracked. His lips were so blistered that his mouth looked like an infected wound. She saw her own concern reflected in his eyes, for she looked just as bad.

"I'll read to you to pass the time," Selome offered, and Mercer shot her a queer look, suspecting that she had finally fallen away from reality.

Yet as he watched, she grabbed a leather-bound book from the cave floor, resting it on her lap, and cracked it open to a random page. She stared at it blankly for just a second. "Hey, this is Shakespeare. It's in Italian, but I'll translate it for you."

"What else?" He was too wasted to feel emotion other than the desperation of the near dead.

"What?"

"What else is in the cave?" Was it possible? A hope flared dimly in his mind.

Selome looked around their mausoleum. "Oh, God! Food! Water!" He could hear her crying.

The air in the cave tasted sweeter when she unstoppered a flask. When she held it to her lips, Mercer watched clear water dribble down her chin, softening the dried scabs on her lips and bringing moisture to her seared tongue. The sensation closed her eyes in ecstatic pain.

Mercer was overwhelmed. Not because the water would save his life; that wasn't his first thought. That Selome would be saved was much more important than his own well-being. He wanted to take credit for getting her through this, but it was her own guts that had carried them, her uncomplaining determination to continue. Trying to inspire her with his strength, she'd turned around and done the same to him. Even as he faded into oblivion, he saw her half fill her mouth with water and press her lips to his, forcing his mouth open to allow a little water to pass into him. She drank again herself and then gave Mercer another mouthful. A minute later, he was unconscious, but his breathing evened and sounded less labored, a tiny but noticeable smile on his face.

The Monastery of Debre Amlak

An unfamiliar sensation brought Mercer awake, and it took him a moment to recognize what it was. *A mattress! Oh, Jesus!* Worn to little more than the thickness of a blanket and covered with sheets of the roughest cotton, it still felt as if he were resting on clouds. His whole body ached, his feet and legs especially. However, it was a reassuring pain that told him he was still alive. He shifted under the bedding; the blisters on his feet smeared open against the sheets. He gasped and shot up in bed, grabbing for his stinging heel. Instantly, his vision clouded over and his head swam. He collapsed back against the flat pillow, his sore feet all but forgotten.

Selome! Her image flooded his mind, and once again he struggled upright, his arms flailing to free himself from the sheets' tangling embrace. He had to find her; nothing else mattered. Then he heard a voice and he looked to his right. The room was just large enough for the bed, a desk, and a chair. The walls were white and clean, the floors were bare and well swept, and through the single window he could see it was twilight. A crucifix above the desk was the room's only decoration. A young boy dressed in a long robe stood at Mercer's bedside. He spoke again in Tigrinyan, ignoring Mercer's incomprehension.

"Selam," Mercer finally croaked.

"Selam, Selam," the youth greeted. *"Kemayla-ha?"*

The boy must have been asking about his condition. *"Hmak."* Bad. It was one of the few words Mercer had learned.

"Shemay Tedla iyu," the boy said, pointing at his chest. *"Men shem-ka?"*

Mercer understood the boy's name was Tedla. He pointed to himself. "Mercer," then added, "Selome?"

The boy gave a lengthy reply, but Mercer understood none of it. He let out a frustrated breath. Tedla poured water from a pewter pitcher and held it for him.

After draining the cup, Mercer settled under the coarse blankets and was asleep in moments. The next time he woke, he was alone and his room was dark except for a single candle burning on the desk. In its glow, he saw that a plate of fruit had been left for him. He had recovered enough to be hungry and reached for it, wolfing two mangoes and a banana before weakness overcame him and he was back asleep.

The candle had gone out when he regained consciousness again. A haunting sound echoed beyond his chamber. Mercer was disoriented, nearly panicked by the darkness, his own weakness, and the faint noise. Slowly his mind brought him back to the present, and his heart rate eased. He recognized the noise as a song, a chant. Then he remembered everything in a rush, the march through the desert, Selome's finding the water in the cave. Fuzzy pictures flashed in his mind of men carrying him and Selome from the cave up a steep trail to an ancient building. He lay in the darkness and smiled, letting the monks at their midnight prayer serenade him back to sleep. They'd made it to the monastery!

When the sun woke him, Mercer had enough strength to lever himself out of bed and dress. His clothes had been laundered and lay in a bundle on the desk. He was surprised to find he needed to use the chamber pot sitting under the bed. At least his kidneys were still functioning.

Once in the hallway, Mercer began to weaken but he continued past several closed doors until he came to the refectory, a large cleared table dominating the room. He sat at one of the chairs and lay his head on the tabletop, his breath coming in uneven gasps. Selome. He needed to find her.

He must have passed out again because suddenly Tedla was taping at his shoulder and speaking to him gently. "Where is everybody?" Mercer asked.

Tedla held up a finger to indicate Mercer was to wait and scampered from the room. A minute later, he returned with another, older monk. There was a reassuring air about the man, a comforting quality that radiated trust. It wasn't just the gray beard and the long dark robe. There was something behind his eyes that spoke of compassion and understanding.

"Selam," Mercer greeted. "Do you speak English?"

"Selam. No. Italiano?"

Mercer shook his head. *"Parlez-vous français?"*

"Un peu." A little.

Mercer switched effortlessly into French, but he spoke too fast for the monk and had to slow. "My name is Philip Mercer. I'm a mine engineer working here in Eritrea."

"Selome Nagast is awake for many hours, Monsieur Mercer. I know who you are. My name is Brother Ephraim."

"How long have we been here?" Mercer could barely understand the monk through his thick accent.

"Last night was your second."

Mercer had slept through nearly thirty-six hours! The Eritrean refugees would be reaching the mine soon; maybe they were already there. He felt his chest tighten with a new panic. "I need to leave."

Ephraim spoke to his acolyte and Tedla ran off, leaving Mercer alone with him. It was clear that they would need a translator if they were to continue their conversation. Soon after, Selome entered. Her ordeal had dulled her eyes some, but she was still beautiful. The weight loss made her already high cheekbones more prominent and her eyes larger. Relief flushed through Mercer and he closed his eyes, opening them again to drink her in. When he tried to stand and meet her embrace, she held him to his chair, her arms twined around his neck, her cheek laid against his. "How are you?" she asked softly.

Before Mercer could reply, Brother Ephraim coughed, drawing their attention. Selome pulled away and adopted a demure attitude in front of the ascetic. He spoke for several minutes, Selome thinking through her translation before turning back to Mercer.

"Brother Ephraim is the monastery's abbot and he welcomes us to Debre Amlak. He says it is highly irregular for a woman to be allowed within the compound, and he is concerned about our relationship." She spoke to Ephraim for a moment and then switched back to English. "I told him that you are a man of honor and I am a chaste woman who is promised to another."

"You lied to a priest?"

"What should I have told him?"

"You shouldn't have said I'm a man of honor, that's all." Mercer suppressed a grin. "Tell our host that any carnal thoughts in my condition are impossible. Thank him for his hospitality and for carrying us up from the cave and ask him how he managed to find us."

"He says that the cave is his retreat from the monastery, a place for him to enjoy an even greater sense of solitude. He discovered us himself and went to get other monks to bring us here."

"A retreat from a retreat?" Mercer wondered aloud, thankful nonetheless.

"He and I spoke yesterday when you were still unconscious, and I told him about our search for an ancient mine. He seemed to know all about it."

"What, the mine?"

"That, yes, but us too. He acted as though he'd been expecting us, or at least you."

"Don't go mystical on me, Selome."

"I'm just telling you what happened." Selome was interrupted by Ephraim. The elder cleric spoke for a few minutes.

Mercer watched Selome's reactions. Whatever the abbot was saying stunned her. She asked Ephraim a few questions before translating for Mercer's benefit.

"Brother Ephraim was never meant to be the monastery's abbot. He fell into the position by default when the monks returned home during the war. He told me this by way of explaining why he did what he did, why he read a book that was never meant to be seen again."

"What are you talking about?"

Selome ignored Mercer's questions. "There is a book here titled *Shame of Kings.* Ephraim said that only one other man has read it, Debre Amlak's previous abbot, a man whose faith it destroyed. Ephraim says the former abbot died believing God's punishment for his sacrilege was Eritrea's years of struggle and suffering.

"Brother Ephraim read it a few weeks ago because another monk predicted that an ancient secret was about to be revealed and that someone would come to question the priests about it. I think he believes that someone is you."

Feeling like cold death, Mercer didn't know what to say. When he looked at Ephraim, he saw the priest was serious. It sent a superstitious shiver up his spine. "Why me?"

"For one thing, you and I are the first outsiders to visit this monastery in decades. Also, when I told him that you're a miner, he said that your presence here and your professional skills make perfect sense when you consider the subject of the book."

"My being a mine engineer relates to some old religious book?"

"The *Shame of Kings* is more of a history than a religious text; the chronicle of an ancient diamond mine in Eritrea first worked by the priests of King Menyelek. It's the story of the mine we just discovered."

"Menyelek, not Solomon?"

"Yes. He was the first-born son of the Queen of Sheba and Solomon, the King of Israel. The diamonds that Menyelek found are certainly the basis of the King Solomon's Mine legend, only the fable was off by a generation." She paused. "But there is something even greater at stake here."

Mercer caught an undertone in Selome's voice and remembered he'd felt that she had been holding something back from him. Something she'd known all along. And he knew he was about to find out what it was.

"The tale begins in another book, the *Glory of Kings,*

which is the Ethiopian version of Sheba's visit to Solomon. It's a very different story from what is written in the Old Testament. You see, she was duped into sleeping with Solomon by a trick played on her by the King. Afterward, Sheba returned to Ethiopia with their baby, Menyelek, but the boy's destiny was to return to Israel. He was twenty-two when he visited his father in Jerusalem. There, a high priest told Menyelek that God had commanded him to remove the Tabernacle of the Word of God and carry it back to Ethiopia, transferring the Seat of God from Israel to Africa."

Seeing his bewilderment, she explained in simpler terms. "Solomon's son stole the Ark of the Covenant from the Temple and spirited it back to his own kingdom."

Mercer could not believe he'd heard correctly. "The Ark of the Covenant? That's what this is all about?" He could tell that she hadn't wanted to reveal any of this, and his anger mounted. This was what she'd been hiding from the beginning. "The diamonds are meaningless to you. You're all after the Ark and think it's hidden in the mine."

"Yes. Defense Minister Levine's agents are in Eritrea to find it and return it to Israel." Selome's voice took on a strident note, full of emotion and fear. "It will give him the moral authority to destroy the Dome of the Rock and erect the Third Temple."

Mercer was thoughtful for a moment. "I'd make him Emperor for Life if he pulled off a feat like that. But the Ark of the Covenant? You can't be serious. Selome, I'm not doubting your faith, but the Old Testament and this *Glory of Kings* aren't historical fact. They're stories."

"So was the *Iliad* until Heinrich Schliemann used it as a reference book," Selome countered hotly, "and discovered the city of Troy, a place many archaeologists said existed only in folklore. If you'll hear me out, you'll see Ephraim's story lends credence to Levine's plan."

"How so?" he asked with little interest. This was too much to believe.

"Soon after returning to Ethiopia with the Ark, Menyelek became embroiled in a number of wars, expanding Ethiopian territory as far as India. The revenue from trade caravans weren't enough to pay for his campaigns, so one of his priests, Azariah, told him of a mountain of diamonds far to the north of their capital.

"The *Shame of Kings* describes the discovery of this fabulous mountain and the history of the mining operation. The priests in charge used soldiers captured during Menyelek's battles to do the actual work. After the wars had ended, the priests turned to slave labor brought from Kush, modern-day Sudan. According to the book, the conditions were terrible and the worst was yet to come. After a hundred years, the workers had exhausted the diamonds that could be recovered from the surface and they were forced to tunnel into the earth. At first they used pygmies because of their smaller stature, but they died quickly in the shafts. One passage of the *Shame of Kings* laments this, for it had seemed like a promising idea."

"And it was still the priests using slaves to dig?"

"Yes." Selome obviously didn't want to continue, but she did, her voice heavy. "Because the pygmies didn't work out, the mine's overseers started using children. Boys and girls as young as six were herded into the mine, never to return. Female slaves were used as breeding stock to replenish the losses. It sounds like a system more cruel than what the Nazis did during the Holocaust, and the mine was in operation for over four hundred years. Countless tens of thousands of innocent lives were snuffed in a subterranean hell and the perpetrators of this atrocity were followers of Judaism."

"Selome, it happened two thousand years ago."

"Brother Ephraim says they were proud of what they did. Not only does the book describe some of the huge gems they found, but it also talks about the inhuman conditions and the practices used to get more work out of the children. If hate groups and anti-Semites found out that the first concentration camps were built by Jews, do you think it would matter how long ago it was? This can never be revealed!"

Mercer wanted to disagree, but he had a suspicion that

she was right. Hate was an easy commodity to sell. "Okay, I'll grant you the *Shame of Kings* is right about an ancient mine in northern Eritrea," he conceded. "The awful working conditions ring true and I know using children in mines was a common practice until just a hundred years ago, but what does this have to do with Levine and the Ark?"

"Levine's quest dates back two decades. He's always been obsessed with holy relics, especially the Ark. When Operation Moses rescued Ethiopian Jews in 1984, he had the refugees questioned about religious artifacts left in their home country. Rumor surrounded a particular church, St. Mary of Zion in Aksum, Ethiopia's ancient capital. Some said the Ark was still there. Levine secretly sent a team of agents to break into the church, but they found nothing to convince them that it had ever been a resting place for the Ark."

"And he *still* thought it was in Ethiopia?" he scoffed.

"Goddamn it, Mercer! It doesn't matter if you believe this or not. Levine does, and as long as he's holding your friend Harry, that's all that's important. Enough people have died in the past weeks to convince you that your doubts don't mean anything."

Mercer's scientific background made him naturally skeptical, but he suddenly realized she was right. It was Levine's motivation that mattered, not its validity. And even if he didn't believe, he knew he shouldn't close his mind to the possibilities. Hadn't the *Shame of Kings* been correct about the mine? "I'm sorry, this is all so . . . Anyway, you were saying Levine thought the Ark was here."

"Ethiopia is the oldest Christian country in the world and has Jewish ties that date back even further. Besides, he was certain it wasn't in Israel. There isn't much of our country that hasn't been combed by archaeologists. Levine started to investigate some of the less-credible rumors the refugees brought with them. He learned that the Ark might have been on an island on Lake Tana but that also turned out to be a false lead. The only other reference he got to the Ark was a story about a golden chest placed in an ancient mine to help ward off an evil that was killing the workers long, long ago. When Levine saw the kimberlite pipe on the Medusa photographs, he was sure he'd find the mine the refugees spoke of. He also felt that somewhere near the pipe, he'd discover the Ark's final repository."

"He doesn't know that the mine was dug by Solomon's son?"

"He wouldn't care. It's the Ark he's after."

"Does the *Shame of Kings* say that the Ark's in the mine?"

"Not in so many words. The rumor of the golden chest Levine is following probably came from it, from someone who read it ages ago. The *Shame of Kings* does talk about a curse that killed the children, a mysterious illness caused by Satan that made it impossible to continue work in the tunnels. To combat it, a powerful talisman was brought to the mine and placed in a special chamber that was dug to the exact specifications of the Ark's original tabernacle in Jerusalem. It says nothing about it ever being removed."

"Did it work? Did the talisman prevent the disease?"

Selome asked Ephraim. "The children died in greater numbers, and soon afterward the priests realized that God was punishing them for what they'd done. They sealed the mine and never revealed its location."

For a moment Mercer allowed himself to speculate. Since the mine they discovered was undoubtedly the same one written about in the *Shame of Kings,* was it possible that the rest of the story was also true? The mine had lain undisturbed for two thousand years, and if the talisman it mentioned was indeed the Ark of the Covenant, then it could still be there, buried under countless tons of rock, waiting to be discovered. He took his silent musings one step further and considered the consequences if Levine managed to find it and return it to Israel. The Mideast would explode in a religious war that would make the past fifty years of conflict seem like petty squabbling. Selome was right when she said that Levine would use its symbolism to raze the Dome of the Rock, the third most sacred site in Islam. If that happened, Mercer imagined the ensuing war would go nuclear as Muslims from all over the globe used their numerical superiority to overpower the Israelis and recapture the Temple Mount. It was a doomsday scenario that Mercer knew could happen, would happen, if he didn't stop it.

This was all too much. Just days ago he found he might have discovered King Solomon's mine, and now Mercer found that he was in a race to find the Ark of the Covenant. If he wasn't so weak and tired, he would have been terrified. The desert trek had left him in a worse condition than Selome, and his mind was beginning to fade again. He couldn't absorb any more information. "I bet the Sudanese don't know anything about this. Their backers are after the diamonds while Harry's kidnappers, Levine ultimately, want an archaeological artifact lost thousands of years ago."

"Yes, and they're both located in the Valley of Dead Children."

Suddenly the meaning behind the valley's name became shudderingly obvious.

"We should be thankful we still have time. Judging by the excavating we did before coming to the monastery, it'll take weeks to reopen the mine." And then Mercer remembered. "Oh shit! There are about two hundred refugees there right now. The Sudanese who attacked us are probably using them as forced labor as we speak. They might already have it opened!"

Mercer hadn't told her about the displaced Eritreans he had coming from the camps in Sudan, and her expression registered her shock. "Where'd they come from?"

"When we were with the nomads in Badn getting fuel, I hired one of the headman's sons to get them and bring them to the valley." Guilt cracked Mercer's voice, but beneath it was a grim determination to see them freed.

Selome spoke with Brother Ephraim for a few minutes, then turned back. "He says it's impossible to reach any town until after the Adobha has subsided. The river is impassable for at least three weeks."

"We have no choice. We have to cross it."

Ephraim seemed to understand Mercer's foul expression and his defiant outburst. Selome performed an almost simultaneous translation. "The river moves with the speed and force of a truck, and it's littered with debris washed down from the highlands. The flood would destroy any raft we could build. Every year, dozens of people die trying to cross it. Be sensible."

"I don't have that luxury. People's lives depend on us, not only those refugees but also Habte, the two drivers, and my friend Harry White. And if, somehow, the Ark really is in the mine, then maybe the rest of the world, too. I'll be sensible when the Eritrean military arrives at the mine and arrests anyone holding a gun."

Selome asked the monk a couple more questions, the priest's response seeming to calm her anxiety. "He says the talisman spoken of in the *Shame of Kings* was placed in the deepest part of the mine, buried so deeply that it would take an army of workers many months to find it." She looked into Mercer's eyes. "Think about it. The Sundanese don't know about the Ark. Once they reach the diamonds, they'll stop exploring the tunnels and begin mining. They'll never know what's buried in some deeper chamber. Remember how many Sudanese troops that headman said were waiting on the border?"

"Fifty," Mercer said, beginning to understand what Selome was saying.

"Levine doesn't have enough people to attack a force that size. They'll have to wait until after the rebels leave before starting their own search. We have weeks or even months to warn the authorities."

"More time to save the world?" Mercer sounded almost flippant, then his mood darkened. "That still leaves two hundred refugees. I'm leaving in the morning."

"You can't even stand right now," she shot back. "Mercer, I've been to those refugee camps, and I can tell you that in the short term those people are going to be better off at the mine."

"How can you say that?" He was surprised she'd put to words that he was just beginning to consider.

"They may be worked as slaves, but they're going to be fed and provided with clean water. Whoever's running the operation has to take care of the refugees if he expects them to work."

In his condition, Mercer knew there was a good chance he wouldn't make it to civilization. His effort would be a wasted, empty gesture that would help no one. It took just a second to come to the only logical option. "All right, we'll rest up for a couple of days, but no more. Ask Ephraim if he can provide us with a guide to Ila Babu. Maybe someone there owns a two-way radio."

"He says that Tedla will guide us. It's about forty miles, but he says he knows of no one in town who has a radio."

"We'll worry about that when the time comes."

Ephraim and Selome took him back to his room and saw him to bed. After the monk left, she sat with him, wiping his brow with a wet cloth. There was such tenderness in her motions that Mercer took her hand and kissed each of her fingertips.

"What's that for?"

"Because I've wanted to do it since we met and couldn't until I trusted you."

She kissed his lips lightly, but there was a greater passion in her eyes. "So you trust me now?"

"No more secrets." He tried to smile and then he was asleep.

Selome watched him a few minutes, her hand spread on his chest, fingers splayed as if to possess more of him. She kissed him again. "No more secrets."

For the next two days Mercer rested and drank water more than he thought possible. His strength returned slowly but steadily. By the end of the afternoon on the second day, he felt strong enough to walk the grounds surrounding the monastery, careful to remain on the inside of the stakes that delineated land that had been cleared of mines. He saw little of Selome; she showed enough respect to the monks and their traditions to keep herself out of sight. He spent some of his waking hours thinking about the inhumanity described in the *Shame of Kings,* but mostly he considered how to rescue the Eritrean refugees and how to stop Levine from using the Ark. If it *had* survived the ages, he wouldn't be surprised if it was buried in the ancient mine. *Jesus!*

It was well past sunset. Mercer was lying on his bed when he heard someone walking outside his window, which opened onto the monastery's small cloister. It was too dark to see more than a shadowy form, so he threw on his pants and boots and slid from his room. The cloister's entrance was off the refectory, and he was aware of the wooden floors creaking as he walked. He feared that he would wake the monks.

Selome stood at the center of the pillared cloister, her body barely illuminated by the moon and stars. She kept her eyes locked with his as he crossed to her slowly.

"I was hoping it would be you," she whispered. "Despite his status as an acolyte, I'm afraid Tedla has taken a fancy to me."

"I was hoping that it was you, too," Mercer replied softly. "I want to say thanks. You were right. I'd never have made it to Ila Babu."

"How are you feeling?"

"Much better, but I'm still as weak as a kitten."

"How weak?" she asked with a huskiness that Mercer recognized immediately. She moved a few paces closer to him, the heat of her body soaking into his skin.

"As weak as a cat." Mercer tried to keep the catch out of his voice. It had been a couple days since he'd seen her, and the sexual tension that they had sparked before their trip to the monastery returned with a fury.

Her arms went around his neck, one knee cocked forward so it slid between his legs. "How weak?"

"How about a tired lion?"

"Better," she smiled. "We'll be leaving the monastery tomorrow, and Tedla is going to be with us every step of the way. Once we contact the government, it'll be a long time before we'll have a moment to ourselves. I'm sorry, but if we are going to make love, it has to be tonight. Now."

"Pretty forward of you."

She placed a slim finger to his lips. "No jokes."

"Selome, I—" His next words were cut off by her hungry kiss. She pressed herself to him, fitting almost perfectly, knees matching knees, hips to hips, chest to chest. He felt her breasts swell and harden against his naked chest, more and more heat pouring against him the longer they kissed.

"I was going to say," Mercer muttered, "I think it would be a good idea if we found a more private place. This is a church, after all."

That dam he'd felt cracking when Selome told him about her involvement with Shin Bet gave way completely. For the first time in months, since the split with Aggie, Mercer gave himself over to another human completely. It was liberating and frightening at the same time, but also very right.

He returned to his room for a shirt and his bedding, and they walked down the narrow path hacked into the cliff. With the moon reflecting off the sandy plain, they could clearly see the cave no more than a quarter mile south. Both were surprised at its proximity to the monastery. Mercer lit a candle and spread the sheets and blankets on the cavern floor. She motioned for him to stretch out and watch as she undressed.

He expected a hint of self-consciousness from Selome, but there was none. She pulled her shirt over her head in one fluid motion, her high breasts bouncing as they came free. Her nipples looked painfully erect, and his body reacted. Her pants fell around her ankles with just the tiniest bit of urging. She kicked out of them and hooked her thumbs in the waist band of her panties. With deliberate slowness, she slid them down her thighs, bending deeply until they lay at her feet in a rippled puddle of silk.

She stood proudly, a dusky Venus, her body taut and perfect, her skin so flawless and waxy smooth in the candlelight that she looked like marble. Mercer couldn't help but stare at the shallow cleft that rose from the juncture of her thighs, her body's most secret place veiled by only a thin down. His heart pounded and his breath matched the shallow heaving of Selome's chest. Her arousal perfumed the air.

Mercer began shedding his clothes, but Selome dropped to her knees next to him, brushed away his hands, and began working at the buttons and zippers, her fingers stroking each newly exposed section of his body until he was nude and she held him firmly in her palm. She squeezed him every so slightly, and his hips bucked involuntarily. It was only then that she kissed his mouth again.

"You are so beautiful," Mercer said, and Selome smiled.

"So are you."

She would not let him do any of the work that first time, not even sheath himself with one of the condoms Mercer's doctor made him stash in his wallet. For Mercer, it felt incredibly decadent not to have to worry about his partner's pleasure, for her expression told him that her arousal came solely from his enjoyment. For the ten minutes they were joined, they freed each other from the world as Selome rocked her body on his, drawing him in deeper and deeper. Mercer's climax left him dizzy and gasping. Then, in a feat he hadn't been capable of since college, they made love again almost immediately. Mercer had only seconds to put on another condom before Selome drew him on top of her. Her orgasmic screams echoed far outside their intimate cave.

They were so lost in their lovemaking, neither heard the convoy of trucks approaching from the east. Half an hour after the vehicles passed, they were packing up the bedding and adjusting their clothes for the walk back to the monastery when distant machine-gun fire shattered the night. The crashing explosion of sound stripped away the euphoria they had just built and brought them back to the ugliness of reality.

Tel Aviv, Israel

Danny Silver was twenty-three years old, an American by birth who had moved to the Jewish state with his parents when he was sixteen. He liked Israel well enough so long as he stayed in the country's largest city. A few years ago, he'd tried kibbutz life for a summer and found the back-to-nature, communal living to be a bore. He liked the action of Tel Aviv with its late-night discos and cosmopolitan aura. Besides, being a bartender at one of the big hotels on the beach ensured he could get laid almost any night he wanted. American girls on break from college or spending time in Israel to discover their "Jewishness" were invariably fascinated by his stories, especially the ones he made up about his compulsory tour in the army.

But it was a Tuesday night, not yet eight, and the cocktail lounge was slow. His only customers were a group of Israeli businessmen in one corner and two old women from a New Jersey tour group near the bar's entrance. Danny busied himself behind the long bar, polishing glasses that were already spotless and wiping down bottles that didn't need to be cleaned. Sara, the waitress, stood casually at her station, one eye on her customers and the other on a college textbook. Danny really didn't like her. She did nothing to hide her disdain for any Jew not born in Israel.

Screw her, he thought absently, unable to tear his eyes away from the perfect swell of her breasts under her white uniform blouse.

A crash from the lobby turned Danny away from Sara's cleavage. An old guy had toppled a sign board in the lobby, sending it to the floor, but the fool didn't stop to right it again. He charged into the bar like a Merkava battle tank, his hard eyes drilling through Danny to the display wall of liquor behind him.

The man resembled a scarecrow, thin and wrinkled. He looked almost comical, but there was nothing funny about his expression. Had the guy been Arab, Danny would have run for his life. But he was white, probably American, and certainly nuts. He rushed straight for the bar, heaving himself onto a stool with an explosive grunt. Hunching his shoulders like a vulture, he glared at Danny until the Israeli sauntered over to ask what he wanted.

"Drink." American, for sure.

"What kind of a drink, sir?" *What an idiot.*

"Give me anything with alcohol or so help me Christ, I'll tear you apart and get it myself."

Normally, Danny would have laughed at him, but the customer spoke with such force that he believed the crazy old bastard would have tried it. "Sure thing, sir, anything you say."

Danny poured a measure of brandy into a snifter, but before he could set the drink on the bar, the American lunged for the bottle. The man snapped off the speed pourer with a practiced twist and upended the bottle to his lips. Three swallows vanished in as many seconds before the geezer set the bottle carefully on the bar top.

"Sorry about that, son," Harry White rasped. "But you were taking too damn long. If you knew what I've been through in the past couple weeks, you would've done the same thing."

"Yeah, sure. Whatever." Danny backed away.

"Tell you what, kid, if you've got any bourbon back there, Jack Daniel's preferably, I promise not to bite. Deal?" The expression of madness was transformed into a smile that was almost grandfatherly.

Danny poured a shot of bourbon and wisely left the bottle on the bar. Stealing a glance at Sara, he saw her watching the whole bizarre exchange with a smirk. She looked as if she expected such repulsive behavior from Americans. *Bitch.*

Harry gulped down the bourbon and helped himself to another, pouring until the glass could not hold one more alcohol molecule. When he brought it to his lips, he didn't spill a drop. "You're a lifesaver, my friend. A goddamned lifesaver." The liquor filed the sharper edges off Harry's voice. "Eight or ten more of these and I might feel human again."

"Mr. White?" a female called from the lobby. She was poised at the entrance to the bar with a startled look. Her chest heaved because she had been forced to run into the hotel, chasing after the octogenarian. Wearing a conservative gray suit with an off-the-rack blouse and a ridiculous bow, to Danny she was the picture of a government employee. She trod across the marble lobby floor, her sensible shoes clacking with a horse-like clomp. "Oh, thank God, Mr. White. I was afraid I'd lost you for a second."

Harry nodded at his drink. "A second was all I needed."

The harried young woman was Jessica Michaelson. She worked for the CIA under the cover of a cultural attaché and had been assigned the job of minding Harry White until his flight back to the United States. As the lowest-ranking CIA agent at the embassy, she had been saddled with Harry for nearly a week now. While not involved with his debriefing, she had to keep the curmudgeon occupied when he was not in meetings with the more senior officers, including the station chief.

Jessica had read the report of what Harry had been through in the past couple of weeks, and even in its sanitized version his experiences were harrowing. But after a week with him, she felt her pity wearing thin and was hoping the terrorists would come and take him away again.

From a portion of the report that Jessica Michaelson had read, Harry's own words from a stenographer's transcript described what had happened to bring him to the care of the CIA:

> *I'd just escaped the gun fight and was real tired. I smelled like hell and my whiskers were itchin' something fierce. I think I picked up some critters in that cell too. Anyway,*

I was walking along, looking for something, anything that I could recognize, but all the signs were written in squiggly letters that looked like they were done by a blind two-year-old. Then I saw one sign I could read, and damned if fate isn't one cruel bitch. It was on a church bulletin board, and it was for an Alcohol Anonymous meeting that was going to start a half hour after curfew had been lifted. I hid out for the night in an alley a couple blocks away. The next morning, I went to the church at the appropriate time, but it was hard to step inside. This being the Holy City and all, I expected lightning to strike me dead at any moment.

Well, I went in and the group looked at me like they'd been expecting me. I sat quiet for a while and listened to the men and women, most of 'em were Americans or British. After twenty minutes of waiting for God's wrath for desecrating the meeting. I stood up and told the group that my name was Harry and with my fingers crossed behind my back told them that I was an alcoholic. I said I'd been sober for a couple of hours now, having come down from a thirty-seven-day binge that started in De Moines, Iowa, and ended in the Church of the Holy Sepulcher. I told them that most of the details in between were still a bit fuzzy.

I know what I was doing was wrong, you understand. I think AA is one hell of a fine program, and it does some amazing things for folks who want to get their lives back together but I needed help pretty badly and I figured these people, seeing me in the state I was, would have a little pity. They all listened, actually they were hanging on my every word. They seemed to know each other's stories pretty well, and I was laying something entirely new on them. They fell all over themselves offering support and advice. Well anyway, after the meeting, a guy came up, told me his name was Walt Hayes from Missouri, and that he was a reporter for Newsweek.

Walt said he'd help me figure out how to get home. Said he had some friends at the American embassy. Later that day he took me to the embassy, introduced me to some attaché or other, and after I told her the true story, she sicced all you CIA flunkies on me. Hey, how about that drink now?

Interviewer: In just a little while, Mr. White. Tell us again about the woman holding you who you thought was a nurse.

For the rest of the details of Harry's adventure, Jessica had broken a few security protocols and listened to the old man's ramblings when she spent dinners with him at the embassy cafeteria, including his dim recollections about the shoot-out at Dulles Airport and the names of a few of his captors.

Her superiors had acquiesced only partially to Harry's continuous entreaties for alcohol and allowed him a drink after each day's debriefing, saying they wanted him fresh for the next session. But now that Harry was finally being returned to the United States, he had bolted from the car transporting him from the embassy to a hotel in Tel Aviv prior to his flight. Because Harry wasn't in any sort of custody, and those that had taken him had gone deep underground, the CIA had agreed to give him a few hours of free time provided that he was under constant surveillance. This also gave the operatives a convenient place away from prying eyes to hand Harry over to agents of the FBI, who would actually be accompanying him on his flight home.

Hot on Jessica's heels into the bar were two additional CIA minders, both men wearing lightweight jackets to conceal their weapons. They too were breathing heavily and looked at Harry with mild shock, for he had managed to outrun them all.

"Mr. White, you weren't supposed to do that," Jessica chided. She moved close so only he could hear when she continued. "We're here for your protection."

Harry turned and pinned her with his stare. "It's not my fault you guys can't keep up. If there had been something to drink in that car of yours, I wouldn't have needed to get in here so quickly. I told you to get me one with a minibar." He shot a smile toward Danny. "How about a little ginger ale?"

"Harry, you are still in danger," Jessica Michaelson whispered. "You should stick by us until we have you safely in the FBI's care."

"Or what? I'll be in trouble?"

"No, Mr. White. You might be dead."

"Ehh!" Harry dismissed the comment with a wave, a lit cigarette magically appearing in his claw-like hand.

One of the male agents tapped Jessica on the shoulder and pointed toward the ceiling. "Harry, let's go up to the room we have waiting," she said. "The FBI should be here in a few minutes, and it would be best if we all met upstairs."

"Okay," Harry agreed, pouring more bourbon into his nearly finished drink. "Let me just freshen this last one and we'll go and see what room service can do for us."

"Mr. White. Harry. Do you really think it's wise to get drunk before your flight?" Jessica Michaelson had no children, yet she had the "mother voice" down perfectly.

Harry had been playing up his situation a bit, he admitted. But he'd done what everyone had asked of him and wanted very little in return, and now his patience was about gone. "Listen, sweetheart," he deliberately taunted. "I've been through hell in the past few weeks and I managed to get myself out of it without your assistance. Indeed, I've managed to survive eighty years without your help, for what that's worth, and I've been in worse scrapes than this. You may recall World War Two from your history books—the chapter usually ends with a picture of a mushroom cloud. I appreciate your concern, it's touching really, but you're a few weeks too late.

"Now, I promised your superiors that I would keep this affair quiet when I get home. But so help me God, if you say one more word, I'm going to sell my story to the nearest magazine and let the chips fall where they may. Everyone says that the Middle East is a powder keg. Well, I just spent a few weeks with the bastards who made the fuse and are currently standing over it with a lit match."

Jessica looked chastened. She wasn't expecting an eloquent outburst from her charge.

Harry continued. "I'm going up to the room with you and I'm going to allow myself to be passed off to the FBI and I'm going back to Washington to let Dick Henna's boys debrief me again. But if you think for one second that I'm going to spend the few hours I have between you and them in any kind of sober state, then you have a lot to learn about me, Ms. Michaelson. I'll do my patriotic duty, honey, but right now I'm on my time."

He lifted himself from his bar stool and glanced at Danny. "She'll be paying my tab and make sure she gives you a good tip."

Monastery of Debre Amlak

Mercer identified the sound of a machine gun a fraction of a second quicker than Selome. He'd heard that noise many times before. He dropped the bundle of bedding and ducked his head out of the cave. The sound had originated above them on the cliff, near the monastery, but he kept his gaze at ground level, searching for a rear picket or a scout party. The open desert was still.

"Who is it?" Selome whispered.

Mercer didn't answer. It wasn't possible that Levine's agents could have found them here, so the gunmen were undoubtedly connected to the Sudanese who'd chased them from the Valley of Dead Children. Mercer hated to think what they'd done to Habte to get this location from him. However, identifying the terrorists didn't help. Another burst of gunfire echoed down from the monastery.

Mercer quickly ran through his options and found he had only one. He couldn't let the monks pay for his blundering into their sanctuary. His presence had attracted the Sudanese, and it was up to him to force them out. If he couldn't, he would surrender and trade himself for the lives of the priests. Once captured, he was certain the rebels would take him to the mine. He'd just have to hope he'd find a way to escape again so he could derail the Israelis.

"Stay here," he ordered, his voice calm but forceful. He turned left once outside the cave.

"Mercer, the path to the monastery is the other direction."

"I know, but we approached from the south, and that's where I dumped the pack. I'll be right back."

He kept to the irregular cliff wall, moving slowly and deliberately, his khaki clothes blending with the sandstone. He expected to search for at least half a mile but he came upon the pack after only three hundred yards. He thought of that last push before he had stumbled into the cave with Selome on his back. He'd made it on will alone, his strength totally depleted, his mind all but gone. But three hundred yards? He was positive he'd carried Selome farther than that. That short distance represented an hour of agonizing labor, perhaps the most difficult hour of his life, and he realized that had the cave been even a few yards farther, they would have died huddled against the cliff.

There was enough moonlight for Mercer to familiarize himself with everything in the satchel. Much of it was worthless, but there was Selome's pistol charged with a full clip of ammunition. He grabbed up the pack and tramped back to the cave, keeping alert for a flash of light reflecting off a weapon or an upturned face on the open plain. Selome was waiting for him at the cave's entrance.

"How'd you find it so quickly?"

"I'm not the superman I thought I was. The pack was only a couple hundred yards away." He secreted items from the bag into his pockets. "I'm going up to the monastery. If I can't draw the terrorists away from the priests, I'm going to give myself over to them."

"And what about me?"

"I don't think they want you. Just me. Remember, I'm the geologist."

"That's not what I meant," Selome said sharply. "What am I supposed to do while you're off playing hero?"

"I'm not doing this to prove how tough I am." *That's an understatement.* Mercer's fear made it difficult for him to swallow. "I have to go, and you have to warn the authorities about what's been happening. I want you to head south again. Stay along the cliff and drag our blanket behind you to sweep away your tracks. Find somewhere to hide for the day. If I don't come down looking for you in a couple of hours, it means I probably won't. Wait until sunset before returning to the monastery. I'm willing to bet the Sudanese will be gone by then."

Her eyes glared. "Don't even consider leaving me out of this, Mercer. I'm even more responsible than you. If you have a plan, count me in."

"Selome, I—"

She cut him off, her voice raised dangerously loud. "I said don't think about it and I mean it. I am coming with you. Like you said, you're the geologist—well, I'm the trained agent. You did pretty well in Asmara, but I have more experience in situations like this."

He was about to list a few of the gunfights he'd been in, but before he could, an unholy scream pierced the night, a sharp keening wail that dropped down the cliff, growing louder and louder until it was suddenly cut off. The silence that followed was more terrible than the scream.

There was no more time to argue.

Mercer led Selome back toward the trail leading up to the monastery. About thirty feet from where the path rose into the rock, a dark shape revealed itself on the ground. They both knew that it was a body. A spray radiated from the corpse like a diffused shadow. The sheer volume of the bloody splashes made it unnecessary to check if the victim had survived the fall.

They crossed the narrow entrance to the ascending path and continued along the cliff, the monastery now behind and above them. Mercer could feel Selome's questioning stare at his back, but he didn't take the time to explain his plan. Keeping a sharp eye for a place they could climb the hundred feet to the plateau above, Mercer considered what he'd do once they were in sight of the monastery. He had no idea how many gunmen had come here, nor how they were positioned. His only advantage was surprise and even that was relatively worthless. By throwing one of the priests off the cliff, the terrorists were telling him they knew he was here. They were expecting him. He could only hope that by coming up behind them rather than climbing the established path, he could gain something.

A quarter mile farther, Mercer found a suitable spot to

make their climb. The cliff still soared in a near vertical massif, but its face was scarred with deep fissures and scaly projections that would act as hand and foot holds. And most important, they were out of earshot of the monastery.

"Wait here." He moved away from the cliff so he could study the whole wall, mapping a route to avoid climbing into a dead end. A more experienced climber would have been able to judge the features of the stone in the moonlight and possibly pick a safe route, but Mercer was, at best, a climber by necessity. He'd never had a burning desire to hang hundreds of feet above his death. He allowed himself only a few minutes, his mind absorbing every possible detail before rejoining Selome.

"Well?"

"Have you ever climbed before?"

"No."

"All right, you'll lead. I'm going to be right behind you so I can give you directions." He couldn't afford to have her freeze below him. "It looks a lot worse than it is, so just move where I tell you and everything will be fine."

"I have to tell you that I'm afraid of heights," she said in a small voice.

"Well, I'm afraid of spiders and that's the real reason you're going first. You get them for me and I'll make sure nothing happens to you. Okay?" His grin seemed to give her that last bit of confidence she needed.

"Okay."

Their progress was smooth at first. The base of the cliff had a shallower pitch than what lay ahead, and the stone had been cleaved by erosion. They kept three points on the rock at all times, cautious but moving well. After thirty feet the face steepened, and they could no longer climb in a stooped position. Forced to stand upright, they pressed themselves to the cool stone, the void sucking at them from below. Mercer could sense Selome's panic rising, and he touched her ankle gently, reassuring her that he was still with her.

"Veer to the left more," he whispered. "There's a natural chimney that should take us up another twenty feet. It leads to a shelf where we can take our first break." He didn't add that after the shelf, the climb would become more difficult.

The chimney was wide enough for Mercer to jam his shoulders against both sides and wriggle his way upward. Selome had a better strength-to-weight ratio, so she could climb even faster. They reached the shelf a half hour after beginning their assault and lay side by side, both panting from the exertion. "Keep moving your fingers or they'll stiffen," Mercer warned as he sucked the blood from where he had scraped two of his knuckles.

"How am I doing?"

"You're wonderful."

"You aren't so bad yourself." Selome kissed him. "Ready?"

"You bet," he replied, heartened by her positive attitude. "You'll want to move to the right. There's a thin lip of stone about six feet above us. It'll be tricky getting to it, but we'll be able to walk along it until we reach another vertical fissure."

She looked above them to see the features Mercer was describing, but a rocky bulge blocked her view.

"You're going to have to trust me on this one."

She placed her hands on the wall, toed her boot into a shallow cup in the stone, and lifted herself. The rock brow pushed her out over empty space, and her balance shifted almost too far. Mercer could hear her nails digging into the stone and his heart raced, fearing she would panic. Seconds trickled by. The only sounds were a caressing breeze, Selome's labored breathing, and the rasp of her clothes against the stone.

"I've got it," she finally wheezed.

Mercer followed and in a moment he was beside her, a ten-inch-wide strip of stone under his feet. Immediately, Mercer saw his miscalculation. From the ground, the narrow ledge looked as if it continued for a dozen yards to the next crack, but it narrowed after just a couple of feet until it was nothing more than a band of shadow against the cliff. It vanished completely for about four feet before reappearing again, if anything even narrower than where they now stood.

He saw nothing but glass-smooth stone for twenty feet above them. They couldn't climb up from here, and backing down was next to impossible. They were trapped.

"What are we going to do?" Selome saw their predicament reflected in Mercer's eyes.

He stared at the problem before answering. "We're going to have to jump to the next ledge. Do you see that knob of stone at chest height in the middle of where the ledge disappears? You have to lean out and grab it with your left hand and then swing across. You're tall enough so your feet will land on the other side."

"No way!" she cried.

"If you see a better option, I'm open to it."

She looked around. The stone protrusion Mercer had seen was fist-sized, jutting from the wall no more than four inches, but it could provide an anchor point for them to pendulum across to the remainder of the ledge.

She kept her shoulder pressed tightly to the stone, her eyes fixed on the knob rather than the sixty feet of nothing beneath them, then reached out, her palm encircling the knob completely. Without allowing herself even a second to think, she eased her weight further onto her hand until her body was bowed backward. She kicked off gently, swinging smoothly, her clothes hissing against the rock. Her right foot landed on the ledge first, and she quickly shifted her weight, twisting so her left knee touched down next to her foot, her free hand clutching the wall. She let go of the knob and grinned over at Mercer.

He smiled back and was readying himself to repeat her feat when a stone sailed past his head. He looked up. A dark figure loomed at the top of the cliff, silhouetted against the night sky. Mercer could see another stone in the man's hand and the outline of an automatic weapon over his shoulder. The man saw Mercer's gaze and waved him up eagerly, taunting him by tossing the stone from hand to hand. Mercer lunged for the stone protrusion, arcing violently through the air.

The stone thrower was a moment too late. Mercer landed on the narrow ledge just as the other rock sailed behind him. He hustled Selome along the ledge, only his toes and the balls of his feet finding purchase on the lip. The next vertical fissure was wide and angled into the cliff. Once they had climbed high enough into it, it was possible to move up it like a ramp. There was no way they could reach the top before the gunman saw them again, but Mercer hoped to get high enough to give him a nasty surprise.

Fifteen feet from the top, Mercer grabbed Selome's leg. "Duck."

He climbed over her so he could take the lead. He saw the gunman waiting at the head of the eroded fissure, his gun now cradled in his hands. Had the man wanted to, he could have shot them both, but Mercer suspected his orders were to capture, not kill. The stone throws had been intentional misses. Mercer had prepared for this contingency by making sure their climb was far enough from the monastery to prevent a guard from shouting for reinforcements. If the Sudanese rebel wanted backup, he would be forced to run back to the church, giving Mercer and Selome a chance to escape.

"Stay flat and hold on tight," Mercer whispered.

He was climbing up the steep defile like a machine, his legs pistoning, propelling him forward deceptively fast. Mercer wished he could use Selome's pistol, but a shot would alert everyone within a mile. He was ready to implement a plan born in desperation. The lighting was poor enough for him to get closer to the Sudanese than the rebel suspected. The soldier didn't recognize the danger until it was too late.

Before leaving the cave, Mercer had secured a geologist's rock hammer to a fifteen-foot length of nylon rope and kept it coiled under his arm, its handle sticking from his unbuttoned shirt. The angle was nearly impossible, but he yanked the tool from its hiding place, twisted to allow for a side-armed throw, and let loose, holding on to the rope's free end. The hammer sailed cleanly, the tether trailing it like the exhaust of a rocket. At full stretch, the nylon line wrapped around the terrorist's neck and arced back again, the tool neatly returning to Mercer's waiting left hand. He heaved with all of his strength, yanking the man off his feet. Torquing his body, Mercer jerked the man up and over himself, releasing his grip on the rope and sending the soldier crashing into the defile a few paces from Selome. The African bounced once and then flew right over her, tumbling down the crevasse until he fell into empty space. His scream lasted less than two seconds.

His AK-47 had become wedged behind a rock just a few feet from where Mercer lay.

Mercer waited for several minutes, but no alarm was raised, and when he peeked over the top of the cliff, he could see nothing but more desert. Selome joined him a few seconds later. "Now what?"

"I'm afraid this is as far as I've taken the plan," Mercer admitted, and handed Selome her pistol, keeping the assault rifle for himself. He tucked the hammer into his belt.

In the far distance, the fortress-like walls of the monastery were washed by the headlights of several vehicles. Occasionally, a figure would bisect the shafts of light and cast shadows against the building. There were at least three trucks that he could see, and Mercer estimated at least a dozen terrorists. The AK held thirty rounds in its banana magazine. He would have to make every one count.

"I guess the best thing to do is sneak up to them and take the rebels as opportunities present themselves."

"Mercer, the first time we fire, they'll be on us in seconds," Selome reminded him grimly.

"Well, whatever we do, we need to get closer."

He led Selome along the edge of the cliff, using the sheer drop to ensure that they couldn't be outflanked. The craggy lip also provided a scant amount of cover for their approach. Thirty yards from the complex of buildings, they could see at least ten armed Sudanese milling around the trucks. Several monks were lined up against the monastery wall, their dark faces shining with sweat and their eyes bright and frightened in the headlights' glow. Mercer watched for several minutes, waiting to see what would happen next and fearful that he already knew. Suddenly the rebels stiffened to attention. Another party entered the circle of light, four men, three of them cradling weapons. The fourth was unarmed and walked with the relaxed arm-swinging gait of a natural leader. The fourth man was white! *One of Levine's?*

Confused, Mercer watched as the white man spoke to one of the blacks and waited for his orders to be translated to the others. Several men hopped into one of the idling trucks and drove off. Mercer assumed they were heading for the base of the cliff to try tracking where he and Selome had gone. The white and several rebels went into the monastery, herding the monks ahead of them. Another soldier walked to the cliff, casting along the escarpment with a powerful flashlight in hopes of spotting their quarry. He turned and started straight for where Mercer and Selome lay hidden. They had only moments before the rebel found them huddled in the darkness.

Mercer pressed his mouth to Selome's ear so his whisper was almost unaudible. "Stay behind me."

He moved forward on his stomach to get closer to the approaching Sudanese, then eased into a shallow depression, the sharp hammer in his right hand, the AK clamped under his body. His mouth had gone dry as the soldier came nearer.

The flashlight beam shone along the ground with an untutored randomness. Mercer knew that if the soldier turned it on him, he would have to surrender, but the African seemed more interested in what lay below the cliff edge. The soldier studying the drop was ten paces away when Mercer made his move, hoisting himself into a crouch and rushing forward faster than the startled soldier could react. One swift blow from the hammer was enough to kill, and Mercer dragged the African back into the dust. The entire maneuver had been silent.

He went back to Selome and led her away from the cliff, circling wide around the monastery so they could approach from a less likely direction. If the white man was an Israeli agent, that meant they'd put aside their differences with the Sudanese and pooled their resources. It was an option that he didn't want to consider.

But what if he's the rebels' original backer, the moneyman behind their operation? And then the answer came to him. *Italian!* Someone with a connection to the mine shaft Mercer had explored had returned to carry on that work. An Italian with ties to Eritrea's colonial past would never be allowed back into the country, but using Sudanese mercenaries would allow him to secretly work the old mine with minimal direct involvement. *Shit, I led them right to it and provided the labor.*

He thought about the African who had opened fire in the Rome airport. The gunman must have worked for the Italian. He had seen the Israeli agent shadowing Mercer, perceived him as a threat to Mercer's life, and murdered him. That would have been the beginning of the struggle between the Sudanese and the Israelis, a battle that had continued outside of Mercer's hotel room in Asmara.

Mercer was still left with the question of how the Sudanese and their Italian backer knew about his coming to Eritrea and the purpose behind it, but that would have to wait.

After walking a wide circle, he led Selome back toward the compound, one hand gripping hers, the other holding the AK. Hunkering down a short distance from the buildings, he watched the back of the monastery, waiting to see any sign that there were Sudanese guarding the flank—there was nothing. He guided Selome to the compound, dashing the final hundred yards in a dead run, the sound of their feet absorbed by the tilled soil of the monks' garden. It took only a second to find a window with an unlocked shutter. He hefted Selome through the opening and scrambled in after her.

They were in a monk's cell, similar to the one in which Mercer first awoke, same plain bed and desk and the ubiquitous crucifix. He cracked open the door and listened. Voices reverberated throughout the monastery, angry shouts and an occasional grunt, as if someone had just been struck. The voices were too distorted to hear clearly, but

Mercer recognized the language as Italian. He waved Selome closer so she too could listen.

"Can you understand what they're saying?"

Selome concentrated, tucking her hair away from her small ear. "Father Ephraim is being questioned about us. He's being asked where we are. The man speaking has a Venetian accent, and sounds like he's used to getting his way. I think that it's another monk who's getting hit every time Ephraim says he doesn't know where we've gone. What are we going to do?"

Mercer's expression matched the desperate look in Selome's eyes. They couldn't allow the interrogation to continue. Already tonight one priest was dead.

"You're going to have to cover me. Stay close." He opened the door before Selome could say anything.

Mercer's sudden appearance in the hallway startled a Sudanese who was walking past. Mercer reacted instinctively and struck out with the butt of the AK-47. The wood cracked against the rebel's jaw, shattering bones and spraying blood and teeth against the wall. Before the unconscious man hit the floor, Mercer was in motion. Easing into the dining room, he could feel Selome at his shoulder.

Father Ephraim was stooped over the prone form of one of his brothers, blood pooled around the ruined mouth of the other priest. Three more monks stood against one wall, guarded by several soldiers. The Italian stood close to where Mercer remained partially hidden. He faced away from Mercer, and in the fraction of a second it took a Sudanese to spot him, Mercer raised the AK by its pistol grip, grabbed a handful of the Italian's bush shirt, and rammed the barrel of the assault rifle into the man's lower spine, nearly bringing him to his knees with the force.

The Italian shouted a name. "Mahdi!"

One of the Sudanese raised his own pistol, locked back the hammer with his thumb, and leveled it at Mercer's head.

"Selome!" Mercer shouted, and she came into the room, her weapon covering Mahdi with chilling calm. "One more gun goes up, friend, and your guts are going to decorate the walls," Mercer said.

Mercer suspected that his prisoner spoke English, but he twisted the barrel of the AK further into the man's spine for emphasis.

"I think you call this a standoff, yes?" Giancarlo Gianelli said casually, not a trace of fear in his voice. "Let me end it for us now, Dr. Mercer."

A shot rang out, a sharp crack that split the air, and Brother Ephraim was slammed backward against the wall. A tendril of smoke coiled from the pistol Gianelli had kept in front of him, out of Mercer's view. "Go ahead and shoot, Doctor. None of us have anything to gain by standing around."

Ephraim breathed in shallow gulps, his face drained to an unnatural gray. He held his hands over the massive wound in his belly, blood cascading over his fingers.

"There are another dozen priests here," Gianelli continued conversationally. "I give you my word that they will not live five seconds after you kill me."

Gianelli had played the end-game so quickly that Mercer had no choice. He could kill the Italian and would end up killing himself and Selome as well, gaining nothing. Or he could lower his weapon and hope for another opportunity. Since the beginning, he'd felt he was one step behind the other players, and true to form, he was behind again now.

Mahdi sneered when Mercer released Gianelli, a contemptuous twist of his mouth that told Mercer he would have welcomed the suicidal gunfight. Selome lowered her own pistol, letting it drop with a metallic clatter. She moved to Ephraim's side, settling herself so that the priest's limp head lay in her lap. Gianelli showed no interest in restraining Mercer as he joined her on the floor. One of the Sudanese retrieved Selome's gun and the AK.

"I'm sorry," Mercer whispered to the dying man, knowing how empty the apology sounded.

Ephraim was losing his fight as they watched. When he spoke, it was a wet wheeze that brought blood to his lips.

"The children," Selome translated softly. "The children

who died in the mine. They were killed by . . ." His last word was not even loud enough to be a whisper.

"What did he say?"

"I'm not sure. It sounded like he said the children were killed by sin."

"We've wasted enough time tonight," Giancarlo said. Mahdi and another rebel hauled Selome and Mercer to their feet. "Dr. Mercer, we've been looking for you for the past couple days. You have some questions to answer for me about that ancient mine."

Mercer guessed that the Italian had completed the work he and Habte had started. They had opened King Solomon's mine but probably didn't recognize the find. That was his only advantage if he hoped to stop Levine. He knew if he expected to keep himself and Selome alive, he was going to have to make himself indispensable.

"I'll tell you what you want to know." It wasn't hard to let defeat creep into his voice.

"I know you will."

"Tell me first, who are you?"

"My name is Giancarlo Gianelli, and it was my uncle who opened the barren shaft you discovered." Gianelli shook his head. "Poor Enrique knew there were diamonds in the region, but he was apparently off by a couple of miles, sinking his mine in the wrong place. But someone long ago discovered the kimberlite pipe and, judging by the depths we explored before coming to find you, had worked it for many years. And now it's time for me to take up where my uncle failed and you, good doctor, are going to help."

Mercer knew what Ephraim meant about the children being killed by sin. He saw it in every fiber of Giancarlo Gianelli; it lurked behind his urbane veneer like a monster. The sin that Ephraim spoke of was one of the original deadly seven. Greed.

Valley of Dead Children

Answers to the dozens of questions swirling through Mercer's mind had to wait until the column of Giancarlo Gianelli's trucks ground back to the mine site. Mercer was in the back of one of the rigs with six heavily armed Sudanese while Selome rode in the back jump seat of another with Gianelli himself. He hoped that her proximity to the Italian was for her protection from the lewd intentions of the troopers and not for the magnate's own carnal thoughts.

Mercer knew of Gianelli. The name had been synonymous with European finance for centuries, almost as famous as the house of Rothschild. He couldn't recall how many of Europe's wars the Gianelli family had funded, but much of their fortune had been soiled with the blood of countless thousands. He did remember that they were heavily involved with the Facist movement during the 1920s and '30s and after World War Two had come under the protection of the United States because of their strong anti-Communism. Of the current head of the family dynasty, he knew little except that the ambition that had made them so powerful ran in Giancarlo's veins.

It was mid-morning when the caravan entered the Valley of Dead Children. They drove past the open shaft bored by Gianelli's ancestor and headed to the ancient mine. When they stopped, a guard in Mercer's truck flipped up the soft canvas flap above the tailgate and jumped to the ground, covering Mercer with his rifle as he too leapt from the vehicle. Mercer had lost track of the number of days he'd been away from the mine, but was staggered by the amount of work that had taken place in his absence.

It took his ears a moment to adjust from the clamor of the truck to the sharper and significantly louder sounds of the work area. Apart from the large truck-mounted generators pounding away a short distance from the mine, Gianelli had two bulldozers, several Bobcat skiploaders, the Caterpillar excavator that Mercer had brought, and an Ingersoll-Rand rotary drill rig for pulling core samples. The equipment's din echoed and reechoed off the bowl of mountains into a deafening racket that shook the dusty air. Amid this mechanical maelstrom, Mercer saw perhaps fifty Africans—the Eritrean refugees—toiling by hand with shovels, picks, and reed baskets.

He couldn't believe the sheer volume of dirt they had managed to move. The mountain that he and Habte had dynamited had been clawed up by the machines and carted away by the African laborers one basket at a time. The mine that Brother Ephraim had spoken of had been exposed, a dark shaft driven into the side of the mountain. It was wide enough for the skiploader to charge into the earth and return again with its bucket loaded with overburden. The operator would dump it into a mound, and a stream of men attacked it with their hands, filling baskets which they hoisted to their heads and carried away.

Mercer thought about the heavy equipment that would be arriving soon, machinery he had either leased or bought on behalf of the Eritrean government. Alone, the 5130 hydraulic shovel could have moved the same amount of dirt in about an hour. Still, the Eritreans' endeavor was miraculous.

A guard prodded him with an ungentle thrust of his assault rifle toward where Gianelli waited near the mine entrance. Mercer watched as one of the troopers, bothered by the slow pace of an Eritrean, knocked the worker to the ground, his heavy basket of dirt falling onto his chest as he lay defenseless in the dust. The rebel kicked the refugee several more times before turning to keep his eye on the rest of the laborers. None of the other workers had come to the aid of their countryman. They had all bowed themselves to the task of surviving.

Slavery was back.

"What do you think, Doctor? Impressive amount of work, wouldn't you say?" Gianelli called. Selome was with him, and another white man stood with their little group, a hulking figure, big in the shoulders and gut.

"Yeah, and I'm sure union reps are having a hard time recruiting new members from your workers."

Gianelli gave a genuine laugh. "I want you to meet Joppi Hofmyer, my supervisor. Joppi, this is Philip Mercer, the famous American mining engineer."

Neither man made a move to shake hands, but Joppi's expression betrayed the fact that he had heard of Mercer. There was respect behind his dim eyes.

"Before you tell me what you know about this mine," Gianelli said breezily, "why don't I give you a tour? I'm curious myself about the progress that's been made while I've been gone."

The mine opening was six feet tall and about the same width. The Bobcat's roof scraped the rough stone ceiling as it emerged from the square aperture. Joppi spoke to the white skiploader driver for a second, and the man shut down the engine. Gianelli and Hofmyer each were handed lighted mining helmets by one of the Sudanese guarding the mine shaft. Neither Selome nor Mercer got one.

"We've managed to remove another seventy feet of over-burden from the tunnel," Hofmyer told Gianelli. "But the deeper into the mountain we go, the more packed the material seems to be. It's as if whoever sealed the mine wanted to make sure it was never opened again. Pretty soon we may even have to blast away some of the stones and impacted dirt."

"Any deviation on the direction or slope? Have you found any branches or chambers?"

"It's still as straight as a string and sloping downward at fifteen degrees. I think I should wait and let you see the rest for yourself."

Twenty feet into the shaft, Hofmyer and Gianelli switched on their headlamps. The light cut into the gloom, yet the tunnel was oppressively dark and the air was heavy and fouled by the skiploader's exhaust. The hanging wall, or ceiling, was low enough to force Mercer to bend slightly as he and Selome lagged behind the Italian and the South African miner. Two Sudanese took up the rear, both carrying pistols.

They continued for over fifteen minutes, Mercer estimating that the tunnel was at least a mile and a half long. While Hofmyer and Gianelli marched with a single-minded purpose, Mercer studied the rock walls and ceiling under the bouncing light from his guards' lanterns, pausing when a particular feature caught his eye. He picked up his pace only when prodded by one of the two guerrillas.

"What are you looking for?" Selome whispered.

"An escape route," he responded cryptically.

Selome looked behind them, but all she saw was an endless tube of featureless rock.

The tunnel ended on a ledge that overlooked the floor of a chamber, a huge vaulted space that had been created eons ago by the natural process of the kimberlite pipe's formation. Molten magma, driven by the engine of the earth, had risen to this level during an eruption before cooling and solidifying. The diamond-bearing material injected into the three-hundred-foot-wide dome had settled over time, lowering the floor of the chamber until the ceiling lofted fifty or more feet over their heads. This was the working area of the ancient mine, and the floor was scarred by man's rapacious appetite for diamonds.

A generator hummed near where the tunnel entered the chamber, tripod-mounted halogen lights running off its power and illuminating nearly every square foot of the cavern. The early miners had divided the cave's floor into square grids, probably to better track the progress of the slaves who had worked here. While much of the floor was uniform, some areas had been mined deeper than others, so the floor resembled a three-dimensional chessboard. Some of the deeper areas were lost in the penumbra below where the party stood at the lip of the subterranean pit. Mercer had no way to guess how many tons of ore had been pulled from the chamber. For all he knew, the entire space had once been solid rock. But he began to believe that Brother Ephraim's claim that the mine had been active for four hundred years was conservative.

"My God! It's the blue ground!" Giancarlo gasped, looking to Hofmyer for confirmation. The big South African nodded.

The entire blue-tinted floor of the chamber was composed of the tough ultramific lodestone for diamond. There was no way of knowing the assay value—the ratio between kimberlite ore and diamond—until samples were taken and analyzed, but it was safe to say that they were all standing on a fortune. Mercer thought about the crushed samples of kimberlite he had discovered shortly before leaving for the monastery and how thoroughly it had been worked to extract every possible carat. That was pretty good proof of the value of the ore. Yes, he thought. A fortune. One that belonged to the people of Eritrea. Apart from everything else, Mercer knew that if he didn't act, it would end up in Gianelli's hands. He kept his anger behind a stony mask, but the effort cost him.

"We found it the day before yesterday. I've had the men busting some ass to clear it of dirt before you arrived." Hofmyer's voice shattered the wonder and astonishment Gianelli was obviously feeling as he looked at the mine for the first time. "Whoever worked this place first did a pretty good job of filling it back up too. It's at the far side of this chamber that we may have to blast away some of the *kak* dumped back in here."

"How deep are those vertical shafts from the working floor of the pit?" Mercer asked.

"I had a couple of *kaffirs* dig into one, and they hadn't hit bottom after pulling up thirty feet of overburden."

"Paystreak in the kimberlite?"

"My thought too," Hofmyer agreed. "Way back when, they must have hit one particularly rich diamond-bearing section and dug into it like dogs."

"This is better than anything I could have possibly hoped for," Gianelli breathed. He turned to Mercer. "Now, tell me about this mine."

Mercer could feel Selome stiffen next to him. He, too, was reluctant to tell the Italian anything, but knew he had to if he wanted to keep them alive.

"The mine was opened about three thousand years ago."

"Don't be ridiculous," Hofmyer exploded. "Look at this place. Only machinery could have tunneled this deeply. This chamber can't be more than a hundred years old."

"I assure you this is an ancient working." Mercer kept a smirk off his face as he studied Hofmyer. *Just keep showing your ignorance, you stupid bastard.* "I found a stone hammer before leaving for the monastery. It was badly chipped and looked as though it had been discarded with the tailings. You'll find it in a leather bag in my tent. I doubt miners with access to machinery would use Stone-Age tools. What's more, look at the tunnel itself. It was bored using a technique that dates back millennia.

"Judging by the texture of the walls and ceiling, the mining of the tunnel must have been hellish work. If you look closely, you can still see the cracks created when the original miners used fires to heat the rock, then flash-quenched them with water and vinegar acid. The thermal shock would shatter the stone and allow them to cart out the debris. I wouldn't be surprised if every foot of that shaft represented a day or more of work. I'd guess about twenty-five years just to drive that one tunnel."

"Is it possible?" Giancarlo asked his mine engineer.

"*Ja*, maybe," Hofmyer muttered.

"Possible, my ass. Haven't you ever read Pliny's account of the gold mines in Asturias, Spain?" Mercer doubted Hofmyer had even heard of the Roman historian. "He called it the 'Destruction of a Mountain.' Starting around 25 B.C., the Romans forced tens of thousand of slaves to tunnel into the Las Medulas Mountains using the technique I just described. On the tops of the mountains, huge reservoirs and canals and aqueducts were constructed, then filled with water. When enough interconnecting tunnels were dug—and I'm talking miles and miles of them—a torrent could be released into the galleries. The water's hydrostatic pressure literally blew the mountains apart, and gold-laden earth was washed down into a plain where it could be easily retrieved. The Romans worked those mountains for two hundred years, forever changing the landscape, and recovering an estimated twelve billion dollars' worth of bullion. Believe me, this mine was worked in a similar fashion and a lot longer ago."

Mercer shot a deadly look at Gianelli. "This leads me to my final piece of evidence. The monk you shot last night told me he knew of this mine from one of their ancient texts, a book lost long ago, but its oral tradition had been maintained." Mercer hoped he was spinning enough fact with the fiction to satisfy Gianelli. "He said that this mine was worked for centuries until there was an invasion. The people who operated it sealed it entirely rather than see it captured."

"My God, it sounds like King Solomon's Mine," Gianelli gasped.

"Maybe, I don't know." The Italian had gotten too close to the truth, and Mercer had to derail him. "It could be that this was the basis for the legend, but as I'm sure Yappy here can tell you, there are countless spots all over Africa that also claim that distinction."

Joppi Hofmyer growled at the bastardization of his name.

"Fascinating," Gianelli said. It was evident that he was more impressed with his prisoner than with the man he had hired to excavate the mine.

Mercer saw this and started to make it work to his advantage. "If I may make a suggestion. You mentioned bringing explosives into this chamber. I wouldn't. The dome may look solid, but unless you have blast mats to deflect the shock of a detonation down the tunnel, you may find yourself proving the hard way that it's not."

"Do we have blast mats?" Giancarlo demanded of Joppi.

"No, sir, but it would only take a few days to get them from Khartoum." Hofmyer seethed at being so easily undercut.

"And while you're at it," Mercer continued, taking an almost casual command of the conversation, "I saw outside that you're about to resift the original tailings for diamonds that might have been missed by the original workers. Don't bother. The tailings I checked had been crushed down so fine that unless you brought a portable fluoroscope with you, it'll be a complete waste of time and manpower that I doubt you can spare."

Hofmyer shot Mercer such a scathing look that it appeared he would physically attack him. Sorting through the tailings had been his idea.

"Sounds logical," Giancarlo said, enjoying the frustration on his overseer's face. "If I had gone through the difficult task of mining the ore, I imagine that I would also make certain not a single stone had been overlooked." He smiled. "Fetching you back here was a good idea. I think it would be another good idea if I kept you around for a while longer. For the time being, you will be my chief among slaves."

For a fraction of a second, Mercer's thoughts played openly across his face, but fortunately Gianelli had looked away. Mercer didn't want the Italian to see the hatred or the resolve that flashed in his eyes. Those he was keeping to himself, knowing that they would help him when the time came. Slave, he'd been called. And slave he would be. Right up to the moment he would slip his hands around Gianelli's throat and squeeze until the son of a bitch was dead.

The Mine

Two weeks passed. Two weeks in which Mercer saw a man beaten to death. Two weeks in which he saw others drop dead from exhaustion. Two weeks in which men and machine toiled endlessly to yank the kimberlite from the womb of the earth, tearing it free with picks and pneumatic drills and bare hands. Two weeks in which his own body was pushed mercilessly.

Gianelli and Joppi Hofmyer worked the male refugees, including Mercer and Habte, in twelve-hour shifts, allowing just ten minutes every two hours for a little food and a meager water ration. The pace wasn't enough to kill a healthy adult, but many of the refugees had arrived at the mine on the verge of starvation and the labor pushed several of the older ones over the edge. Because of his expertise, Mercer was named an underground manager for his shift, watched over by one of Hofmyer's South Africans, a man named du Toit. At least ten armed Sudanese also guarded the work. The pit echoed with the machine-gun rattle of compressed air drills and jackhammers, a deafening roar of man's fight against earth's strength. It was impossible to look across the workings. The air was thick with dust and fumes, and the miners were covered with so much grit that it was difficult to tell white from black. A flexible ventilator tube with high-speed fans had been rigged along the tunnel leading to the work, but it did little to alleviate the dust or the incredible heat in the chamber.

Taking a lesson from the British prisoners of war who had built the Kwai River bridge, Mercer dedicated himself to mining the kimberlite to the best of his ability. He selected those refugees with the strength and stamina to work the drills and jackhammers, teaching them the basics and a few tricks to make their task easier. Others he employed as pick men and priers, and still others to haul the ore back to the surface, where more people hammered it apart to search for the elusive diamonds.

But the stones weren't that elusive. The kimberlite here was the richest Mercer had ever seen. While he was not allowed in the secure area near the mine's entrance where the ore was crushed and the diamonds were stored in a safe, he learned enough to guess that the mine was paying out better than twelve carats a ton, an astronomically high value. He did have the opportunity to see a few stones that were found right in the mine. At first the Eritreans were dumbfounded at the value placed on the small symmetrical lumps of crystal when Mercer pointed them out, because there is little of a diamond's hidden fire to be seen before the stone is cut and polished. The biggest stone Mercer saw for himself was a nice twenty carats, but he'd heard rumors about a monster stone, some said the size of a man's fist, that had been found by one of the women sorting the ore.

It was in the pit that one of the guards beat an Eritrean to death. It wasn't known if the refugee had broken one of Hofmyer's numerous rules or if the young Sudanese had just done it for the thrill. The reason didn't matter to the victim, nor did it really matter to those who witnessed the Sudanese using the butt of his AK-47 to split open the man's head.

Mercer had been on break when it happened, and he sprang to his feet at the first blow. Habte was next to him. He recognized the danger Mercer was about to put himself in, and Habte wrapped his arm around Mercer's leg, tumbling him back to the ground.

"Don't, Mercer, just don't. That man is already dead and you are still alive," Habte whispered. "I learned during the war that no man's life is worth a defiant gesture."

The beating lasted at least a minute, and when it was over, du Toit ordered the crew back to work. The corpse lay where it had fallen until the end of the shift, the workers ducking their eyes reverently as they passed by.

For two weeks the mining went on, a continuous chain of men burdened with baskets of kimberlite wending their way along the tunnel to the surface and returning to the workings for more. By the end of the second week, Mercer realized that Gianelli intended to work everyone to death, not only to ensure their silence, but to make certain that every possible diamond could be found in the time he'd allowed himself.

Late at night, when Mercer and Habte were lying on the ground in the barbed-wire stockade that acted as their quarters, they would discuss theories behind Gianelli's rushed schedule. Habte maintained that the Italian was afraid the location would be discovered by someone else and reported to the government in Asmara, but Mercer suspected that there was another purpose behind the killer pace.

"Habte, be reasonable," Mercer said. "We never saw another person when we were first searching for this place, and the nomad in Badn said this region is avoided because of some superstition. And don't forget, the landmines act as one hell of a deterrent. Shit, I haven't even seen a plane fly over."

"All this is true," Habte murmured tiredly, rolling so he could pluck a sharp stone from under his back. "But why is Gianelli pushing so hard?"

"I don't know," Mercer admitted, too tired to think through the problem.

It had been plaguing him from the start of the mining operation, but at night it took all of his concentration just to eat the weak stew served by the wives of the refugees.

The other thought dogging him was Selome's safety. They hadn't been able to speak to each other. She was in a separate compound with the other women, forced to cook for the workers, a slave as surely as he. Whenever Mercer saw her as he was getting his stew, he tried to smile and put up a brave front, but knew that concern darkened his eyes. He could see that she had been hit a couple of times, for purple bruises showed on her arms and face. Each night Mercer and the others could hear guards drag a few of the women off for their own pleasure. He didn't know if Selome had been similarly treated, and his inability to help her, or the others, ate at him like cancer.

On the morning that started his fifteenth day of captivity, the sky was dark with storm clouds. The veiled sun didn't even cast shadows. The men waiting in line for their breakfast shivered miserably in the damp chill.

"It will rain before the sun sets again," Habte said to Mercer, clutching a tin plate for more of the ungodly stew.

"If we're going to make a break for it," Mercer replied, first making sure that none of the guards were close enough to overhear, "it'll have to be soon. I doubt they'll give us tents, and the refugees won't last more than a day or two in the rain."

"Neither will we," Habte grunted. "Do you have a plan?"

Mercer paid no attention to his friend. He looked at the women tending the cooking fires, watching for Selome to turn from her task so he could offer a smile. When she looked at him, he noticed that exhaustion had bent her once erect carriage and dulled her expression. He studied her for second and saw the old defiance flash from behind her eyes. As gently as he could, he nodded her over to him.

She looked about cautiously before hoisting a platter of *injera* to her head and moving to the long trestle table that served as the buffet. Mercer saw that her willowy body was so thin he could see the bony projections of her hips though the fabric of her pants. She did not meet Mercer's eyes as she placed the platter on the table.

"We are getting out of here tonight," Mercer whispered fiercely, his anger making his quick decision easy. "Be ready two hours after my shift ends."

"We'll never make it. The guards will be on us the moment we start running from the camp. Wouldn't it be wiser if you got out alone and went for help from some village?"

"It would take me a week to reach a town, and the workers here won't last another two days. Besides, we won't be leaving the camp. Trust me, I have an idea. It's nuts, incredibly dangerous, but we have to try."

"I'll be ready. I've even managed to horde a little food and water for us."

Beaten, possibly raped, and enslaved, yet she still had managed to keep alive a spark of hope. Mercer ached to touch her. He felt his heart squeeze and a burst of adrenaline course through his system when he thought of her courage. He drew strength from her refusal to give up. "I'll see you tonight."

The crew was given only ten minutes to wolf down the food before heading back into the mine. While the surface activities ceased at night to conserve fuel for the generators, underground, the men worked around the clock. The outgoing shift passed Mercer's team in the tunnel, each man watching his own feet, too exhausted to care that another day was done.

There was little that Mercer could accomplish until nightfall except have Habte alert as many workers as possible. The escape party would have to be small for any chance at success, but Mercer wanted the others forewarned, in the hope that when he went into action, they could help add to the confusion.

Yet the cursed luck that had shadowed Mercer was still with him. Joppi Hofmyer was working in the mine and, after two weeks of subtle needling by Mercer, was ready to exact his revenge. No sooner has Mercer descended the particular shaft that he'd been working only hours before, than Hofmyer approached.

"Mercer, get your fookin' ass up here," Hofmyer shouted from the top of the fifty-foot-deep hole in the mine's working floor, his voice booming over the shattering sounds of the equipment.

As slowly as possible, Mercer climbed the rope ladder rigged to the side of the pit until he was standing on the original floor level. He chanced a look at the long tunnel leading to freedom, then rounded back to the South African. "What's on your mind? Another lesson in hard rock mining?"

"Aye, it'll be a lesson, all right." Hofmyer stood close enough for Mercer to be staggered by his rancid breath. "Gianelli's gone for the morning, so I'll have hours to think of an excuse for why you died today."

Hofmyer was a few years older than Mercer, but that was in no way a disadvantage. The Boer stood half a head taller and weighed a solid fifty pounds more. His shoulders were broad, his chest like a barrel, and his fists were larger than sledgehammers. The knuckles were crisscrossed by numerous white ridges of old scar tissue. Joppi Hofmyer was in peak physical condition—while Mercer was on the verge of collapse.

Knowing his first shot would most likely be his only, Mercer struck. His move was slowed by his condition, but it caught Hofmyer off guard. Mercer's fist slammed into Joppi's mouth, snapping two teeth and crushing his lip against the jagged stumps so his blood flowed. Hofmyer fell back several steps, bothered more by the suddenness of the attack than the pain of his injury.

The workers on the mine floor stopped to watch the drama. Even the Sudanese slackened their vigilance. Hofmyer grinned at Mercer, a bloody display of snapped teeth and ruined flesh. "That's the spirit," he said wetly, spitting to clear his mouth. "This'll be a lot more fun if you put up a fight."

Mercer got into a combat stance and prepared to fight for his life. As he expected, Hofmyer stood solidly, his arms open. He was so accustomed to using his size and strength to overpower opponents that he'd never learned the subtleties of unarmed combat. Mercer hoped that he knew enough to at least survive the pounding that was coming. He had no illusions of actually winning.

Hofmyer's first punch missed Mercer by an inch as he ducked away, but the follow-up landed, blowing the air out of Mercer's lungs and rocking him on his heels. It felt as if he'd been struck by a baseball bat and the punch had been from in close, using just a fraction of Hofmyer's strength. The South African laughed again, feigning blows that Mercer had no option but to dodge. Even a glancing shot would land him on his backside.

For ten minutes Hofmyer threw punches, some landing, some brushing by, and some missing completely. Mercer managed only a single counterpunch, a weak swing that hurt his hand more than Hofmyer's temple where it struck. The Eritrean laborers had been cheering at the start of the fight, but upon seeing Mercer's ineptitude at defending himself, they quieted. As each punch slammed into him, they cringed, for no man could withstand the brutal punishment Mercer was enduring.

But Mercer had a reason behind his apparent lack of defense. Every time Joppi came at him, he allowed himself, through retreat or landed blows, to move closer and closer to the idling skip loader. Its replacement driver had not yet shown for work, and the squat excavating machine rested near the middle of the domed chamber, its wide bucket elevated off the ground. If Mercer had any chance of surviving the fight, he would need the Bobcat's power to augment his own flagging strength.

Hofmyer never became aware of Mercer's intentions, but he also never moved to the exact spot that Mercer wanted him. Three times Mercer was beaten to within a foot of the skip loader, and every time Joppi moved out of the fray to catch his breath and enjoy the cheers of the Sudanese rebels. Three times, with an undeterred patience, Mercer was pushed and beaten and kicked until they abutted the Bobcat again. His face was bloodied and swollen so he could barely see and he kept one arm low to protect what might be broken ribs, but still he took the punishment. It was during the fourth time that Mercer judged everything was right.

There was a small spark left in him, that last bit that gave him a burst of speed and strength. Joppi came in for a devastating series of body blows, twisting his horny fists into Mercer's flank in order to increase the pain of the battered ribs. Hofmyer expected Mercer to fall back, gasping as he had for the past three such attacks, but Mercer didn't. Straightening as best he could, Mercer lashed out with his fist, a ranging shot that forced Joppi off balance and then, so quickly no one even saw it happen, Mercer threw himself to the ground, extending his leg in a sweep that brought Hofmyer crashing to the stone floor. Before Joppi could recover, Mercer was on his feet again, reaching across to the controls of the Bobcat. With a skillful flick of his wrist, he pivoted the vehicle in place so the hydraulic bucket centered over Joppi's head and lowered the blade until it exerted just enough pressure to pin the South African. Had Mercer wanted, he could have crushed Joppi's skull like an overripe melon.

The Sudanese guards finally realized what had happened, and their weapons came up.

"Back off," Mercer shouted in English, his tone carrying his meaning. From under the bucket of the skip loader, Joppi Hofmyer shrieked. Mercer glanced down at his prisoner. "That's right, you bastard, tell them how much it hurts. Tell them you don't want to die."

Joppi screamed again, a horrid sound that pierced every corner of the cavern. His body wriggled as the blade kept his head mashed against the floor.

"Habte?" Mercer shouted, and a second later the Eritrean was at his side. "Can you speak to these Sudanese?" The Eritrean nodded. "Good. Joppi, I want you to tell them to back out of the tunnel. If they're still here in thirty seconds, your brains are going to decorate this cavern."

The South African repeated the order, his voice shrill with fear yet muffled by the weight of the machine. Habte translated, and the Sudanese did as ordered, forming up in a ragged line and retreating from the cavern.

"You'd better hope," Mercer spoke to Hofmyer, "that Gianelli returns soon, because you aren't getting up until he gets here."

He handed the control of the skiploader to Habte so he could wipe away the blood on his face. "If he twitches more than you like, go ahead and put a little more pressure on his head." Mercer revved the diesel to punctuate his order and drowned out Joppi's pleas for mercy.

Giancarlo Gianelli entered the cavern about an hour

later with a retinue of guards. He wore fresh khakis and he smiled disarmingly at Mercer, who sat slumped in the control seat of the small earthmover. "I see we have a slight problem."

"Not if you don't mind me squeezing Joppi's head like a grape, we don't," Mercer replied nonchalantly.

"Well, we can't have that, can we?"

"You're right." Mercer revved the engine and eased up on the bucket, freeing Hofmyer. "I wanted you to see that I could have killed him and didn't. Every man present, including your troops, can confirm that I didn't start this. I just want it to end. He goes his way and I go mine."

"And just where do you think you are going?" Gianelli seemed amused by the apparent ease Mercer had subdued Hofmyer and just as casually let him go.

"You know what I mean, Gianelli. Call him off and I'll go back to work."

"So this wasn't some elaborate effort to escape?" Giancarlo arched an eyebrow.

Mercer looked at him flatly. "You'll be the first to know when I'm ready to escape."

"Your bravado is impressive," Gianelli chuckled. Hofmyer was sitting on the ground, his head cradled gingerly between his hands. "No more, Joppi. You want to beat Mercer to death, do it when we are finished here. Am I clear?"

Hofmyer's reply was a moan.

"Good."

"Gianelli, tell me." Mercer eased himself from the Bobcat and stood in front of the Italian industrialist. It was the first opportunity he'd had to speak with him. "What's this all about? Working this mine, I mean. You don't need the money, and you've already proved there are diamonds here just like your uncle said there were. Why work these people to death for a couple thousand carats? I know I'm not getting out of this alive, so what's the harm in telling me?" A thought struck Mercer that moment, and he voiced it. "After all, do you think the Central Selling System is going to let you move these stones? They're going to come down on you like a ton of bricks."

"Very astute," Gianelli said. "You hit upon the crux of my plan on the first try."

"What is this Central Selling System?" Habte interrupted.

Gianelli rounded to Habte and spoke in a patient tone. "The CSS is the secret arm behind one of the most recognized corporate names in the world. Unlike any other industry, the diamond market is dominated by a tight-fisted monopoly that controls every aspect of the trade: mining, cutting, and selling. Nearly everyone in Europe and America is well acquainted with their artful television and print advertisements that espouse the everlasting quality of their stones. The CSS is a shadowy organization that keeps rein on who gets diamonds, who is able to sell them, and for exactly how much. Through their policies the value of diamonds is kept artificially inflated." He turned to Mercer. "Correct me if I'm wrong, but you're thinking the CSS will find out about my little operation and close down the mine in order to maintain their monopoly?"

"That's about right," Mercer said. "They know down to the individual stone how many diamonds are mined worldwide and not only in the facilities that are part of their consortium. If previously unknown stones from an unknown source suddenly appear, their investigative branch is going to find out and put an end to it, through any means necessary. You know the power they have. The CSS has contacts in the highest echelons of South Africa's and England's government. They operate with near impunity."

"That's what I'm relying on. You see, *I'm* the person who's going to tell them about this mine." Mercer's eyes went wide with this admission and Gianelli gave a delighted laugh. "I have neither the desire nor the resources to take on the CSS. They, of course, don't know that. The inherent flaw with any monopoly is their fear of competition, and it's astounding the lengths they will go to maintain their supremacy."

Mercer finally understood at last. "You're going to bluff them?"

"Not bluff them exactly. I'm going to show them the stones we've recovered so they can see my seriousness. When I hand over a bucket of diamonds they won't be able to trace, they'll know there's a new player in the game. I don't know if they will pay me more to know the mine's location or more to ensure I don't work it anymore. Either way, they must control this site. Consider my actions extortion. I'm using their greed against them."

Mercer kept his face neutral, but he had to admit it was a brilliant plan, elegant and simple. Gianelli would reap billions. The CSS wouldn't know he didn't really own the mine until they had paid him off. "And when your actions force the CSS to raise the price of stones worldwide in order to pay you off and send South Africa's economy into a tailspin?"

"Who cares? So what if pimply-faced boys have to pay a few thousand dollars more for engagement rings for their stupid girlfriends? As for South Africa, I hope the country falls apart and the whites retake control. I made a lot of money down there before the blacks were given power. While part of my motivation was to reinstate my uncle's name in the family annals as the true genius he was, I certainly wouldn't have spent so much money without some financial recompense."

Mercer knew that South Africa's fledgling democracy wouldn't survive the shock of tens of thousands of men out of work. Anarchy would run rampant as people fought to stay alive. "You sick bastard. These are lives you're playing with."

"The cheapest commodity in the world."

"So how much is enough? You must have a couple thousand carats, and there's a rumor going around about a mammoth stone. Why keep working these people?"

"The more stones I dump on the CSS, the more they'll pay me to get out of the diamond industry. I'm sure you know I'm walking somewhat of a tightrope between my need for the stones and the chance of being discovered. But the efficiency of the men hasn't diminished much in the past two weeks, thanks to you, so we'll remain a bit longer.

"To give you a little motivation, I'll make you a bargain. At the end of say, three more weeks, if I haven't been forced to leave prematurely, I'll make my deal in London. I imagine my negotiations shouldn't last more than a few minutes. Once completed, I'll have the refugees released. After I sell my knowledge of the mine, that information no longer has value and they are free to go and tell whomever they wish. Does that sound fair?"

"In three weeks there won't be ten men left alive," Mercer spat.

Gianelli's eyes glazed angrily. "That's not my concern." He turned to Hofmyer, who had finally gained his feet. "Go get yourself tended to and see that du Toit comes in here to watch these monkeys."

Mercer went back to work, his mind reeling. The Mideast, South Africa, the refugees, Selome, Habte and Harry. With stakes this high, he had no choice but to succeed.

The Mine

The noise was like the pounding of drums, a deep bass that rattled the chests of the men heading down the tunnel at the end of their shift. Even before they were close enough to see the outlet, they recognized the sound. They had been farmers once, these men, and they knew when the rains came.

It was eight at night and so dark that the delineation between the black tunnel and the outside was just a fraction of a shade, no more than a ghost's glow. Water poured over the mouth of the tunnel in a continuous waterfall, a solid sheet that every few seconds would disgorge the soaked form of a man heading into the working pits. Conversation was impossible as Mercer and his fellow miners coming off shift approached the cascade. The sudden appearance of the replacement workers was startling and eerie.

"Will the rain help us or hurt us?" Habte had to shout in Mercer's ear to overcome the noise of the tremendous runoff.

Mercer could only shrug. He was focused on things other than the storm. He'd told Selome to be ready two hours after his shift ended, and he and Habte had a great deal to accomplish in that time. Just before it was their turn to step into the torrential night, Mercer pulled Habte aside. The closest Sudanese guard was still a good five hundred yards down the drive herding the stragglers from Mercer's team. It would be impossible for him to see or hear Mercer and Habte's conversation.

"Are you set with everything you have to do?" Mercer

asked tiredly. He'd rested as much as he could during the shift, but he was still weary, a bone fatigue that felt like it would be with him forever. The only bright spot was that Hofmyer hadn't broken any of his ribs.

"Yes. I'll be waiting just outside the tunnel. Everything will be rigged and ready to go."

"If it's not, this is going to be the sorriest escape in history," Mercer growled. "Does everyone know what's expected of them?"

"They will know what to do when the time comes. Those I didn't speak to directly today, like the men headed to the mine now, will hear from the others. Don't worry, they will be ready."

Mercer was relying on a hunch, a thin one at best, and if he was wrong, Hofmyer and Gianelli would probably take turns roasting his testicles over an open fire and machine-gun everyone else.

"Are you set with everything *you* have to do?" Habte grinned, trying to cut through Mercer's black mood.

Mercer gave a gallows chuckle. "We'll both know in two hours."

As Mercer suspected, Gianelli hadn't provided tents for his laborers. Yet the Italian, the other whites, and the Sudanese troopers were waiting out the storm in separate tents, huge affairs that hummed with air conditioners to cut the humidity and glowed feebly through the silver streaks of wind-driven rain.

None of the women were forced to serve food during the storm, but they had laid out a meal for the returning workers. The *injera* was so soggy it oozed from Mercer's hands like mud, and the stew kettles overflowed with rain water. Rather than waste his time with a meal he was too nervous to eat, Mercer made his way to the barbed-wire stockade. Big blue tarps had been spread on the ground, and he could see countless lumps beneath the plastic ground cloths. They were the men huddled together for warmth and protection. The sky cracked with thunder and lightning, piercing explosions that shook the earth. Following every blow of thunder, he heard the moans of the terrified Eritreans.

Three Sudanese had been given the job of watching the refugees, but as Mercer passed the tent they had erected for shelter, he saw one of them already asleep and the others looking about ready to nod off. On a night as foul as this, they weren't expecting trouble from their prisoners.

That's right, boys, Mercer thought as he entered the enclosure, *no one out here but us sheep bunking in for the night. You have yourselves a good nap.*

The Eritreans had reserved a corner of a tarp for Mercer and Habte, and he was directed to the spot with quiet gestures. He rolled under the top piece of reinforced plastic to wait until Habte finished his waterlogged meal. Despite the adrenaline beginning to wend its way through his system, he slept for a few minutes until Habte appeared at his side.

"You can sleep?" Habte remarked. "I guess you are not too worried."

"If you're as ugly as I am, you need all the beauty rest you can get." Mercer turned serious. "Do you have it?"

Habte showed him a small miner's hammer tucked in the waistband of his pants. "They never knew it was missing."

"And you've got the two men to help?"

"One man. I will help get us out."

"Forget it, Habte. We can't risk your hands getting too cut up. You have some delicate work to do after we get out of the stockade."

Habte nodded. "Okay, I have another who will do it."

The fencing that kept the Eritreans prisoner was concertina wire, heavy coils of razor-sharp barbed wire laid in a pyramid ten feet wide at its base and over eight feet tall. The snarled strands were wrapped so tightly, the obstacle resembled a steel hedgerow protected with tens of thousands of inch-long teeth that could cut cloth or flesh with equal ease. Mercer's plan was simple, but it needed the courage of two refugees and a tolerance for pain that was almost beyond comprehension.

When they were ready, the first refugee lay on his stomach before the coils and slowly began to worm his way under the mound. He moved with care, but even before he managed to extend one whole arm into the spirals of steel, he was cut and bleeding. He didn't cry out or complain or try to remove his limb. Instead, he started working his other arm in. He had borrowed clothing from other miners, so he wore several layers to protect himself, but as he crawled deeper into the fence, the cloth split, and seconds later blood as dark as his skin welled up and was washed away by the downpour. He cried out only when a barb pierced his face, snagging against his chin and tearing a long gash that would require stitches if it was ever to heal properly.

For ten minutes, Mercer, Habte, and another refugee watched the man's progress, holding their breath when he stuck himself in the groin and exhaling when he removed the tiny dagger and whispered back that it had missed everything critical. Five more minutes passed before all that remained of the Eritrean in the stockade was his bare feet. Then it was time for the second refugee to broach the wall of razor wire.

The second man dug himself under the first Eritrean's feet and like a snake wriggled under him, using his predecessor's body as a shield from the barbs. He snagged only a couple of times, minor snarls that he could dislodge with a quick shake of an arm or leg. It took him only a few minutes to cover the distance the first volunteer had paid for with his pain and blood. They waited another twenty minutes while the second African crawled farther forward, tunneling and burrowing slowly and carefully. His passage was marked with bits of clothing and flesh stuck on the barbs. He stopped only when his knees bracketed his comrades' head, though there was still another eighteen inches of wire to cover.

Mercer didn't hesitate. He put himself to the task with the same fatalism of the Eritreans. He slithered under first one refugee and then the other, his much broader shoulders taking the brunt of the steel thorns. *"Yakanyelay,"* he said when he reached the second man's head. "Thank you."

Moving slowly, feeling time slipping away, Mercer began to work himself under the remaining wire. His hands were slick with a mixture of blood and rain. Water was streaming into his eyes, so he worked nearly blind. Only when a bolt of lightning flared could he see how pitifully small his progress had been. The two Africans had covered twice his distance in half the time while he appeared to be lying completely still. He quickened his pace, but a careless move rammed a barb under his fingernail all the way to the cuticle. A lancing needle of pain shot up his arm, exploding in his skull, and he had to bite down not to scream out.

He pulled out the barb and continued, closing his eyes to the agony. Suddenly his probing hands moved against nothing. He had reached the end. He wriggled forward, clearing both arms of the entanglement before whispering for Habte to follow. It took Habte just three minutes to reach Mercer, snaking under the obstacle with sinuous ease. Mercer felt at least a dozen barbs sink into his back as Habte crawled under him, pressing him up against the heavy coils. It took an act of will for Mercer not to shout for his friend to hurry.

When Habte was finally free, he helped Mercer clear the last of the tangle, plucking wire from his back and legs as Mercer slithered those last few feet. The rain fell in a biblical deluge.

"There are going to be others following our route," Habte said as they tasted freedom for the first time in weeks. Rainwater washed the blood from their faces, hands, and arms.

"If those two men don't get help, they may bleed to death."

"They know it's the price if more of us can be freed."

Mercer studied Habte and knew the Eritrean was speaking the truth as an African saw it. He wondered if the Ethiopians who'd once occupied these lands really believed they could have defeated an enemy with that kind of mettle. "Their sacrifice isn't going to be in vain. Are you ready?"

"Yes."

"I'll meet you at the mouth of the tunnel in—" Mercer looked at his watch, dismayed by the amount of time that had elapsed. "One hour and twenty minutes. You'll be able to do everything?"

Habte thought for a moment. "Yes, it will be tight, but I'll be waiting."

"See you in a while." Mercer and Habte shook hands, and in seconds they were swallowed by the storm.

Mercer looked into the darkness beyond the mining camp. It would be easy for him to just walk away. He could be miles from the valley by morning, and the rain would make it impossible to track him. He could be back home in a couple of days. He knew now that Harry White was being held by Israelis, and he had enough contacts in the government to secure his friend's release. The two of them could be enjoying a drink at Tiny's in a week. Mercer shook the image from his head angrily and looked away from the beckoning desert.

In order to stop Levine, he had to stop Gianelli first. To do that, he had to free some of the refugees so they could cover his attempt to contact Dick Henna. Besides, he'd led the Eritreans into slavery, and it was his responsibility to get them out again. He also thought of Selome and what she'd been through. For the first time since Aggie Johnston had left him, Mercer felt that old slow burn in his chest. At this point it didn't mater if it was love—maybe that would come, maybe not, but it gave him the strength to go on. He started in the direction of Giancarlo Gianelli's camp.

The camp for the whites was about a quarter mile from the prisoners' stockade, upwind from the open-air latrines the Eritreans were forced to use. The night was inky black, and the light spilling from the clutch of tents was like a beacon as Mercer slogged through the mud. The rain masked any sound he might have made as he slipped and slid toward his destination but it would not shield him if he stumbled into a patrolling Sudanese.

An armed soldier loomed out of the tinsel of rain so suddenly that Mercer doubted his own vision. The Sudanese wore a wet poncho and was facing away, his AK-47 held under protective cover. Mercer's throat went dry, his breath shallowing until he was holding that last inhalation like a souvenir of a less-frightened moment.

He came up on his toes, silently urging the soldier not to turn. He moved fast, making his strides as long as possible in the circumstances. With three feet to go, the soldier, a veteran guerrilla, sensed something behind him and started to whirl, clearing his assault rifle to engage.

Mercer covered those last few feet like a wraith. He brought his elbow up to his head and, using his momentum and the soldier's spin to increase the power of the blow, smashed it down on the side of the man's neck. The force of the blow drilled the Sudanese into the mud. Dead or out, Mercer didn't take the time to care. He snatched up the AK, rifled the man's uniform for spare magazines, and continued toward the encampment.

He released that held breath, returning to his focus, shutting the violence from his brain.

Armed and feeling a measure of control, Mercer approached the tents. They were laid out in two distinct groups, the larger ones aligned in four rows, the other five grouped in a circle. A crack of lightning revealed tables and chairs in the center of the grouping and a ring of stones for a fire pit. Guessing that the four smaller tents were for the whites, Mercer dodged around the encampment to approach as far away from the Sudanese tents as possible.

The storm hid him as he worked his way to the back of them. Nearly choking himself on an invisible guy rope, he fell heavily in the mud. He lay still for a slow count of twenty, waiting to see if his ineptitude had drawn attention, but no alarm was raised.

Mercer rested his ear against the tent's nylon shell, listening for voices. He had snapped one of the barbs from the razor wire, which he could barely hold without slicing his fingers. When he was satisfied that the tent was empty, he used the little blade to slit open a gash where the wall attached to the floor.

He had to strain to make out any details once he was inside. Light from the adjoining tents cast just the feeblest glow. As soon as he realized there were two beds, he knew he had the wrong tent. He was looking for Gianelli's, and it was doubtful the billionaire would bunk with anyone else. This one must belong to a couple of the South Africans currently in the pit, he thought.

At the next tent, he heard Gianelli and Joppi Hofmyer talking. The rain made it impossible to hear what was being said, yet there was no mistaking the voices. Mercer slid to the opposite side from where the voices were loudest and used his blade to cut a tiny eyehole. His vision was obscured by a piece of Louis Vuitton luggage. Rather than stare inanely at the leather, he put his ear to the hole.

"Better than using the Bobcat, why not the mechanical arm of the excavator?" Gianelli laughed, and Mercer guessed they were discussing the manner of his own murder.

"I think it would be more fun to turn him over to the Sudanese and let them rape the fooker to death," Hofmyer boomed.

"I didn't think Christians did that sort of thing."

"Aye, but remember these monkeys are Africans first. Raping your vanquished enemies is about the oldest custom around here."

"It's nine-thirty," Gianelli exclaimed. "I lost track of time. I need to call Venice. You will have to excuse me."

"Sure, Mr. Gianelli. Sorry to make you late for your call."

"Not late yet, but I've got to use the toilet again. Boiled water, imported food, and no ice for weeks and my stomach is still fouled."

"Touch of Menyelek's revenge, eh?"

"Not funny, Hofmyer."

Mercer heard a tent fly zip open like the sound of tearing silk and then the voices faded. The last words he could discern were a curse by Gianelli about the rain.

He had maybe ten minutes before Gianelli returned, and he wasted none of them. He enlarged his peep hole so he could slip into the tent. His movement unsettled the mound of matching luggage, tumbling the pile to the floor. "Son of a bitch," Mercer hissed, massaging the back of his head where a valise had caught him.

He began a systematic search of Gianelli's tent, pawing through the trunks and cases. Gianelli had brought several pieces of furniture with him on the expedition, including an antique ironwood canopy bed complete with mosquito netting. Mercer searched under the mattress and box spring and rifled the two built-in drawers beneath it where he found the sat-phone he'd given Habte at the nomad village of Badn. *One item down, one to go.* The desk was also an antique. It had ten drawers, and Mercer went through them all, fruitlessly shuffling through mounds of papers.

He glanced at his watch. Eight minutes had passed. Panic was beginning to hurry his movements. Next to the camp chair was a small table. Its top was piled with more papers. Mercer plucked them up to see if anything was hidden beneath—again he turned up nothing. Gianelli would be back any second, and if Mercer failed in his search, his plans for escape were finished. He would be better off returning to the stockade and trying again the following night.

The rain pattered against the nylon roof, making it impossible to hear anyone approaching. Mercer checked the time again. Eleven minutes; he had to leave. It would take him another minute to right the stack of luggage, and he'd already stayed too long. Just then the gas powered refrigerator to his left gave a little shudder as it cycled off. Mercer realized it was the one place he hadn't looked. The fridge was small, designed for camping. Mercer opened it. Set on the bottom shelf was Mercer's leather kit bag. He took just a moment to make sure the folded Medusa photographs were still amid the clutter. *Oh, thank you, Christ!* Had they not been there, Mercer's escape plans would have crumbled.

Gianelli must have put them in the fridge to protect them from the brutal humidity, he realized, slinging the kit bag across his shoulder. He had begun stacking the luggage, leaving just enough space for him to crawl back out again, when Gianelli's voice made him freeze. The Italian sounded as though he was just outside his tent, calling something to one of the Sudanese guards, Mahdi perhaps. Mercer didn't move.

Ignoring the remaining cases, Mercer ducked for the hole just as the tent fly zippered open, the metal tag climbing the wall as if by magic. He threw himself to the ground, scrambling to get out of the tent before Gianelli spotted him. At the last second he hooked his foot on the precarious mountain of Vuitton, sliding it in place just as Giancarlo entered his temporary home.

Mercer lay panting next to the tent, the rain washing away the nervous sweat that slicked his face and hands. He could hear Gianelli begin speaking on the satellite phone hooked to his computer. Five seconds, Mercer thought. Five seconds and he would've been nailed. He snatched up the AK-47, transferring the spare magazines into his satchel, and raced back to the compound. He had only fifteen minutes to free Selome and link up with Habte.

"Shit!" he breathed. He had anticipated a cushion of a half hour.

As he ran, he wondered if it wouldn't have been smarter to seize Gianelli and use his life as a bargaining chip to free the remainder of the Eritreans. That might have worked, he conceded, slipping in the clinging morass, his eyes straining against the darkness in hopes of spotting any guards before he himself was seen. But if Gianelli either refused to cooperate, which was a distinct possibility given the man's instability, or if the soldiers got trigger-happy, then Mercer's action would lead to the deaths of a hundred innocents. No, he thought, his original idea was better. Mercer felt he couldn't win a head-to-head with Gianelli, so he would hide, and fight only when he was ready.

The women's stockade was smaller than the men's. There were only about thirty women and girls in it along with those male children too young to work in the mine. Mercer had studied it in the early-morning hours before his shifts and knew its only weakness was the guarded entrance. He didn't have the luxury of time to burrow under the coils of razor wire as he had done earlier.

Like the men's enclosure, the guards here had erected a

tent to shelter themselves from the elements and to give privacy to their nightly rapings. There was just enough light for Mercer to see the gleam of brass when he snapped the banana mag from the AK to check its load.

The guards' tent was quiet as he approached. He had no way to disguise his clothes and white face, so he simply ducked in. The first Sudanese to notice him was sitting on a wooden stool. When he stood to challenge, Mercer cracked the butt of the AK between his eyes, sending him sprawling. Another guard dodged away when Mercer twisted to repeat the attack, rolling to the floor next to a low pallet the men used for sleep. The Sudanese hadn't had the time to arm himself and Mercer ignored his supplicating hands. The gun butt made a sickening crack when it landed on the soldier's skull. Of the third guard, there was no sign.

"Damn." The guerrilla was either at the latrine or inside the women's stockade selecting a victim for the night. Mercer couldn't spare the time waiting for him.

He looked into the enclosure, but the rain obscured his vision beyond ten feet. Everything farther was a murky curtain of darkness. The lock on the barbed wire gate was off, suggesting the Sudanese was inside. He stepped in and cleared his eyes of water. But it was his ears that gave away his quarry's location.

A sharp, feminine scream lanced out from the far side of the stockade, and Mercer took off to track down the source. There was a large square of plastic on the ground, shiny wet and glossy, and Mercer knew the majority of the women were beneath it, huddled like their male counterparts a short distance away. He skirted the tarpaulin and came up to where two dark figures struggled in the rain. From a few feet away, it was impossible to make out who was who, and Mercer committed his charge to taking down the taller of the two combatants.

Then, at the moment before he jammed the AK barrel into the Sudanese's kidney, he realized that it was the shorter figure who was the man. The taller person was Selome! Redirecting his aim slightly, the rifle barrel caught the rebel in the lower back, rupturing his skin until the steel was buried in the man's flesh up to the forward sight. The African arched his spine in agony. As he bent back, Mercer released his hold on the assault rifle, grabbed the man by the throat, and slammed him to the ground. He clamped a hand over the man's nose and mouth until his struggles ended.

"Hope I'm not too late?" he whispered to Selome.

She composed herself. "I'd say you were right on time."

"We've got about three minutes to meet up with Habte. Come on." They ran from the stockade.

"The other women are going to make a break for it," Selome said as they passed the guards' tent. "They'll try to free the men and scatter into the surrounding hills."

"That should make Gianelli's job of finding the rest of us a little more difficult." He prayed that the Italian's revenge when he rounded them back again would wait until after he'd dealt with Mercer's group.

Near the mine opening, another large razor-wire enclosure encircled the area where the women and children crushed the kimberlite ore. It was deserted now except for a couple of guards standing under the cover of a metal shed erected to hold the safe Gianelli was using to store the diamonds. A generator hummed nearby, and a single floodlight shone in the rain. Mercer and Selome approached cautiously, using the big Caterpillar excavator as cover.

They were late. Habte should be around here someplace, waiting for them, having worked his way into position from above. Before their dash to the mine, Mercer had to meet up with him because the Eritrean had another task to perform tonight, something more important than anything else.

"What now?"

Mercer's eyes rested on the Bobcat sitting a short distance away. "Ah, instant tank. Follow me."

As they reached the skiploader, Habte raced from behind a mound of mining debris to join them.

"I was starting to wonder if you had gone off to elope," he said, struggling with the unfamiliar word.

"Thought about it, but she wanted a big ceremony. You

know how women can be." Mercer clasped Habte's hand. "Everything ready?"

"Detonator is lying behind that hill where I was waiting, and there are thirty pounds of explosives rigged above the mine entrance."

"Any trouble?"

"No. You were right. It was easy to smash into the explosive locker with the hammer."

"They were relying on the guards to prevent us from getting to them and didn't bother with a stronger lock."

"Lucky guess," Selome quipped.

"Elementary, my dear Selome." Mercer reached into his kit bag and extracted his Iridium satellite phone. He handed it to Habte. This was the one with the stronger charge, so he wasn't concerned about draining the batteries when he powered it up. "The number is programmed into the phone, just hit this button here and dial 25. You may have to get away from the surrounding mountains to get a signal, I'm not sure. The man you'll be talking to is named Dick Henna. If he needs verification that you're with me, remind him about our conversation in his car and tell him that if he and his wife do get a dog, they should get a tailless Pembrooke corgi. He'll know what it means. Tell him what's been happening and to send troops here as soon as possible. He can get our exact location by contacting the NSA. They'll be able to determine our position by triangulating which communication satellites are handling the call. Make sure he notes the exact time of your call. It'll make the technician's job a hell of a lot quicker.

"Tell him that Harry White is being held by Israeli extremists linked to Defense Minister Chaim Levine and to start working on getting him freed. Make sure he knows that we're in a bad way here, and the longer it takes to get the Marines on the ground, the more people are going to die."

"Shouldn't Selome make the call? Her English is better than mine."

"No, I'm going to need her." Mercer turned to Selome. "Unless you want to go and do it."

"No, I'm staying with you."

"Okay. Habte, as soon as we're twenty feet from the mine entrance, I want you to blow those explosives."

"But with this phone we can contact the authorities, and by tomorrow the Eritrean military will be here."

"In an hour the guards I killed tonight will be discovered, and you can believe the refugees will pay for their deaths. Gianelli's going to realize I took the phone, and he and his band of bastards will be safely across the Sudan border by the time the army arrives. We need to keep them here. This is the only way. Get into position at the detonator, and after you seal the mine, get away from here and make that call." Mercer hopped into the bucket seat of the skiploader and motioned Selome to get on his lap.

Habte vanished back into the storm, and Mercer handed the AK-47 to Selome. "As soon as you see someone notice us, take them out."

The key was in the overhead ignition, and Mercer gave it a twist, timing the firing of the diesel with a rolling boom of thunder. He feathered the throttle to its lowest setting and eased the twin control arms forward. The heavy tires clawed into the mud, slipping for a full revolution before finding purchase, and the Bobcat was under way. Twisting the wrist actuators on the controls brought the bucket up to partially shield them from gunfire.

When the skiploader entered the glow from the tall spotlight atop the shed, the guards saw the unauthorized vehicle and opened fire, winking eyes of flame jetting from their weapons. Selome shrieked as a fusillade rattled against the bucket, sparks shooting off the metal. "Fire back!" Mercer screamed.

The Bobcat was taking a pounding, both front tires deflating when struck, though the vehicle continued to crawl forward. Mercer rammed the throttle to its stops. Despite the increased speed, it was obvious he'd underestimated the number of guards at the mine entrance and their accuracy. Selome was returning fire, controlled three-round bursts that pinned men behind cover, but had yet to diminish the Sudanese ranks.

Mercer chanced a look under the bucket just as one of the guerrillas caught a bullet and flew back into the mud. He was about to congratulate Selome on her shot when he realized she was changing clips. Another Sudanese went down, punched through the mouth so his entire skull erupted as the round passed through. Mercer thought Habte was shooting from his cover behind the mound of tailings, but the angle was all wrong. It was during a second-long pause in the murderous exchange of fire that he heard the sharp, distinctive whip crack of a high-powered rifle.

There was someone else involved in the fight! A sniper helping Mercer and Selome make it to cover, and he knew who it was. The Israeli commandos, the men he'd thought, hoped, he had lost weeks ago. He had no idea how long they had been watching the camp or what their plans were, but Mercer wasn't about to lose the advantage they were giving him.

"Empty the clip as fast as you can. This is it!"

They were twenty feet from the entrance, and as they drew closer, more Sudanese fell, gunned down from above by the unseen assassin. Mercer realized that the Israeli had positioned himself in the middle of where Habte had planted the explosives. He felt nothing that the man who had just helped them was about to die.

He drove the hearty little excavator into the tin shack that housed the safe, crushing one guard between the blade and the metal wall. The building collapsed under the grinding pressure, falling apart like a house of cards. The safe was white and very high-tech, about the size of a steamer trunk. Mercer lowered the blade and scooped it up. Its weight was almost too much and the Bobcat's engine seethed, but they continued forward with the safe nestled in the bucket.

Fifteen feet from the entrance, Mercer felt the ground shudder. Ten crimson blooms erupted in the darkness above the mine entrance. Habte had fired the charges he'd planted, and the stability of the rock face was gone. The overhanging mountain started to come down in an avalanche. They had ten feet to cover, and the Bobcat's motor was missing every few moments, an ominous skip that signified a bullet had pierced something critical. Mercer lowered the blade and released the thigh restraints that had locked over him and Selome.

"Be ready to run!" he screamed, seeing a solid wall of dirt, rock, and mud rushing down the mountain, hundreds of tons of debris that forced the air ahead of it in a gust.

The Bobcat surged again, finding a bit of power that carried them into the mine just a fraction of a second before the first of the avalanche plummeted to the desert floor. Mercer kept the throttles to their stops, racing ahead of the debris that started to fill the tunnel itself. The ground continued to shake, rock falling from the ceiling. The tunnel was about to collapse.

"Mercer!" Selome gasped.

The explosion had weakened the ancient tunnel, and it started to come down in huge slabs, cracks and fissures appearing in the walls, the rents racing forward faster than the Bobcat could possibly move. Mercer considered abandoning the excavator, but he needed the safe and the diamonds inside it for bait. Pressure bursts erupted just behind them, chunks of rock exploding down the shaft with the speed of bullets, more rubble clogging the tunnel. Stones rattled off the skiploader's safety cage.

They drove for two hundred yards with a surging wall of debris chasing their heels. The engine began coughing again just as they started to pace ahead of the wending fissures in the walls. Mercer's lips worked in a silent entreaty for the rig to keep moving.

After a few more seconds, the sound of falling stone receded. He looked behind them. The cave-in had stopped, though he could still feel the earth shifting as the mountain settled.

He shut down the Bobcat and silence rushed in, he and Selome panting in the dust-choked air.

The string of lights in the tunnel were powered by a generator in the main chamber, and they danced in time with the man-made earthquake. A few of the bulbs had smashed against the ceiling and plunged the drive into shadow. Behind them stood a packed jumble of stones, some as large as automobiles, others mere shards, but still the drive was completely sealed.

"What in the hell was that all about?" Selome coughed, stunned by the ferocity of the avalanche.

"Our entombment," Mercer replied, unconcerned by the destruction around him.

Valley of Dead Children

Yosef couldn't believe his eyes when the mountain beneath his sniper's position suddenly began sliding downward in an unstoppable rush. He was a quarter mile away, higher in the hills that surrounded the valley, and he watched the whole thing through night-vision glasses. Even in the greenish distortion of the second-generation optics, the sight was unbelievable.

One moment, he saw his man work his rifle, the long silencer fitted to the American-made Remington, eliminating all telltale signs of his location while cutting just a fraction off the deadly weapon's accuracy. And then the hill heaved upward in multiple gouts of earth. The sniper was caught unaware, vanishing into the maelstrom of debris so quickly that Yosef couldn't track his position as he was swallowed by the avalanche. Nor could he tell if Selome Nagast and Philip Mercer had made it into the tunnel. It was possible they'd been crushed by the tons of rock and dirt.

He radioed his other team, thinking that the mine was under attack. The two-man team reported that nothing was happening at their sector.

If it wasn't an attack, then Yosef had no idea what had happened. He'd watched Mercer's escape from the barbed-wire enclosure and tracked him as he moved stealthily around the mining camp, first to a cluster of tents and later to free Selome. Their dash for the mine in the small digging machine was dismaying. Yosef couldn't understand why they hadn't tried to escape the valley. And then came the avalanche. He considered that perhaps the explosions were the result of a trip-wire booby trap designed to prevent unauthorized entry into the mine. There could be no other explanation.

Then came the full realization. The ancient mine had been sealed by the landslide! He gaped at the mounds of rock and earth that blocked the entrance and was struck dumb. All the work that had gone into the opening of the mine was lost, and it could only be the fault of Philip Mercer. Yosef prayed that the American had been smeared into a wet stain. Mercer had destroyed Yosef's chance for ever recovering the Tabernacle of the Lord, the sacred Ark in which Moses had carried the Word of God into Israel.

The Israeli team had kept the mine under observation since the column of equipment had arrived from the west, followed shortly by hundreds of refugees. They had found the valley from the plane they'd rented in Asmara, using the map supplied by Rabbi Yadid. They'd landed twenty miles away, and Yosef and the others had taken only a day to march to the mine and establish observation posts that they'd manned around the clock for the past weeks.

In all that time, none of them had seen anything remotely resembling the Ark of the Covenant removed from the mine, and Yosef assumed that the artifact was still buried inside. The miners would have a better chance than the commandos at finding it, so he had hoped to make his assault when it was discovered and removed from the tunnel. The superior training of his small team would ensure they'd have little trouble stealing the Ark once it was on the surface.

But things back home had changed all that.

During his last contact with Levine, the Defense Minister had told him that his agents in Israel had failed to find Harry White. It was crucial that Yosef find the Ark before White's debriefing, or the operation would fail. So far no alarms had been sounded within the intelligence community, but both men knew that once the old man told his story, it was only a matter of time before an investigation implicated the minister. Levine ordered Yosef and his men to make a direct approach by taking over the mine and finding the Ark themselves. Yosef noted the strong odor of desperation in Levine's plan.

At first Levine had wanted the Ark to secure his election to the prime minister's office, but now the discovery might be needed to protect him from prosecution. He'd promised Yosef that he could still count on close air support from the CH-53 Super Stallion standing by. Levine needed just four hours' notice to get the chopper and an in-flight tanker into the air and en route.

Choking down his own emotions, Yosef continued to watch the camp below him. He saw the two white leaders of the expedition take charge of the pandemonium. He assumed one of them was Giancarlo Gianelli and the larger man with him was a mining engineer. Yosef couldn't hear their voices, but the gestures and the speed in which the orders were carried out demonstrated total control. Within minutes, additional lamps had been brought to the landslide and the large crawler excavator was up and running, its twin lights piercing the rain. The mechanical arm began tearing into the loose rubble, ripping out long trenches of debris.

Yosef saw some of the armed Sudanese lope off into the night and assumed they were chasing the few Eritreans who had escaped the stockades after Mercer and Selome. Only twenty minutes after the disaster, nearly a quarter of the detritus had been cleared. The Israeli was amazed at the efficiency with which the white men worked the crews.

Perhaps, Yosef thought, hope remained. They looked as though they would get the shaft cleared in just a few hours. This meant Yosef and his people could still sneak in later to search for their prize. Even as he watched, more Eritreans were put to the task, crawling over the mounds of rubble with shovels and picks, adding their labor to the machine's.

Yosef lay cradled in a hollow between several boulders. Rain pounded mercilessly, turning the top layer of soil into a slipping mass that oozed downhill. He hated that the Ark was going to become just another political tool, its very symbolism tarnished by the manner of its recovery. Yet as long as it went to the people of Israel, he felt justified. With Levine now backed into a corner, recovering the artifact could mean the difference between prison and freedom for all of them.

A noise pulled his attention from the workers clearing the mine. Someone was on the mountain with him, moving laterally to get away from the encampment. He thought it was one of the fleeing Eritrean refugees. He hunkered a little deeper into his burrow. If either an Eritrean or one of the armed guards stumbled onto his position, he would kill without hesitation. If he remained undiscovered, he would leave them to their nocturnal fumbling.

He put the noise out of his mind and redirected his attention to the mine when a voice disturbed him again. He thought maybe two Eritreans had linked up in the dark and was about to turn back to his vigil when he realized he could hear only one voice. A man was speaking on a phone.

And he was speaking in English.

Inside the Mine

No sooner had the earth stopped trembling than Mercer began smashing the light bulbs that had survived the collapse with the butt of Selome's AK-47. She took no notice of his peculiar behavior. Instead, she stared down the drive, her eyes misted with emotion. This was only the second time she had seen the interior of the mine, and it filled her mind with wonderment about the people who had built it. She knew it had been dug by slaves, children who were worked to death, but it still represented a tangible piece of her history, and as a Jew, she knew how little physical evidence remained of her faith.

"Selome," Mercer called.

"What?"

"Get hold of yourself. The guards down in the pit are going to come to investigate, and we need to be ready." He came up to her in the dark, touching her hand to reassure her of his location in the darkness. "Take this light." He handed her a small penlight he'd kept in his kit bag and settled them next to the dead skiploader. "When I squeeze your hand, I want you to turn it on and shine it down the tunnel."

The drive was a mile and a half long, and it took a few minutes for the Sudanese guarding the slave workers to send someone to see what had taken place and for the hapless guard to reach the end of the shaft. Mercer could hear tentative steps shuffling on the dusty foot wall as the rebel drew nearer, crossing into the darkened section of the tunnel where he waited with Selome. When he gauged the guerrilla was about twenty feet away, probing the wall like a blind man in an unfamiliar place, he gave Selome's fingers a gentle squeeze.

The penlight wasn't powerful, but after the total blackness, its beam was blinding. Motes of dust hung in the air as thick as a New England blizzard, and at the far reach of the light, a soldier paused, peering into the glow. As soon as Mercer saw the armed figure, he triggered off a single shot.

"One down, four more to go." Earlier, Gianelli had used ten Sudanese to guard each shift, but the number had dropped to five since there had been no trouble from the slave workers. He stood, handed the rebel's AK to Selome, and started walking toward the domed chamber.

"Mercer, how are we going to get out of here? There must be a thousand tons of rock blocking the exit." Selome didn't know Mercer well enough to appreciate one of his insane plans, so panic put a raw edge to her voice.

"Don't worry. When we're done tonight, there's going to be another thousand tons in this tunnel."

The light bulbs lining the hanging wall were in little metal cages, and as they moved closer to the working pit, Mercer smashed them to eliminate the chance he and Selome were back-lit to other investigating soldiers. After twenty minutes of quiet walking, they reached a spot about forty feet from the chamber. Still no one had come to see what had befallen their comrade or the mine entrance.

"Damn," Mercer cursed bitterly. "They're better disciplined than I thought. I was hoping to catch another of them in the tunnel."

As usual, the pit was well lit and echoed with the sounds of the generators, which had probably masked Mercer's earlier rifle shot. The tools, though, were now idled. The Eritreans leaned against the pneumatic drills while their guards looked blankly at each other. All work had stopped while they waited to see what happened next. The South African miner appeared to be the only one not immobilized by the catastrophe. He was shining one of the halogen lamps on the dome arching over the pit, checking to see if it had been damaged by the explosions and avalanche.

"That cave-in may have looked bad," Mercer whispered, "but Gianelli will get it cleared pretty quickly. We have a lot more work to do."

"What next?"

"We need to immobilize the rest of the guards, and then we're going to do a disappearing act."

"What do you mean, a disappearing act?"

"I'm going to make every one in this chamber vanish into thin air." He noted the disbelief in her expression and grinned. "Don't you believe in magic?"

Outside the sealed mine entrance, the men worked feverishly in the rain, pushed on by the brutal prompts of the Sudanese and by the sharp tongues of Joppi Hofmyer and Giancarlo Gianelli. The Italian was frantic, screaming at everyone and kicking piles of dirt like a spoiled child. He yelled at Hofmyer and the other three South Africans not trapped in the mine, and he yelled at the Eritreans and the Sudanese, even though the natives couldn't understand a word he said. By now he knew what had happened. Mercer was gone from the men's compound, and only a few of the feebler women remained in theirs. They'd found two corpses under the barbed wire of the men's enclosure, and a dozen male workers had vanished into the raging storm. Gianelli felt that the avalanche was a diversion on Mercer's part to redirect interest from the refugees and force a reopening of the mine while they made their escape. However, Gianelli still had more than enough men to both capture the runaways and clear away the avalanche.

In all, Mercer had done little to derail Gianelli from his plan. Hofmyer assured the industrialist that he would have the tunnel reopened in short order. The trapped men should be in good condition, and it was possible that du Toit, who was the overseer inside, would keep them working, confident that his comrades would rescue him.

"I bet we don't lose more than a few hours because of this," Hofmyer said. "And Mercer's trapped in the mountain. Apart from the couple of guards he killed and a little inconvenience, he did nothing to us, I swear."

"Yes, well, there are a couple thousand carats of rough diamonds in the safe that bastard buried inside this mountain, and this whole operation will be a waste if we don't recover them. I call that more than a *little* inconvenience."

"Mr. Gianelli, I bet that safe is no more than a couple of feet into the tunnel. A guard at the mine entrance said that just before the avalanche, the skiploader was running very rough."

Gianelli whirled. "You had better well hope so!" Spittle flew from his lips. "Mercer's satellite phone is missing, which means the government is going to know about us shortly. I need those stones. We still have time, but not much."

The men and machines continued to rip apart the mounds of dirt and rock that covered the entrance. If anything, Hofmyer's time estimate was too generous. To Gianelli's eye, it appeared that the tunnel would be cleared in two hours, maybe less. One of the South African miners had come up with the idea of using the pumps brought to empty the earlier Italian workings and use them to power a water cannon. The apparatus was turned on while Giancarlo watched, water drawn from a rain-created lake that had grown to enormous proportions. The high-pressure jet tore into the debris like a drill, washing away soil and smaller rocks.

Yes, he thought, *maybe this won't be too bad after all.* He hoped Mercer had survived the cave-in so he could watch the man die a much slower death. The idea gave him a grim satisfaction.

Mercer didn't have a good plan for eliminating the four other Sudanese guarding the pit. He wanted to avoid a firefight, since he and Selome had only two guns and a finite amount of ammunition. While waiting for inspiration, providence provided for him. The white miner—Mercer recalled the man's name was du Toit—started up from the pit floor, heading for the tunnel exit and his own investigation. Hidden as they were, the miner wouldn't see Mercer and Selome until he was almost on top of them.

Selome read Mercer's intentions and crossed the tunnel to take up a position to prevent du Toit from bolting. The South African walked between them, his flashlight aimed straight ahead. Mercer stepped from around a large boulders, his AK held low across his belly, the barrel pointed at du Toit's groin.

The South African raised his hands so quickly that his knuckles scraped on the low ceiling. Selome made a tiny scuffing sound as she came up behind du Toit, and if anything, the miner's hands pressed tighter against the hanging wall.

"Smart choice," Mercer said softly. "Now, we're going back to the pit and see if you can convince the guerrillas to do the same thing. Nod if you think that's a good idea."

Du Toit bobbed his head vigorously, though his eyes never left the 7.62mm aperture of the AK leveled at his genitals.

"That's good, because if you aren't convincing, you'll be the first to die."

Mercer stood at the top of the working pit, holding du Toit by the shirt collar, and gave a bellowing, primeval yell. The four Sudanese swiveled their guns to the duo standing ten feet over their heads but held off firing. Selome quickly crawled forward to cover the guards with her own AK.

"Drop your weapons!" she shouted in Tigrinyan, and when one of the Sudanese who understood the language did so, the others followed suit. Eritreans near the guards scrambled to retrieve the assault rifles.

Many of them had been freedom fighters just a few years earlier, and they handled the weapons with easy familiarity, forcing the Sudanese to their knees and asking Selome if they could kill them.

"No," she called. "We need the ammunition for later, and these dogs may have value when we get out." She looked at Mercer and repeated what she'd just said in English. "I didn't think you wanted them dead."

"Good assumption." Mercer released du Toit and trotted down the ramp that led to the floor of the mine. He sat at a table used as the underground office, clearing away rock samples and mining gear with a sweep of his arm. "I estimate we have another three hours before Gianelli breaks through, so first we need to put another roadblock in his way. And then we've got some serious mining to do."

"What's your plan?" Selome joined him.

"First thing is to send some men to drag that safe in here with us. Then we need to drop more of the tunnel hanging wall, close to where it reaches the pit. There's more than enough explosives here for the job."

"Didn't you say something to Hofmyer about needing to channel the explosions away from the chamber to avoid destroying the main dome?"

Mercer chuckled,. "Hofmyer might be a miner, but he's no geologist. That dome's been here for a billion years, sitting near some of the most active fault lines on the planet. If earthquakes haven't destroyed it by now, it'd take a nuke to damage it today."

"So we replug the tunnel. I'm guessing that's to slow Gianelli again?"

"Correct."

"And what will we be doing while he's digging?"

"I told you, we're going to vanish into thin air." Mercer slid the Medusa pictures from his kit bag and carefully unfolded them. When he found the one he wanted, he showed it to Selome.

She studied the unintelligible jumble of lines and swirls and splashes of color. "I'm sorry, but those pictures make no sense to me."

"If Alice had a photograph like these, she never would have gotten lost in Wonderland." Mercer grinned. "I'll explain it all in a while, but first we need to get these men working. We'll split into two teams, so you'll have to do double duty interpreting for me unless anyone else here speaks English."

Twenty minutes later, Mercer had a gang of ten men standing in the tunnel. He'd used a can of fluorescent spray to mark where he wanted holes drilled into the ceiling and fashioned a piece of metal wire as a depth gauge. There were about thirty bright orange spots spread along a hundred-foot section of the tunnel. Through Selome's translations, he explained that he wanted half the holes drilled straight upward and the other half at an angle. Angling the holes would direct the force of their explosives in a more random destructive pattern. The holes didn't need to be any deeper than the wire gauge. He left instructions to be told when the first fifteen holes had been drilled so he could place the charges needed to bring down the hanging wall.

He watched for several minutes to make certain the men knew what he wanted and was pleased at how proficient they had become with the drills. Each one weighed a hundred pounds and they were as long and unwieldy as railroad ties, yet the Eritreans worked them with the expertise of seasoned professionals. Water from a tank lubricated the drill's cutting heads, and chips of rock and mud began pouring from the ceiling in a steady drizzle. One of the men paused to wave at Mercer when he removed the drill from the first completed hole.

"Hit it again, man." Mercer slapped him on the shoulder and the miner started boring into another of the painted marks.

Mercer left them to their task and returned to the table with the Medusa photographs. Selome had laid out some food and water for him and he ate while studying one particular picture. She sat close by, watching him as he worked but he paid her little heed. His face was a mask of concentration, and when he looked up from his task, his eyes were hard and his expression grim.

Without proper tools and measurements, Mercer had set himself a nearly impossible task, and amid the din of the workers rigging the tunnel, he felt the responsibility weighing heavily. He needed a plug that would slow Gianelli, not deter him entirely. Mercer knew there was a chance that when they collapsed more of the tunnel, its entire length would come down. If the Italian abandoned the diamonds Mercer had stolen, there wasn't enough fuel for the drills or explosives for them to tunnel themselves back out. He'd intentionally buried them alive, and if he continued with his plan, he might seal them in forever, murdering Selome and the other forty people in here with him.

Selome touched Mercer on the back of his scarred hand, and he looked into her dark eyes. "For what it's worth," she said, "I believe in you."

"This time I don't think it's going to be enough," he replied, but hauled himself to his feet and waved over the cluster of miners waiting for instructions.

They walked to one of the deeper shafts that had been dug into the working floor of the mine. The bottom of the fifty-foot hole was lost in the gloom. Mercer scrambled down the ladder, followed by Selome and the Eritrean who was the gang's leader. He shook the can of spray paint he'd carried with him, the tiny ball bearing clattering like the tail of a rattlesnake. Glancing again at the Medusa picture he'd brought, Mercer painted two bold crisscrossing diagonal lines near the south corner of the shaft.

"X marks the spot." He tossed the can to the ground. "We dig here faster than Mike Mulligan and his steam shovel, and just maybe we'll make it out of this mess alive."

Selome's next question was lost in the bustle of men lowering equipment into the hole. Minutes later, Mercer had stripped off his shirt and stood poised over one of the big drills, its tip resting on the rock floor. "Our only saving grace is there's no kimberlite down here. The early miners dug like bastards but didn't find anything. The rock is a much softer matrix; otherwise my plan would never work."

"What's beneath us?"

He looked at her. "The real King Solomon's Mine." With that, he opened the compressed air valve on the drill. It was as if the shattering sound alone splintered the stone as the cutter head sank into the earth.

Valley of Dead Children

Within a few minutes of leaving the camp, Habte Makkonen knew that he had been spotted and followed, yet he did not change his pace or direction. Doing so would alert the stalker. The man who shadowed him was good, an expert actually, and the storm made his job that much easier, but Habte hadn't survived so many years in the front lines of the rebellion without becoming better still.

There were two other problems besides the fact he wasn't armed and his pursuer most likely was. First, the mountains ringing the valley were steep and too treacherous to climb in the rain, and the valley floor offered little cover. As he moved away from the mine, he was terribly exposed. Second was that the pursuit had been taken up much too quickly for the stalker to be one of the Sudanese guards. The rebels hadn't had the time to mount an organized search by the time Habte fled the camp. This left only the snipers who'd opened fire moments before the explosives had buried the mine. Habte was also certain his watcher had a pair of night-vision goggles and his rifle's scope had similar capabilities.

The sniper, certainly an Israeli agent, was interested in the mine—according to what Mercer had said—but Habte could guess at the man's interest in him now. He had made an earlier, unsuccessful call to Dick Henna on Mercer's satellite phone. He'd spoken for a few seconds before realizing that the recorded voice he heard was telling him he had a bad connection and to try the call again. The Israeli must have overheard him responding to the unfamiliar device. Habte cursed his own stupidity for not calling farther from the mining site. If he was going to alert Henna quickly, Habte didn't have much leeway to wait out the sniper. He had to get clear to make that call.

Skirting an ancient landslide, Habte saw something across the plain that gave him an idea, and he wondered if the sniper would allow him to do it. Walking across a thousand yards of open land with a sniper's scope on his back was not the most brilliant tactical solution he'd ever devised, but he hoped that if he kept his gait even and unthreatening and waited for the sniper to close range every few minutes, he might just make it.

The old head gear sat forlornly on the open expanse, the buildings next to it darker shadows in the night. Lightning illuminated the eerie site every few seconds, outlining the skeletal structure that had once hauled workers and worthless ore out of the Italian-built mine. As casually as a man on a stroll, Habte veered from the hills and made for the old facility. He expected a bullet in the back, but when none came after the first forty yards, he paused to allow the sniper to move into a better shooting position. As long as the sniper felt he wasn't trying to bolt, Habte prayed that he wouldn't take the shot.

The mine was far enough from the other workings to ensure that if the sniper wanted, he could pin Habte with a few well-placed shots and close in for an interrogation. That was what Habte was betting his life on: that the sniper was more interested in his intentions than his death. He continued to walk slowly, his pace almost ambling as if the storm didn't matter. Once he thought he heard the sniper moving along a hillside, the sliding hiss of loose stones betraying both his position and the fact that he was closing.

And then a sudden thought struck Habte and he took off at a full run, legs flying, arms pumping and his breath heaving against years of cigarette smoke. A silenced shot winged by, ricocheting against the ground well behind and to the right. The shot was made in desperation; it was an inaccurate estimation of Habte's position because the sniper didn't have him in his sights. Habte then realized that the sudden bursts of brilliant electricity that cut through the storm would blind him if viewed through any light-amplifying device.

The sniper couldn't use the starlite scope or the night-vision goggles! While the Israeli was still armed, the playing field had been leveled by a common atmospheric phenomenon.

Habte dove into the building they had used as a camp when they first arrived at the valley. He had only moments before the pursuer reached the dilapidated structure, and Habte needed all of them to put his plan into motion. He stripped out of his clothing, dumping the soaked garments on the floor and, nude, scrambled back out of the building. His black skin would be shiny in the rain, but for his purpose he was invisible.

The Israeli sniper might have received the finest military training in the world, but his experience was nowhere near Habte's. As he loped silently toward the head gear, his bare feet silent in the mud, the Eritrean felt the odds were evening out. One of the things that had kept him alive all those years fighting the Ethiopians was an understanding of human nature. He could anticipate what others were going to do long before they knew themselves.

Ignoring the hundred-foot hole beneath the head gear's lattice of struts, Habte leaped onto one of the supports, scampering up ten feet without pause, ignoring the slashes in his skin made by the scaly surfaces. He nestled the satellite phone into the crotch of two beams and clung tightly, his silhouette hidden in the tangle of metal. He doubted the Israeli had seen this mine before and was certain the sniper would not be able to resist the urge to peer into the stygian mine shaft.

The sniper had shouldered his long rifle and moved slowly, an Uzi rucked hard against his flank, the bulbous night-vision gear resting on the top of his head. His body was shrouded in a ghillie suit, a camouflage garment made of hundreds of sewn-together rags that from a distance of a few feet looked like an innocuous shrub. With the amount of rain that had soaked the suit, Habte estimated the soldier was carrying an additional thirty pounds, and his movements would be slowed by the encumbrance.

A bolt of lightning cast a sizzling light across the sky,

and the Israeli rolled to the ground, coming up against the camp building, covering his exposed right side with the machine pistol. Habte's suspicions were confirmed; the man's movements appeared lethargic. At this range, there was enough ambient light for Habte to watch the Israeli clip the goggles over his eyes for a moment to peer around the camp and into the building before slipping them off again. He'd studied the head gear for an instant but didn't notice Habte.

As predicted, the sniper seemed more interested in the mine shaft as the only other logical place for his quarry to hide and began crawling over for a better look. Habte estimated he had only a few seconds to wait before springing on the soldier.

The sound was sharp enough to carry over the storm's fury and so incongruous that Habte waited until it sounded again before reacting. The sat-phone was about to ring for a third time when Habte snatched at it, clumsily dislodging it from its resting place and knocking it from his perch. The Israeli was equally startled, but there was nothing clumsy about his movements. He rolled on his back, bringing his Uzi to his shoulder, and when the phone rang again, he adjusted his aim. His reactions were instinctive. He fired off a quarter of the magazine, a long tongue of fire leaping from the compact weapon as bullets pinged off the steel scaffold.

His aim, however, was directed at the falling phone and not at the dark figure poised in the murk above. Habte leaped from the tower, propelling himself out into the night, landing yards short of where the Israeli lay on the muddy ground. The sniper scrambled to trigger the Uzi at the apparition rolling toward him. He took just a second too long, and while Habte's lunge lacked force, it was enough to foul the weapon's aim. A harmless spray of 9mm rounds streaked into the sky.

The phone had survived the drop and hadn't been hit by the opening fusillade so it rang again.

With the Uzi clamped between the two struggling figures, Habte had the advantage. The Israeli grappled with him, but Habte's wet skin gave him no handhold. The Eritrean grabbed a hank of the ghillie suit and started to shake the sniper vigorously, slamming his head into the mud. Even when the sniper tried to hook an ankle around Habte's and roll them to gain the upper hand, his feet just slid up Habte's bare leg. Yet Habte couldn't get enough of a grip to force the writhing agent's face into the ooze to drown him, so they continued in a macabre parody of love-making, both moving against each other, arms and legs entwined.

The advantage shifted when the Israeli grasped the dangling bunch of Habte's genitals and squeezed them with all of his strength. Habte howled, arching his body in an effort to break the grip, but the sniper held on with the tenacity of a remora. Managing to free one hand, Habte wrapped his fingers around the Israeli's throat and angled the sniper for a vicious head butt that shattered teeth and forced blood to pool in the soldier's mouth. Choking on his own blood and with his wind pipe almost crushed, the sniper started to die, his grip on Habte's balls loosening.

Habte maintained the pressure long after the sniper stopped struggling and only stood when he felt that all the life had been crushed from the body. He studied the face and recognized him as the driver of the car parked outside the Ambasoira Hotel when the Sudanese and the Israelis had clashed in Mercer's room. Habte wished it was the Israeli team's leader lying here covered in mud and soaked with his own blood, but that would have to wait.

The phone's ring shocked Habte, and he lifted himself painfully from the ground and found the small device half buried in the mud. It had landed about an inch from the lip of the mine shaft.

Habte snapped it open and pressed the button to accept the call. His voice was a painful wheeze. "Hello, you have reached the phone of Philip Mercer. He's been buried alive. May I help you? My name is Habte Makkonen."

* * *

The men working to clear the mine entrance heard and felt another explosion deep within the earth, a jolt that shook the ground. In the pause that followed, Gianelli asked Joppi Hofmyer if he knew the origin of the subterranean detonation. The South African had no answer, and rather than speculate, as Gianelli seemed to want, Hofmyer put the crews back to work. It took another forty minutes to clear the entrance enough for a man to slip inside.

Hofmyer went first, a powerful flashlight supplementing the lamp on his miner's helmet. Gianelli scrambled after him, and the two started down the near-black tunnel. Hofmyer kept his eyes on the walls and ceiling, looking for new cracks in the rock. Every few feet he would tap the stone with a hammer, listening for a dull thud that would indicate a rotten place. In contrast, Gianelli stared into the gloom ahead of them, his mind focused on recovering his diamonds.

"They must have tried to blow open the safe. That's what we heard," he told an uninterested Hofmyer. "Mercer warned about using explosives under the dome without blast mats, so it couldn't be anything else."

The lights cut just a few feet into the choking veil of dust that mingled with the chemical stench of explosives. So far the path into the mountain was clear. Nothing seemed out of place amid the dressed stones that lined the walls and ceiling.

Hofmyer was the first to see a new plug in the tunnel, when he estimated they were only about two hundred feet from the pit. Rubble blocked the drive from floor to ceiling, but this avalanche wasn't as tightly packed as the first one. The rock was loose and shifted with just a tap of his foot, and when he levered a few pieces out of the pile, nothing new fell from above.

"What's this all about?" Gianelli asked.

"No idea, but if Mercer thinks this'll stop us for long, he's out of his bloody head," Hofmyer sneered. "It'll take nothing to move this out of the way and get to the pit."

"Are you sure?"

"Yeah, the ceiling seems stable, but just to be safe, we'll shore this lot up as we clear the muck outa the way." Hofmyer finished his examination of the pile of debris and turned to his employer. Gianelli had promised him a bonus commensurate with the speed in which the diamonds were recovered, so he had a newfound desire to get into the mine. "I told ya I heard of this Mercer before from some of the trade magazines and from mates back in South Africa, and I expected a hell of a lot more from him. Blocking the tunnel like this is child's play. I don't know what he's playing at, but this is starting to piss me off."

"When we get our hands on him, he'll wish he had died in the avalanche."

Once the entrance to the main tunnel was completely cleared, Hofmyer ordered the Eritreans to remove the debris from Mercer's drop mat. The explosives had rendered the waste into easily maneuvered chunks, and a human chain was quickly established to transfer the debris outside. It still took nearly two hours because of the distance to the surface and because Hofmyer used specially designed screw jacks to prop up the hanging wall.

Gianelli was standing next to the South African when they broke through to the pit. Hofmyer poked his head into the chamber, a pistol held in his fist, just in case. He was silent for a long moment.

"Well?" Gianelli panted.

Hofmyer didn't answer. He directed a couple of workers to clear away the last of the rubble and crawled into the domed chamber. Emboldened by Hofmyer's actions, Gianelli dogged his heels. They found themselves standing on the ledge above the ancient mine floor. Lights still blazed brightly, running on internal battery power because the generators were silent. In fact, they had been destroyed, their mechanical guts spread around them in pools of oil. The drills were lined up next to the generators, and they, too, had been wrecked, the couplings for the air hoses smashed beyond repair.

Apart from the equipment, the chamber was empty.

"Gone," Gianelli said, not believing his eyes. "They are all gone."

Hofmyer stood next to him, slack-jawed incredulity on his face. There was no sign of Mercer or the Eritrean miners or the Sudanese guards. Mercer had made the entire group vanish.

On the far wall of the pit, written with neon yellow paint in letters five feet tall was a simple six-word message composed, no doubt, by Philip Mercer. It sent a deep chill through Hofmyer and especially Gianelli. They both felt that somehow it was true.

I'M WAITING FOR YOU IN HELL

The Mine

An hour before Gianelli broke through the first avalanche and encountered the drop mat, the working floor of the mine had been far different. Machinery thrummed and ratcheted, echoing off the arched roof and drowning the shouts and oaths of the Eritrean workers. The activity was frantic as they strove to reach Mercer's nearly impossible deadline. They tore into the deep shaft like madmen, jack-hammering out chunks of stone that had to be muscled from the pit. They had bored a man-sized hole a further fifteen feet into the soft stone, deflected at an angle from the main shaft in strict accordance to Mercer's instructions.

In the entry tunnel, the scene was less hectic but just as noisy, the crew continuing to drill ten-foot-deep holes into the hanging wall. Mercer had left the work in the pit and joined this crew, following behind them with bundles of explosives. He placed each charge carefully, not letting the pressure of time rush the delicate process. Selome worked with him, handing him the cylinders of plastique from a cart they had dragged into the tunnel. The drillers were far enough ahead so they could hold a shouted conversation.

"Are you finally going to explain what we're doing?" she asked.

Mercer didn't look up from the charge he was wiring. "Yeah. This drop mat is going to buy us a few more hours before Gianelli reaches us."

"You already told me that," Selome replied. "And you said you're going to make us all disappear, but what do you mean?"

Mercer answered her question with one of his own. "Did

you notice something incongruous between the mine that Brother Ephraim described and this tunnel here?" Selome shook her head. "He said that Solomon's mine was excavated by children working in slave conditions, right?"

"Yes."

"Then explain to me why the children needed to dig this tunnel so wide and so tall. Also, how could they have dug it straight to the kimberlite deposit? The odds against that are about one in a trillion."

"I have no idea." It was obvious that she hadn't considered either of these points.

"This tunnel was built *after* the kimberlite had been discovered in order to make extracting the ore more efficient. It was sized for adults, not children, dug so that two men carrying baskets of ore in their hands could pass each other comfortably. The kimberlite had already been located through another set of tunnels that run beneath this one, and that's the mine that *The Shame of Kings* describes."

"Oh, my God," Selome breathed. "It was staring in front of me all along and I never saw it."

"Hey, I do this for a living," Mercer said. "This one was dug when the mine's high assay value made it economical to drive a tunnel directly to the ore body rather than haul it out through the smaller, children's tunnels below us."

"So the other team is digging where you think the two mines intersect? You found the location from the satellite photographs?"

"Yes." Mercer finished with the charge he'd been wiring and inserted it into the hole over his head, tamping it gently to seat it properly. "Those Medusa pictures finally had some value after all. When I first saw them in Washington, I noticed that white lines covered some of them and assumed they were either distortions or veins of a dense mineral giving back a strong echo to the positron receiver. What I figured out since coming here is that they represent hollows in the earth, tunnels like this one."

"And you found a way back to the surface?"

Mercer looked a little sheepish. "Well, not exactly. Remember, the resolution on those pictures was terrible. It's not quite guesswork on my part, but damn close. Still, I think where those men are drilling will lead to the older tunnels, the ones Ephraim told us about."

"I'm not saying I don't believe you, but what if it doesn't?"

"Then Gianelli's going to break into this mine and gun down everyone he sees." Mercer shrugged. "I've gotten us this far, haven't I? Maybe our luck will hold."

They blasted the drop mat as soon as Mercer had rigged the last charge, everyone having taken an impromptu vote to either surrender to Gianelli or try to find a way out on their own. Mercer felt he owed them that. He explained the pitfalls and the danger, but the vote was unanimous to seal off the mine again.

When the crew had finished blocking the tunnel, Mercer shifted them to the pit. They drilled for another hour, the men working with machine-like efficiency, Mercer in the thick of it. He was operating one of the drills when the bit struck a void in the rock and the entire rig sank up to its couplings. Not wanting to hope too much, but feeling a building excitement, he hauled the drill back up, aligned it a few inches away, and fired in another hole. A section of floor collapsed and he found himself standing above a black hollow that hadn't seen light in three thousand years. His triumphant whoop alerted the other men, and they crowded around, recoiling at the fetid, decaying odor that belched from the depths.

Mercer shut down the drill and signaled to a man above to silence the generators. In moments the shaft was filled with excited voices as those workers not otherwise engaged clambered to look into the darkness.

"You did it," Selome shrieked, and threw her arms around Mercer's shoulders. Her passionate kiss brought a round of cheering from the workers and a delighted smile to Mercer.

"Little early for the champagne," he warned. "There's something I forgot, and it may already be too late. Cave disease."

"Cave disease, what's that?"

"Cryptococcus. It's a fungus that lives in undisturbed areas like caves and abandoned mines. Once inhaled, it germinates in the lungs and can cause fatal meningitis if not treated quickly. The main tunnel was safe because Hofmyer vented it before sending in workers, but this other mine may be rife with the stuff." Mercer paused, assessing the odds. "We've already breathed the air blowing out of the hole, and we don't have a choice but to continue."

"Is there a cure?"

"Yeah, um, amphotericin and flourocytosine, I think. But we don't have time to worry about that now. Gianelli should be working on the blast mat, and we have to get everyone into the original mine and hide every trace that we were ever here." Mercer then added with a fiendish grin, "And that includes the safe full of diamonds."

Another twenty minutes and they were ready to abandon the chamber. Mercer had rigged a coffer dam above the pit that led to the old mine and loaded it with tons of rubble. He configured it so its contents could be dumped into the shaft after they had escaped through the hole in its bottom. He also ordered the destruction of the remaining mining equipment and scrawled a personal greeting to Gianelli and Hofmyer for their arrival. Dropping the safe into the hole widened it enough for the men to begin lowering themselves into the cramped tunnels below.

Mercer considered leaving du Toit and the Sudanese behind, but they would give away the escape route the instant Gianelli reached the chamber. He couldn't bring himself to murder them. They were prisoners and deserved some sort of fair treatment. He made sure they were securely bound and well guarded before allowing them into the tunnel.

He was the last one to descend into the children's mine, dragging the lanyard that would breach the coffer dam behind him. Once in the cramped tunnel, he moved away from the hole connecting the two mines. When he judged he was far enough, he yanked the line and held his breath as debris filled the pit above them. Unless Hofmyer possessed a photographic memory, he would never know the pit had been filled or how Mercer had taken his people out of the main chamber.

It was only after the last of the rubble settled that he took a moment to investigate their surroundings. In the beam of his flashlight, the tunnel was only three feet tall and maybe as wide, circular rather than squared. All the surfaces were rough, showing the marks where they had been worked by primitive stone tools. The air was just rich enough to breathe, but it was a struggle. In the few moments since the tunnel had been sealed, the air was starting to foul. Mercer realized he had to string out the forty men with him if he was to avoid depleting the oxygen in one section, yet he couldn't have them too far apart for fear of losing someone.

From where he sat, he could see three branch tunnels meandering off, one to left, one to right, and one rising up and over this one. The claustrophobic tunnels reminded him of pictures he'd seen of the myriad branches in a human lung or the den of some burrowing rodent. A man could become hopelessly lost after only a few feet. He crawled over the supine men until he had reached the front of the group, passing the Sudanese guards, oblivious to their wrathful stares. Selome waited for him with her own flashlight. They had only two others, but these lights were powered by hand crank mechanisms that required no batteries so there wasn't any danger of them dying. Still, the tunnel was so dim that it was impossible to see beyond just a couple of yards.

"What now, fearless leader?" Selome asked, her pride in Mercer evident in her eyes and smile.

Mercer's kit bag bulged with items he thought he might need for the ordeal to come. He dug out one of the lighters. He sparked the wheel and watched the flame until the metal top was too hot to touch. The flame remained in a solid column, not flickering in the slightest. "No air movement, but that doesn't mean we won't find some. It just means we are too far back to feel it. What I want to do is find a place to leave everyone behind, a chamber like the children would have used as a dormitory. Chances are it will be situated near a natural air vent."

"And then?"

"You and I find the way out of here. We'll be able to move a lot faster if we don't have to worry about stragglers and our prisoners." Mercer glanced back into the darkness, listening to the coughing fits of the men. The air was rank. "Now you know why I didn't want Habte with us. As much as he smokes, he wouldn't last five minutes in here. By the time we get out, he should have reached Dick Henna and a couple hundred Marines will have landed, taking care of our former Italian slave master."

"And then we come back for the rest of the miners?"

"You got it."

They started out, Mercer in the lead with Selome right behind. They followed the erratic beam of his flashlight as he crawled through the serpentine tunnels on his hands and knees. After an hour, all of them were feeling the effects of the dust their motion kicked up, and the tunnel echoed like a tuberculosis ward. The Eritreans were drinking water at a prodigious rate to salve their burned throats. Mercer was becoming concerned. They needed to find a small chink in the earth's armor that allowed a seep of air to reach the dark maze.

Another two hours of uninterrupted agony followed as the party oozed through the warren with wormlike slowness. Every few hundred yards, Mercer would test the air for movement, but each time the lighter's flame held steady. He studied the Medusa pictures at many of the major junctures. Their resolution was so poor that the lines on the photos did not correspond with the three-dimensional map he was creating in his mind. After the fourth frustrating time, he angrily tucked them back in his bag. Their only hope lay with Mercer's instincts and his intimate knowledge of mines and mining. He was the only one who could navigate this subterranean realm, ignoring large branches and side tunnels that might have tempted another and leading them through tiny crawl spaces that someone else would have ignored.

They were well into their fourth hour when Mercer sparked his lighter again. The small flames swayed away from him, its movement so slight that had he not been staring, he never would have noticed it. Selome saw the expression on his face and grinned.

"I think we're going to be okay," he said.

The chamber they found fifteen minutes later was about twenty feet square, and while the quarters were cramped, everyone fit. Mercer noted that the cavity was a natural formation, one that the child miners had discovered and exploited for themselves. It was like a warm womb deep underground, a sanctuary from the agonizing labor they endured until their young lives ended in the darkness. The ceiling of the cave was about six feet tall and was scarred with hundreds of cracks. Through one of these fissures and through a labyrinthine twist in the living rock, a trickle of air descended into the earth, freshening the atmosphere. After the foul odor of the tunnels, the air in the chamber was sweet and joyously refreshing.

Selome settled against Mercer's chest as he lay against one wall, taking a much needed break. The men were tangled around them like a litter of exhausted puppies, too tired to sort themselves out. Many minutes would pass before the last coughing spell ended with a wet expectoration of blood.

"It's all downhill from here," Mercer said.

"You mean it gets easier?"

"No." Mercer shook his head. "We've been climbing toward the surface for the past hour so these tunnels will have to slope downward again if we're going to find an exit we can use."

"Okay, mister." Selome looked at him with mock severity. "You've been giving cryptic answers and telling only half the story since we entered the mine, and every time you pull some trick out of your hat. So what's your trick this time?"

Mercer laughed. "Found me out, did you? Yes, I have another trick. Remember when we first entered the mine after Gianelli caught us at the monastery? I said I was looking for an escape route." Selome nodded. "I noticed a section of wall a hundred feet from the surface that looked as if it had been rebuilt. The stone was a shade lighter than the blocks used to line the rest of the tunnel. I'm betting our lives that there's another tunnel behind it that had been covered over, hidden."

"You think these old mine shafts lead to it."

He nodded. "But if they don't, we are seriously screwed."

They rested for another half hour before Mercer decided that if he delayed any longer, he'd be too stiff to continue. He roused Selome and spoke with the gang leaders, again asking her to translate. He laid out his plan and the Eritreans agreed. Their faith in his abilities was an inspiration for Mercer, but also a burden. First it was Harry's life which depended on what he did, then Selome's and Habte's, and now he'd added forty more people, plus the others still in the slave compounds. He cleared his mind of creeping defeatism. It was much too late to doubt his decisions, even if he led them into a possible, and quite literal, dead end.

"Are you ready?" Mercer asked.

"Have I ever said no?"

"That's my girl."

They started out of the chamber, exiting through one of the larger tunnels. In only a few seconds, they could no longer see the glow from the two flashlights they'd left with the Eritreans. The beam of their own single light seemed puny in the mounting blackness of the unnatural maze. And as Mercer crawled ahead of Selome, the single AK-47 he'd taken with him seemed just as ineffective if they managed to reach the surface and had to face Gianelli again.

Mahdi had bided his time. He was not a patient man and the quiet waiting had been frustrating, but now it was all about to pay off. He lay with the three other Sudanese soldiers, men who had been under his command for years, men who would kill or die for him. Just having him with them had given his troops the necessary discipline to wait out the American and his Eritrean whore. Lying amid the stinking pile of humanity, Mahdi congratulated himself for getting this far.

Of course, it was pure chance he'd been in the mine talking with his troops when Mercer appeared. He was the soldier to drop his weapon first, sensing that even with superior firepower, Mercer had taken the tactical advantage by holding the white miner. When he saw the whore appear a moment later, her own weapon leveled, Mahdi knew he'd made the correct choice.

Another element of chance at work tonight was the large bandage that swathed the upper half of his face and dressed his right cheek. He'd been practicing fighting moves against one of his lieutenants with unsheathed knives, as was their habit, when the soldier slipped and the blade slashed Mahdi's face. The wound would heal nicely, adding a new scar to the older wounds marring his body. The bandage his medic had applied hid enough of his features to prevent anyone from recognizing him, and since neither Mercer nor the Eritreans had looked too closely, they hadn't realized their prisoner was the commander of the Sudanese guard detail.

Mahdi had allowed himself to be taken, cowed like the rest of his men and shepherded along with this suicide mission for no other reason than to see Mercer choke to death on his tongue when there was the chance to cut it out and feed it to him. Maybe he'd have a piece of the whore before he killed her too. He smiled in the dark chamber, a tightening of his facial muscles that on a normal person would look like a grimace. He wondered if he could work it so Mercer was still alive when he stuck it to the Eritrean slut, but he doubted it. Better to just kill the American and then have his fun.

He needed to get after them first. While it would be easy to track them in the dusty tunnels, he didn't want them getting too far ahead. Waiting for more of the slave laborers to fall asleep, Mahdi used subtle hand signals to communicate with the other guards, a secret code of gestures that they'd used countless times during the civil war in Sudan. Mahdi ordered one of his men to sacrifice himself in a blatant escape attempt that would give him the opportunity to make a break for it. He'd considered trying to overpower their captors but the Eritreans were armed with the guards' AK-47s. A silent retreat would work the best, and even if Mahdi got out without one of the Kalishnikovs, he still carried a throwing knife in his boot.

Waiting for the right moment, he glanced at the boots and remembered the fat bald man who had once owned them. That had been a boring hunt but a very satisfying kill, he recalled. Hadn't his victim said he was an archeologist? Clever cover, but Mahdi had already been warned by Gianelli that the man was searching for the lost mine. Mahdi knew now that the man need not have died; he had been searching fifty miles from the mine. But Mahdi liked the boots.

When three quarters of the Eritreans were asleep, including one of the armed ones, he decided that it was time. Mahdi showed his comrade the old cavalryman's signal of a closed fist and the waiting soldier gave a sharp nod. Charge.

The trooper didn't hesitate. He leaped to his feet, kicking sleeping miners as he rushed toward a side tunnel away from where Mercer and Selome had disappeared, screaming unintelligible curses as he went. Mahdi too was in motion, using the other Sudanese as shields as he twisted away from the group, blending himself into the darkness beyond the feeble glow of the single lit flashlight.

The Eritreans came awake, one of them taking aim in the gloom and gave the trigger a quick tap. Three red explosions appeared on the diversionary guerrilla's back, and he pitched forward, his body collapsing against the wall next to the exit. In the confusion, Mahdi rolled away from the group, the rope binding his hands making it difficult to move, but still he managed to grasp the spare light on his way out of the cavern.

He regained his feet and stumbled on. The tunnel was so dark he walked with his eyes closed, keeping his arms stretched to one side so he could brush along the wall. After passing several side branches, he ducked into another one and snapped on the light. It took him only a moment to pluck the knife from his boot and cut through the hemp securing his wrists. His men would destroy the other flashlight left with the Eritreans in the melee following his escape, so he was now immune from pursuit. He, and he alone, was the hunter in this hellish world, and Mercer would never know what was coming.

If Mercer thought the early part of their trek was torturous, it was nothing compared to the past couple of hours. It seemed he could do no wrong leading the miners to the fresh air chamber, but since then he'd led Selome up two long blind alleys and had been forced to wriggle through areas that even the children who'd dug these galleries would have trouble negotiating. It was as though they were trapped in the body of some enormous creature not willing to give up its latest meal. As they corkscrewed through the twisting intersections and aimless shafts, Mercer was beginning to think he would get them hopelessly lost. So far their motion had created a trail in the dust, but if they passed a spot that was clean, it would be impossible to backtrack to where the Eritreans waited.

Finally they entered another tall cavern, one that lacked fresh air but had been mined extensively. The flashlight's beam revealed a sight that would haunt him for the rest of his life.

Unlike the bodies he'd discovered in the Italian mine, these were not neatly laid out. It appeared they had been left where they had died. Their poses were agonizing. There were maybe a dozen of them, desiccated mummies with skin stretched tightly over screams of pain. The corpses were all of children, the oldest not more than ten or twelve. Even in death, their suffering transcended the millennia.

"Oh, God." Selome gagged.

Mercer said nothing. He looked at the pitiable remains of the slave children, trying to keep emotions from clouding his judgment. By the ore piled around a couple of them, he could see that work had continued without pause next to the bodies. No attempts had been made to give the children any kind of burial. They had been abandoned, worked to death, and left to rot where they'd died. Selome began praying.

Still in shock, Mercer forced himself to make a closer

examination of one of the bodies, wanting to know the exact cause of death. He didn't dare disturb the fragile corpse, but from the areas he could study, he saw no signs of injury; no broken bones or blunt trauma. The only bizarre feature was the unnatural curling of its hands, arms, and feet. They were coiled so tightly they looked as if they had no bones in them at all. Mercer noted that the other bodies were all in similar positions.

What the hell could have done this? he thought. He noted the child still had its teeth, so he discounted scurvy, but rickets was a possible candidate. Then the clinical side of his brain shut down and he felt pity wash over him in tidal surges. What did it matter how they died? They were gone, murdered by a nameless slave master long ago who'd probably been rewarded for his efficiency. Mercer had to force himself to breathe. He said a silent prayer for the children, and when he raised his eyes and took note of the vein of ore they'd been working, a sickening realization came to him.

He wanted to escape this macabre cave, but the scientist in him had to be sure, even if he knew the results could be a death sentence for him and Selome. She continued to pray as he crushed down a small sample of the ore left on the footwall. He unclipped the protective steel casing off the boxy flashlight and poured a measure of the ore into it. He ignored the coils of fuse in the bag and withdrew a stick of dynamite. He worked the explosive until he could pour the powder onto the ground beneath the container. Only when he was finished did she notice his efforts and join him.

"What are you doing?"

"An experiment," he replied, and Selome recognized the fear in his voice.

He laid their full canteen onto the metal case so it acted as a lid. "Do you remember what Brother Ephraim said about the children who worked the mine being killed by sin?"

Without a tight constraint, the explosive burst into flame when he touched it off with his lighter, illuminating the cavern in harsh white light. When the fire burned out, he tapped the canteen several times and stuck it back into his bag. The reddish ore in his makeshift apparatus had darkened considerably. He dumped it onto a jagged rock and waited. It took just a few seconds for silvery beads to ooze out of the ore and pool on the ground next to him.

"He wasn't warning us about sin with a S, but sin with a C, as in cinnabar, also called red mercuric sulfide. It's the principal ore stone for raw mercury." They both stared at the shimmering pool of liquid metal.

"But isn't mercury—"

"One of the most toxic substances on the planet. It can cripple, paralyze, or kill just by breathing its fumes."

"That's what killed the children?"

"That's what going to kill us, too, if we don't get out of here. It's so deadly that miners who dig this stuff today only work eight days a month. Every second we delay can have permanent effects." He was already leading Selome down another tunnel.

"Is there anything we can do?"

"Yeah, sweat a lot. Believe it or not, perspiration can cleanse the body of mercury if it's not allowed to bond to the cell proteins. After every shift, miners spend time in a room called 'the beach' to sweat out the toxins under powerful heat lamps."

The mine was stuffy and hot already, so there wasn't a problem keeping their pores open, but they only had that single canteen of water, and when that ran out, their bodies would no longer waste fluids on temperature control. The mercury would then begin its absorption process, and the consequences after that might be irreversible.

They encountered several more horror chambers as they wound through the mine, one of them containing at least a hundred mummified victims. Mercer could see that many of the children had been exposed to mercury through their mothers when they were in the womb. The poison had done terrible damage to their chromosomes, and they suffered horrifying malformations. Some were barely recognizable as human.

"Somehow the kimberlite vent came up through a vein of mercuric sulfide. I've never heard of a geologic feature like this but I can understand why they thought the Ark of the Covenant may have helped the children," Mercer said.

"How?"

"Even at the time the Ark was brought to Africa, metallurgists knew that mercury bonded with gold. I think they were hoping it would absorb the mercury vapor and stop its debilitating effects. Remember, apart from any mythical properties it may have had, the Ark was covered with gold."

"But this much mercury?"

"I didn't say it was a good idea."

They continued through more endless passages for another hour until Selome had a disturbing thought. "Mercer, the tunnel leading to the working pit was about a mile and a half long, and even at a slow crawl, we must have covered five times that distance on our way back." Her voice was muffled by the tight passage as the walls soaked up the sound.

"You noticed that, too?" he replied. "I'm beginning to get a little concerned myself. These tunnels were constructed through softer material to make the mining easier, but it doesn't seem possible that they'd meander as badly as this. I'm starting to think we may be in another dead end."

"We're lost?" She started to panic.

Mercer stopped, twisted around so he could see her with the flashlight. Her face was tiger-striped by beads of sweat cutting runnels through the dust caked to her skin. He could see she was starting to lose confidence. Mercer cupped her chin in his palm. "There are two inevitabilities in life, death and taxes. You have my word that come next April, you'll be cutting a big check."

She forced bravery into her voice. "Americans pay taxes in April. I'm Eritrean."

The next chamber they found was high enough for them to stand, and unlike the others, it was enormous. Their flashlight could penetrate only a fraction of the way across, but by gauging the echoes, Mercer estimated the cavity was nearly the size of a football field. He immediately recognized the mining technique used to excavate the space. Room and pillar mining called for huge spaces to be gouged into the ore while leaving support columns of undisturbed rock to hold up the hanging wall. It was a common technique in coal mining, but not very efficient in a diamond mine, and he was surprised it had been used to work this kimberlite vein. The pillars were so numerous, it felt as if they were walking among the trunks of a dense petrified forest or in the eerie catacombs under an ancient cathedral. He was stunned that the mine overseers had conceived and engineered the system as he led Selome across the expanse. Over their heads, the hanging wall was in terrible shape, cracked and scored by the enormous pressure of the earth bearing down on it. He guessed that in another hundred years or so, the pillars would succumb to the strain and the entire room would collapse.

Halfway to the other side of the room a shadow caught Mercer's eye, and when he turned to investigate, Selome gave a startled scream and was thrown to the floor. Mercer was flattened by a rushing apparition that materialized out of the darkness. His head cracked against the ground, his mind spinning. It was impossible that anything alive could be down here with them; the mine had been sealed for thousands of years. A vicious kick to his stomach pulled him back to reality. It didn't matter who or what was with them, they were about to be killed. A knife glinted sharply in the beam of the flashlight that had flown from his stunned hands. The AK-47 lay out of reach beyond the penumbra.

The thing jumped on Mercer as he lay stunned. He managed to raise a hand and deflect the blade plunging at his chest. He twisted his assailant enough for him to counter with a crushing punch, the blow snapping a couple of short ribs. Rather than being slowed by the shot, the attacker went wild, striking Mercer across the jaw with his elbow, and the darkness of the cavern rushed into Mercer's brain. He would have lost the fight right then had Selome not leaped on the assailant's back, drawing him off Mercer for a moment.

For her effort, Mercer saw her catch a savage punch in the face that sent her reeling, her body falling like a deflated balloon. He scrambled to find his assault rifle and the attacker was on him again, this time sinking the knife into the fleshy part of Mercer's thigh. Screaming with the needle-hot pain, Mercer torqued and back-handed the creature across the cheek. To his horror, he felt his hand sink into its putrid face and saw a chunk of flesh fly off. The wound did nothing to deter the assault and Mercer realized he really was fighting some demon who roamed the labyrinth.

He scrambled out of the monster's reach, dodging around a pillar and into total darkness. From his vantage point he could see the creature shuffling to the abandoned light. The beam caught the apparition in the face, and Mercer recognized Gianelli's principal henchman, the leader of the rebels, Mahdi. He remembered one of the guards he'd taken prisoner had worn a bandage—that was what he'd wiped off Mahdi's face.

Mercer had no time to consider how he had escaped the Eritreans or managed to track them. He knew Mahdi would go for the AK next, and he had to get to the gun first. He concentrated on his exact position when Mahdi had first hit him and the most logical direction the gun would have sailed. A glint in the distance caught Mercer's attention, but it was too far away to be the gun. He struck out boldly, his hands in front of him to avoid slamming into one of the stone columns. In the darkness, Selome was still screaming as if she believed that some specter stalked these galleries.

Both men spotted the weapon when it caught the light's beam. Mahdi had a shorter distance to run to reach it, but Mercer's reactions were quicker and they both dove and got a hand on it at the same time.

Mercer had a better grip on the AK and used it to twist the weapon away from the soldier. Mahdi kneed him viciously in the inside of his forearm and Mercer's entire hand went numb. Suddenly the gun was in Mahdi's control. Struggling under the man's weight and only able to use his bad arm to deflect the gloating Sudanese, Mercer reached into the kit bag still slung around his shoulder.

He'd planned to use the high-speed fuse in conjunction with the dynamite he carried if they'd needed to blast any obstacles that got in their way, but now it had a more urgent purpose. Mahdi either didn't notice or didn't care as Mercer dropped the two-hundred-foot coil of fuse over his head. The rebel was laughing, knowing he had the advantage, but when he spied a tiny flame shooting from the Zippo in Mercer's fingers, his eyes went wide with terror. In those last seconds he understood what Mercer had looped over him.

The fuse burned at twenty-two thousand feet per second, so the entire coil cooked off faster than the eye could see. Even under its protective coating, the temperature of the burning chemicals skyrocketed. The smell was almost as bad as the screech when the veins in Mahdi's throat burst under the pressure of his blood turning to steam. His flesh roasted like a joint of meat.

Mahdi's finger tightened on the AK's trigger even as his eyes rolled back into his skull. A full clip arrowed into the ceiling, ricocheting and filling the chamber with deadly lead. The crashing shots and the echoes weakened a section of the scaly hanging wall, and a fifty-ton slab of stone crashed to the floor a short distance away, followed seconds later by several more.

The whole ceiling was giving way! Mercer rolled out from under the struggling terrorist, grabbed up the assault rifle by its hot barrel, and grasped the flashlight in his other hand. More stones let go, huge chunks whose impact loosened even more of the ceiling in a domino effect. It was as if the earth had come alive and they were caught in its jaws. With the weight shifting its balance, one of the pillars exploded like a bomb, crushed beyond its structural tolerance, hurtling rock like grapeshot.

Mercer heaved Selome off the floor as if she was no more than a child. As more debris rained around them, they ducked into a side tunnel. He took just a second to look back and watched a slab of rock larger than an automobile land squarely on Mahdi as he writhed with the pain of his burned neck. The weight of the stone forced the contents of his torso toward his head, but they could not erupt through the cranium. Mercer saw Mahdi's throat expand like that of a bull frog's until the entire bulbous mass exploded in a red mist and the body lay still.

He trained the light to the far end of the gallery where he had seen the distant glint. Just before his view was obliterated by the crumbling chamber, he watched an eerie blue light radiate from the gloom, burning brighter and brighter until a chunk of stone crashed right in front of him, sealing the room forever.

The side tunnel's roof was lower than most of the others they'd encountered, and Mercer had to ease Selome to the ground and coax her to follow as more of the chamber behind them collapsed. Huge clouds of dust blew into the tunnel, enveloping them, choking them until they could no longer open their eyes and every breath was torture. And still more of the room fell, a roaring sound that filled their world and threatened to tear away their sanity. They scrambled from it, ripping skin from their hands and knees as this tunnel began to fill with debris.

They covered fifty yards before the cave-in ended. The sudden silence left their ears ringing. Looking back the way they'd come, Mercer saw that they were cut off from the others by untold billions of tons of earth. Even if they had wanted to, there was no way they would ever be able to return.

What the hell was that glow? The blue light had to be a static discharge, he thought. When rock is crushed, it can give off a small amount of electricity. Given the amount of moving stone, the phenomenon could easily explain what he'd seen. Or maybe it was a pocket of methane catching fire after being ignited by a spark. He had several other naturally occurring explanations, but deep in the back of his mind, he knew there was also an unnatural one. *No, it couldn't be.*

"What happened in there?"

"Mahdi suffered a crushing defeat," Mercer rasped, waiting for Selome to take a drink from their canteen. He wanted to give her time to recover before telling her that this tunnel went in the opposite direction from where they wanted to go. There was no way he was going to tell her what else he'd seen.

"You have no idea what I was thinking in there when he attacked us," Selome replied, wiping her lips against the delicate bones on the back of her hand.

"Can't be any weirder than what was going through my mind," Mercer agreed. "Are you okay?"

"My jaw hurts and I'm sure it'll be black and blue in a few hours, but I'm fine. You?"

Mercer removed his pants and began working on the knife wound in his leg. He didn't waste any of their precious water cleaning the gash but slapped a fragment of his shirt over the incision and secured it with a strips of silvery duct tape from his bag. "Dr. Mercer's antiseptic surgery, secondary infections are our specialty."

"Is it bad?"

"Nothing major was hit," Mercer said, then added with dark humor, "and it'll stiffen long before we get to see your black and blues."

The dust was still too thick to rest this close to the cave-in, so Mercer donned his pants and they started out of the area. Particles lay heavily in the air, and the powerful light could cut only a feeble swath through it. After a further hundred yards, the tunnel had shrunk in diameter so that their backs scraped the ceiling as they crawled. Still they were dogged by chocking clouds of grit.

"This may take a while to settle." Mercer gagged each time he opened his mouth and his nose felt scored by acid.

They were forced to lower themselves even more as the tunnel continued to shrink. In moments the shoulders of Mercer's shirt were ripped through and the abraded skin began to bleed. Without choice or option, they continued, using their elbows and toes to propel themselves forward.

"Mercer, what's happening?" Selome cried.

"I don't know."

The tunnel was no larger than a coffin, just wide enough for them to squirm on their bellies, and in the murky light Mercer could see its diameter constricting even further. For the first time he considered that this tunnel might pinch out into solid rock. As if reading his thoughts, Selome called his name again, her voice teetering on the edge of hysteria.

"I know, I know." It was becoming tougher for him to move. He'd taken off his kit bag a while back and pushed it and the AK-47 ahead of him. He had to twist and struggle to gain every inch.

For a while, the tunnel remained the same size, neither growing or shrinking, but their progress was cut to a snail's pace. Rock encircled Mercer completely; not one section of his body was out of contact with its jagged embrace. The tunnel walls were pure, blood-red mercury ore. In a few places, raw mercury had worked itself from the ceiling and dripped into little hollows and troughs on the floor.

"How long did you say we could stay in here?"

"I'm not sure." The light revealed a stretch of tunnel glittering with hundreds of tiny pools of quicksilver. "Remember, mercury can be absorbed through the skin, so don't let it touch any open wounds you might have."

"My entire body is an open wound."

They made it through the severely contaminated section and started down a gentle slope. Mercer could see where the mercury had cut canals in the floor as it flowed downhill.

His coughing fits were becoming less frequent, but their severity was punishing. Unlike Selome, who had a little room between her body and the tunnel walls, Mercer was so constricted that every cough seemed stillborn in his chest, exploding within his body without finding a proper outlet. He had to prepare himself for the pain when he felt one coming. Already he could taste the coppery salt of blood in his mouth from ruptured lung tissue.

Mercer jammed.

Fighting panic, he rolled his shoulders and tried to work them forward, but the more he struggled, the more it seemed the walls tightened around him like the remorseless coils of a python. The tunnel floor was compacted dirt, and he tried to tear into it with his hands, but it was as hard as cement and left his fingers bleeding.

Selome saw his frantic movements and slid back to avoid his flailing feet. "What's happening?"

"I'm afraid I'm stuck."

"What do you mean stuck?"

"I mean I can't move. I can't go back and I can't go forward."

"Well, try!" In the confines of the tunnel, her voice was muted, dead, like she was speaking from the other side of a wall.

"And you think I've been lying here taking a nap," Mercer snapped, but he couldn't draw a deep enough breath to give force to his words. He felt like he was drowning.

"I'm sorry," Selome said. "What do you want me to do?"

"Grab my feet and pull as hard as you can." He needed to breathe. He wanted to scream. The rock wouldn't let him.

It took five minutes to pull him back enough for him to gain some working room. Mercer calmed again, but he could feel panic clawing at the back of his thoughts. His shoulders and back were flecked with blood. "Now we go back again."

"But that way is blocked by the cave-in."

"Not that far back. We need to find a place where you can crawl over me and take the lead. I think you will be able to squeeze through."

"What about you?"

"We'll burn that bridge after we cross it."

It took two hours of slithering backward for them to find an area with enough ceiling height for Selome to crawl over him. When she was lying on his back, she rested her head against his neck for a moment, her breath in his ear.

"God, be careful," Mercer cried. "I don't have the room in here to get an erection."

With Selome leading the way, they slowly returned to the area where Mercer had gotten stuck. "What happens now?"

"You keep going. Take the light and the gun, and try to

find a way out of here." Mercer sounded emotionless when he spoke but was glad that she couldn't see his face.

Panic was a reaction to the unfamiliar, he told himself. But this time he had no experience to give him the confidence to keep from losing his grip with the rational.

"I can't."

"You don't have a choice." Even as he knew he might not escape alive, he thought about the others. "There are forty trapped miners waiting to be rescued, and if we both die right here, they die too."

"I don't care about them, dammit, I care about you." She was sobbing.

Mercer reached out and stroked her ankle, pulling down her sock so he could touch her smooth skin. "And I care about you, too. But unless you get moving and find some help, I'll never be able to take you on a sex-filled vacation in some exotic place."

"Is that a promise?"

"I haven't let you down yet." Mercer felt another racking cough coming. The last words came out in a painful gasp.

"I can't leave you."

Her cry made him wince. He didn't want to die alone, but he hardened himself, pushing aside his own needs. He struggled to regain his breath and purged his mouth of more blood. "Just go. You have to find a way out of here. I can't have your death as the last thing on my conscience. You can't do that to me."

She sniffed back tears. "What about the canteen and the flashlight?"

"Take them."

"Philip, I think that . . . I . . ." He could hear her struggling with the words and her own feelings, and before she committed herself, she changed her mind. "I think that we should go to Egypt, maybe a Nile cruise. I've always wanted to see the ancient monuments."

"I'll call my travel agent when you're gone."

Selome slithered away, vanishing from sight after a couple of yards. Mercer could see that a few impossible feet in front of him, the tunnel tantalizingly widened. The rock held him tighter than a straitjacket, and he struggled between panic and frustration. He'd never suffered claustrophobia, but he felt its icy tentacles reaching for him, grabbing him around every inch of his body and squeezing until his lungs convulsed. He drew shallow gulps of air so fouled with dust that he retched.

He was alone, shrouded in a darkness worse than death. He tried to wriggle forward but became more tightly trapped, the tunnel pressing him from all sides, holding him in a grip it would never relinquish. The blackness was so complete he could taste it as it filled his mouth and smell it as it invaded his lungs. His skin crawled with the silence of his tomb. His mind screamed for release from this prison, to move just a fraction of an inch. He could barely swivel his head, and when he did, crumbly mercury ore scraped off the ceiling, more poisonous dust for him to draw into his body.

"Okay, well, this is interesting, isn't it?" It would only take a few days before his words became the ravings of a madman as he fought against the darkness and the silence and the isolation of his death.

Another spasm of coughing took him. His chest was unable to expand properly and the internal pressure threatened to shatter his ribs like glass. He wondered if pneumonia would develop and kill him before the mercury he was breathing destroyed his motor control and rotted his brain. He remembered that the beginning stage of mercury poisoning was a tremor in the extremities, and he couldn't tell if the quiver in his legs was real or imagined.

Rather than dwell on the inevitable, he let his mind drift to the blue glow. What if he hadn't seen a static discharge or a methane explosion? What if it really was the Ark, now crushed beyond recovery? "I've got the rest of my life to figure it out."

Washington, D.C.

Dick Henna broke years of training when he made that call. Since the early days of their marriage, Fay had worked tirelessly to get a little culture into her workaholic husband's life. She had started out easy on him, the occasional foreign film or ethnic restaurant, and over time she had him going to musicals and actually enjoying the opera. Her only major setback had been a too-early introduction to ballet that had soured him forever, but the night he made the call to Mercer's phone, she'd crossed another invisible line. It wasn't that he didn't care about the plight of Tibet, but two hours of gongs and chanting and dance moves he couldn't identify by the Tibetan National Troupe were just too much.

He'd mumbled an apology to Fay about needing the rest room and slid from the box at the Kennedy Center, dodging out of the huge theater and into the red-carpeted lobby. His Secret Service escorts seemed equally relieved at their temporary escape from the performance. Next to the bronze bust of the late President Kennedy, which to him was the ugliest statue he'd ever seen, he snapped open his cell phone and dialed Mercer for the hundredth time in the past weeks. It was a fruitless gesture, he knew, but he hadn't had word from his friend and State Department reports about violence in Asmara had him concerned.

He was about to cut the connection after the fifth ring, when an unfamiliar voice answered in accented English. "Hello, you have reached the phone of Philip Mercer. He's been buried alive. May I help you? My name is Habte Makkonen."

Their fifteen-minute conversation cut short Henna's concert. He sent an agent back to his seat to apologize to Fay. Like just about every other husband in the country, he figured he'd spend his retirement making up to his wife for the years of broken promises. The phone in his limo was more secure than his cell phone, and the attached scrambler had the latest in encryption software. He was on it for the entire drive to the Pentagon.

After alerting Marge Doyle, he called the Pentagon and had them track down C. Thomas Morrison. The limo reached the Department of Defense's sprawling headquarters just as Admiral Morrison was located.

"Evening, Dick, how're you doing?" the Joint Chiefs' chairman asked jovially.

"I've got a present for you, but you're going to have to unwrap it," Henna replied. "Where are you right now?"

"Home. My son's in town looking at colleges for his daughter. She wants Howard because it's a black school, and he wants her at Georgetown because of its reputation."

"Tell them they're going to have to thumb through the catalogs without you. I'm at the Pentagon and you're going to want to be here too."

"What's happening?"

"I found your Medusa photographs and we're going to need some firepower to get them back."

Admiral Morrison's voice went serious the instant he heard the word *Medusa.* "Say no more. I'm putting on my shoes right now. I should be there in half an hour."

Leave it to a military man to know the exact time of his commute no matter what the traffic situation. Twenty-nine minutes later, Morrison strode through the entry doors closest to his E-ring suite of offices, two uniformed aides pacing behind him in an arrowhead formation. He and Henna shook hands and strode to the elevators, arriving at Morrison's office just an hour after Habte's call. That hour was the longest delay in the chain of events to follow. Henna quickly outlined his conversation with Habte and the circumstances surrounding it.

"Northern Eritrea, huh?" Morrison studied the world

map behind his desk. He chuckled. "Isn't that a coincidence. Since our last conversation, a detachment of Force Recon Marines found themselves rotated to an amphibious assault ship off the coast of Somalia. There are two hundred soldiers on that ship who'd been planning a piece-of-cake tour in Italy and are mighty pissed off at their new deployment. I bet they'd love to vent some of that anger."

Henna's reply had the same mocking tone. "Coincidences are compounding as we speak. I called Lloyd Easton at the State Department while I was waiting for you. Right now he's convincing the president of Eritrea that an American training exercise in his country would be in his best interests."

"What about authorization from the president?"

"As soon as we're done here, I'll contact him. In light of our conversation with Israel's prime minister, he's been expecting that something like this might happen. He'll be astounded when he hears Gianelli is involved. Marge pulled his file for me when I was in my limo and it must be a foot thick. Interpol has never been able to directly link him to anything illegal, but if we're quick here, we'll nail the bastard to the wall. It'll be a feather in the president's cap during the next G-7 summit if we can haul him into a courtroom."

"As long as the political end's covered, I'll handle the military side. It'll take some time to get this ball rolling." Morrison snatched up a phone and ordered a call put through to the National Security Agency and the National Reconnaissance Office. He offered Henna a zeppelin-sized Cohiba when he finished. "We're going to need some photo intelligence of the area, and the Marines are going to need some prep time."

"I've got to call Habte Makkonen back and give him a time line. What do you think?"

"Six hours minimum and even that's pushing it too hard."

"Not from where Mercer's sitting," Henna said through a cloud of fragrant cigar smoke.

The phone rang, and Morrison spoke with the duty officer at the NRO. "There's a civilian on the ground reporting a heavy cloud cover in the area, but there's a lot of machinery working at the site. If you can't get clear pictures, switch to IR and we'll find the bastards by their heat signature." He clamped his hand over the mouthpiece and spoke to Henna. "This is going to take a while. If you want, use the phone on my secretary's desk to brief the Old Man and reach Makkonen. Tell him what to expect and to get his butt under cover when the Marines hit the mine."

Henna left Morrison coordinating satellite coverage and planted himself at a desk in the outer office. He figured he could afford a little time, so he placed a call he felt was equally important. He'd personally met the plane carrying Harry White from Israel at Dulles, driving into the city with the octogenarian and seeing him ensconced at an FBI safe house until the situation settled. True to his word, Harry was stone sober and didn't complain through the subsequent hours of questioning. It wasn't until after Henna's agents had finished that Harry demanded to know what had happened to Mercer. His glare had spoken volumes when Henna admitted that they had no idea where he was or what had happened to him.

"Hello."

"Harry, it's Dick Henna. We've found Mercer."

Harry heard Henna's declaration, but it took a few seconds for him to absorb it. "You really found him?" he asked at last.

"He's at an abandoned mine in Eritrea. He's okay."

"No, he's not," Harry snapped. "He's in deep shit or you wouldn't be calling me, he would."

"Harry, really, he's all right."

"I've been more than cooperative with you. The least you can do is be honest with me. What the hell is really going on?"

Henna couldn't fathom how Harry knew he was lying. It was just one of those things, part of that bond that Mercer and Harry shared. He blew out a breath. "Okay, you're right. I'm sorry. He is in Eritrea, but he's the prisoner of a group of Sudanese rebels who're working for an Italian industrialist who's a known criminal. From what we know so far, he's buried himself in the mine with some Eritrean refugees as a way to buy us some time to get Marines into the area."

"And?"

"And what?"

"Do you have Marines going in?"

"I'm at the Pentagon right now with the Chairman of the Joint Chiefs. Harry, we're moving heaven and earth to get him back."

"He's pulled your asses from the fire a couple of times now. You had goddamned better move a lot more than that or so help me, Christ, by the end of the week I'll be on every talk show in the country."

"Harry—"

"I'm not fooling around. You get Mercer back or you can kiss your job and this Administration good-bye. I know enough to bury all of you."

"Jesus, Harry, it doesn't need to come to that."

"I know it doesn't because you'll rescue him. End of discussion."

Seven and a half hours later, a swarm of UH-60 Blackhawk helicopters thundered into Eritrean airspace, the Marines on board eager for a good fight.

King Solomon's Mine

At first it wasn't a noise—merely the absence of the all-consuming silence. Mercer strained to listen, his ears ringing with the effort and his eyes watering as he stared into the sable blackness. There! A tiny sound existing only in the deepest level of his consciousness, a hissing like a gentle whisper. He tried to shout, but his mouth was cemented closed by his thirst and he could manage only a hoarse croak.

Time might have passed, he had no way to tell, but he was sure that the mysterious hiss was growing louder. He wouldn't let himself hope. He couldn't do that if he was wrong. Then he saw a light, just a muted flicker. To him, it was like a blinding star burst. He drank it in, his eyes streaming with the joyous pain of it.

"Hello?" he rasped.

"Hello yourself," Selome called cheerily from a short distance away. "I'll be with you in just a few minutes."

"What are you doing?" Mercer's question was too quiet for her to hear, so there was no response.

It took ten more minutes, but he didn't care. Selome was coming for him. The tears behind his eyes were no longer caused by the light. As he waited in his stone cocoon, he had a thought that tempered his joy. He'd given up on himself. He'd actually believed that he was going to die. He'd never, ever been one to quit until the very end, but this time he'd really thought he was finished. Even as he was about to be rescued, he was furious with himself, and even worse, disappointed.

Mercer suddenly felt the dirt beneath him begin to shift.

The constricting pressure against his chest slackened. He could hear Selome more clearly now. She was digging furiously, using some sort of heavy spade, and with every slash into the dirt ahead of him, Mercer felt the tunnel floor sink a fraction of an inch. When he tried to wriggle, he gained ground, his shoulders scraping against the walls, his back no longer squashed to the ceiling.

Then in a rush like childbirth, he was free, sliding forward dangerously fast, gaining speed as the slope steepened and the ceiling vanished above him. He started to tumble, caught in a cascade of loose soil and rocks that scored his eyes and nose and jammed solidly into his ears. He banged against the walls as he fell, wanting to cry out at the agony of a smashed shin, but there was so much dirt boiling around him that if he opened his mouth, he would suffocate. Then his headlong plunge stopped, and he lay still as more rubble poured over him, the weight of it increasing with every second.

He was about to black out when the dirt blanketing his body was thrust aside. He felt a hand grasp his belt and shake him. Dirt flew like water from a spaniel and he could breathe again. He cleared the filth from his eyes and peered around. His first sight was of Selome standing over him.

"I should dig for buried treasure more often. It's amazing what a girl can find." She looked radiant even in the glimmer from the flashlight.

"Gold doubloon I'm not."

He couldn't believe how good it felt to be sore. It meant he was still alive. He swayed to his feet, reaching to brush a tendril of hair from Selome's face. "I didn't think you were coming back." His voice was thick. He wanted to tell her what had happened when she left him alone, but he couldn't. What he felt went beyond words. He simply stepped into her embrace, soaking up the heat of her body. "Thank you."

There was just enough amber incandescence from the flashlight for him to visually explore the chamber they occupied and to understand how she had gotten him out of his tomb. The gallery was roughly rectangular and at least thirty feet tall with a shallow alcove at one end. Its walls had been covered with blocks of dressed stone. Mercer recognized the stones used in the closet-sized niche. He had seen them before. They were the same type as those lining the main tunnel from the surface. This room had been a staging area, a link between the direct path to the kimberlite ore beds and the older, more meandering tunnels. Behind him, a towering pile of dirt reached almost to the ceiling. At its summit, he saw the tiny round hole that led to the rest of the old mine and had held him prisoner for so long.

When the new, straighter drift had been driven into the mountain, the workers must have back-filled the passageway to the room and pillar mine chamber. In the thousands of years since then, the fill had settled enough for Mercer to crawl almost to the point where it emptied into this room. Of course, Selome had recognized that if she dug into the base of the mountain of dirt, it would collapse into the room and free him.

"I'm sorry it took so long, but when I fell into this chamber, I cracked my head against the floor and blacked out." There was an angry bruise above her left eye.

"You won't hear me complaining." Mercer gulped half the remaining water from their canteen and examined the shovel Selome had used to loosen his earthen constraints. "It's a shame you had to use that. It's a beautiful example of a bronze-aged tool."

"Then I'm glad you're not an archaeologist. I ruined about five of these things getting you out."

There was a collection of primitive tools in one corner of the room, picks and shovels, some scaled for an adult's use, other miniature versions for the child slaves. Next to them sat rotted piles of leather that had been buckets and water flasks. A little bit off lay stacks of clay lamps.

"We can bemoan lost artifacts later," Mercer said. "Right now I want to get us out of here and take care of some business."

He rigged the stones blocking the alcove exit with explosives from his kit bag, careful to use just enough to take down a section of the wall and not blow it apart. He had no idea what was happening in the main tunnel beyond the barrier and didn't want to advertise his presence until he was ready.

"What about fuse? Didn't you use it against Mahdi?"

Mercer plucked another coil from his bag and snipped off a length. "Second rule of hard rock mining: you can never have enough fuse."

"What's the first rule?"

Mercer held up more dynamite. "You can never have enough explosives."

The fuse was much slower than the one he'd used to disable Mahdi, so they had plenty of time to make it to the trench redoubt he'd dug with Selome's help. He covered his head with one arm, keeping his body over Selome. When the charge blew, the concussion pelted them with debris.

He looked up and blinked. The wall hadn't crumbled, but there was a three-foot crawl space at its bottom and light from the outside spilled into the chamber. Neither of them had ever thought they would see sunshine again and they embraced in its comforting aura.

"Now, let's see this put to an end." Mercer slung his bag over his shoulder, snatched up the AK-47, and led Selome into the tunnel.

The echoing sounds of a gun battle reverberated down the length of the shaft, stray tracer rounds winking by. Mercer quickly shoved Selome back into the chamber.

"Stay here and don't move until I come for you. You just saved my life. Now it's my turn." He stepped out, keeping low to the footwall, the AK at the ready.

Mercer couldn't tell who was using the mine as a cover position so he started crawling forward as more rounds streaked over his head. His eyes adjusted to the sunlight filling the shaft, but the haze of cordite smoke was nearly blinding and he had to get close to recognize the men firing out toward the camp. They were Sudanese soldiers. Habte must have made the call because he guessed the return fire ricocheting down the drive was from the Marines.

The rebels held an unassailable position against the American soldiers as long as they had ammunition. Unless a rocket launcher was used, there was no way to dislodge them. The Marines surely knew Habte's warning to Henna about the trapped miners, so explosives were not an option. Remembering Mahdi's sneak attack in the mine and the brutal raping that had taken place outside the women's stockade, Mercer felt nothing as he brought the AK to his shoulder.

With controlled double taps on semiautomatic, he shot four Sudanese in the back and the remaining two in the chest when they whirled to face the threat that had come unexpectedly from behind. He scrambled up to their barricade and searched frantically for something white to wave at the Marines still pouring rounds into the tunnel entrance. He had to make do with the well-used handkerchief he found in the pocket of one of the dead man. A second after waving it over the barricade, he heard a command in English to hold fire.

He stood. "Don't shoot. I'm an American."

"Dr. Mercer?" a Texas drawl asked over the din of a continuing battle farther from the mine.

"Yeah, I'm Mercer." The euphoria he should be feeling had been suppressed by his desire to make the Sudanese and especially Gianelli suffer for what had happened in the past weeks. "I've got a woman with me, and there are forty miners still trapped in here." He looked to where he thought the Marines had taken cover, but he couldn't see them. There were too many places to hide on the desert floor—behind the scattered equipment boxes or near some of the heavy equipment that hadn't been damaged during the battle or behind one of the countless piles of dirt excavated from the mine.

"Ya'll have to hold tight for a spell longer. This is one hot LZ." The soldier's comment was drowned by the thundering rotors of an AH-64 Apache gunship as it crabbed across the desert, its chin gun pouring a steady stream of 20mm rounds into the far side of the camp.

Mercer spotted the cluster of Force Recon Marines

huddled next to an overturned and still burning D-4 bulldozer. The soldier in charge saw him, waved in acknowledgment, and led his squad across the camp. Mercer drained the contents of two Sudanese canteens, and when the Marines were out of sight, he bolted from the mine, jinxing around toppled lighting towers and mountains of overburden. Though the rain had stopped, the sky was thick with clouds. The heat and humidity made his dash slow, and his bruised chest protested every breath. The knife wound in his leg was a sharp throb. Suddenly, the sky directly overhead exploded. A pressure wave of air slammed him to the earth, the concussion blasting against his eardrums. He rolled to his back and began scrabbling across the ground.

Two hundred feet above him, the flaming carapace of the Apache gyrated out of control, streamers of greasy smoke belching from its engine, its tail rotor assembly coming apart like a shrapnel bomb. One of the rebels had fired a surface-to-air missile into the helo and scored a direct hit. The gunship crashed close enough to throw Mercer again, fiery sheets of aviation fuel raining around him, but incredibly none landed on his clothes or skin.

When he stood, the ribs that had first taken a pounding under Hofmyer's fists and later by Mahdi and the tunnel walls had finally given out. He felt a sharp stab of pain that reached all the way to his heart, and the agony of the broken bones forced him to his knees. He had taken so much physical abuse that he wondered just what he hoped to accomplish. The Marines were here. They would handle the rebels. He was putting his life in danger for absolutely no reason.

Deciding that maybe it was best to wait this one out, he was searching for a good place to hole up when bullets kicked up erratic fountains of dirt at his feet. Clutching his ribs with one arm, Mercer ran as best he could, reaching cover behind a big portable generator. He squinted into the haze created by the dozens of smoke grenades, their clouds of smog cutting visibility to almost nothing. He didn't see who had opened up on him, but spotted a Sudanese ambush set up for a squad of patrolling Marines. The American soldiers were alert and moved well, but they were about to be diced in a surprise cross-fire.

The AK bucked in his hands, stitching two of the guerrillas and then the clip ran empty. Mercer fumbled to slam home a fresh one, dodging to the other side of the mobile generator as rounds pinged off its metal hide. The Marines dropped to the ground, entering the melee and killing three more Sudanese. Mercer was joined a second later by the four young Americans.

"Thanks, pal," the leader of the patrol wheezed, slumping against the Ingersoll-Rand.

"My pleasure. Can't tell you how glad I am to see you."

"You're Mercer, right?"

"Yeah."

"We were briefed to look for you when we landed, but weren't you buried or something?"

"I was until about ten minutes go." Mercer took a protein bar the Latino corporal offered and devoured it in three bites. "What's the situation?"

"Shit, you know more than we do. Briefing said about fifty armed troops guarding this camp with minimum equipment and arms. Bastards capped an Apache just a minute ago with a portable SAM, and there seem to be a lot more than fifty."

"The number's about right," Mercer countered. "But these guys have been fighting for years in the Sudan. They've got combat experience to spare, and their former commander was one mean son of a bitch."

"Yeah, well, anyway, we've taken heavy losses. If it weren't for all the civilians mixed up with the bad guys, the captain would've called in some close air support and bombed the shit out of this place."

Any chance for a continued conversation was shattered by a chain of detonations at the fuel tank farm. The eruptions of flame and smoke towered into the leaden sky, building and blooming like deadly flowers. The ground shook so hard that Mercer felt his teeth were going to loosen from his jaw.

As he was recovering, the Marine seated on the far side of the corporal jumped spastically and the paintwork of the generator behind him splattered with clots of blood and the back of his skull. The Marines reacted even before they knew where the shot had originated, sending out a scathing return fire and racing from their cover. Mercer had no choice but to follow. He ran in a doubled-up position, aiming the AK behind his hip and unleashing a fusillade of his own.

They slogged up a mound of overburden, the soldiers slowed by the pounds of equipment each carried and Mercer by his own condition. Another shot blew a geyser of dirt just an inch to the left of Mercer's shoulder, grit lashing his face as he clawed his way to the summit. In the protection of the artificial hill's flat peak, he realized just who was shooting at them and why.

The Israeli team was still here. The two shots were so accurate that they could only come from a sniper rifle. They were either firing to add to the confusion so they could slip into the mine or they were planning on an evacuation and wanted to keep the combatants occupied while they escaped. For Mercer, both options were unacceptable.

Chancing a look over the parapet of their earthen fortress, he could survey the entire camp and the clusters of men fighting below. It looked as if the Sudanese's numbers were greatly diminished. He could see a few holdouts near Gianelli's big transporters. In the distance, there were figures running away from the battle, but he guessed they were Eritreans. Of the bodies he could see littering the ground that weren't dressed in American desert BDUs, two were white, but from this range he couldn't tell if either was Gianelli.

"Say again?" the corporal was shouting into the radio built into his combat helmet. "Roger that, Sky Eyes. Keep us posted."

"What's happening?" Mercer clipped his last banana magazine into the well of the AK-47.

"AWACS plane circling off the coast reports a low-level

contact about six klicks east of here and moving in at a hundred miles an hour."

"Shit!"

"What is it?"

"There's a team of Israelis in the area. They've been after this mine for a while, but I think they're cutting their losses and bugging out."

"Well, they're going to make it," the Marine said, not really interested in another enemy with his hands so full of Sudanese. "We don't have any more gunships to go after it, and if that AWACS only now just spotted it, you can believe it'll disappear just as easily."

Mercer knew the soldier was right. Flying nap of the earth, a good chopper pilot could evade even the most sophisticated airborne radar systems. He got an idea. "How'd you guys get here?"

"Blackhawks. There are a half dozen of them on the ground about ten miles north. We hoofed it the rest of the way in."

"Can you radio for one to pick us up?"

"Yeah, but it won't do any good. Those birds are just troop ships. No guns."

"Just get one. We'll be the firepower." Mercer tapped the corporal's M-16A1 with the butt of his AK.

The corporal switched the channel on his radio. "Captain Saunders, this is Chavez. I'm with Mercer. He says the bogey Sky Eyes just painted is an evac chopper for some uglies. I want permission to go after it in a Blackhawk." He paused, his gaze on Mercer. "Yes, sir. I know. We're on top of a hill, and it looks like things are dying down in our sector . . . Yes, sir, I'll keep an eye on him . . . No, sir, I'll ask him. Dr. Mercer, where are the rest of the Eritrean nationals?"

"Still trapped in the mine. There's a woman in the main tunnel who knows exactly where they are."

The soldier nodded and activated his mike again. "In the mine, sir . . . Yes, sir, we're standing by."

"Well?"

"The captain's calling a chopper. We'll pop some green

smoke when the bird gets here. We're going to drop you at our staging area and go after the Israelis ourselves. It's not my place to ask, but what kind of international situation are we getting ourselves into here?"

"Think of the deepest pile of shit you can imagine and then double it," Mercer grunted. "Only bright spot is, we're the good guys for a change."

The soldier carrying the heavy Squad Automatic Weapon spotted a target and ripped off about fifteen rounds, empty brass arcing from the 5.56mm in a tight necklace. Chavez and the other Marine scanned the camp for more targets but only indistinct shapes moved in the smoke and they couldn't chance a friendly-fire kill.

"Whad'ya have, Moose?"

"Two of them with AKs at ten o'clock, moving clockways. They're behind that ten-wheel truck."

"Keep 'em pinned," Corporal Chavez ordered. Moose gave the SAW's trigger another long pull. "But watch your ammo discipline."

"How long till the chopper gets here?"

Chavez clicked to another frequency on his radio. "Inbound helo, this is Charlie One. Give me an ETA to sector seven, about eight hundred yards north of the mine entrance . . . Copy. We'll pop green when we hear you." He turned to Mercer. "About six minutes."

Moose fired another barrage with the SAW and the two other Marines started to pour lead down the hill, screaming unintelligible curses. Mercer saw half a dozen rebel soldiers advancing from their left flank. Four were armed with AK-47s and two carried RPG-7 rocket launchers. One went down before he could fire; the other took a snap shot with the bazooka-like weapon and a section of the hill erupted like a miniature Mount St. Helens.

The Squad Automatic Weapon fell silent. Moose had been killed by blast debris. Mercer, Chavez, and the other Marine dodged for cover, and even as dirt continued to rain down, they fired back. When Mercer emptied his last clip, he tossed aside the AK and reached for the SAW.

The machine gun was huge, almost too heavy to carry into combat, but its effectiveness was unquestionable.

Three charging guerrillas were hit in the hail of gunfire, snapped back by the pounding gun in near perfect sequence.

"Keep the fuckers back!" Chavez screamed as he worked on a gash in the leg of the other soldier. The man's desert camo uniform was soaked through with blood from a point just below his groin.

Mercer continued to fire the weapon, traversing the barrel in tight sweeps to keep the Sudanese pinned. Another rocket slammed into the hill, and part of its peak blew away, exposing their flank. He had no idea how many rounds were in the boxy magazine clamped under the SAW, but he prayed it was enough to cover them until the chopper arrived.

"Evac flight." Chavez was on the radio with the helicopter again. "We need some help here . . . Roger."

Chavez unclipped a smoke grenade from his combat harness, slipped the ring, and tossed it to the other side of the hill's summit. A second later, putrid green clouds boiled off the mountain, marking their location to the approaching Blackhawk.

Bullets raked the top of the hill, explosions of dirt and lead that sent Mercer and the two surviving Marines reeling. Yet over the din they could still hear the chopper as it came in, its rotors whipping the smoke in violent eddies. The copilot had opened the helicopter's side door, but as they began their hover for the pickup, he was forced to return to the cockpit.

"The pilot can't land, not enough room up here. You'll have to jump in first," Chavez screamed over the rotor blast, his dirty hand still clamped over the entrance wound in his squad mate's leg. "I need to hold pressure on this dressing."

Mercer emptied the SAW's clip, a further thirty rounds chewing up the camp. He commandeered the wounded soldier's M-16 and, as the Blackhawk lowered even closer to the hillock, leaped for the open door.

A surge of air grabbed the chopper at that instant, and Mercer's chest slammed into the bottom of the door frame. In the split second before the pain struck, he felt the ends of his ribs grind against each other like corroded machine parts. The Blackhawk had been pushed away from the mountain of overburden, and Mercer found himself dangling above seventy feet of empty space, his legs bicycling uselessly as the pain loosened his grip on the door sill.

The pilot must have seen what happened. Ignoring the turbulence and the whirling blades' proximity to the ground, he heeled the nimble chopper nearly onto its side, throwing Mercer bodily into the aircraft. By the time Mercer recovered enough to crawl to the doorway, the Blackhawk was once again on station over the hill. Chavez was ready to pass the wounded Marine up to him.

They came under renewed and intense fire, the chopper taking a dozen rounds, ricochets scoring the cabin like hot coals. Mercer fired his M-16 one-handed, the stock braced against the helo's body as he lay half in and half out to help Chavez. He had his free arm under the young Marine's limp arms when a third RPG rocket hit the top of the hill. The Blackhawk lurched with the explosion and the Marine slid from Mercer's tentative grip. The soldier and Corporal Chavez disappeared in a hellish world of flame and smoke and debris.

The Blackhawk pilot lifted his craft away from the hill and out over the open desert, well beyond the range of any weapons the Sudanese might have. Mercer sat numb, unmoving, staring downward as if he could bring back the two dead soldiers by freezing his position. It took all of his strength to blink, to wash away part of the horror he saw in Corporal Chavez's eyes in the instant of his death. He sat immobile for two minutes before he could reach up and slip a pair of headphones off the firewall that partially protected the cockpit.

"How's the ship?" His voice sounded as if it came from someone else, a different person who could still function, still think rationally, still care about what happened next.

"We're okay," the pilot responded. "I'm sorry about

your buddies back there. There was nothing I could do." It wasn't really an apology, just a statement of fact in war.

"What's the status of that bogey?"

"Hold on," the pilot said, and Mercer guessed he was switching frequencies to talk with the circling AWACS. "Bogey vanished from radar about five minutes ago roughly a mile from the camp, then was spotted again moving eastward about two minutes later. Sky Eye lost the signal right after that. Sounds like someone made a pickup."

"Start flying east as fast as this thing can go. I suspect the helicopter we're chasing is much bigger than this one, a cargo ship that won't have your speed." Mercer's assumption was based on the Israelis' deluded plan to recover the Ark of the Covenant. He had no idea how big the artifact was reported to be, but he guessed that the Israelis would provide a large enough machine, no matter what its size.

Mercer ducked his head into the cockpit.

"Who in the hell are you?" The pilot was startled that his passenger was a civilian.

"Philip Mercer. I'm the guy you were brought in to rescue."

"Hey, we've got orders to drop you at the staging area," the copilot said.

"Fine by me, but you do that and there's no way we'll catch that other chopper. Chavez told me the AWACS can't track it, and we're the only other pairs of eyes in the area."

The twin General Electric T700s screamed at their maximum rating, pushing the lightly laden utility helicopter at over two hundred miles per hour. The ground under the roiling sky rushed by in a nauseating blur. Mercer buckled himself into the seat closest to the open door, acting as another observer for the pilots, scanning their starboard side for the fleeing Israeli craft.

The pain in his chest was excruciating. He found an emergency medical pack under his seat and choked down some painkillers. He then used the pocket knife from it to slice off two seat belts. He tied the cut ends together and wrapped the belts around his chest, using the buckle mechanism to ratchet his makeshift binding tight. It was a dangerous mend, but for the first time since the Apache had exploded over his head, he could breathe with a degree of normalcy. He wiped sweat from his face and no longer feared mercury poisoning. He didn't think he'd stopped sweating since his first mad dash into the mine with Selome and the diamonds.

"There!" the copilot called out. "At our one o'clock position about two miles ahead."

The Blackhawk was fast approaching the Red Sea coast, and the weather had deteriorated. Wind whistling into the back cabin of the craft carried a deluge of rain, and drops peppered the wind screen like pebbles. The massive escarpment that protected the African coast from the ravages of the ocean dropped from under the helicopter in a gut-wrenching swoop, and the pilot mirrored the dramatic plunge perfectly. In another minute they would be over the Red Sea and shortly after that, if the fleeing helicopter didn't change direction, they would fly into Saudi Arabian airspace south of Mecca.

The American chopper was gaining on the Israeli Super Stallion, but the huge khaki helicopter had a big head start and Mercer knew they couldn't catch it until they reached the Arabian peninsula.

"If we maintain pursuit, we're going to have to alert the Saudi Air Force," the pilot pointed out.

"So do it," Mercer replied, exasperated by the details.

"I've got a transmission on an emergency channel," the copilot called. "I think it's from the Super Stallion."

The voice over the radio was accentless and the transmission was clear. "American helicopter, American helicopter, this is Mercy Flight One en route to Mecca with victims from the Sudan famine. Why are you pursuing us?"

"You want to handle this?" the copilot asked Mercer.

"Yes," he replied tightly. "I've got it. Mercy Flight One, this is a United States Marine Corps helicopter. We do not wish to open fire, but you are carrying international fugitives wanted for terrorist acts. Over."

"Negative, Marine flight. We are contracted to the relief agency Médecins Sans Frontiers. We are carrying starving children to a hospital in Mecca."

"If you do not return to Eritrean airspace and land at Massawa, we will have no choice but to shoot down your craft. Over," Mercer bluffed. With just an M-16, he couldn't do more than dent the fleeing craft.

The coast of the Arabian peninsula was fast approaching, and the Blackhawk pilot was reluctant to broach the sovereignty of a friendly nation.

A new voice came over the net, one Mercer recognized immediately. Anger boiled up within him. "Dr. Mercer, how good to hear from you again," Yosef said. "I was hoping you were listening. I've learned that you may be erratic, but you can also be very predictable too."

"You are going to die, you son of a bitch," Mercer seethed.

"I don't think so," Yosef replied mildly. "You see, we're still holding your friend."

Mercer felt as if the helicopter had hit the side of a mountain. He'd forgotten they still held Harry. At that moment he knew the fanatics were going to get away with everything.

Switching to intercom mode, he asked the pilot if their communications gear could make a satellite call, and when he received an affirmative, he asked him to contact Dick Henna's cell phone.

"I take your silence as acknowledgment," Yosef said across the airwaves. "Very reasonable. Calling in the Marines was poor form, Doctor. Since the sniper I sent after your friend with the phone didn't return, you forced my hand a bit early, and without the Ark, there is no way to guarantee Mr. White's safety. In fact, my last order to my people was that he is to be killed. Unless I rescind that order, your friend's life is at an end. Give me and my team free passage, and when we arrive in Israel, I'll have White released. Don't consider this a failure on your part, just a stalemate."

The pilot cut off Yosef's speech by switching channels

from the cockpit, and Mercer heard Dick Henna's voice saying hello.

"Hi, Dick. It's Mercer."

"Jesus H. Christ. Where in the hell are you?"

"I'll tell you in a second, but first, have you made any progress finding Harry?"

"Yeah, he's back in Washington. He's been here for a while now."

"I'll call you later." Mercer killed the connection and slumped. *Oh, God, thank you.*

The guilt and the fear and the responsibility fell off Mercer in a liberating wave, leaving his mind clear for the first time since Harry's abduction. It was over. He was finished. Nothing else mattered anymore. Harry was safe. Selome was safe. The Eritreans were free. Even Gianelli's plan to blackmail the diamond cartel was over. He knew if he let it, his relief would cut through his resolve. But he wasn't quite done yet. Mercer wasn't going to allow Yosef to escape. He didn't want it for his friends or for anyone else. He wanted this for himself.

The pilot spoke before he could switch the radio back to the fleeing chopper. "We've got two problems here, Dr. Mercer. One is we'll enter Saudi airspace in about four minutes. The other is a pair of fast movers just came up on radar. They're closing at mach one from the north. ETA is ten minutes."

"Whose are they?" Mercer had a sinking suspicion he knew the origin of the approaching jets.

"I've got no IFF signature off either of them." The pilot referred to the Identify Friend or Foe transponders carried by the military aircraft of the United States and her allies.

"So they're not Saudi?"

"I doubt they'd shut off their IFFS over their own territory, especially since the coastline's covered with SAM installations."

"In other words, we've got ten minutes before that helicopter's fighter escort arrives."

"Yup."

"Let's take 'em down."

"Hey, listen, Doc, is that such a good idea? I mean, whoever has the clout to wrangle up fighter cover must be legit."

Mercer grunted. "We're about to be one of the checks and balances of the Israeli democracy. Maneuver us directly over that helicopter. I've got an idea."

Two miles from where the land met the sea, the Israeli renegades banked north to meet up with the jet fighters, skirting the outer reach of Saudi Arabia's coastal defenses. There was no chance the lumbering Super Stallion could outrun the Blackhawk, but they certainly were trying. It took only three more minutes for the American helicopter to take up a position above the Israeli's huge rotor.

"You'd better have a damn good idea," the copilot shouted. "Radar has those jets down our throats in four minutes."

Mercer worked furiously. "When I shout, break left as hard as you can, then land this pig. Fast. Those jets may take a shot even after I destroy the Stallion." He keyed his mike to speak to Yosef. "Listen up, you son of a bitch, and listen good."

"Ah, the good doctor is back," Yosef replied mockingly. "I thought you'd already left us."

"I've always preferred roulette, but I know enough about poker to know that when your bluff gets called, the game's over."

Yosef's voice was strained and his reply took just a fraction too long. "And you think I'm bluffing? Remember, it's not your life you are gambling with but that of your friend, Harry White."

"Asshole, I know you're bluffing." Mercer estimated how long it would take a two-pound object to fall from the door of his helicopter and land on top of the other. Gauging as best he could, he cut ten seconds' worth of fuse from the coil in his kit bag and seated it into his last stick of dynamite. "And in about a minute you're going to pay the highest stakes of all."

"Bravado, Dr. Mercer," Yosef replied. "In one minute, if I'm not given free passage, two F-16s are going to blow you from the sky. I may die, yes, but so will Harry White. Your revenge may be gratifying, but it will also be short-lived."

"You should have known when to fold 'em, partner," Mercer drawled. It took a few tries to light the fuse in the air whipping around the cabin, but once it was burning evenly, he shouted, "Now!"

The Blackhawk pilot had anticipated Mercer by a crucial half second, and when he released the explosive, he realized it would miss the upperworks of the Israeli helicopter. While an explosion near the hull of the Sikorsky would be damaging, it was doubtful it would cripple the huge cargo chopper.

Mercer's mouth opened for a scream of frustration even as the Blackhawk twisted and fell from the sky so fast that he became momentarily weightless. Yet his gaze never left the Israeli helo or the little package tumbling torward it.

A helicopter's rotor produces lift by creating a pocket of high pressure below the blades and low pressure above. For a chopper the size of the CH-53, tons of air rush into the vortex around the rotor, centering the craft like the eye of a hurricane. Into this maelstrom fell the dynamite. The little bomb would have fallen harmlessly past a conventional aircraft, but when it felt the relentless draw of the turbine-powered blades, it changed direction in midair. The millisecond before the packet was shredded by the rotor, the fuse touched the chemical explosives.

The helicopter vanished behind an expanding blossom of fire, and when it finally reemerged, the six rotor blades and the top third of the aircraft were gone. The Super Stallion was dead in the air, only its forward momentum carrying it in a flagging parabola. Mercer didn't blink until it slammed into the cobalt-blue sea, fire from its ruptured tanks washing away on the waves spawned by the impact. In a second it was gone.

"Get us to the Arabian coast and under their radar umbrella," Mercer shouted to the pilot, but the veteran was way ahead of him. The chopper settled into a flight path scant feet above the sea, the engines torqued for maximum speed.

"Those jets are breaking off and returning north," the copilot yelled a minute later.

Mercer was too tired to care, but he gave a weak cheer for the crew's benefit. "Let's get back to the mine. We're not done yet."

It took forty minutes, and on the inbound flight they heard radio chatter from other Blackhawks ferrying the injured to the amphibious assault ship.

Habte was the first to greet Mercer on the ground, shaking his hand solemnly, then enfolding him in a brotherly hug that would add another day or two to the recovery time for Mercer's broken ribs.

"I didn't think I'd see you again." Habte tried to keep the emotion out of his voice but failed.

"Came damn close."

Selome was next to reach the little group huddled near the Blackhawk. She too hugged Mercer, much more gently, but her kiss was consuming—as if she was trying to fit every possible emotion into that one gesture. Mercer's response was no less enthusiastic.

"I'm fine, don't worry." She preempted his question. "The Marines have already freed the miners, and they've been sent with the worst of the injured to their base ship."

Mercer was still on an adrenaline high. Everything felt otherworldly. An hour ago he had been fighting for his life, and now he was holding hands with a beautiful woman, surrounded by grimy but satisfied soldiers. It would take a long time for everything to soak in, the horror and the pain, but for just a few minutes he felt like he was invincible, and the thought made him grin.

"That's great, but I was about to ask if you are ready for that vacation yet?"

A Marine approached, extending his hand to Mercer. Behind him, two guards held Giancarlo Gianelli and Joppi Hofmyer. The smile vanished from Mercer's face, his gray eyes going deadly flat.

"Captain James Saunders, USMC," the redheaded Marine introduced. "It's an honor to meet you, Dr. Mercer."

"Honor's mine, Captain." Mercer grasped the outstretched hand. "On behalf of all of us, thank you."

"Just doing our job, sir," the Marine demurred. "I thought you might want to see these two characters before I shipped them out of here. The FBI already has agents in Asmara to escort them to Europe, where they're going to stand trial."

"I've seen enough ugliness in the past weeks to want to pass up this last opportunity. Thanks anyway."

"Fair enough." Saunders gestured for the guards to take the two to a waiting helicopter, but when they were just a couple of steps away, Mercer reconsidered. "One second, Captain."

Both captives were filthy and looked ravaged by their attempt to flee the battle, yet both were also uninjured. Mercer addressed Hofmyer first. "I've already kicked your ass once, so I'm not even going to bother with you." Then he directed his hatred at Gianelli. The Italian yelped when Mercer's murderous eyes fell on him.

"You, on the other hand, well, this I'm going to enjoy." Mercer cocked his fist, centering Gianelli's face perfectly, but he stayed his hand. "Screw it. You're not worth the effort."

Gianelli sagged with relief and stared goggle-eyed when Mercer turned away.

"Like hell you're not." Mercer twisted back and slammed Gianelli, the punch rolling the industrialist's eyes into his skull and laying him flat in the dirt. "Thank you, Captain Saunders. I think I needed that."

Selome ducked under one of Mercer's arms and Habte braced up the other, so he walked between the two of them, using them for support. Then he straightened, the old fire returning, his face lit with a devilish thought. "What do you say we go find Gianelli's safe and see what all this fuss has been about?"

Masada, Israel

In a land where nearly every building and hillock and cave has significance, few sites are as awe-inspiring or sacred as King Herod's fortress at Masada. It sits atop a diamond-shaped mountain, commanding a view unlike any other in the world. The Dead Sea—earth's deepest spot—lies in its shadow, over a thousand feet below sea level, the salty haze reflecting off the lifeless waters making it impossible to distinguish the Jordanian coast just seven miles away.

Masada had been built as an unassailable defensive fort but became a favorite retreat to King Herod, who'd spared nothing in making its opulence legendary. It had two separate palaces and a swimming pool that was kept full year-round despite the brutal Judean summers. However, it's not the architecture that makes Masada so significant, it's what happened there during the Great Revolt in the first century A.D. when Jewish Zealots battled with their Roman masters.

During the revolt, Masada was captured by Menachen Ben Yehuda and became a retreat for the Zealots. And after four years of warfare and another three of siege, it also became their last stand. Using Jewish slaves, the Romans constructed a huge ramp to the top of the mountain, an impressive engineering feat for the time, and when they finally broached the fortress walls, they discovered a funeral pyre. Surrounded by the Roman Tenth Legion under the command of Procurator Flavius Silva, 967 Jews chose suicide rather than submit to the army who'd besieged them.

Like the Western Wall, Masada has become a tangible

link to Jewish history, a site of pilgrimage and reverence. Today, every soldier inducted into the Israeli Defense Force has his swearing-in ceremony on the windswept thirty-acre shrine, a reminder of the heroism and strength of his people.

That was why Prime Minister David Litvinoff was so angry as his Aerospatiale helicopter descended through the night, its landing lights shining brightly on the sandy hill top. How dare Levine soil this spot by agreeing to his surrender here? His brazenness knew no bounds.

Levine had disappeared shortly after Harry White had been taken back to the United States. He'd narrowly missed an arrest, and since then, Shin Bet had been unable to locate him. Litvinoff was assured it would only be a matter of time, but after two weeks, it seemed the Defense Minister would never resurface, even as he continued to work to his goal of recovering the Ark of the Covenant. Levine had even managed to get fighter jets scrambled on his orders and a cargo helicopter sent to Eritrea to rescue his team there. The fighter pilots hadn't known their mission wasn't government sanctioned but they had still been dismissed from active duty pending a further investigation.

Litvinoff's chopper settled lightly and two soldiers sprang out, night-vision goggles scanning the parade ground south of Herod's principal palace, weapons at the ready. The engine spooled to silence, the rotor blades beating the air slower and slower until they sagged like limp palm fronds.

Litvinoff unhooked his seat belt and stepped to the ground. "If Levine wanted me dead," he reassured one of his personal guards, "he wouldn't have let us land."

Levine had called that morning, acting like he hadn't a care in the world and told Litvinoff that he would surrender himself, but only if the Prime Minister met him at Masada.

"Wait here." Litvinoff ignored the expression on his guard's face. "He wants to meet me alone at the upper terrace of Herod's villa. I'll be back shortly."

He was quickly swallowed by the night, the beam of his flashlight jerking as he walked north. Litvinoff tried to keep his mind blank as he rounded the walls of the ancient storerooms and the crumbling foundations of the Roman administration building. The night was warm, but the salty breeze was cooling. His sparse hair blew around his eyes and the wind whipped dust from the ground.

Passing the stairs that led to the lower terraces of the villa, Litvinoff continued through a stone maze until he came to a semicircular wall that hung over the northern tip of Masada like the prow of a great ship. It was too dark to see anything below him, but Litvinoff could feel the emptiness reaching out from just a few feet away.

"I knew you'd come," a voice called from the darkness.

Litvinoff turned to face the voice, his back to the starless void. "How dare you desecrate this place by coming here. You almost destroyed everything Masada stands for." He didn't want to get into this with Levine, but his emotions were too much. His hate. His outrage.

"Destroyed, David? No, I almost made everything worthwhile. I almost succeeded returning to Israel its most coveted artifact." Levine stepped into the flashlight's beam. Nothing about his posture looked like he was sorry about what he'd done. He even wore his uniform. In comparison to his striking figure, Litvinoff was short and gray, a tired old man who looked out of place anywhere other than an office.

"Well, it's over."

Levine laughed. "Do you really think it's over? Are you that naive? This wasn't all my doing, you know. There are others working with me, powerful men and women, many of them in your own government. We failed this time, but that doesn't mean we won't continue. We will find the Ark and restore the Temple and then we will do away with the Palestinians. You can't stop us."

"Maybe I can't, but that doesn't matter," Litvinoff said and saw that his words confused his Defense Minister. "Symbols can be powerful, Chaim, but only if people give them power. Even if you had found the Ark, do you think you would've been able to do all the other things you wanted? The excitement about its discovery would last only as long as the next scandal or the next war. No one cares anymore. They don't want symbols."

"You're wrong," Levine snapped. "Symbols are needed more than ever. The world is falling apart. America is turning our planet into a homogenized strip mall. We need to maintain our differences. We need something to remind us all that we are Jews first and foremost, then Israelis or Americans or Europeans. It's all we have left."

"I won't disagree with you, but this isn't the way."

"David, we've been friends for a long time—"

"We've never been friends," Livtinoff said evenly. "You were nothing but a political necessity to me, a way to keep a coalition government going. Don't mistake that for friendship."

Levine nodded slowly, surprised by the frank declaration. "Very well, we have worked together for many years. You know I would do nothing to harm Israel. That is why we are out here tonight. I failed at my quest and I know that my continued involvement in politics will only harm your government."

"How kind."

"Don't think it's for your sake. I told you before, the people working with me will continue. I've been exposed and I can't let that jeopardize their efforts." A gun appeared in Levine's hand. He'd kept it in a holster behind his back. "This is the only way."

The shot was brutally loud, a crashing explosion of light and sound that assaulted Litvinoff's ears like thunder. He hadn't fired a pistol since the Six Day War and his hand stung.

He'd fired his own weapon, pulling it from his pocket in front of Levine, but the Defense Minister hadn't seen the action because of the flashlight beaming in his face. Chaim Levine looked at the wound in his chest even as he struggled to raise his own pistol to his temple. Litvinoff fired again and Levine fell back, hitting the stone wall and slumping to the ground, his automatic slipping from his fingers.

"You won't become a symbol, Chaim," Litvinoff said to the corpse. "I won't let you martyr yourself and add your ghost to the spirits that haunt Masada. You don't deserve it, and despite what you thought, you never did."

Egypt

Many factors made it inevitable that the Nile River would become one of civilization's cradles. There were the yearly floods that deluged the river valley with such fertile soil that farming could continue year-round. And then there was the quirky fact that while the river flowed northward, the prevailing winds blew south, guaranteeing easy passage in either direction. It was this wind that gently moved across the wooden deck of the luxury barge, flicking at the canvas awning over the upper salon and drying beads of sweat dotting Philip Mercer's face and bare chest, soaking into the waistband of his shorts.

His upper body was still bruised multiple shades of purple and deep breaths bothered him, but he was healing well and the physician who had visited the boat in Luxor a week ago said that he'd make a full recovery. Thankfully, neither he nor Selome had any lasting effects from their exposure to mercury, and Mercer's fears about cryptococcus had been unfounded.

He and Selome had been on the barge for three weeks, cruising up the river from the bustle of Cairo. The boat belonged to a former client of Mercer's who'd made a fortune after contracting his geologic services and was more than willing to allow the use of his vessel. From the shore she looked unremarkable, sixty-eight feet long and nearly twenty wide, with a flat bottom and squared bow and stern. Her pilot house was a square block haphazardly placed too far forward to be aesthetically pleasing. It was only when one stepped onto her decks that she revealed her true beauty and luxury appointments.

The upper deck was mahogany, sanded so smooth that it shimmered in the desert sun. The small swimming pool and the Jaccuzi looked like miniature oases. Amid the palm planters, a wet bar beckoned. Apart from the crew, Mercer and Selome had the barge to themselves. Below decks were six cabins, including the master's suite with a bed big enough for a polo match and a gold and marble bath. The dining room and main salon were equally lavish, and while the decor wasn't Mercer's style, he appreciated its beauty.

He wiped perspiration from his eyes and opened them slowly, enjoying the sight that lay before him. Selome Nagast was stretched out on a wicker chaise longue, her dusky skin like oiled stone in both firmness and gloss. Her hair was bunched atop her head, but still cascaded around her shoulders, the henna dye glinting like a pillow of rubies. The only other color on her body was a wisp of a bikini bottom that vanished in cords around her narrow hips and flashed just a tiny triangle between her legs. Her breasts, perfect in any position, were spread by her relaxed pose, riding high and peaked so delicately that Mercer felt his lower body shift as he studied them.

Moving only a hand, for he did not want to disturb her sleep, he plucked a gimlet from the table behind him. He estimated, sipping the biting lime and vodka mixture, that this was his third and it wasn't yet noon. Mercer knew some people searched for excitement to escape the doldrums of their lives while on vacation. He wanted just the opposite.

On the river side of the anchored luxury barge, called *Aga Khan,* a steady procession of tourist cruise ships paraded in both directions, loaded with Americans, Japanese, and Europeans. Opposite sat the temple of Kom Ombo, a sandstone complex dedicated to Horus and Sobek, the crocodile god. The temple looked similar to the Acropolis in Athens with sturdy columns in the shape of lotus plants and crowned with massive rock lintels. Mercer and Selome had spent the day before walking through the ruins, admiring the Ptolemaic hieroglyphics and the mummified remains of sacred crocodiles. The temple had once been a pilgrimage destination for the lame and injured, and many of the pictographs depicted medical procedures and prayers.

Today was their last day alone together. Here at Kom Ombo, they were being joined by Dick Henna and his wife, Fay. Later, in Aswan, the two couples would leave the boat for another week of sightseeing, including a privately chartered plane trip to the massive Ramses II temple at Abu Simbel.

No sooner had Mercer thought about the impending end to their solitude than there came a disturbance at the gangplank. At first he thought it was another curio merchant trying to sell souvenirs, but then he heard Dick Henna's voice and Fay's excited exclamation as she got her first look at the true nature of her ride south.

"Selome, wake up," Mercer called, and her eyes fluttered open. He tossed her the bikini top. "Company's arrived."

She gave a little moue of annoyance and slipped the bikini over her chest, settling her breasts in the twin cups just as Henna and Fay came out to the sundeck.

Mercer was on his feet in an instant, shaking Dick's hand and kissing Fay's cheek. "Welcome to Mercer's Barge of Sin. Your whim is our command."

"I said it before and I'll say it again, I got into the wrong line of work." Henna drank in the barge's opulence until his gaze fell on Selome. He gaped.

"Selome Nagast, this is Dick and Fay Henna." While Dick was shaking her hand, Fay shot Mercer an approving wink that made him smile. "How was your trip?"

"Great," Dick replied. "First-class from Dulles to Cairo, private jet from there to Aswan and a limo here. Who could complain?"

Mercer had paid for it all as thanks to Dick for his help and Fay for her patience.

"And Harry?"

"He'll be here the day after tomorrow. He's in Israel now, helping Mossad identify the people who held him captive. I can't believe he has that much energy. His constitution is like iron."

"While his heart's gold and his liver is lead," Mercer

laughed. "Why don't you two get settled? We can talk over lunch."

An hour later, they sat at one of the outside tables, Henna and Fay dressed in shorts and loose shirts. Mercer had thrown on a T-shirt and Selome had covered up with a colorful wrap. As they ate, two lateen-rigged feluccas dashed by the barge, the traditional craft still a regular sight on the river after countless hundreds of generations.

After the stewards cleared the table and refreshed everyone's drinks, Mercer finished his nearly textbook history of the temple behind them and turned the conversation more serious. "We might as well get the working part of your trip out of the way so we can enjoy the rest of the week in peace."

"I agree," Fay chimed quickly.

"Fair enough." Henna looked lovingly at his wife of thirty-five years. "Okay, we'll do the bad stuff first and work our way to the good news.

"Three of the miners trapped when you escaped the mine pit have died from mercury poisoning, and four others aren't expected to make it. Most, however, responded well to treatment and will make a full recovery."

Mercer said nothing. He didn't think of the thirty he had saved, only the ones he'd lost, and Selome put a hand over his.

Henna continued. "Only four Eritreans were killed during the Marine assault, and autopsies proved they were all killed by the Sudanese. Out of the Marine detachment, we lost eight men with another twelve wounded. Only three Sudanese survived the battle and are being held in Asmara awaiting trial. The minister of justice assures me their execution will be swift. In a deal between Interpol and the Eritrean authorities, they also get to keep Joppi Hofmyer and the other South African mine engineer, but Giancarlo Gianelli went to Europe. The board of directors for Gianelli SpA have been forthcoming about his other illegal activities in an attempt to stave off bad publicity. Even with good behavior, he'll be in prison long after the next ice age."

"Has he shown any remorse?"

"None."

"I should have killed him when I had the chance," Mercer grunted. He knew even a life sentence was too lenient for what Gianelli had done.

"Now for the good news. I'll save the best stuff for last. As I'm sure you heard, Defense Minister Levine died mysteriously a couple of weeks ago. The official cover story is heart attack, but the truth is, Prime Minister Litvinoff shot Levine himself. Litvinoff called for a postponement of the elections, but it looks like when they are held, he will retain the prime ministership with a Labor Party majority in the Knesset. The other conspirators we know about will be tried in secret. Israel's government is keeping this whole affair quiet, but our President knows exactly what transpired and he's going to use that for leverage during the next round of peace negotiations if they balk at old promises again."

"Carrot and stick diplomacy?"

"Not my concern, I'm just a cop." Henna smirked. "Now for the really good parts.

"That heavy mining equipment you had ordered from Washington arrived in Eritrea the day after you and Selome came here. The Army Corps of Engineers gave them a hand getting it to the mine site as part of a cooperative loan package. Habte Makkonen has been named as the mine's general manager, and he'll have it in operation soon. Of course, they're calling it the King Solomon Mine. Makkonen and the minister of mines have already struck a deal with the London diamond cartel for distribution. Within another few weeks the first stones will be shipped. No one can predict how much this will change Eritrea, but everyone agrees that their cycle of poverty is over."

"Tell him the other part," Fay prompted.

"Oh, yeah. Remember that safe, the one you couldn't open at the mine?"

"Mercer tried everything short of dynamite on that stupid thing," Selome offered.

"Gianelli refused to give us the combination, so the safe's

manufacturer was contacted and they sent one of their technicians. I guess that little pig was the latest in strongbox technology because it took the safe-cracker a full week to open it."

"And?" It was Fay who was showing more excitement than anyone else, even though she knew the story.

"You probably heard rumors about a huge stone that had been found when you were working in the pits. Well, they were true. Rough, it weighs one hundred and twenty carats. Diamond-cutting experts who have it in Antwerp say it'll polish out at over sixty."

"Jesus Christ!" Mercer was stunned. "A stone that size is priceless. A collector will pay a fortune for the right to name it."

"It's already been spoken for."

"Who?" Mercer asked, guessing it would soon adorn someone's trophy wife.

"The people of Eritrea have donated it to the Smithsonian's Museum of Natural History. It will be displayed next to the Hope Diamond in the Hooker Hall of Geology." Henna beamed. "It's going to be called the Mercer Diamond."

Mercer felt a prick of tears behind his eyes and turned away before the others could see how touched he was by the gesture. When he recovered, he looked at Selome. "You knew about this?"

"I learned about it the last time I called the Minister of Mines." She couldn't keep the smile from her face. "On behalf of all my people, we wanted some way to thank you for what you did for us."

Such gratitude made Mercer look uncomfortable, but there was a glint of self-satisfaction behind his expression.

Later that night, Mercer and Selome made love in the big master suite. As they lay in the damp tangle of sheets, Selome rested her head on Mercer's chest so he could not see her face when she spoke. "You've changed since this morning. Was it the diamond?"

He respected her enough not to evade the question. "No, it isn't that."

How could he explain it to her? What words could tell her that despite all they had been through, he wanted to go home and pick up where he'd been before that first call from Prescott Hyde. He had to forget about this nightmare. It wasn't fair or right to include her too, but she was part of it. Everything was just too painful, images of Gibby and Brother Ephraim and the mummified children, the sight of bodies he'd found in the other mine, Chavez's face when the hill exploded. It would take years for the horror to dissipate, and some of it would be with him forever.

"It is Dick and Fay then," she said. "They remind you that life exists away from here and you are now eager to return."

"Selome, I—"

He wasn't eager, but he had to go. He had to sever every tie with what had happened. He had to make a clean break if he hoped to start the long healing process.

"I know, Philip. I understand. You are ready to go home. Don't think I didn't know this was coming. I expected it." Her voice caught. "When we met, I sensed you were carrying an old pain, something from your recent past that you could not get rid of. It's gone now, but maybe you're afraid that this experience will follow you too."

Mercer smiled. "You were the one who made the old memories fade. I think I'd given up on people, shut myself off, but you reminded me that I'm still alive inside. I can never repay you for what you've done for me." And then Mercer realized he could. "I made a promise with myself that I wouldn't tell anyone what I'm about to tell you and you have to promise that the secret stays here, in this room."

Selome twisted so she could look at him, his serious tone demanding her full attention.

"In the chamber where Mahdi died, I saw something, something I can't explain." He could see her searching his eyes. "I've been trying to rationalize what I saw, come up with a scientific explanation in my mind, but I can't."

"What was it?" Selome asked, already sensing she knew. Her body quivered.

"It was unlike any natural phenomena I'd ever seen, an otherworldly blue light that glowed and pulsed as if it was alive. I didn't actually see what caused it, but I'm pretty sure that the Ark of the Covenant was down there with us. Levine was right."

"We have to tell someone! My God, we have to go get it. Do you know what this means?"

"Yes, I do," Mercer said. "How many people have died because of it already? If the search continues, more will be killed until all of Israel is destroyed, maybe the world. No, Selome, we shouldn't go get it. It was crushed under a billion tons of rock, and that's exactly where it should stay." He paused. "Do you remember that Ephraim said God commanded Menyelek to take the Ark to Africa? Maybe it was for just this reason. It was meant to be a tool for God's veneration, not a means for men to destroy each other. We aren't ready for it yet, we can't handle it."

"But . . ." Her voice trailed off. She knew Mercer was right.

"I told you this so at least you would know the truth. That's my gift for your help."

She could see what it had cost him to reveal this secret. The internal conflict etched his face and tightened the muscles in his body. "Thank you," she whispered. "I think my gift was much less painful to give. I'm now in your debt."

"No more debts. We're even."

"So what will you do once you get home?" Her serene expression told Mercer that they really were even. "Will you find some new adventure to occupy your mind and help you forget about me?"

"I'll never forget you, but no more adventures," Mercer said. "I'm teaching mine rescue in Pennsylvania in a few weeks. After that, I hope to be heading to Greenland as part of a scientific expedition. Compared to what you and I have been through, it'll be a cakewalk."

Selome studied his eyes, a secret little smile on her lips. "In all of your questing, have you ever really found what you're looking for?"

Mercer considered for a minute. "It's not the goal that interests me, it's the quest itself."

"In that case, promise me that for our last week together, I am your sole quest."

He did.

ABOUT THE AUTHOR

Jack Du Brul is a graduate of the Westminster School and George Washington University. Trying to add as much adventure to his life as he does to his novels, Du Brul has climbed Masada at noon, swum in the Arctic Ocean off Point Barrow, explored war-torn Eritrea, hiked in Greenland, and was gnawed on by piranhas in the Amazon River. He collects zeppelin memorabilia, and when not writing or traveling (twenty-three countries and counting), he can be found in a favorite chair with a book and a brandy. Jack Du Brul lives in Burlington, Vermont.